THIS EDITION IS LIMITED TO 550 SIGNED COPIES

THE STOKER WINNERS:

The Horror Hall of Fame

THE STOKER WINNERS:
The Horror Hall of Fame

Edited by
Joe R. Lansdale

CEMETERY DANCE PUBLICATIONS

Baltimore

2012

Cemetery Dance Publications 2012
ISBN: 978-1-58767-026-8

Dust Jacket Art: © 2012 by Alan M. Clark
Interior Art: © 2012 by Glenn Chadbourne
Dust Jacket Design: Gail Cross
Typesetting and Design: Bill Walker
Printed in the United States of America

Cemetery Dance Publications
132-B Industry Lane
Unit 7
Forest Hill, Maryland 21050
http://www.cemeterydance.com

First Edition

Contents

INTRODUCTION

Joe R. Lansdale

ONCE UPON A TIME I was asked to edit a book of stories from the Bram Stoker winners. Which meant, of course, that there wasn't any real editing to do. The stories were already chosen by the awards committee, and they were all good.

I wrote an intro to that collection, and then went about my business, looked up many years later, only to realize that the book had never been published. The first publisher decided against it, for whatever reason. It was picked up by another publisher, but it didn't happen there either, and I have no idea why either publisher bailed, but bail they did, leaving these Bram Stoker award winning stories high and dry, marooned in the wasteland. The intro I wrote long ago for that volume was not a survivor of that wasteland. It was lost. Now, many years later, as this marooned collection has been rescued, I've been asked to write another.

Before I go any farther, let me say this: once I was a member of the Horror Writers Association, then called The Horror Writers of America, but frankly, I bailed. There are a lot of reasons for this, and this isn't the place to discuss them. Besides, I'm on record elsewhere as to why. So we'll let that dog lie.

But, a brief history lesson. The Bram Stokers grew out of the Horror Writers Association. Something not known to many, except for those who

9

were there, is the fact that my wife, Karen, founded the organization at the request of Robert McCammon. Rick, as he is known to his friends, came up with the idea, and originally he wanted to call the organization, H.O.W.L., which stood for The Horror Occult Writers League, but he didn't have the time to establish it.

Karen did.

It was decided the name needed to be less cute, (though I admit a fondness for the original name) and it was agreed to call it The Horror Writers of America, and once this was in place, Karen went at it hammer and tongs. What she did was she built an organization on a mailing list and a newsletter that was cheaply put together and mailed out as frequently as she could manage—which was frequent (I wonder if anyone out there still has copies). There were articles by various writers, including me and McCammon and Dean Koontz, and others. It was a good start.

Dean Koontz, good man that he is, took it on himself to take over the newsletter and make it professional. If my wife brought it into being, Dean raised it up and gave it dress clothes. It was then up to everyone else to teach it manners.

Originally, none of us, the founders, so to speak, wanted there to be awards. We felt it would be a distraction from other aspects of the organization. It was. But that doesn't change the fact that the awards have been very good examples of the best of horror fiction, and I think this has been true of short fiction in particular, as this volume will prove, and those of us who work, or have worked in the field, like the fact that the horror genre is taken seriously enough to have its own recognition for excellent writing. I hasten to add that many stories not included here, stories that didn't win awards, might well deserve to share the stage with these, but these are the ones chosen, and we celebrate them here.

Now, I have fiction included here as well, and as editor, that makes me feel mildy uncomfortable, even if I never had anything to do with the awards, and am actually no longer a member, and haven't been for years, but be that as it may, you can take my contributions out of the mix if you like. With or without me, this is a fine grouping of horror tales, and they are unique and show how horror has evolved over the years, as it must if it is to survive. These stories have been on the shelf for a long time, and as they still seem fresh and progressive, it speaks to the nature of their continued prominence. They age well, and they will continue to do so. They prove that horror fiction is much broader than a bump in the night, the rattle of bones in a closet, and that not all horror has to have a supernatural element. These stories cut a wide swathe through the field, and that makes this book a wonderful primer for would-be horror writers, or for writers of any ilk, because good stories and good writing do not belong to genre; they belong to readers.

As I said before, it's a shame this book has been on a shelf for so long. It's awful and wrong and inexplicable that it hasn't appeared before now, and there's no excuse for it. But finally, it's here, the stories gathered together like fine chocolates, all in one symbolic box, and this box of chocolates has something that a real box of chocolates does not have. These fine delicacies do not diminish with consumption; this box is always full, and you can always dip back into it and consume it again.

Enjoy.

And try not to smack your lips. At least in public.

It's rude.

Joe R. Lansdale
Nacogdoches, Texas

THE SCENT OF VINEGAR

Robert Bloch

EVERY SATURDAY NIGHT TIM and Bernie went bowling at the whorehouse.

"It didn't look like a whorehouse," Bernie said. "At least not any more than the places most of us lived in back then. And the damn thing was perched so high above Beverly Hills you'd have to look down to see King Vidor's spread." The old man glanced at Greg, the cigar in his hand semaphoring apology. "Sorry, I keep forgetting we're talking 1949. You've probably never even heard of the man."

"King Vidor," Greg paused. "He directed *The Big Parade*. And Bette Davis in *Beyond the Forest*, the picture where she says 'What a dump!' Right?"

Bernie aimed the cigar at Greg. "How old are you?"

"Twenty-six."

"I'm seventy-six." Bernie's eyes narrowed behind his hornrims. "Where'd you hear about Vidor?"

"Same place I heard about you," Greg said. "I'm a student of Hollywood history."

"And whorehouses." Bernie's dry chuckle rose, then ceased as pursed lips puffed on the cigar.

Greg Kolmer grinned. "They're part of Hollywood history too. The part I couldn't find in books."

Bernie was nodding. "In those days everything was hush-hush, and if you didn't keep your mouth shut, Howard Strickling shut it for you."

"Wasn't he publicity director at MGM?"

"Right again." Bernie's cigar gestured benediction. "He's the guy who said the first duty of a publicity man is to keep the news out of the paper." Another chuckle. "He knew everything. Including where Tim and I did our bowling."

"Was it really that big of a deal? I mean, all those stories about living it up out here—"

"—are true." Bernie said. "You think sex was invented by Madonna or some hot-dog computer hacks over at Cal Tech? Let me tell you, in the old days we had it all. Straights, gays, bi-, tri-: anything you wanted, you could get. You bring the ladder, we furnish the giraffe."

"Then why were you covering up?"

"Censorship. Simple as that. Everybody knew the rules and cooperated, or else. Tim and I were in management at the same studio; not top-level, but our names were on parking slots. So we weren't going to risk the 'or else' part, if you follow me."

Greg nodded, concealing his impatience. Because that was the only way to get Bernie to tell him what he really wanted to hear. And Bernie would tell him, sooner or later, because he had nothing else to do, sitting in this rundown old house on the wrong side of Wilshire with no friends to talk to, because you can't talk to the dead. Which is probably why he'd agreed to talk to Greg, was talking to him now.

"You take the stars," Bernie was saying. "The smart ones never fooled around with anybody under contract on their own lot. Getting involved with somebody you were liable to see every day was too risky; too much pressure, and you couldn't just walk away. So they patronized the hook-shops." Bernie's face crumpled in an old man's grin. "What do you suppose the folks in Peoria would say if they knew their favourite loverboy had to pay to play, just the guy next door?"

"I doubt if many people in Peoria went to brothels in those days," Greg said.

"Maybe not." Bernie flicked cigar ash as he spoke. "But we did. Tim and I hung out at Kitty Earnshaw's. Great old broad, a million laughs."

Greg leaned forward. *At last. Now it's coming.* "The one who had this house up in the hills you were talking about?"

"Right. Kitty was the best. And her girls were user-friendly."

"Where was this place?"

Bernie spiralled his cigar in a northerly direction and more ash fell carpetward. "Way off Benedict Canyon somewhere, past Angelo. Been more than forty years since I've been up there, I don't remember—"

"Why'd you stop going?"

"Kitty Earnshaw retired, got married or religion or something. The new management was different, everyone Oriental. Not just Japs or Chinese, but girls from places like Burma, Singapore, Java, all over. Woman in charge never showed her face when I was there, but I heard stories. Marquess de Sade, that's what they called her."

"Marquis de Sade?"

"Marqu*ess*. A gag, I guess. But the place was getting a little too kinky for me. Like the night I met some drunk down at the bar and he says, 'You pick a girl yet? Take the one with the glass eye—she gives good socket.'"

Bernie shrugged. "Maybe that was a gag too, but I saw enough to make me start wondering. The chains and bondage scene—you know, with the little ships and the handcuffs on the bedposts, all four of them, and the Swiss Army knives. Anyhow, I stopped going there."

"And your friend Tim?"

"I don't know. Studio dropped him when television took over out here. What happened to him after that I can't say."

"Did you ever try to find out?"

The old man stubbed his cigar in the ashtray. "Look, Mr. Kolmer, I'm getting a little tired, so if you don't mind—"

"I understand, sir." Greg smiled. "And I want to thank you. You've been very helpful." He rose. "Just one other thing. The location of this place we've been talking about. If you could be more specific—"

Bernie frowned. "All I remember, it was east of Benedict. Dirt road, probably been washed out for years now." He hesitated. "Come to think, the place must have been burned out in that big fire back in the Sixties."

"I could look it up," Greg said. "Fire Department records."

"Don't waste your time. The place wasn't even in Beverly Hills city limits, or L.A. either. Area up there is no-man's-land, which is why the house could operate. Nobody was sure who had jurisdiction."

"I see." Greg turned. "Thanks again."

The old man walked him to the door. "Don't do it," he said.

"Do what?"

"Don't try going up there. Look, it's none of my affair. But for your own good I'm telling you—"

"Telling me or warning me?"

"Call it advice. From somebody who knows."

"Knows what?"

The old man smiled, but his voice was somber. "That house up there is no place to take a bowling ball."

Greg didn't go up there with a bowling ball.

He didn't even take a Thomas map, because the place Bernie Tanner had told him about wasn't on the map. The area was blank, which meant there was no access unless Greg could locate that dirt road, which might or might not still exist.

It took Greg almost two hours of cruising up and down Benedict before he found the path. And it was scarcely more than that, at best a winding trail. The entrance was so overgrown with scrub that it couldn't be seen from the lane leading to it, and the stretch spiralling around the hillside was invisible from below, choked with weed and sage.

At first Greg wasn't sure it was wide enough even for his small car, but he had to chance it; chance the ruts and ridges and clumps of vegetation that punished tires and driver alike as the little hatchback went into a slow low. Without air conditioning it was like trying to breathe with a plastic bag over your head, and by the time he was halfway up the hillside he wished he hadn't started.

Or *almost* wished. Only the thought of what might be on the summit kept him going, through the stifle of heat and the buzz of insect swarm.

The car stalled abruptly, and Greg broke into panic-ooze. Then the transmission kicked in again, and he sweated some more as a bump in the road sent the hatchback veering left, pitching Greg against the door. Beneath underbrush bordering a curve he caught a sudden sickening glimpse of the emptiness just beyond the edge, an emptiness ending in a tangle of treetops a thousand feet below.

Greg fought the wheel, and the car lurched back on an even course. The road must have been better in the old days; even so, it was one bitch of a trip to make just to go bowling. But that was Bernie Tanner's business and Bernie Tanner's road.

Greg's own road stretched back a lot farther than the bottom of this hill, all the way back to Tex Taylor, a onetime cowboy star at the Motion Picture Country Home. He had all those stories about the old days in Hollywood, and that's all Greg had wanted at first; just some kind of lead-in he could work up into a piece for one of those checkout-counter rags. He'd been selling that kind of stuff long enough to get used to the idea he'd never win a Pulitzer Prize.

But what the dying western wino told him gave sudden startling hope of another kind of prize—one that might have awaited presentation for nearly half a century up there at what Tex Taylor called the House of Pain. That's what he said its name was, after the Asian woman took over and began to give quality time to S-and-M freaks. Maybe it was all a crock, but it sounded possible, certainly worth a trip up there to find out.

Trouble was that Tex Taylor was borderline senile and couldn't remember exactly where this weirdo whorehouse was located. But he did, finally, come up with the name of somebody he'd seen there in the glory days. And that's how Greg got hold of Bernie Tanner.

Greg wondered if Bernie had any money. Today anything with a

Beverly Hills address could probably fetch a mil or so on the current market. Maybe Bernie would pay him a mil or so just for old time's sake, just out of pride.

And there were others like Bernie still around, stars and directors and producers who were bankable way back when; some of them had saved their money or put it into real estate and led comfortable, quiet lives in Bel Air or Holmby Hills. If Bernie would pay a million, how much would all the others be willing to fork over, given the proper motivation?

Greg grinned at the thought. And then, as the car swung around the last curve, his grin widened.

He had reached the summit. And on the summit was the house.

Hey, it wasn't the Taj Mahal or Buckingham Palace or even the men's washroom at the Universal Tour. But the bottom line was it hadn't burned or gone down in an earthquake or been bulldozed by a developer. It was still here, standing in shadowy silhouette against the late afternoon sun.

Greg took a flashlight from the glove compartment and clipped it to his belt. Then he reached into the compartment again and found there was just enough left in the envelope for a little toot, enough to keep him bright-eyed and bushy-tailed while he did whatever he'd have to do up here. He waited for the rush, then got out and lifted the hood to let the steam escape. There'd be no water up here, and probably no gas or electricity; they must have had their own generator.

He stared up at the two-story structure. Frame, of course; nobody could have hauled machinery here for stone or concrete construction. The roof had lost its share of shingles, and paint peeled from boards that had once been white, but the building's bulk was impressive. Half a dozen boarded-up windows were ranked on either side of the front door; tall windows for a tall house. Greg closed his eyes and for a moment day was night and the windows blazed with the light of a thousand candles, the front door opened wide in welcome, the classic cars rolled up the driveway, headlights aglitter, wheels gleaming with chrome. And off behind the distant hills the moon was rising, rising over the House of Pain.

It was the toot, of course, and now moonlight shimmered into sunlight and he was back in the teeth of searing heat, radiator-boil, insect-buzz.

Greg walked over to the double door. Its weathered, sun-blistered surface barred intrusion, and at waist level the divided doors were secured by lock and chain. Both were rusty; too much to expect that he could just walk up and yank his way in.

But it happened. The chain gave, then came free in his fist, covering his palm and fingers with powdery particles of rust from the parted links. He tugged and the door swung outward. Hinges screeched.

Greg was in the house and the house was in him.

Its shadows entered his eyes, its silence invaded his ears, its dust and decay filled his lungs. How long had it been since these windows were first boarded, this door locked? How many years had the house stood empty in the dark? Houses that once were thronged with people, throbbed to their pleasure and their pain—houses like this were hungry for life.

Greg withdrew the flashlight from his belt, flicking it on and fanning the beam for inspection. *What a dump!*

He was standing in a foyer with a solid wall directly ahead, archways opening at left and right. He moved right, along a carpet thickly strewn with dust long undisturbed, and found himself in a room that he imagined must take up most of this wing. A huge Oriental rug covered the floor; its design was obscured and fraying, but Greg thought he could detect the outline of a dragon. Sofas and chairs were grouped along three sides beneath gilt-framed paintings which, Greg noted, might have served as centerfolds for the *Kama Sutra*. Angled at the far corner was a piano, a concert grand. Once upon a time somebody had spent a lot of money furnishing this place, but right now it needed maid service.

Greg's flashlight crawled the walls, searching for shelves and bookcases, but there were none. The fourth side of the room was covered by a row of tattered drapes hung before the boarded up windows. The drapery may also have displayed the dragon pattern, but outlines had faded, its fiery breath was long extinguished.

19

Greg crossed the foyer and went into the other wing. It turned out to be a bar, and at one time may have resembled Rick's place in *Casablanca*, but now the set was struck. The room was a tangle of upended tables and overturned wooden chairs, flanked by booths on two walls and tattered drapery on the third. Along the fourth wall was the bar, with a big mirror behind it, bordered on both sides by shelves and cupboards that had once displayed bottles and glasses but now held only heaps of shard. The mirror itself was cracked and mottled with mold. *Here's looking at you, kid.*

At one side of the bar a door led to what must have been the kitchen; on the other side an archway framed the base of a staircase beyond. Skirting the maze of tables and chairs, Greg headed for the archway.

Upstairs would be the bedrooms and maybe the private quarters of the Marquess or whatever she called herself. The place looked as if it had been abandoned in a hurry; the padlocked door and boarded-up windows may have been the results of a return visit. But why leave all the furnishing? Greg had no answer, but he hoped to find one. And find what else might also have been abandoned.

The stairs' worn padding muffled his footsteps, but creaking began when he reached the long hallway off the upper landing. It echoed again as he opened and closed the doors lining both sides of the corridor.

All led to bedrooms, each with its own indecorous décor. Here lay a round bed surrounded and surmounted by mirrors, but the sumptuous bedspread was riddled with moth-holes and the mirrors reflected only the light of Greg's flashlight beam. In another room stood a bare marble slab with metal cuffs and an assortment of chains hanging from ends and sides. The marble top was flecked, the metal attachments reddened with rust, not blood. And the whips on the wall rack dangled impotently; the case of knives and needles and surgical shears held pain captive through the empty years.

Empty years, empty rooms. Wall-mural obscenities turned into absurdities by the crisscross of cracks, the random censorship of fading over decades of decay.

But where were those private quarters: an office, someplace to keep the books, the files, the cash, and maybe—just maybe—what he was looking for? He hadn't gone through all this just to chase shadows. What the hell was he doing here anyway, prowling through a deserted whorehouse at sunset? The johns didn't come to these places looking for starkness and desolation; tricks were supposed to be welcomed. But what had he found except rot and ruin, a bar full of broken bottles, a parlor piano that grinned at him with keys like rows of yellowed teeth? Damn it, why didn't somebody tend to a customer? *Company, girls!*

Greg came to the end of the corridor, reached the last room on the left. There was nothing here now, and maybe never had been. Tex Taylor was lying, the old rummy had no proof, and he was just doing a number like the old ham he was, using Greg as an audience for the big deathbed-revelation scene. Who said people had to tell the truth just because they were dying?

He opened the door on a bedroom just like all the others, dark and deserted: bare walls and bare bureau top, empty chair and empty bed.

At least that's what he thought at first glance. But when he looked again he saw the shadow. A dark shadow, lying on the bed.

And now, in the flashlight's beam, the shadow turned to gold.

There was a golden girl lying on the bed, a golden girl with a jet-black halo of hair framing an almost feline face—slanted eyes closed in slumber above high cheekbones, coral curvature of lips relaxed in repose. The flashlight beam swept across her nudity, its light lending luster to the gold of her flesh.

Only one detail marred perfection. As Greg stared down he saw the spider. The big black spider, emerging from her pubic nest and crawling slowly upward across her naked belly.

Greg stifled his gasp as he realized the girl was dead.

She opened her eyes.

She opened her eyes and smiled up at him, opened her mouth and flicked a thin pink tongue in a sensual circle over the coral lips. Her smile widened, revealing twin razor-rows of teeth.

Now, still smiling, the girl sat up. She raised both arms, hands coming to rest on either side of the throat hidden by the dark tumble of her hair. The long fingers splayed, tightening their grip as if trying to wrench the head free.

Then the girl tugged, lifting her head off her neck.

She was still smiling.

And Greg was still gasping as he turned, stumbled from the room, down the hall and the stairs, through the littered bar below, the cobwebbed foyer. Then the door at last: *open fast, don't look back, slam it tight.*

The house had been dark, but now it was dark outside as well, and Greg was grateful he'd somehow managed to retain his flashlight. He ran to the car, keyed the ignition, sent the hatchback circling to the spot where the road wound down, down in the dark, around narrow curves, twisting trees. It didn't matter as long as he kept going down, going away from there, that place and that thing he'd seen—

Or *thought* he'd seen.

Someone doesn't just reach up and lift her head off her neck; nobody can do such a thing, loosening the red-blood-choked strands of the arteries and the darker filaments of veins all twined against the central cord of the oesophagus with a flashlight beam shining on its coating of slime. You don't imagine details like that; you have to see them. And he *had* seen, it had happened, this was real.

But what was it?

Greg didn't know, but Bernie would. That had to be why the old man warned him about going up there, going to where it waited in the dark.

The clock on the dash told Greg it was 9:30. Most elderly people go to bed early, but a few stay up for the news. And tonight Bernie would be one of them, because Greg had news for him.

It took a half-hour to get down, but by the time he pulled up, parked and knocked on the front door his course was clear: this time he was going to get some answers.

The door opened on Bernie Tanner's startled stare. "Mr. Kolmer?" There was surprise in his voice, whisky on his breath.

"Didn't think I'd be back?" Greg said. "Thought she'd get me, is that it?"

"I don't know what you're talking about."

"Don't hand me that!" Greg's voice rose.

"Please, not so loud. I got neighbors—"

"You'll get new ones in Forest Lawn if you try to dump on me again." Greg tugged at the door. "Open up."

Bernie obeyed quickly, then closed the door even more quickly after his self-invited guest had entered. Turning, the old man lurched toward his chair. Greg noted the bottle on the table and the half-filled tumbler beside it. The old man picked up his glass and gestured. "Drink?"

"Never mind that." Greg seated himself on the sofa; its faded fabric reeked of alcohol and stale cigar smoke. "Let's have it," he said.

Bernie avoided his gaze. "Look, if something's wrong it's not my fault. I told you not to go up there."

"Sure. But it's what you didn't tell me that made trouble."

The old man shook his head. "I didn't think you'd go. I didn't think you or anyone else could find the place, even if it was still standing after—"

"After what?"

Bernie tried to push the question away with his hand. "Look, I told you all I can—"

"Maybe you'll have more to say after I steer the law up there to take a look around."

Bernie gulped air, then gulped the contents of his glass. "All right, I'll level. That place didn't close down because the madam got married. She got murdered."

"Keep talking."

The old man poured himself another drink. "This fella Tim, the one I told you used to go up there with me. I said I didn't know what became of him after I quit going. Well, I lied."

"Why?"

"I didn't want to get involved. It happened so long ago and it wouldn't do any good. You'd figure I was crazy, the way I figured Tim was when he told me."

"Told you what?"

"About the hookers up there, the Orientals the new madam brought in. He said they were some kind of vampires. If you dozed off, fell asleep, they'd suck your blood."

The old man paused. "He showed me toothmarks on his neck."

"He should have gone to the police."

"Do you think they'd believe him any more than I did? Instead he went to Trenk, Ultrich Trenk—you wouldn't remember him, he did some horror flicks for the indies back then."

"*Blood of the Beast.*" Greg nodded. "*Crawlers.* I know the titles but I never saw them."

"Nobody did," Bernie said. "They got shelved before release. And so did Trenk. His stuff was too strong for those days. Trouble with him, he believed in what he did—not the lousy scripts, but the premises. Ghosts, vampires, werewolves, all that crap. And he believed Tim, because he'd heard some other things about the place up there, about the way bats flew around and—"

"Never mind that. Tell me what happened!"

Bernie reached for his drink. "Word was that Trenk went up there with Tim and three other guys who'd been customers and got suspicious of what, God only knows. But there was some kind of hassle and the bottom line is the place closed down, everybody left, end of story."

"I thought you said the madam was murdered."

Bernie frowned. "Tim told me he'd been the one who killed her. He told me because he was dying down at the old Cedars of Lebanon hospital, with what they thought was some rare kind of blood disease. They'd only let me talk to him for five minutes; when I leaned on him for details he said to come back tomorrow."

"And—?"

"He died that same night." The old man swallowed his drink. "Maybe it's just as well I didn't hear the rest. Nobody else who went up with Tim ever said a word about it. Trenk went back to Europe, but he'd kept his mouth shut too."

"What about those bats?"

"All I know is what Tim told me, and what he said didn't make much sense. Don't forget, he was dying, probably hallucinating."

"Probably," Greg said. He wondered if he should ask another question, but it wasn't worth the risk. The way Bernie talked, it didn't sound as if he even suspected, and if that was the case there was no sense giving him a clue.

The old man thought Tim was hallucinating. If Greg told him about the girl in the house, would he say that was a hallucination too?

Could be. After all, Greg did have himself a toot before going in, and it wasn't as little as he liked to tell himself it was. Maybe that washed-up cowboy actor was on something too—either that or just jiving him. But the cowboy was dead, Bernie's friend was dead, and Bernie looked as if he'd stayed up way past his bedtime.

Greg stood up. "I'll be going now," he said.

Bernie blinked. "Aren't you going to tell me what happened to you up there?"

"Nothing. It's just a spooky old house, and I guess I got carried away." Greg walked to the door, opened it, then glanced back at the old man slumped in his chair. "Just in case you've been worrying, let me relieve your mind. I didn't see any bats."

So much for his good deed for the day.

Now it was time to do a good deed for himself. It had been a long time since lunch. Driving off, Greg turned onto Olympic and headed for a mini-mall offering a choice of franchised junk food. He chose the place with the best grease-smells and wolfed down more than his diet dictated: two burgers with everything, extra fries, coffee and a shake. He hated pigging out like this, but right now it was all he could afford. If tonight had been different he might be eating at Morton's.

As it was, perhaps he ought to consider himself lucky just to be alive. There was no sense stewing about the rest.

Driving home he reached his decision before he reached his destination. Whether what he'd seen was real or the product of his imagination, one thing was certain; he didn't want to see it again.

When Greg pulled into his parking space under the apartment it was close to midnight. The close-to-witching hour when the unholy hosts rise from their graves—Leno, Letterman, Arsenio, reading their ad-libs to the cackling crowd, welcoming their guests with all the grace of Dracula greeting Renfield, then draining their blood—

Now where had all that come from? Riding the elevator up to the third floor, he had the answer. Damn Bernie and his vampire talk. And as for what Greg had seen, or thought he'd seen, there was an answer for that too—an answer he'd have to face sooner or later. And after tonight he knew it had better be soon. When the spiders come out of their hiding places and the sleeping beauties start taking off their heads, you'd better stop. Going up there had been enough of a bad trip in itself.

First thing he got into the apartment, he'd flush the rest of his little stash down the tube. If not, he'd be going down the tube himself one of these days. The time to think about it was over; this was *do it* time.

Only it didn't quite work out that way. When Greg opened the door and reached for the light switch, a voice from the dark said "Freeze" and that's what he did.

Footsteps sounded softly behind him and a faint gust of air fanned his neck as someone closed the front door.

Beside him a switch clicked on. Against the background of the cluttered little living room, the light of a lamp in a corner framed the outline of a man wearing jacket and jeans. But Greg's attention focused on the glint of a gun in the intruder's hand.

The gun gestured.

"Hands behind your head. That's right. Now move to the sofa and sit."

As Greg obeyed he got another glimpse of the gun. *Piece like that could blow your head off. God, what's happening? I need a fix.*

The intruder edged into a chair on the other side of the coffee table, and now the lamp highlighted eyes and cheekbones and skin tone.

For a moment Greg evoked an image of the golden girl he'd seen—or had he?—earlier this evening. But what he was seeing here was unquestionably real. A middle-aged man with coarse, close-cropped black hair: obviously an Asian or Asian-American, obviously not the friendly type. A man with an attitude, and a gun.

Just a snort, a sniff, anything—

The man's stare was cold. So was his voice. "Put your arms down. Both hands in your lap, palms up."

Greg complied and the man nodded. "My name is Ibraham," he said.

"Abraham?"

"Perhaps it was once, when Muslim rule began. But I'm called Ibraham in Kita Bharu."

· "I don't know that country."

"It's a city. The capital of what used to be Kelanton, in Malaya." The man frowned. "I'm not here to give geography lessons."

Greg kept his palms up, his voice steady. "What are you here for?"

"I want you to take me to the house."

"House? I don't know—"

"Please, Mr. Kolmer. Your friend told me you went there earlier this evening."

"When did you see Bernie?"

"About an hour ago. He was kind enough to furnish your address, so when I found you were not home I took the liberty of inviting myself in."

The bathroom window, Greg told himself. *Why do I keep forgetting to lock it when I go out?*

That wasn't the question which needed answering at the moment. There was another one more important, so he asked it. "What did Bernie tell you?"

"Everything he knew." Ibraham's slight shrug didn't cause his aim to waver. "Enough for me to guess the rest." A nod didn't jar the gun either. "That story about researching an article—it's not true, is it, Mr. Kolmer? You went to that house looking for something you didn't find."

"How do you know?"

"If you found it you wouldn't have gone back to Tanner. Of course he didn't know what you were looking for, or he'd have told me that too." Ibraham lifted his gaze: eyes of onyx in slanted settings. "Tell me what you were after."

"I can't," Greg said. "Swear to God, I don't know."

"But you have some idea?" Ibraham leaned forward. "The truth—now."

Greg stared at the gun and its muzzle stared back. "The cowboy who told me about the place said there was a blackmail operation. This new madam was bugging rooms, getting pictures, filming with hidden cameras, using two-way mirrors and whatever else they had back in those days.

"There was a market then; magazines like *Confidential* paid plenty for such stuff, particularly if stars were involved. But nothing about the place ever showed up—I know, because I waded through library files. So my hunch was the material—photos, film, audio tape, whatever—never was submitted. Something happened to close the house down before the stuff could be peddled. Which meant—"

"It could still be there," Ibraham said, and nodded.

"How did you hear about all this?" Greg asked.

"From my mother. She was there when it happened."

"At the house?"

"She worked as a maid." For the first time there was a hint of amusement in Ibraham's eyes. "You must understand she was very young. The lady, the one they called the Marquess, adopted her after both my grandparents were killed in the war. When my mother came with her to this country she was only fifteen. Some of the other girls, the ones who did what was expected in such a place, weren't much older. But the Marquess

28

protected my mother from everything, including full knowledge of what she was involved with. Of course she learned in time. But when she did, it was too late." Ibraham's eyes were somber now. "She was lucky. On the night everything happened she wasn't at the house. The Marquess' chauffeur had driven her down to a Westwood Laundromat. I don't know how they found out about what took place, but news got to them somehow and they never went back. The chauffeur had a substantial bank account; he'd been the Marquess' lover. On the journey back to Kelanton he became my mother's lover as well. He died in a Johore brothel the day I was born.

"I never knew any of this until just before my mother died, several years ago. What she told me made me suspect the same thing you did, but I couldn't get over here immediately." Ibraham glanced at the gun. "In my country there is still a war going on."

"You're in the army?"

"The military became my career after I graduated from university in Singapore. Now I wish to retire."

Greg shifted cautiously. "Look, do you have to do this *shtick* with the gun?"

Ibraham lowered the weapon. "Probably not. After all, we're partners."

Greg fought for self-control, and lost. "No way!"

"It's the only way," Ibraham said. "You know how to find the house. And my mother told me what's hidden there. We go together. Tonight."

Greg shook his head. "Didn't Bernie tell you what happened to me— what I saw?"

"I know." Ibraham seemed to have no problem with self-control, Greg noted—but then, he had the gun. "My mother warned me. I know what to do."

Greg took a deep breath. "Maybe so. But do it tomorrow, when we can go up there in daylight."

"No. We can't afford delay."

"Do you think Bernie might start talking—"

"Only through a *Ouija* board." Ibraham glanced down at his gun.

29

Fear iced Greg's spine. "Why?" he murmured.

"The old man was the only one who'd know where we were going. No sense taking chances."

"How can you say that, knowing what we might run into up there?"

"What we're going after is worth the risk. I'm sure you're aware of that or else you'd never have gotten into this in the first place. That house holds a fortune, and we're going to get it."

Greg glanced at the gun. "And when we get it, you'll get me," he said.

"I give you my word." Ibraham rose. "Either go with me or stay behind. Like Bernie."

Greg swallowed hard. "Look, man, I've had a rough night, you know? Let me get my medication—"

"What are you on?"

Greg told him, and Ibraham gestured quickly. "You're not going up there stoned," he said. "Could be bad for your health."

A muzzle moved to press against Greg's spine; that was bad for his health too.

"Move," said Ibraham.

And they did, in Greg's car, with him behind the wheel, Ibraham at his side, and the gun riding against his rib cage. The midnight air was humid; both men were perspiring moments after the car swung out into the deserted street.

"Roll down your window," Greg said.

"Don't you have an air conditioner?"

"Can't afford it."

"You can, after tonight."

Ibraham was smiling, but Greg frowned. "This thing I saw up there— what is it?"

"*Penangallan.* A kind of vampire, but not exactly."

"Meaning what?"

"A *penangallan* doesn't need to rest in grave-earth or coffin. Like your western vampires it seeks human blood for nourishment, but it can hibernate for years if necessary. Maybe the difference is in the metabolism. Vampires require a greater supply of energy to walk abroad each night. But the *penangallan* survives indefinitely in some sort of suspended animation. And when it does move, it flies."

Greg nodded. "You mean it turns itself into some kind of a bat."

Ibraham shook his head. "That's just superstition. The *penangallan* still retains human form—or part of its human form."

"I don't get it."

"These creatures can detach their heads from their bodies. And the head has the power of flight. When the head is removed, the stomach and intestines are pulled out and stay attached to it, receiving the blood it drinks."

The words triggered Greg's memory—just a flash, but enough. *The golden girl, sitting up and lifting her head from the open stump of the neck.* He'd seen it. It was true.

He felt a jarring movement and beside him Ibraham stirred in his seat. "Watch what you're doing," he said.

What Greg was doing was turning onto the concealed side road. Had they really come this far this quickly? Of course there was no traffic up here, no lights. Strange how easy it was to locate the hidden opening this second time around, even in the dark. But then again, it was associated with something he wasn't likely to forget.

The car entered and moved upward in a tunnel formed by the overhanging trees lining the roadway. Greg switched headlights, but even the brights were of little help here. Then the trees thinned, but the underbrush thickened and the car began to lurch around the sharp curves.

"Watch it!" Ibraham warned.

But Greg had already warned himself with the memory of what lay ahead. *A head—*

"I can't cut it," he said. "We've got to wait. Tomorrow. We'll do it tomorrow."

"Now." The gun jabbed against his ribs; Ibraham's voice jabbed his ear. "You're going now. Either behind the wheel or dumped in the trunk."

"You're bluffing—"

"That's what the old man thought."

Greg's hands were wet on the wheel, but they stayed there as the car inched forward over the rutted roadway and climbed around a curve. Now he glanced at the Malayan. "Suppose we're wrong. Suppose we don't find anything there?"

"I told you what my mother said. It's there and we'll find it."

"One thing I don't understand," Greg said. "If the stuff they had on their customers was so valuable, why wasn't it used?"

"My mother wondered about that too, but she didn't learn the plan until later, from the Marquess' lover."

"Plan?"

"Bit by bit the pieces fit together. The Marquess had bought the place with more than just profit in mind. Back in Kelanton she had a reputation as a *pawing*—a sorceress, you'd call it—and she gathered together and brought the *penangallans*, which she controlled for her own purposes. Which were to use blackmail money to take over other vice operations and gradually gain political power in the area. The *penangallans* would deal with those who stood in her way. She was ready to carry out her plan when the end came. You know the rest."

Greg frowned. "Your mother could have gone to the police—"

"She was a fifteen-year-old girl, an illegal immigrant with forged papers, who spoke almost no English. Even if she'd found a way to contact the authorities—do you think anyone would go along with what she said about hookers who remove their heads, and all the rest of it?"

Greg had no answer for that, only another question as they angled up the torturous trail. "The thing I saw," he said. "Why would it still be there after all these years? Why didn't it leave the place when the Marquess was killed?"

"The *penangallan* flies low," Ibraham said. "It can't soar like a bat, and it must protect its dangling stomach sac and intestines from harm. In Malaysia, homes are often guarded by garlands of *Jenyu* leaves hung on doors and windows. The *penangallan* fears the *Jenyu* plant's sharp thorns." He glanced at the looming pines and the clumps of underbrush clustered beneath them. "Here your hillsides are covered with cacti and all kinds of spiky vegetation. It would rip the creatures' guts if they tried to escape."

"But they wouldn't have to fly," Greg said. "They could go down staying in their bodies just as they did up there."

Ibraham shrugged. "A *penangallan* preserves its body by drinking fresh blood. Without it the body will decay just like any other corpse. So if they did try to come down in human form before decay set in, there'd be problems. I don't think they'd last very long if word got out that human heads were flying around Beverly Hills and sucking blood in Bel Air. Besides, they'd have to have a place to hide. And to store the vinegar."

"Vinegar?"

"If the *penangallan* flies, its entrails swell up when exposed to the open air. So afterward it must soak its lower parts in a jar or vat of vinegar to shrivel the stomach and bowels to normal size. Then it fits them back into the body when the head is replaced."

No way, Greg told himself. *Either this guy is crazy or I am. There are no such things, no such place, no house—*

They rounded the turn and there it was.

If the place had looked ghostly by day, it looked ghastly in the grayish shroud of moonlight filtering through lowering clouds. Its dark silhouette seemed to slant toward them as the hatchback halted amidst spirals of steam from the hood. Greg stared numbly at the house. If it was real, then what about the rest—

"Out," Ibraham said.

Greg hesitated, then took a deep breath. "Look, I've told you everything I know, everything that happened. There's no reason for me to go in again with you now."

"What about the material you were looking for?"

Greg took another deep breath. "I've changed my mind. I don't want any part of it."

33

"Afraid?"

"After what you told me? Damned right I am."

"You expect me to go in by myself?" Ibraham asked. "So you can drive off and leave me stranded?"

"I'll wait, I swear it. Hey, you can take my car keys—"

"I'm taking you."

The gun rose, and so did Greg. Ibraham tensed as Greg's hand went to the glove compartment, then relaxed as the younger man brought out his flashlight.

Together they left the car and moved to the entrance in silence. Even the sound of the wind had died; everything had died here.

Greg halted before the door, and his companion eyed the broken lock. "You're making a mistake," Greg said. "If what you told me is true, a gun won't protect us from that thing I saw."

"There are other ways," Ibraham said, raising the weapon as he spoke. "Inside."

Inside was pitch blackness pierced by the pinpoint flashlight beam. Greg adjusted it so that they stood in a wider circle of radiance, but the light was dim against the darkness beyond. The silence itself seemed more intense than outside; there was nothing to disturb it here, nothing until they came.

"Leave the front door open," Greg whispered. "We might want to get out of here in a hurry."

Ibraham shrugged. "As you wish." Moving forward, he peered toward the right archway. "What's in there?"

Greg described the parlor, and his captor nodded.

Now he glanced to his left. "And here?"

"The bar."

The two men halted just past the archway as the flashlight beam roamed the room.

"All that damage," Ibraham said. "This must be where the fighting took place." He peered at the stairs on the far side.

34

Greg spoke quickly. "You don't have to go up there. I told you there's nothing in those bedrooms."

"Except the last one," Ibraham countered. "That's reason enough. We've got to go up."

"You know what's there. You admitted your gun won't help."

Ignoring him, Ibraham scanned the tile shambles of the littered floor. His eyes swept over the topped tables, overturned chairs and broken glass. His eyes halted. "This will do," he said.

Greg followed his gaze to a chair turned upside down, two of its legs wrenched half-free from the base of the seat. "What do you mean?"

Ibraham told him what he meant. He told him what to do, then watched, gun in hand, while Greg did it. Getting the chair leg loose wasn't difficult, and locating a sharp knife in a drawer behind the bar wasn't a problem for him either. The hard part was whittling away at the wooden chair leg until the end was trimmed into a tapering shaft with a narrow point. It was Ibraham, rummaging through shelving beneath the bar counter, who came up with the bung-starter.

"Good," he said. "We're ready."

Greg didn't feel ready. He felt he needed out of here. Ibraham had already goaded him to the base of the stairs, and it was there that he turned.

"Hey, man," he said. "I thought we came here to look for that stuff."

"We will."

"You're wasting your time. It's not upstairs."

"But something else is. And we won't be safe looking around here until we dispose of it."

The gun muzzle guided Greg up the staircase. In the upper hallway the floorboards creaked, and so did the doors as Ibraham opened them in turn. But it was the sound of his own heartbeat that Greg heard as they reached the end of the hall and stood before the last door on the left.

It was Greg who opened the door, but Ibraham was the one who gasped as the flashlight beam encircled the burnished golden beauty of the naked girl on the bed.

35

Her eyes were closed, and this time she did not stir. Ibraham gestured impatiently, but Greg stood immobile at the bedside, staring down at the golden girl.

This was what he'd needed. Proof that he hadn't freaked out from dropping acid, that what he'd seen here before was real.

And if it was real, then so was the rest of what he'd seen, what had sent him screaming down the hillside. That's why he was standing here now, holding the sharpened stake. He knew what he must do, and this was the worst reality of all.

He took a step backward. He couldn't go through with this, no way, now was the time to get out of here—

The muzzle of the gun bit against his spine. Greg heard the faint click signalling the release of the safety catch.

The girl on the bed heard it too, for she stirred for a moment, stirred but didn't awaken.

Once she did, once she opened her eyes, it would be too late. Greg remembered the rows of pointed teeth, remembered the hands that tugged the head away from the neck swiftly, so very swiftly. Which meant he had to be swift too.

He belted the flashlight.

He lifted the stake with both hands.

Gasping with effort, he plunged it down into the cleft between the golden breasts.

Then her eyes did open, wide. Her lips retracted and he saw the teeth, saw the talons rise to slash at his face, claw at his wrists as he held the stake fast.

Snakelike she squirmed, and like a snake she hissed, but Ibraham was standing on the other side of the bed and he brought the broad head of the bung-starter down, driving the stake deep.

The golden hands tore frantically at the shaft imbedded between the golden breasts, but Greg's grip remained unbroken. He held the stake firmly as Ibraham hammered it home. There was a single shattering shriek as a gout of crimson geysered upward, then sudden silence.

Talons loosened their hold; the golden face fell back on the pillow, its slant-eyed stare veiled by the billowing black hair. No sound issued from the open mouth, and the blood around the base of the stake ceased further flow. Mercifully, there was no movement or hint of movement to come. The golden girl was dead.

Greg turned away, panting after his exertion, filling his labouring lungs with the acrid odor of blood. His stomach cramped and for a moment he thought he might pass out. Then he became aware that Ibraham was speaking.

"—not finished yet. But it should be safe to go now."

Greg unhooked his flashlight. "Go where?"

"To get what we came for." Ibraham motioned him to the door, and Greg noticed that he was again holding the gun.

So nothing had changed, really. Except that they'd come here this crazy midnight to pound a stake into the heart of a dead girl or an undead girl; it didn't matter which, because she was dead now. *We killed her and the stake went in and the blood spurted out just like in those horror movies only this wasn't a movie just a horror, God I need a fix—*

But there was no fix, not in the hall or on the stairs or down at the bar.

Ibraham's gun urged him along to the hall before the mottled mirror on the back wall. "Should be just about here," Ibraham said. He reached out and ran his free hand across the inner edge of the bar, muttering, "If my mother was right." A panel under the bar slid back silently, revealing a black rectangular opening.

"She was," Ibraham said.

Greg's flashlight dipped toward the darkness. "Lower," his captor said. "Must be some stairs."

There were. Greg descended first, beam fanning forward until he reached the bare stone surface below the fourteenth step. Ibraham followed, but this time his gun wasn't aimed at Greg. Like the flashlight, it swerved and circled, as if seeking possible targets in the cavernous cellar before them.

The two men moved slowly, silently. Nothing to hear but the thud of their own footsteps, nothing to see but the beam tracing a path along the stone floor beneath their feet.

Here the air was cooler, but the odor it carried, a mingling of dust and decay, was almost stifling. There was another smell, faint but pungent, which Greg couldn't identify.

Now Ibraham identified it for him. "Vinegar," he said. "Remember, I told you the *penangallan* shrinks its entrails in vinegar in order to squeeze them back down into the body? I was wondering where they kept their supply."

"But we didn't find any others—"

"My mother thought there could be a dozen among the Marquess' girls."

Greg started to speak, but Ibraham waved him to silence. "The scent is almost undetectable here. Probably evaporated."

"I'm not worried about the goddamn smell," Greg said. "But if there are more of those things down here—"

Suddenly his foot struck something, something that clattered as he stumbled back. The flashlight beam dipped down toward the stone surface, sweeping over the sprawled length of arm and leg bones, the ridged rib cage and nacreous neck of the skeleton.

It had no skull.

The rush came so quickly that Greg almost dropped the flashlight. Its beam wavered because his hand was shaking. No skull. No head. It was one of them.

Ibraham moved forward; his harsh whisper echoed through darkness: "Here's another."

Greg raised the flashlight, semi-circling its dim beam, then wished he hadn't.

The floor ahead was littered with bones. Some, heaped against the walls, were partially joined: a leg attached to a pelvis, a collarbone to a humerus, radius and ulna to the metacarpals. Two other skeletons were fully articulated but, like the first, they lacked skulls. Greg's stare swept across the scatter, but Ibraham's attention was elsewhere. He skirted the bonepile, threading his way between heaps and jumbles, then approached the makeshift wooden shed rising along the right side of the cellar. More skeletal fragments lay there, piled almost at random, amidst shreds of rotted cloth.

There was a door at the far end of the shed's wall, and Ibraham pulled it open slowly, revealing the wooden shelving ranged along the far side within.

"Get some light over here," he said. Greg started toward him, raising the flashlight. Its beam sought the shelves—long, low shelves bearing wide-mouthed, deep-bodied clay bowls. There were perhaps a dozen pots of them resting side by side like the pots in a florist's shop, but what bloomed in each were not flowers.

Greg stared at the rows of human skulls. And they grinned at him in greeting, grinned as though sharing some grisly secret that only the dead can know.

Ibraham moved beside him. "You see what's happened here? Those bowls must have been filled with vinegar."

"To shrink the intestines." Greg nodded. "But why didn't it work?"

"You can't store liquids in leaky containers," Ibraham explained. "And every one of these bowls is cracked."

Now, peering more closely, Greg could see what he meant. Most of the cracks were visible just above the base of each bowl to form a pattern, almost as though they'd been gouged out by some sharp tool or instrument.

Greg frowned. "Didn't they realize it was wrong to use these?"

"They had no other choice," Ibraham said. "She must have broken them after the raid. Probably that's how they escaped the madam's fate—they hid down here while the raid was going on. Maybe the raiding party killed the bartender too. Stands to reason they took the bodies away and got rid of them." He glanced down at the scattered bones. "But the *penangallans* were safe here. They must have stayed in hiding a long time, and when they came out they were hungry. And you know what happens when there's no food in the house."

Greg nodded. "You go out to eat."

"Exactly. They flew off to try their luck at hunting. But there's not much around, just birds and perhaps some small game. Since they couldn't fly down from here, that's all they could find. The only way they could survive was to hibernate." Ibraham gestured. "The one upstairs was smarter. She must have known how little success they'd have out there, because she didn't go. And when they returned and came down here she had a surprise for them."

"Like you said, she'd broken the bowls."

"That's what I figure. While their bodies rested out in the cellar, they settled their heads and entrails in the bowls here, but most of the vinegar leaked out quickly; before it could be effective it was gone. The girl we saw upstairs was gone too, after locking them in. She probably had her own bowl and vinegar supply tucked away somewhere upstairs, because she'd already planned what she was going to do."

"But what *could* she do?" Greg said.

"You still don't get it." Ibraham glanced down. "Don't these bones and skeletons tell their own story? The heads rested helplessly in those dried-out jars while the stomachs burst and rotted away. And trapped out here, the headless bodies, blind and squirming in the dark."

Greg grimaced. "And the thing upstairs—?"

"She ate them," Ibraham said. "That's what kept her alive all these years." He nodded at the skeletons and the piles of bones. "She didn't need to fly in search of food. Not with a dozen bodies down here, bodies that still moved, bodies filled with blood. She stripped the flesh from these bones bit by bit, sucked arteries and veins dry. It must have been done over a long period, and most of the while she slept, just as we found her."

Greg's stomach knotted convulsively. "I'm outta here," he panted, turning to seek the stairs.

"First we get what we came for." Ibraham's weapon pressed against

Greg from behind as he climbed. And back upstairs the gun prodded Greg to the rear of the room.

"Take a look behind the staircase," Ibraham ordered. "The madam could have had her office under there."

Greg swore silently. Of course the office would be in some place like that, close to the action but not easy for outsiders to spot. If he'd only looked around more carefully before going upstairs on the first visit, chances are he might not have had to go upstairs at all. The office would be where the madam kept the stuff. If he'd used his head and thought things through, he wouldn't be here now in the middle of the night, middle of nowhere, this crazy house with that crazy thing upstairs and a crazy gook downstairs pushing a gun into him for half of what they'd find.

"Let's go," the crazy gook was saying. "I tell you it's got to be here."

And that's where they found it, under the stairs. The door was metal, closed but unlocked, and behind it was the office. Or had been, until the intruders burst in, tore the drawers out of desks and filing cabinets, smashed them with crowbars and an axe that still lay atop shelving wrenched from a battered bookcase on the right wall.

Across from it, on the left wall, was an open safe.

Open, and empty.

Greg blinked at the bare steel shelf. "Gone; those bastards took the stuff with them—"

"Take another look," Ibraham said softly.

Greg followed his gaze, traveled with it across the bare concrete floor to the center of the room. His eyes followed a paper trail—or a trail of what had once been paper. Now it was just a brownish-gray muddle of charred shreds speckled with tiny glints from flecks of burned photos. From the trail rose an odor, faint as the scent of vinegar; the reek of long-dead ashes in which all hope lay buried.

"Outta here," Greg whispered.

Ibraham shook his head. "You think I don't know how you feel? I want

41

to forget it ever happened. But before we put it behind us, there's one more job. The *penangallan*—"

"It's dead," Greg said. "We killed it. You know that."

"Not so. Remember, the *penangallan* isn't like other bloodsuckers. As long as the head remains attached to the digestive tract it can still fly and feed. A stake is not enough."

"It's enough for me," Greg told him. "I'm not going to tangle with that thing."

"The stake probably paralyzes it, at least for a time," Ibraham said. "But we can't take chances. We must cut off the head."

"Forget it. I'm finished."

Ibraham ignored him, but his weapon did not.

Would he shoot? Greg thought of Bernie Tanner for a moment and he didn't need an answer. Instead he asked another question. "What do you want me to do?"

Ibraham nodded toward the toppled shelving at his right. "Over there," he said. "Get the axe."

Greg turned, imagining the impact of a bullet in his back. And perhaps it wouldn't have been imagination if they'd found that blackmail material intact. No reason for Ibraham not to shoot him then, kill him and take all the loot; nobody'd ever know. But that could still be true now. If they got rid of the *penangallan*, Ibraham would get rid of him too—because Greg was the only one who could tie him to Bernie Tanner's murder.

So there really wasn't much choice but for Greg to do exactly what he was told: reach out and pick up the axe. But it was his own idea to turn swiftly, raise the axe and bring it down right between Ibraham's eyes.

The gurgle was still dying in his victim's throat as Greg ran, reeling through the office doorway, the barroom, the hall, the open front door.

He squeezed into the car, fumbling for his keys, cursing the broken air conditioner but grateful for the breeze from the windows. The air was still warm and moist, but it was clean, free of must and dust, the scent of vinegar, the mingled odor of stale ashes and fresh blood.

Blood. He'd killed a man; he was a murderer. But nobody knew, nobody would ever know if he played it cool. Even if somebody wandered up to the house there was nothing to connect him with what they'd find. Get himself a set of tires tomorrow and the old tread marks wouldn't match the new. They might get prints off the doorknobs and axe handle, but they'd have nothing to match them with; he'd never been fingerprinted. And they wouldn't be looking for him in the first place, with nothing to go by.

So he was home free, would be now that the car had started, now that he was wheeling down the hillside, with every twist and turn taking him farther away from that damned house and that damned thing; taking him closer to the lights and the streets, streets where you could find a fast fix, find it and forget what had happened. It would just be like a bad trip, he didn't really kill anyone, and there wasn't really anything like that thing with the golden face and the almond eyes and the gleaming, pointed teeth in the crimson mouth he was seeing now in the rearview mirror, rising up from the backseat.

Greg screamed, and so did the brakes of the car as he spun the wheel, spun and lost because there was no way to win, no way to turn from that narrow, tangled trail.

And then the thing was hovering behind him, rising up and swooping forward, its viscera lashing and looping.

The slimy coils twirled and tightened around Greg's neck, and from the stalk-like stem above it the golden face dipped, lips fastening on Greg's flesh as the fangs found his throat. Ibraham had been right, after all.

Now Greg knew why a stake through the heart was not enough.

THE CALLING

David B. Silva

It never stops.

The whistle.

The sound is hollow, rising from a cork ball enclosed by red plastic. His mother no longer has the strength to blow hard—so the sound comes out as a soft song, like the chirping of a cricket somewhere off in another part of the house, just barely audible. But there. Always unmistakably there.

Blair buries his head beneath his pillow. He feels like a little boy again, trying to close out the world because he just isn't ready to face up to what is out there. Not yet. Maybe never, he thinks. How do you ever face up to something like cancer? It never lets you catch up.

It's nearly three o'clock in the morning now.

And just across the hall…

Even with his eyes closed, he has a perfect picture of his mother's room: the lamp on her nightstand casting a sickly gray shadow over her bed, the blankets gathered at her feet. Behind her, leaning against the wall, an old ironing board serves as a makeshift stand for the IV the nurse was never able to get into his mother's veins. And the television is on. And the bars on the side of the bed are up to prevent her from falling out. In his mind, Blair sees it all. Much too clearly.

He wraps himself tighter in the pillow.

The sound from the television is turned down, but he still thinks he can hear a scene from *Starsky and Hutch* squealing from somewhere across the hallway.

Then the whistle.

A thousand times he has heard it calling him…at all hours of the night…when she is thirsty…when she needs to go to the bathroom…when she needs to be moved to a new position…when she is in pain. A thousand times. He hears the whistle, the soft whirring call, coming at him from everywhere now. It is the sound of squealing tires from the street outside his bedroom window. It is the high-pitched hum of the dishwasher, of the television set, of the refrigerator when it kicks on at midnight.

Everywhere.

He has grown to hate it.

And he has grown to hate himself for hating it.

An ugly thought comes to mind: *why…doesn't she succumb? Why hasn't she died by now?* It's not the first time he's faced himself with this question, but lately it seems to come up more and more often in his mind. Cancer is not an easy thing to watch. It takes a person piece by piece…

"My feet are numb."

"Numb?"

"Like walking on sandpaper."

"From the chemo?"

"I don't know."

"Maybe…" Blair said naively, "maybe your feet will feel better after the chemo's over." He had honestly believed that it would turn out that way. When the chemo stopped, then so would her nausea and her fatigue and her loss of hair. And the worst of the side effects *had* stopped, for a while. But the numbness in her feet…that part had stayed on, an ugly scar left over from a body pumped full of dreadful things with dreadful names like doxorubicin and dacarbazine and vinblastine. Chemicals you couldn't even pronounce. It wasn't long before she began to miss a step here and there, and soon she was having to guide herself down the hallway with one hand pressed against the wall.

"Sometimes I can't even feel them," she once told him, a pained expression etched into the lines of her face.

She knows, Blair had thought at the time. She knows she's never going to dance again. The one thing she loves most in the world, and it's over for her.

The heater kicks on.

There's a vent under the bed where he's trying to sleep. It makes a familiar, almost haunting sound, and for an instant, he can't be sure if he's hearing the soft, high-pitched hum of the whistle. He lifts his head, listens. There's a hush that reminds him of a hot summer night when it's too humid to sleep. But the house seems at peace, he decides.

She's sleeping, he tells himself in a whisper. Finally sleeping.

For too long, the endless nights have haunted him with her cancerous likeness. She is like a butterfly; so incredibly delicate. She's lying in bed, her eyes half closed, her mouth hung open. Five feet, seven inches tall and not quite ninety pounds. The covers are pulled back slightly, her nightgown is unbuttoned and the outline of her ribs resembles a relief map.

She's not the same person he used to call his mother.

It's been ages since he's seen that other person. Before the three surgeries. Before the chemotherapy. Before the radiation treatments. Before he finally locked up his house and moved downstate to care for her...

She cried the first time she fell. It happened in her bedroom, early one morning while he was making breakfast. He heard a sharp cry, and when he found her, her legs were folded under like broken wings. She didn't have the strength to climb back to her feet. For a moment, her face was frozen behind a mask of complete surprise. Then suddenly, she started crying.

"Are you hurt?"

She shook her head, burying her face in her hands.

"Here, let me help you up."

"No." She motioned him away.

He retreated a step, maybe two, staring down at her, studying her, *trying* to put himself in her position. It occurred to him that she wasn't upset because of the fall—that wasn't the reason for the tears—she was crying because suddenly she had realized the ride was coming to an end. The last curve of the roller coaster had been rounded and now it was winding down once and for all. No more corkscrews. No more quick drops. No more three-sixties. Just a slow, steady deceleration until the ride came to a final standstill. Then it would be time to get off. The fall… marked the beginning of the end.

It had been a harsh realization for both of them.

He began walking with her after that, guiding her one step at a time from her bedroom to the kitchen, from the kitchen to the living room, from the living room to the bathroom. A week or two later, she was using a four-pronged cane. A week or two after that, she was using a wheelchair.

Everything ran together those few short weeks, a kaleidoscope of forfeitures, one after the other, all blended together until he could hardly recall a time when she had been healthy and whole…

She's going to die.

Blair has known that for a long time now.

She's going to die, but…

but…

How long is it going to take?

It seems like forever.

A car passes by his bedroom window. It's been raining lightly and the slick whine of the tires reminds him of that other sound, the one he's come to hate so much. He hates it because there's nothing he can do now. There's no going back, no making things better. All he can do is watch…and wait...and try not to lose his sanity to the incessant call of the whistle.

He bought the whistle for her nearly two and a half weeks ago in the sporting goods section of the local Target store. A cheap thing, made of plastic and a small cork ball. She wears it around her neck, dangling from the end of a thin nylon cord. Once, when it became tangled in the pillowcase, she nearly choked on the cord. But he refuses to let her take it off. It's the only way he has of keeping in touch with her at night. Unless he doesn't sleep. But he's already feeling guilty about the morning he found her sleeping on the floor in the living room...

When he went to bed—sometime around 1:30 or 2:00 in the morning—she'd been sleeping comfortably on the couch, and it seemed kinder not to disturb her. Seven hours later, after dragging himself out of the first sound night's sleep in weeks, he found her sitting on the floor.

"Jesus, Mom."

She was sitting in an awkward position, her legs folded sideways, one arm propped up on the edge of the couch, serving as a pillow. No blanket. Nothing on her feet to keep them from getting cold. And to think—she had spent the night like that.

He knelt next to her.

"Mom?"

Her eyes opened lazily. It wasn't terribly rational, but he held out a distant hope that she'd been able to sleep through most of the night. "I'm sorry," she said drowsily. "I couldn't get up...my legs wouldn't."

"I shouldn't have left you out here all night." He managed to get her legs straightened out, to get her back on the couch, under a warm blanket, with a soft pillow behind her head.

That afternoon, he bought her the whistle.

"When you need me, use the whistle. You got that?"

She nodded.

"Night or day, it doesn't matter. If you need me for something, blow the whistle." He paused, hearing his own words echo through his mind, and a cold, shuddering realization swept over him. He didn't know when it had happened, but somewhere along the line they had swapped roles. He was the parent now, she the child.

"What if I can't?"

"Try it."

Like everything else, her lungs had slowly lost their strength over the past few months, but she was able to put enough air into the whistle to produce a short, high-pitched hum.

"Great."

That was—what?—three weeks ago?

Blair sits up in bed. The streetlight outside his window is casting a murky blue-gray light through the bedroom curtains. The room is bathed in that light. It feels dark and strangely out of balance. He fluffs both pillows, stuffs them behind him, and leans back against the wall. Across the hall, the light flickers, and he knows the television is still on in his mother's room. It seems as if it's far away.

He shudders.

Let her sleep, he thinks. Let her sleep forever.

Sometimes the house feels like a prison. Just the two of them, caught in their life-and-death struggle. The ending already predetermined. It feels…not lonely, at least not in the traditional sense of the word…but… *isolated*. Outside these walls, there is nothing but endless black emptiness. But it's in here where life is coming to an end. Right here inside this house, inside these walls.

The television in her room flickers again.

Blair stares absently at the shifting patterns on the bedroom door across the hall. He used to watch that television set while she was in the bathroom. Sometimes as long as an hour, while she changed her colostomy bag…

"I'll never be close to a man again," she told him a few months after the doctors had surgically created the opening in the upper end of her sigmoid colon. The stoma was located on the lower left side of her abdomen. "How could anyone be attracted to me with this bag attached to my side? With the foul odor?"

"Someone will come along, and he'll love you for you. The bag won't matter."

A fleeting sigh of hope crossed her face, then she stared at him for a while, and that was that. She hadn't had enough of a chance to let it all out, so she kept it all in. The subject never came up again. And what she did on the other side of the bathroom door became something personal and private to her, something he half decided he didn't want to know about anyway.

If he had a choice.

"How're you doing in there?" he asked her late one night. He'd had to help her out of bed into the wheelchair, and out of the wheelchair onto the toilet. That was all the help she ever wanted. But she'd been in there, mysteriously quiet, for an unusually long time.

"Mom?"

"I'm okay," she whispered.

"Need any help?"

More quiet.

"Mom?"

"What?"

"Do you need any help?"

"I've lost the clip."

"The clip?"

"For the colostomy bag. It's not here."

"You want me to help you look for it?"

"No. See if you can find another one in one of the boxes in the closet."

"What does it look like?"

"It's…a little plastic…clip."

He found one, the last one, buried at the bottom of a box. It had the appearance of a bobby pin, a little longer, perhaps, and made of clear plastic instead of metal. "Found one."

"Oh, good."

He pulled the sliding pocket door open, more than was necessary if all he had intended to do was hand her the clip. The bathroom was smaller than he remembered it. There was a walker in front of her, for balance if she ever had to stand up, and the toilet had metal supports on each side to help her get up and down. It seemed as if the entire room was filled with aids of one kind or another.

"Is this what you're looking for?"

She was hunched over, leaning heavily against one of the support bars, her nightgown pulled up around her waist. Her face was weighted down with a weariness he'd never seen before and for the first time he understood how taxing this daily—sometimes three or four times a day—process had become for her. When she looked up at him, she seemed confused and disoriented.

"Are you okay?"

"I can't find the clip." She showed him the colostomy pouch for the first time. He couldn't bring himself to see how it was attached to her. Partly because he didn't want to know, and partly because that would have been like checking out her scars after surgery. Some things are better left to the imagination. More important, there was a woman in front of him whose ribs were protruding from her chest, whose face was a taut mask stretched across her skull, whose fingers were frail stick-like extensions of her hands; and this woman, looking so much like a stranger, was his mother. God, this was the woman who had given him birth.

"I've got the clip right here."

"Oh." She tried a smile on him, then glanced down at the bag in her hands. The process was slow and deliberate, but after several attempts she was finally able to fold the bottom side of the bag over.

Blair slid the clip across it. "Like this?"

She nodded.

And he realized something that should have occurred to him long before this: it was getting to be too much for her. As simple as emptying the bag might be, it was too confusing for her to work through the procedure now.

"Okay, I think we've got it."

"Oh, good."

"Ready to get out of here?"

"I think so." She whispered the words, and before they were all out, she started to cry.

"Mom?"

She looked up, her eyes as big as he'd ever seen them.

God, I hate this, he thought, taking hold of her hand and feeling completely, despairingly helpless. I hate everything about this.

"I didn't hurt you, did I?"

Her crying seemed to grow louder for a moment.

"Mom?"

"I didn't want for you to have to do that."

Lovingly, he squeezed her hand. "I know."

"I'm sorry."

"There's nothing to be sorry about. It's not a big deal." He pulled a couple of squares of toilet paper off the roll and handed them to her. "Things are hard enough. Don't worry about the small stuff. Okay?"

By the time he got her back into bed again, she had stopped crying. But he'd never know if it was because of what he'd said, or if it was because she didn't want to upset him anymore. They were both bending over backwards trying not to upset each other. There was something crazy about that.

The whistle blows.

At least he thinks it's the whistle. Sometimes, it's so damn hard to tell. There's that part of him, that tired, defeated part of him, that doesn't want to hear it anyway. How long can this thing drag on? Outside, all of thirty or forty feet away, a man jogs by with his dog on the end of a leash. People who pass this house don't have the slightest inkling of what's going on behind these walls. A woman's dying in here. And dying right alongside her is her son.

He pulls the covers back, hangs his feet over the edge of the bed.

For several days, she hasn't been able to keep food down. That memory comes horribly clear to him now...

"Feel better?"

She shook her head, her eyes closed, her body hunched forward over the bowl. Then suddenly another explosion of undigested soup burst from her mouth.

He held the stainless steel bowl closer, it felt warm in his hands. This had been going on for nearly three days now. It seemed like it might never stop. "You've got to take some Compazine, Mom."

"No."

"I can crush it for you and mix it with orange juice."

No response.

"Mom?"

No response.

"It'll go down easier that way."

"No."

"Christ, Mom, you've got to take something. You can't keep throwing up forever."

"The pills make me sick."

"Sicker than this?"

"They make me sick."

The whistle.

Blair slips a T-shirt over his head, pulls on a pair of Levi's. He tries to convince himself it'll stop. Maybe if he just leaves it alone, the sound will quietly drift into the background of the television set, and he'll be able to go back to sleep again...

"It'll stop on its own," she tried to convince him. "But if it doesn't, you'll dehydrate."

At last the vomiting appeared to have run its course. At least for the time being. She sat up a little straighter, taking in a deep breath. When she opened her eyes, they were faraway devoid of that sparkle that used to be so prominent behind her smile.

"Please, just take one Compazine."

"No."

Her skin began to lose its elasticity a few days later. The nausea stopped on its own, just like she'd said it would. But now, the only liquid she was taking was in the form of crushed ice, and there was the very real fear that dehydration might eventually become too painful for her.

"We can try an IV," the visiting nurse told him. "It won't help her live longer, but it'll probably make her more comfortable."

"Her veins aren't in very good shape."

"I've done this before."

They had to lean the ironing board up against the wall behind the headboard of her bed, because they didn't have an IV stand. The nurse hung the solution bag from one of the legs, and it seemed to work well enough. Then she tried to find a vein in his mother's right arm. It wasn't as easy as she'd thought it would be.

After several new entries, he turned away.

His mother began to whimper.

"The needle keeps sliding off." The nurse switched to her left arm, still struggling to find a workable vein, still failing miserably.

"That's enough," he finally said. "Let's just forget it."

"Her veins are so—"

There was a tear running down the cheek of his mother, and her mouth was twisted into a grimace which seemed frozen on her face.

"I'm sorry, Mom. I didn't mean to hurt you."

She rolled over, away from him...

He's standing at her bedroom door now, and she's in that same position: with her back turned toward him. He can see the black cord of the whistle tied around her neck, but the whistle is out of sight.

"Mom?"

The television flickers, drawing his attention. The scene is from *Starsky and Hutch*, shot inside a dingy, gray-black interrogation room. There's a young man sitting in an uncomfortable chair, Starsky standing over him, badgering him. It seems faraway and unimportant, and Blair's attention drifts easily back to his mother.

"You need anything?"

He moves around the foot of her bed, stops alongside her, the stainless steel bowl on the floor only a few inches away from his feet. "Mom?"

Her eyes are closed. She looks peaceful. Her nightgown is partially open in front. There's a thick tube running up the right side of her body and over her collarbone, running underneath the skin—like an artery— where the doctors had surgically implanted a shunt just a few short weeks earlier. Inside that tube, flowing out of her stomach, up her body, and back into her bloodstream, there's an endless current of cancerous fluid the tumor has been manufacturing for months.

In her left hand, wrapped around a long, thin finger, she's holding the nylon cord. He can almost hear the whistle's high-pitched hum calling to him from somewhere else. Sometimes it sounds as if it's singing his name—*Bl-air*—and he wonders if he'll ever be able to hear his name out loud again without being swept away by the strange concoction of resentment and helplessness that overwhelms him.

He touches her arm.

For a moment, everything is perfect: she's sleeping soundly, the house is quiet, the whistle stilled. Too good to be true.

"Mom?"

He places the palm of his hand over her chest, not believing what's going through his mind now. No intake of breath. No beat of heart. Instead, she feels cool to the touch, and…and absolutely…motionless.

"Jesus…"

"I don't want to talk to anyone."

"You sure?" he asked, holding his hand over the mouthpiece of the phone.

"They'll want to visit."

"Maybe not."

"I don't want anyone to see me like this."

It had happened so gradually: first the phone calls, then the visitors, finally the mail, and before he had realized what had happened, they had isolated themselves from the outside world. It was just the two of them, alone, inside the house, waiting for the cancer to run its course…

One more time, he places the palm of his hand ever so lightly across her chest.

"Mom? Please, Mom."

The wall above her bed flickers with the light from the television set, reflecting dully off the underside of the ironing board. He glances up, staring at the IV tube still dangling from the leg of the board, remembering too clearly, too vividly how much pain she went through the night the nurse had struggled to find a good vein in her arms.

"I never should have let her do that to you."

It feels cold inside the house. The room seems darker, smaller, a lonelier place.

He stands next to the bed, careful not to disturb her, though somewhere in the back of his mind he's already aware that she's finally at peace now. She's lying near the edge, her legs bent at the knees, her arms bent at the elbows. She looks as if she's praying. For a moment longer, he stares, failing to remember a time when the flesh wasn't pulled taut like a death mask across her face. This is the way he'll always remember her. It's all he has left.

The television draws his attention again, and that tiny distraction is somehow enough to stir him. He turns toward the door, wanting to be out of the room, thinking it can't be over…he doesn't want it to be over… maybe if he comes back later…

Then he hears it again.

The whistle. A soft, echoing sound. Calling him.

Bl-air.

"Mom?"

He expects different when he turns back, but he finds her eyes still closed, her chest still motionless. The nylon cord hangs loosely around her neck, the whistle lost somewhere inside her cotton nightgown. He sits on the edge of the bed, studying her, suddenly feeling like a little boy. It's a lonely feeling.

Bl-air.

It sounds again.

The whistle.

With care, he unwraps her finger from around the black cord. Then he opens the front of her nightgown and follows the cord down…down *there*…down to where the whistle is softly blowing, to where the cancer has been growing. The incision from her last surgery is open, the tissue curled back, and inside the cavity—ash gray and darker, pulsing—the cancer is wrapped like a kiss around the mouthpiece of the whistle, exhaling a soft humming song—

Bl-air.

It never stops.

The cancer never stops.

CHATTING WITH ANUBIS

Harlan Ellison

WHEN THE CORE DRILLING was halted at a depth of exactly 804.5 meters, one half mile down, Amy Guiterman and I conspired to grab Immortality by the throat and shake it till it noticed us.

My name is Wang Zicai. Ordinarily, the family name Wang—which is pronounced with the "a" in *father*, almost as if it were Wong—means "king." In my case, it means something else; it means "rushing headlong." How appropriate. Don't tell me clairvoyance doesn't run in my family... Zicai means "suicide." Half a mile down, beneath the blank Sahara, in a hidden valley that holds cupped in its eternal serenity the lake of the oasis of Siwa, I and a young woman equally as young and reckless as myself, Amy Guiterman of New York City, conspired to do a thing that would certainly cause our disgrace, if not our separate deaths.

I am writing this in Yin.

It is the lost ancestral language of the Chinese people. It was a language written between the 18th and 12th centuries before the common era. It is not only ancient, it is impossible to translate. There are only five people alive today, as I write this, who can translate this manuscript, written in the language of the Yin Dynasty that blossomed northeast along the Yellow River in a time long before the son of a carpenter is alleged to have fed multitudes with loaves and fishes, to have walked on water, to have raised

61

the dead. I am no "rice Christian." You cannot give me a meal and find me scurrying to your god. I am Buddhist, as my family has been for centuries. That I can write in Yin—which is to modern Chinese as classical Latin is to vineyard Italian—is a conundrum I choose not to answer in this document. Let he or she who one day unearths this text unscramble the oddities of chance and experience that brought me, "rushing headlong toward suicide," to this place half a mile beneath the Oasis of Siwa.

A blind thrust-fault, hitherto unrecorded, beneath the Mountain of the Moon, has produced a cataclysmic 7.5 temblor. It had leveled villages as far away as Bir Bū Kūsā and Abu Simbel. The aerial and satellite reconnaisance from the Gulf of Sidra to the Red Sea, from the Libyan Plateau to the Sudan, showed great fissures, herniated valleys, upthrust structures, a new world lost to human sight for thousands of years. An international team of paleoseismologists was assembled, and I was called from the Great Boneyard of the Gobi by my superiors at the Mongolian Academy of Sciences at Ulan Bator to leave my triceratops and fly to the middle of hell on earth, the great sand ocean of the Sahara, to assist in excavating and analyzing what some said would be the discovery of the age.

Some said it was the mythical Shrine of Ammon.

Some said it was the Temple of the Oracle.

Alexander the Great, at the very pinnacle of his fame, was told of the Temple, and the all-knowing Oracle who sat there. And so he came, from the shore of Egypt down into the deep Sahara, seeking the Oracle. It is recorded: his expedition was lost, wandering hopelessly, without water and without hope. Then crows came to lead them down through the Mountain of the Moon, down to a hidden valley without name, to the lake of the Oasis of Siwa, and at its center…the temple, the Shrine of Ammon. It was so recorded. And one thing more. In a small and dark chamber roofed with palm logs, the Egyptian priests told Alexander a thing that affected him for the rest of his life. It is not recorded what he was told. And never again, we have always been led to believe, has the Shrine of Ammon been seen by civilized man or civilized woman.

Now, Amy Guiterman and I, she from the Brooklyn Museum and I an honored graduate of Beijing University, together we had followed Alexander's route from Paraetonium to Siwa to here, hundreds of kilometres beyond human thought or action, half a mile down, where the gigantic claw diggers had ceased their abrading, the two of us with simple pick and shovel, standing on the last thin layer of compacted dirt and rock that roofed whatever great shadowy structure lay beneath us, a shadow picked up by the most advanced deep-resonance-response readings, verified on-site by proton free-precession magnetometry and ground-penetrating radar brought in from the Sandia National Laboratory in Albuquerque, New Mexico, in the United States.

Something large lay just beneath our feet.

And tomorrow, at sunrise, the team would assemble to break through and share the discovery, whatever it might be.

But I had had knowledge of Amy Guiterman's body, and she was as reckless as I, rushing headlong toward suicide, and in a moment of foolishness, a moment that should have passed but did not, we sneaked out of camp and went to the site and lowered ourselves, taking with us nylon rope and crampons, powerful electric torches and small recording devices, trowel and whisk broom, cameras and carabiners. A pick and a shovel. I offer no excuse. We were young, we were reckless, we were smitten with each other, and we behaved like naughty children. What happened should not have happened.

⚉

We broke through the final alluvial layer and swept out the broken pieces. We stood atop a ceiling of fitted stones, basalt or even marble, I could not tell immediately. I knew they were not granite, that much I did know. There were seams. Using the pick, I prised loose the ancient and concretized mortar. It went much more quickly and easily than I would have thought, but then, I'm used to digging for bones, not for buildings. I managed to chock the large set-stone in place with wooden wedges, until I had guttered the perimeter fully. Then, inching the toe of the pick into the fissure, I began levering the stone up, sliding the wedges deeper to keep the huge block from slipping back. And finally, though the block was at least sixty or seventy centimetres thick, we were able to tilt it up and, bracing our backs against the opposite side of the hole we had dug at the bottom of the core pit, we were able to use our strong young legs to force it back and away, beyond the balance point; and it fell away with a crash.

A great wind escaped the aperture that had housed the stone. A great wind that twisted up from below in a dark swirl that we could actually see. Amy Guiterman gave a little sound of fear and startlement. So did I. Then she said, "They would have used great amounts of charcoal to set these limestone blocks in place," and I learned from her that they were not marble, neither were they basalt.

We showed each other our bravery by dangling our feet through the opening, sitting at the edge and leaning over to catch the wind. It smelled *sweet*. Not a smell I had ever known before. But certainly not stagnant. Not corrupt. Sweet as a washed face, sweet as chilled fruit. Then we lit our torches and swept the beams below.

We sat just above the ceiling of a great chamber. Neither pyramid nor mausoleum, it seemed to be an immense hall filled with enormous statues of pharaohs and beast-headed gods and creatures with neither animal nor human shape...and all of these statues gigantic. Perhaps one hundred times life-size.

Directly beneath us was the noble head of a time-lost ruler, wearing the *nemes* headdress and the royal ritual beard. Where our digging had dropped shards of rock, the shining yellow surface of the statue had been chipped, and a darker material showed through. "Diorite," Amy Guiterman said. "Covered with gold. Pure gold. Lapis lazuli, turquoise, garnets, rubies—the headdress is made of thousands of gems, all precisely cut...do you see?"

But I was lowering myself. Having cinched my climbing rope around the excised block, I was already shinnying down the cord to stand on the first ledge I could manage, the empty place between the placid hands of the pharaoh that lay on the golden knees. I heard Amy Guiterman scrambling down behind and above me.

Then the wind rose again, suddenly, shrieking up and around me like a monsoon, and the rope was ripped from my hands, and my torch was blown away, and I was thrown back and something sharp caught at the back of my shirt and I wrenched forward to fall on my stomach and I felt the cold of that wind on my bare back. And everything was dark.

Then I felt cold hands on me. All over me. Reaching, touching, probing me, as if I were a cut of sliced meat lying on a counter. Above me I heard Amy Guiterman shrieking. I felt the halves of my ripped shirt torn from my body, and then my kerchief, and then my boots, and then my stockings, and then my watch and glasses.

I struggled to my feet and took a position, ready to make an empassing or killing strike. I was no cinema action hero, but whatever was there plucking at me would have to take my life despite I fought for it!

Then, from below, light began to rise. Great light, the brightest light I've ever seen, like a shimmering fog. And as it rose, I could see that the mist that filled the great chamber beneath us was trying to reach us, to touch us, to feel us with hands of ephemeral chilling ghostliness. Dead hands. Hands of beings and men who might never have been or who, having been, were denied their lives. They reached, they sought, they implored.

And rising from the mist, with a howl, Anubis.

God of the dead, jackal-headed conductor of souls. Opener of the road to the afterlife. Embalmer of Osiris, Lord of the mummy wrappings, ruler of the dark passageways, watcher at the neverending funeral. Anubis came, and we were left, suddenly, ashamed and alone, the American girl and I, who had acted rashly as do all those who flee toward their own destruction.

But he did not kill us, did not take us. How could he…am I not writing this for some never-to-be-known reader to find? He roared yet again, and the hands of the seekers drew back, reluctantly, like whipped curs into kennels, and there in the soft golden light reflected from the icon of a pharaoh dead and gone so long that no memory exists even on his name, there in the space half a mile down, the great god Anubis spoke to us.

At first, he thought we were "the great conqueror" come again. No, I told him, not Alexander. And the great god laughed with a terrible thin laugh that brought to mind paper cuts and the slicing of eyeballs. No, of course not that one, said the great god, for did I not reveal to him the great secret? Why should he ever return? Why should he not flee as fast as his great army could carry him, and never return? And Anubis laughed.

I was young and I was foolish, and I asked the jackal-headed god to tell *me* the great secret. If I was to perish here, at least I could carry to the afterlife a great wisdom.

Anubis looked through me.

Do you know why I guard this tomb?

I said I did not know, but that perhaps it was to protect the wisdom of the Oracle, to keep hidden the great secret of the Shrine of Ammon that had been given to Alexander.

And Anubis laughed the more. Vicious laughter that made me wish I had never grown skin or taken air into my lungs.

This is not the Shrine of Ammon, he said. Later they may have said it was, but this is what it has always been, the tomb of the Most Accursed One. The Defiler. The Nemesis. The Killer of the dream that lasted twice six thousand years. I guard this tomb to deny him entrance to the afterlife.

And I guard it to pass on the great secret.

"Then you don't plan to kill us?" I asked. Behind me I heard Amy Guiterman snort with disbelief that I, a graduate of Beijing University, could ask such an imbecile question. Anubis looked through me again, and said no, I don't have to do that. It is not my job. And then, with no prompting at all, he told me, and he told Amy Guiterman from the Brooklyn Museum, he told us the great secret that had lain beneath the sands since the days of Alexander. And then he told us whose tomb it was.

And then he vanished into the mist. And then we climbed back out, hand over hand, because our ropes were gone, and my clothes were gone, and Amy Guiterman's pack and supplies were gone, but we still had our lives.

At least for the moment.

I write this now, in Yin, and I set down the great secret in its every particular. All parts of it, and the three colors, and the special names, and the pacing. It's all here, for whoever finds it, because the tomb is gone again. Temblor or jackal-god, I cannot say. But if today, as opposed to last night, you seek that shadow beneath the sand, you will find emptiness.

Now we go our separate ways, Amy Guiterman and I. She to her destiny, and I to mine. It will not be long in finding us. At the height of his power, soon after visiting the Temple of the Oracle, where he was told something that affected him for the rest of his life, Alexander the Great died of a mosquito bite. It is said. Alexander the Great died of an overdose of drink and debauchery. It is said. Alexander the Great died of murder, he was poisoned. It is said. Alexander the Great died of a prolonged, nameless fever; of pneumonia; of typhus; of septicaemia; of typhoid; of eating off tin plates; of malaria. It is said. Alexander was a bold and energetic king at the peak of his powers, it is written, but during his last months in Babylon, for no reason anyone has ever been able to explain satisfactorily, he took to heavy drinking and nightly debauches…and then the fever came for him.

A mosquito. It is said.

No one will bother to say what has taken me. Or Amy Guiterman. We are insignificant. But we know the great secret.

Anubis likes to chat. The jackal-headed one has no secrets he chooses to keep. He'll tell it all. Secrecy is not his job. Revenge is his job. Anubis guards the tomb, and eon by eon makes revenge for his fellow gods.

The tomb is the final resting place of the one who killed the gods. When belief in the gods vanishes, when the worshippers of the gods turn away their faces, then the gods themselves vanish. Like the mist that climbs and implores, they go. And the one who lies encrypted there, guarded by the lord of the funeral, is the one who brought the world to forget Isis and Osiris and Horus and Anubis. He is the one who opened the sea, and the one who wandered in the desert. He is the one who went to the mountaintop, and he is the one who brought back the word of yet another god. He is Moses, and for Anubis revenge is not only sweet, it is everlasting. Moses—denied both Heaven and Hell—will never rest in the Afterlife. Revenge without pity has doomed him to eternal exclusion, buried in the sepulchre of the gods he killed.

I sink this now, in an unmarked meter of dirt, at a respectable depth; and I go my way, bearing the great secret, no longer needing to "rush headlong," as I have already committed what suicide is necessary. I go my way, for however long I have, leaving only this warning for anyone who may yet seek the lost Shrine of Ammon. In the words of Amy Guiterman of New York City, spoken to a jackal-headed deity, "I've got to tell you, Anubis, you are one *tough* grader." She was not smiling when she said it.

THE PEAR-SHAPED MAN

GEORGE R. R. MARTIN

THE PEAR-SHAPED MAN lives beneath the stairs. His shoulders are narrow and stooped, but his buttocks are impressively large. Or perhaps it is only the clothing he wears; no one has ever admitted to seeing him nude, and no one has ever admitted to wanting to. His trousers are brown polyester double knits, with wide cuffs and a shiny seat; they are always baggy, and they have big, deep, droopy pockets so stuffed with oddments and bric-a-brac that they bulge against his sides. He wears his pants very high, hiked up above the swell of his stomach, and cinches them in place around his chest with a narrow brown leather belt. He wears them so high that his drooping socks show clearly, and often an inch or two of pasty white skin as well.

His shirts are always short-sleeved, most often white or pale blue, and his breast pocket is always full of Bic pens, the cheap throwaway kind that write with blue ink. He has lost the caps or tossed them out, because his shirts are all stained and splotched around the breast pockets. His head is a second pear set atop the first; he has a double chin and wide, full, fleshy cheeks, and the top of his head seems to come almost to a point. His nose is broad and flat, with large, greasy pores; his eyes are small and pale, set close together. His hair is thin, dark, limp, flaky with dandruff; it never looks washed, and there are those who say that he cuts it himself with a bowl and a dull knife. He has a smell, too, the Pear-shaped Man; it is a sweet smell, a sour smell, a rich smell, compounded of old butter and rancid meat and vegetables rotting in the garbage bin. His voice, when he speaks, is high and thin and squeaky; it would be a funny little voice, coming from such a large, ugly man, but there is something unnerving about it, and something even more chilling about his tight, small smile. He never shows any teeth when he smiles, but his lips are broad and wet.

Of course you know him. Everyone knows a Pear-shaped Man.

Jessie met hers on her first day in the neighbourhood, while she and Angela were moving into the vacant apartment on the first floor. Angela and her boyfriend, Donald the student shrink, had lugged the couch inside and accidentally knocked away the brick that had been holding open the door to the building. Meanwhile Jessie had gotten the recliner out of the U-Haul all by herself and thumped it up the steps, only to find the door locked when she backed into it, the recliner in her arms. She was hot and sore and irritable and ready to scream with frustration.

And then the Pear-shaped Man emerged from his basement apartment under the steps, climbed onto the sidewalk at the foot of the stoop, and looked up at her with those small, pale, watery eyes of his. He made no move to help her with her chair. He did not say hello or offer to let her into the building. He only blinked and smiled a tight, wet smile that showed none of his teeth and said in a voice as squeaky and grating as nails on a blackboard, "Ahhhh. *There* she is." Then he turned and walked away. When he walked he swayed slightly from side to side.

Jessie let go of the recliner; it bumped down two steps and turned over. She suddenly felt cold, despite the sweltering July heat. She watched the Pear-shaped Man depart. That was her first sight of him. She went inside and told Donald and Angela about him, but they were not much impressed. "Into every girl's life a Pear-shaped Man must fall," Angela said, with the cynicism of the veteran city girl. "I bet I met him on a blind date once."

Donald who didn't live with them but spent so many nights with

Angela that sometimes it seemed as though he did, had a more immediate concern. "Where do you want this recliner?" he wanted to know.

Later they had a few beers, and Rick and Molly and the Heathersons came over to help them warm the apartment, and Rick offered to pose for her (wink wink, nudge nudge) when Molly wasn't there to hear, and Donald drank too much and went to sleep on the sofa, and the Heathersons had a fight that ended with Geoff storming out and Lureen crying; it was a night like any other night, in other words, and Jessie forgot all about the Pear-shaped Man. But not for long.

The next morning Angela roused Donald, and the two of them went off, Angie to the big downtown firm where she was a legal secretary, Don to study shrinking. Jessie was a freelance commercial illustrator. She did her work at home, which as far as Angela and Donald and her mother and the rest of Western civilization were concerned meant that she didn't work at all. "Would you mind doing the shopping?" Angie asked her just before she left. They had pretty well devastated their refrigerator in the two weeks before the move, so as not to have a lot of food to lug across town. "Seeing as how you'll be home all day? I mean, we really need some food."

So Jessie was pushing a full cart of groceries down a crowded aisle in Santino's Market, on the corner, when she saw the Pear-shaped Man the second time. He was at the register, counting out change into Santino's hand. Jessie felt like making a U-turn, busying herself until he'd gone. But that would be silly. She'd gotten everything she needed, and she was a grown woman, after all, and he was standing at the only open register. Resolute, she got in line behind him.

Santino dumped the Pear-shaped Man's coins into the old register and bagged up his purchase: a big plastic bottle of Coke and a one-pound bag of Cheez Doodles. As he took the bag, the Pear-shaped Man saw her and smiled that little wet smile of his. "Cheez Doodles are the best," he said. "Would you like some?"

"No, thank you," Jessie said politely. The Pear-shaped Man put the brown paper sack inside a shapeless leather bag of the sort that schoolboys

73

use to carry their books, gathered it up, and waddled out of the store. Santino, a big grizzled man with thinning salt-and-pepper hair, began to ring up Jessie's groceries. "He's something, ain't he?" he asked her.

"Who is he?" she asked.

Santino shrugged. "Hell, I dunno. Everybody just calls him the Pear-shaped Man. He's been around here forever. Comes in every morning, buys a bottle of Coke and big bag of Cheez Doodles. Once we run out of Cheez Doodles, so I tell him he oughta try them Cheetos or maybe even potato chips, y'know, for a change? He wasn't having none of it, though."

Jessie was bemused. "He must buy something besides Coke and Cheez Doodles."

"Wanne bet, lady?"

"Then he must shop somewhere else."

"Besides me, the nearest supermarket is nine blocks away. Charlie down at the candy store tells me the Pear-shaped Man comes in every afternoon at four-thirty and has himself a chocolate ice-cream soda, but far as we can tell, that's all he eats." He rang for a total. "That's seventy-nine eighty-two, lady. You new around here?"

"I live just above the Pear-shaped Man," Jessie confessed.

"Congratulations," Santino said.

Later that morning, after she lined the shelves and put away the groceries, set up her studio in the spare bedroom, made a few desultory dabs on the cover she was supposed to be painting for Pirouette Publishing, ate lunch and washed the dishes, hooked up the stereo and listened to some Carly Simon, and rearranged half of the living room furniture, Jessie finally admitted a certain restlessness and decided this would be a good time to go around the building and introduce herself to her new neighbors. Not many people bothered with that in the city, she knew, but she was still a small-town kid at heart, and it made her feel safer to know the people around her. She decided to start with the Pear-shaped Man down in the basement and got as far as descending the stairs to his door. Then a funny feeling came over her. There was no name on the doorbell, she noticed.

Suddenly she regretted her impulse. She retreated back upstairs to meet the rest of the building.

The other tenants all knew him; most of them had spoken to him, at least once or twice, trying to be friendly. Old Sadie Winbright, who had lived across the hall in the other first-floor apartment for twelve years, said he was very quiet. Billy Peabody, who shared the big second-floor apartment with his crippled mother, thought the Pear-shaped Man was creepy, especially that little smile of his. Pete Pumetti worked the late shift, and told her how those basement lights were always on, no matter what hour of the night Pete came swaggering home, even though it was hard to tell on account of the way the Pear-shaped Man had boarded up his windows. Jess and Ginny Harris didn't like their twins playing around the stairs that led down to his apartment and had forbidden them to talk to him. Jeffries the barber, whose small two-chair shop was down the block from Santino's, knew him and had no great desire for his patronage. All of them, every one, called him the Pear-shaped Man. That was who he was. "But who is he?" Jessie asked. None of them knew. "What does he do for a living?" she asked.

"I think he's on welfare," Old Sadie Winbright said. "The poor dear, he must be feebleminded."

"Damned if I know," said Pete Pumetti. "He sure as hell don't work. I bet he's a queer."

"Sometimes I think he might be a drug pusher," said Jeffries the barber, whose familiarity with drugs was limited to witch hazel.

"I betcha he writes them pornographic books down there," Billy Peabody surmised.

"He doesn't do anything for a living," said Ginny Harris. "Jess and I have talked about it. He's a shopping-bag man, he has to be."

That night, over dinner, Jessie told Angela about the Pear-shaped Man and the other tenants and their comments. "He's probably an attorney," Angie said. "Why do you care so much, anyway?"

Jessie couldn't answer that. "I don't know. He gives me goose bumps. I don't like the idea of some maniac living right underneath us."

Angela shrugged. "That's the way it goes in the big, glamorous city. Did the guy from the phone company come?"

"Maybe next week," said Jessie. "That's the way it goes in the big, glamorous city."

Jessie soon learned that there was no avoiding the Pear-shaped Man. When she visited the laundromat around the block, there he was, washing a big load of striped boxer shorts and ink-stained short-sleeved shirts, snacking on Coke and Cheez Doodles from the vending machines. She tried to ignore him, but whenever she turned around, there he was, smiling wetly, his eyes fixed on her, or perhaps on the underthings she was loading into the dryer.

When she went down to the corner candy store one afternoon to buy a paper, there he was, slurping his ice cream soda, his buttocks overflowing the stool on which he was perched. "It's homemade," he squeaked at her. She frowned, paid for her newspaper, and left.

One evening when Angela was seeing Donald, Jessie picked up an old paperback and went out on the stoop to read and maybe socialize and enjoy the cool breeze that was blowing up the street. She got lost in the story, until she caught a whiff of something unpleasant, and when she looked up from the page, there he was, standing not three feet away, staring at her. "What do you want?" she snapped, closing the book.

"Would you like to come down and see my house?" the Pear-shaped Man asked in that high, whiny voice.

"No," she said, retreating to her own apartment. But when she looked out a half hour later, he was still standing in the same exact spot, clutching his brown bag and staring at her windows while dusk fell around him. He made her feel very uneasy. She wished that Angela would come home, but she knew that wouldn't happen for hours. In fact, Angie might very well decide to spend the night at Don's place.

Jessie shut the windows despite the heat, checked the locks on her door, and then went back to her studio to work. Painting would take her mind off the Pear-shaped Man. Besides, the cover was due at Pirouette by the end of the week.

She spent the rest of the evening finishing off the background and doing some of the fine detail on the heroine's gown. The hero didn't look quite right to her when she was done, so she worked on him, too. He was the usual dark-haired, virile, strong-jawed type but Jessie decided to individualize him a bit, an effort that kept her pleasantly occupied until she heard Angie's key in the lock.

She put away her paints and washed up and decided to have some tea before calling it a night. Angela was standing in the living room, with her hands behind her back, looking more than a little tipsy, giggling. "What's so funny?" Jessie asked.

Angela giggled again. "You've been holding out on me," she said. "You got yourself a new beau and you didn't tell."

"What are you talking about?"

"He was standing on the stoop when I got home," Angie said, grinning. She came across the room. "He said to give you these." Her hand emerged from behind her back. It was full of fat, orange worms, little flaking twists of corn and cheese that curled between her fingers and left powdery stains on the palm of her hand. "For you," Angie repeated, laughing. "For you."

That night Jessie had a long, terrible dream, but when the daylight came she could remember only a small part of it. She was standing at the door of the Pear-shaped Man's apartment under the stairs; she was standing there in darkness, waiting, waiting for something to happen, something awful, the worst thing she could imagine. Slowly, oh so slowly, the door began to open. Light fell upon her face, and Jessie woke, trembling.

He might be dangerous, Jessie decided the next morning over Rice Krispies and tea. Maybe he had a criminal record. Maybe he was some kind of mental patient. She ought to check up on him. But she needed to know his name first. She couldn't just call up the police and say, "Do you have anything on the Pear-shaped Man?"

After Angela had gone to work, Jessie pulled a chair over by the front window and sat down to wait and watch. The mail usually arrived about eleven. She saw the postman ascend the stairs, heard him putting the mail in the big hall mailbox. But the Pear-shaped Man got his mail separately, she knew. He had his own box, right under his doorbell, and if she remembered right it wasn't the kind that locked, either. As soon as the postman had departed, she was on her feet, moving quickly down the stairs. There was no sign of the Pear-shaped Man. The door to his apartment was down under the stoop, and farther back she could see overflowing garbage cans, smell their rich, sickly sweet odor. The upper half of the door was a window, boarded up. It was dark under the stoop. Jessie barked her knuckles on the brick as she fumbled for his mailbox. Her hand brushed the loose metal lid. She got it open, pulled out two thin envelopes. She had to squint and move toward the sunlight to read the name. They were both addressed to Occupant.

She was stuffing them back into the box when the door opened. The Pear-shaped Man was framed by bright light from within his apartment. He smiled at her, so close she could count the pores on his nose, see the sheen of the saliva on his lower lip. He said nothing.

"I," she said, startled, "I, I...I got some of your mail by mistake. Must be a new man on the route. I, I was just bringing it back."

The Pear-shaped Man reached up and into his mailbox. For a second his hand brushed Jessie's. His skin was soft and damp and seemed much colder than it ought to be, and the touch gave her goose bumps all up and down her arm. He took the two letters from her and looked at them briefly and then stuffed them into his pants pocket. "It's just garbage," squeaked the Pear-shaped Man. "They shouldn't be allowed to send you garbage. They ought to be stopped. Would you like to see my things? I have things inside to look at."

"I," said Jessie, "uh, no. No, I can't. Excuse me." She turned quickly, moved out from under the stairs, back into the sunlight, and hurried back inside the building. All the way, she could feel his eyes on her.

⊰⊱

She spent the rest of that day working, and the next as well, never glancing outside, for fear that he would be standing there. By Thursday the painting was finished. She decided to take it in to Pirouette herself and have dinner downtown, maybe do a little shopping. A day away from the apartment and the Pear-shaped Man would do her good, soothe her nerves. She was being overimaginative. He hadn't actually done anything, after all. It was just that he was so damned *creepy.*

Adrian, the art director at Pirouette, was glad to see her, as always. "That's my Jessie," he said after he'd given her a hug. "I wish all my artists were like you. Never miss a deadline, never turn in anything but the best work, a real pro. Come on back to my office, we'll look at this one and talk about some new assignments and gossip a bit." He told his secretary to hold his calls and escorted her back through the maze of tiny little cubicles where the editors lived. Adrian himself had a huge corner office with two big windows, a sign of his status in Pirouette Publishing. He gestured Jessie to a chair, poured her a cup of herb tea, then took her portfolio and removed the cover painting and held it up at arm's length.

The silence went on far too long.

Adrian dragged out a chair, propped up the painting, and retreated several feet to consider it from a distance. He stroked his beard and cocked his head this way and that. Watching him, Jessie felt a thin prickle of alarm. Normally, Adrian was given to exuberant outbursts of approval. She didn't like this quiet. "What's wrong?" she said, setting down her teacup. "Don't you like it?"

"Oh," Adrian said. He put out a hand, palm open and level, waggled it this way and that. "It's well executed, no doubt. Your technique is very professional. Fine detail."

"I researched all the clothing," she said in exasperation. "It's all authentic for the period; you know it is."

"Yes, no doubt. And the heroine is gorgeous, as always. I wouldn't mind ripping her bodice myself. You do amazing things with mammaries, Jessie."

She stood up. "Then what is it?" she said. "I've been doing covers for you for three years now, Adrian. There's never been any problem."

"Well," he said. He shook his head, smiled. "Nothing, really. Maybe you've been doing too many of these. I know how it can go. They're so much alike, it gets boring, painting all those hot embraces one after another; so pretty soon you feel an urge to experiment, to try something a little bit different." He shook a finger at her. "It won't do, though. Our readers just want the same old shit with the same old covers. I understand, but it won't do."

"There's nothing experimental about this painting," Jessie said, exasperated. "It's the same thing I've done for you a hundred times before. *What* won't do?"

Adrian looked honestly surprised. "Why, the man, of course," he said. "I thought you'd done it deliberately." He gestured. "I mean, look at him. He's almost *unattractive*."

"What?" Jessie moved over to the painting. "He's the same virile jerk I've painted over and over again."

Adrian frowned. "Really now," he said. "Look." He started pointing things out. "There, around his collar, is that or is that not just the faintest hint of a double chin? And look at that lower lip! Beautifully executed, yes, but it looks well, gross. Like it was wet or something. Pirouette heroes rape, they plunder, they seduce, they threaten, but they do not drool, darling. And perhaps it's just a trick of perspective, but I could swear"—he paused, leaned close, shook his head— "no, it's not perspective, the top of his head is definitely narrower than the bottom. A pinhead! We can't have pinheads on Pirouette books, Jessie. Too much fullness in the cheeks, too. He looks as though he might be storing nuts for the winter." Adrian shook his head.

"It won't do, love. Look, no big problem. The rest of the painting is fine. Just take it home and fix him up. How about it?"

Jessie was staring at her painting in horror, as if she were seeing it for the first time. Everything Adrian had said, everything he had pointed out, was true. It was all very subtle, to be sure; at first glance the man looked almost like your normal Pirouette hero, but there was something just the tiniest bit off about him, and when you looked closer, it was blatant and unmistakable. Somehow the Pear-shaped Man had crept into her painting. "I," she began, "I, yes, you're right. I'll do it over. I don't know what happened. There's this man who lives in my building, a creepy-looking guy, everybody calls him the Pear-shaped Man. He's been getting on my nerves. I swear, it wasn't intentional. I guess I've been thinking about him so much it just crept into my work subconsciously."

"I understand," Adrian said. "Well, no problem, just set it right. We do have deadline problems, though."

"I'll fix it this weekend, have it back to you by Monday," Jessie promised.

"Wonderful," said Adrian. "Let's talk about those other assignments then." He poured her more Red Zinger, and they sat down to talk. By the time Jessie left his office, she was feeling much better.

Afterward she enjoyed a drink in her favourite bar, met a few friends, and had a nice dinner at an excellent new Japanese restaurant. It was dark by the time she got home. There was no sign of the Pear-shaped Man. She kept her portfolio under her arm as she fished for her keys and unlocked the door to the building.

When she stepped inside, Jessie heard a faint noise and felt something crunch underfoot. A nest of orange worms clustered against the faded blue of the hallway carpet, crushed and broken by her foot.

⚉

She dreamed of him again. It was the same shapeless, terrible dream. She

81

was down in the dark beneath the stoop, near the trash bins crawling with all kinds of things, waiting at his door. She was frightened, too frightened to knock or open the door yet helpless to leave. Finally the door crept open of its own accord. There he stood, smiling, smiling. "Would you like to stay?" he said, and the last words echoed, *to stay to stay to stay to stay*, and he reached out for her, and his fingers were as soft and pulpy as earthworms when he touched her on the cheek.

The next morning Jessie arrived at the offices of Citywide Realty just as they opened their doors. The receptionist told her that Edward Selby was out showing some condos; she couldn't say when he'd be in. "That's all right," Jessie said. "I'll wait." She settled down to leaf through some magazines, studying pictures of houses she couldn't afford.

Selby arrived just before eleven. He looked momentarily surprised to see her, before his professional smile switched on automatically. "Jessie," he said, "how nice. Something I can do for you?"

"Let's talk," she said, tossing down the magazines.

They went to Selby's desk. He was still only an associate with the rental firm, so he shared the office with another agent, but she was out, and they had the room to themselves. Selby settled himself into his chair and leaned back. He was a pleasant-looking man, with curly brown hair and white teeth, his eyes careful behind silver aviator frames. "Is there a problem?" he asked.

Jessie leaned forward. "The Pear-shaped Man," she said.

Selby arched one eyebrow. "I see. A harmless eccentric."

"Are you sure of that?"

He shrugged. "He hasn't murdered anybody yet, at least that I know of."

"How much do you know about him? For starters, what's his name?"

"Good question," Selby said, smiling. "Here at Citywide Realty we just think of him as the Pear-shaped Man. I don't think I've ever gotten a name out of him."

"What the hell do you mean?" Jessie demanded. "Are you telling me his checks have THE PEAR-SHAPED MAN printed on them?"

Selby cleared his throat. "Well, no. Actually, he doesn't use checks. I come by on the first of every month to collect, and knock on his door, and he pays me in cash. One-dollar bills, in fact. I stand there, and he counts out the money into my hand, dollar by dollar. I'll confess, Jessie, that I've never been inside the apartment, and I don't especially care to. Kind of a funny smell, you know? But he's a good tenant, as far as we're concerned. Always has his rent paid on time. Never bitches about rent hikes. And he certainly doesn't bounce checks on us." He showed a lot of teeth, a broad smile to let her know he was joking.

Jessie was not amused. "He must have given a name when he first rented the apartment."

"I wouldn't know about that," Selby said. "I've only handled that building for six years. He's been down in the basement a lot longer than that."

"Why don't you check his lease?"

Selby frowned. "Well, I could dig it up, I suppose. But really, is his name any of your business? What's the problem here, anyway? Exactly what has the Pear-shaped Man *done*?"

Jessie sat back and crossed her arms. "He looks at me."

"Well," Selby said, carefully, "I, uh, well, you're an attractive woman, Jessie. I seem to recall asking you out myself."

"That's different," she said. "You're normal. It's the way he looks at me."

"Undressing you with his eyes?" Selby suggested.

Jessie was nonplussed. "No," she said. "That isn't it. It's not sexual, not in the normal way, anyhow. I don't know how to explain it. He keeps asking me down to his apartment. He's always hanging around."

"Well, that's where he lives."

"He bothers me. He's crept into my paintings."

This time both of Selby's eyebrows went up. "Into your paintings?" he said. There was a funny hitch in his voice.

Jessie was getting more and more discomfited; this wasn't coming out right at all. "Okay, it doesn't sound like much, but he's *creepy*, I tell you. His lips are always wet. The way he smiles. His eyes. His squeaky little voice. And that smell. Jesus Christ, you collect his rent, you ought to know."

The realtor spread his hands helplessly. "It's not against the law to have body odor. It's not even a violation of his lease."

"Last night he snuck into the building and left a pile of Cheez Doodles right where I'd step in them."

"Cheez Doodles?" Selby said. His voice took on a sarcastic edge. "God, not *Cheez Doodles*! How fucking heinous! Have you informed the police?"

"It's not funny. What was he doing inside the building anyway?"

"He lives there."

"He lives in the basement. He has his own door, he doesn't need to come into our hallway. Nobody but the six regular tenants ought to have keys to that door."

"Nobody does, as far as I know," Selby said. He pulled out a notepad. "Well, that's something, anyway. I'll tell you what, I'll have the lock changed on the outer door. The Pear-shaped Man won't get a key. Will that make you happy?"

"A little," said Jessie, slightly mollified.

"I can't promise that he won't get in," Selby cautioned. "You know how it is. If I had a nickel for every time some tenant has taped over a lock or propped open a door with a doorstop because it was more convenient, well…"

"Don't worry, I'll see that nothing like that happens. What about his name? Will you check the lease for me?"

Selby sighed. "This is really an invasion of privacy. But I'll do it. A personal favour. You owe me one." He got up and went across the room to a black metal filing cabinet, pulled open a drawer, rummaged around, and came out with a legal-sized folder. He was flipping through it as he returned to his desk.

"Well?" Jessie asked, impatiently.

"Hmmmm," Selby said. "Here's your lease. And here's the others." He went back to the beginning and checked the papers one by one. "Winbright,

Peabody, Pumetti, Harris, Jeffries." He closed the file, looked up at her, and shrugged. "No lease. Well, it's a crummy little apartment, and he's been there forever. Either we've misfiled his lease or he never had one. It's not unknown. A month-to-month basis..."

"Oh, great," Jessie said. "Are you going to do anything about it?"

"I'll change that lock," Selby said. "Beyond that, I don't know what you expect of me. I'm not going to evict the man for offering you Cheez Doodles."

The Pear-shaped Man was standing on the stoop when Jessie got home, his battered bag tucked up under one arm. He smiled when he saw her approach. *Let him touch me*, she thought; *just let him touch me when I walk by, and I'll have him booked for assault so fast it'll make his little pointy head swim.* But the Pear-shaped Man made no effort to grab her. "I have things to show you downstairs," he said as Jessie ascended the stairs. She had to pass within a foot of him; the smell was overwhelming today, a rich odor like yeast and decaying vegetables. "Would you like to look at my things?" he called after her. Jessie unlocked the door and slammed it behind her.

I'm not going to think about him, she told herself inside, over a cup of tea. She had work to do. She'd promised Adrian the cover by Monday, after all. She went into her studio, drew back the curtains, and set to work, determined to eradicate every hint of the Pear-shaped Man from the cover. She painted away the double chin, firmed up the jaw, redid those tight wet lips, darkened the hair, made it blacker and bushier and more wind tossed so the head didn't seem to come to such a point. She gave him sharp, high, pronounced cheekbones—cheekbones like the blade of a knife—made the face almost gaunt. She even changed the color of his eyes. Why had she given him those weak, pale eyes? She made the eyes green, a crisp, clean, commanding green, full of vitality.

It was almost midnight by the time she was done, and Jessie was exhausted, but when she stepped back to survey her handiwork, she was delighted. The man was a real Pirouette hero now: a rakehell, a rogue, a hell-raiser whose robust exterior concealed a brooding, melancholy, poetic soul. There was nothing the least bit pear-shaped about him. Adrian would have puppies.

It was a good kind of tiredness. Jessie went to sleep feeling altogether satisfied. Maybe Selby was right, she was too imaginative, she'd really let the Pear-shaped Man get to her. But work, good hard old-fashioned work, was the perfect antidote for these shapeless fears of hers. Tonight, she was sure, her sleep would be deep and dreamless.

She was wrong. There was no safety in her sleep. She stood trembling on his doorstep once again. It was so dark down there, so filthy. The rich, ripe smell of the garbage cans was overwhelming, and she thought she could hear things moving in the shadows. The door began to open. The Pear-shaped Man smiled at her and touched her with cold, soft fingers like a nest of grubs. He took hold of her by the arm and drew her inside, inside, inside, inside…

Angela knocked on her door the next morning at ten. "Sunday brunch," she called out. "Don is making waffles. With chocolate chips and fresh strawberries. And bacon. And coffee. And O.J. Want some?"

Jessie sat up in bed. "Don? Is he here?"

"He stayed over," Angela said.

Jessie climbed out of bed and pulled on a paint-splattered pair of jeans. "You know I'd never turn down one of Don's brunches. I didn't even hear you guys come in."

"I snuck my head into your studio, but you were painting away, and you didn't even notice. You had that intent look you get sometimes, you know, with the tip of your tongue peeking out of one corner of your mouth. I figured it was better not to disturb the artist at work." She giggled. "How you avoided hearing the bedsprings, though, I'll never know."

Breakfast was a triumph. There were times when Jessie couldn't understand just what Angela saw in Donald the student shrink, but mealtimes were not among them. He was a splendid cook. Angela and Donald were still lingering over coffee, and Jessie over tea, at eleven, when they heard noises from the hall. Angela went to check. "Some guy's out there changing the lock," she said when she returned. "I wonder what that's all about."

"I'll be damned," Jessie said. "And on the weekend, too. That's time and a half. I never expected Selby to move so fast."

Angela looked at her curiously. "What do you know about this?"

So Jessie told them all about her meeting with the realtor and her encounters with the Pear-shaped Man. Angela giggled once or twice, and Donald slipped into his wise shrink face. "Tell me, Jessie," he said when she had finished, "Don't you think you're overreacting a bit here?"

"No," Jessie said curtly.

"You're stonewalling," Donald said. "Really now, try and look at your actions objectively. What has this man done to you?"

"Nothing, and I intend to keep it that way," Jessie snapped. "I didn't ask for your opinion."

"You don't have to ask," Donald said. "We're friends, aren't we? I hate to see you getting upset over nothing. It sounds to me as though you're developing some kind of phobia about a harmless neighbourhood character."

Angela giggled. "He's just got a crush on you, that's all. You're such a heartbreaker."

Jessie was getting annoyed. "You wouldn't think it was funny if he was leaving Cheez Doodles for you," she said angrily. "There's something... well, something *wrong* there. I can feel it."

Donald spread his hands. "Something wrong? Most definitely. The man is obviously very poorly socialized. He's unattractive, sloppy, he doesn't conform to normal standards of dress or personal hygiene, he has unusual eating habits and a great deal of difficulty relating to others. He's probably a very lonely person and no doubt deeply neurotic as well. But

87

none of this makes him a killer or a rapist, does it? Why are you becoming so obsessed with him?"

"I am not becoming obsessed with him."

"Obviously you are," Donald said.

"She's in love," Angela teased.

Jessie stood up. "I am *not* becoming obsessed with him!" she shouted. "And this discussion has just ended."

That night, in her dream, Jessie saw inside for the first time. He drew her in, and she found she was too weak to resist. The lights were very bright inside, and it was warm and oh so humid, and the air seemed to move as if she had entered the mouth of some great beast, and the walls were orange and flaky and had a strange, sweet smell, and there were empty plastic Coke bottles everywhere and bowls of half-eaten Cheez Doodles, too, and the Pear-shaped Man said, "You can see my things, you can have my things," and he began to undress, unbuttoning his short-sleeved shirt, pulling it off, revealing dead, white, hairless flesh and two floppy breasts, and the right breast was stained with blue ink from his leaking pens, and he was smiling, smiling, and he undid his thin belt, and then pulled down the fly on his brown polyester pants, and Jessie woke screaming.

On Monday morning, Jessie packed up her cover painting, phoned a messenger service, and had them take it down to Pirouette for her. She wasn't up to another trip downtown. Adrian would want to chat, and Jessie wasn't in a very sociable mood. Angela kept needling her about the Pear-shaped Man, and it had left her in a foul temper. Nobody seemed to understand. There was something wrong with the Pear-shaped Man, something serious, something horrible. He was no joke. He was frightening. Somehow she had to prove it. She had to learn his name, had to find out what he was hiding.

She could hire a detective, except detectives were expensive. There had to be something she could do on her own. She could try his mailbox again.

She'd be better off if she waited until the day the gas and electric bills came, though. He had lights in his apartment, so the electric company would know his name. The only problem was that the electric bill wasn't due for another couple of weeks.

The living room windows were wide open, Jessie noticed suddenly. Even the drapes had been drawn all the way back. Angela must have done it that morning before taking off for work. Jessie hesitated and then went to the window. She closed it, locked it, moved to the next, closed it, locked it. It made her feel safer. She told herself she wouldn't look out. It would be better if she didn't look out.

How could she not look out? She looked out. He was there, standing on the sidewalk below her, looking up. "You could see my things," he said in his high, thin voice. "I knew when I saw you that you'd want my things. You'd like them. We could have food." He reached into a bulgy pocket, brought out a single Cheez Doodle, held it up to her. His mouth moved silently.

"Get away from here, or I'll call the police!" Jessie shouted.

"I have something for you. Come to my house and you can have it. It's in my pocket. I'll give it to you."

"No you won't. Get away, I warn you. Leave me alone." She stepped back, closed the drapes. It was gloomy in here with the drapes pulled, but that was better than knowing that the Pear-shaped Man was looking in. Jessie turned on a light, picked up a paperback, and tried to read. She found herself turning pages rapidly and realized she didn't have the vaguest idea of what the words meant. She slammed down the book, marched into the kitchen, made a tuna salad sandwich on whole wheat toast. She wanted something with it, but she wasn't sure what. She took out a dill pickle and sliced it into quarters, arranged it neatly on her plate, searched through her cupboard for some potato chips. Then she poured a big fresh glass of milk and sat down to lunch.

She took one bite of the sandwich, made a face, and shoved it away. It tasted funny. Like the mayonnaise had gone bad or something. The pickle was too sour, and the chips seemed soggy and limp and much too salty. She didn't want potato chips anyway. She could picture them in her head, almost taste them. Her mouth watered.

Then she realized what she was thinking and almost gagged. She got up and scraped her lunch into the garbage. She had to get out of here, she thought wildly. She'd go see a movie or something, forget all about the Pear-shaped Man for a few hours. Maybe she could go to a singles bar somewhere, pick someone up, get laid. At his place. Away from here. Away from the Pear-shaped Man. That was the ticket. A night away from the apartment would do her good.

She went to the window, pulled aside the drapes, peered out.

The Pear-shaped Man smiled, shifted from side to side. He had his misshapen briefcase under his arm. His pockets bulged. Jessie felt her skin crawl. He was *revolting*, she thought. But she wasn't going to let him keep her prisoner.

She gathered her things together, slipped a little steak knife into her purse just in case, and marched outside. "Would you like to see what I have in my case?" the Pear-shaped Man asked her when she emerged. Jessie had decided to ignore him. If she did not reply at all, just pretended he wasn't there, maybe he'd grow bored and leave her alone. She descended the steps briskly and set off down the street. The Pear-shaped Man followed close behind her. "They're all around us," he whispered. She could smell him hurrying a step or two behind her, puffing as he walked. "They are. They laugh at me. They don't understand, but they want my things. I can show you proof. I have it down in my house. I know you want to come see."

Jessie continued to ignore him. He followed her all the way to the bus stop.

The movie was a dud. Having skipped lunch, Jessie was hungry. She got a Coke and a tub of buttered popcorn from the candy counter. The Coke was three-quarters crushed ice, but it still tasted good. She couldn't eat the popcorn. The fake butter they used had a vaguely rancid smell that reminded her of the Pear-shaped Man. She tried two kernels and felt sick.

Afterward, though, she did a little better. His name was Jack, he said. He was a sound man on a local TV news show, and he had an interesting face: an easy smile, Clark Gable ears, nice gray eyes with friendly little crinkles in the corners. He bought her a drink and touched her hand; but the way he did it was a little clumsy, like he was a bit shy about this whole scene, and Jessie liked that. They had a few drinks together, and then he suggested dinner back at his place. Nothing fancy, he said. He had some cold cuts in the fridge; he could whip up some jumbo sandwiches and show her his stereo system, which was some kind of special super setup he'd rigged himself. That all sounded fine to her.

His apartment was on the twenty-third floor of a midtown high rise, and from his windows you could see sailboats taking off on the horizon. Jack put the new Linda Ronstadt album on the stereo while he went to make the sandwiches. Jessie watched the sailboats. She was finally beginning to relax. "I have a beer or ice tea," Jack called from the kitchen. "What'll it be?"

"Coke," she said absently.

"No Coke," he called back. "Beer or ice tea."

"Oh," she said, somehow annoyed. "Ice tea, then."

"You got it. Rye or wheat?"

"I don't care," she said. The boats were very graceful. She'd like to paint them someday. She could paint Jack, too. He looked like he had a nice body.

"Here we go," he said, emerging from the kitchen carrying a tray. "I hope you're hungry."

"Famished," Jessie said, turning away from the window. She went over to where he was setting the table and froze.

"What's wrong?" Jack said. He was holding out a white stoneware plate. On top of it was a truly gargantuan ham-and-Swiss sandwich on fresh deli rye, lavishly slathered with mustard, and next to it, filling up the rest of the plate, was a pile of puffy orange cheese curls. They seemed to writhe and move, to edge toward the sandwich, toward her. "Jessie?" Jack said.

She gave a choked, inarticulate cry and pushed the plate away wildly. Jack lost his grip; ham, Swiss cheese, bread, and Cheez Doodles scattered in all directions. A Cheez Doodle brushed against Jessie's leg. She whirled and ran from the apartment.

Jessie spent the night alone at a hotel and slept poorly. Even here, miles from the apartment, she could not escape the dream. It was the same as before, the same, but each night it seemed to grow longer, each night it went a little further. She was on the stoop, waiting, afraid. The door opened, and he drew her inside, the orange warm, the air like fetid breath, the Pear-shaped Man smiling. "You can see my things," he said, "you can have my things," and then he was undressing, his shirt first, his skin so white, dead flesh, heavy breasts with a blue ink stain, his belt, his pants falling, polyester puddling around his ankles, all the trash in his pockets scattering on the floor, and he really was pear-shaped, it wasn't just the way he dressed, and then the boxer shorts last of all, and Jessie looked down despite herself and there was no hair and it was small and wormy and kind of yellow, like a cheese curl, and it moved slightly and the Pear-shaped Man was saying, "I want your things now, give them to me, let me see your things," and why couldn't she run, her feet wouldn't move, but her hands did, her hands, and she began to undress.

The hotel detective woke her, pounding on her door, demanding to know what the problem was and why she was screaming.

⧈

She timed her return home so that the Pear-shaped Man would be away on his morning run to Santino's Market when she arrived. The house was empty. Angela had already gone to work, leaving the living room windows open again. Jessie closed them, locked them, and pulled the drapes. With luck, the Pear-shaped Man would never know that she'd come home.

Already the day outside was swelteringly hot. It was going to be a real scorcher. Jessie felt sweaty and soiled. She stripped, dumped her clothing into the wicker hamper in her bedroom, and immersed herself in a long, cold shower. The icy water hurt, but it was a good clean kind of hurting, and it left her feeling invigorated. She dried her hair and wrapped herself in a huge, fluffy blue towel, then padded back to her bedroom, leaving wet footprints on the bare wood floors.

A halter top and a pair of cutoffs would be all she'd need in this heat, Jessie decided. She had a plan for the day firmly in mind. She'd get dressed, do a little work in her studio, and after that she could read or watch some soaps or something. She wouldn't go outside; she wouldn't even look out the window. If the Pear-shaped Man was at his vigil, it would be a long, hot, boring afternoon for him.

Jessie laid out her cutoffs and a white halter top on the bed, draped the wet towel over a bedpost, and went to her dresser for a fresh pair of panties. She ought to do the laundry soon, she thought absently as she snatched up a pair of pink bikini briefs.

A Cheez Doodle fell out.

Jessie recoiled, shuddering. It had been *inside*, she thought wildly, it had been inside the briefs. The powdery cheese had left a yellow stain on the fabric. The Cheez Doodle lay where it had fallen, in the open drawer on top of her underwear. Something like terror took hold of her. She balled the bikini briefs up in her fist and tossed them away with revulsion. She grabbed another pair of panties, shook them, and another Cheez Doodle leapt out. And then another. Another. She began to make a thin, hysterical sound, but she kept on. Five pairs, six, nine, that was all, but that was enough. Someone had opened her drawer and taken out every pair of panties and carefully wrapped a Cheez Doodle in each and put them all back.

It was a ghastly joke, she thought. Angela, it had to be Angela who'd done it, maybe she and Donald together. They thought this whole thing about the Pear-shaped Man was a big laugh, so they decided to see if they could really freak her out.

93

Except it hadn't been Angela. She knew it hadn't been Angela.

Jessie began to sob uncontrollably. She threw her balled-up panties to the floor and ran from the room, crushing Cheez Doodles into the carpet.

Out in the living room, she didn't know where to turn. She couldn't go back to her bedroom, *couldn't*, not just now, not until Angela got back, and she didn't want to go to the windows, even with the drapes closed. He was out there, Jessie could feel it, could feel him staring up at the windows. She grew suddenly aware of her nakedness and covered herself with her hands. She backed away from the windows, step by uncertain step, and retreated to her studio.

Inside she found a big square package leaning up against the door, with a note from Angela taped to it. "Jess, this came for you last evening," signed with Angie's big winged A. Jessie stared at the package, uncomprehending. It was from Pirouette. It was her painting, the cover she'd rushed to redo for them. Adrian had sent it back. Why?

She didn't want to know. She had to know.

Wildly, Jessie ripped at the brown paper wrappings, tore them away in long, ragged strips, baring the cover she'd painted. Adrian had written on the mat; she recognized his hand. "Not funny, kid," he'd scrawled. "Forget it."

"No," Jessie whimpered, backing off.

There it was, her painting, the familiar background, the trite embrace, the period costumes researched so carefully, but no, she hadn't done that, someone had changed it, it wasn't her work, the woman was her, her, her, slender and strong with sandy blond hair and green eyes full of rapture, and he was crushing her to him, to *him*, the wet lips and white skin, and he had a blue ink stain on his ruffled lace shirtfront and dandruff on his velvet jacket and his head was pointed and his hair was greasy and the fingers wrapped in her locks were stained yellow, and he was smiling thinly and pulling her to him and her mouth was open and her eyes half closed and it was him and it was her, and there was her own signature, there, down at the bottom.

"No," she said again. She backed away, tripped over an easel, and fell.

94

She curled up into a little ball on the floor and lay there sobbing, and that was how Angela found her, hours later.

Angela laid her out on the couch and made a cold compress and pressed it to her forehead. Donald stood in the doorway between the living room and the studio, frowning, glancing first at Jessie and then in at the painting and then at Jessie again. Angela said soothing things and held Jessie's hand and got her a cup of tea. Little by little her hysteria began to ebb. Donald crossed his arms and scowled. Finally, when Jessie had dried the last of her tears, he said, "This obsession of yours has gone too far."

"Don, don't," Angela said. "She's terrified."

"I can see that," Donald said. "That's why something has to be done. She's doing it to herself, honey."

Jessie had a hot cup of Morning Thunder halfway to her mouth. She stopped dead still. "I'm doing it to myself?" she repeated incredulously.

"Certainly," Donald said.

The complacency in his tone made Jessie suddenly, blazingly angry. "You stupid ignorant callous son of a bitch," she roared. I'm doing it to myself, *I'm* doing it, *I'm* doing it, how *dare* you say that *I'm* doing it." She flung the teacup across the room, aiming for his fat head. Donald ducked, the cup shattered and the tea sent three long brown fingers running down the off-white wall. "Go on, let out your anger," he said. "I know you're upset. When you calm down, we can discuss this rationally, maybe get to the root of your problem."

Angela took her arm, but Jessie shook off the grip and stood, her hands balled into fists. "Go into my bedroom, you jerk, go in there right now and look around and come back and tell me what you see."

"If you'd like," Donald said. He walked over to the bedroom door, vanished, re-emerged several moments later. "All right," he said patiently.

"Well?" Jessie demanded.

Donald shrugged. "It's a mess," he said. "Underpants all over the floor, lots of crushed cheese curls. Tell me what you think it means."

"He broke in here!" Jessie said.

"The Pear-shaped Man?" Donald queried pleasantly.

"*Of course* it was the Pear-shaped Man," Jessie screamed. "He snuck in here while we were all gone and he went into my bedroom and pawed through all my things and put Cheez Doodles in my underwear. He was *here*! He was touching my stuff."

Donald wore an expression of patient, compassionate wisdom. "Jessie, dear, I want you to think about what you just told us."

"There's nothing to think about!"

"Of course there is," he said. "Let's think it through together. The Pear-shaped Man was here, you think?"

"Yes."

"Why?"

"To do...to do what he did. It's disgusting. He's disgusting."

"Hmmm," Don said. "How, then? The locks were changed, remember? He can't even get in the building. He's never had a key to this apartment. There was no sign of forced entry. How did he get in with his bag of cheese curls?"

Jessie had him there. "Angela left the living room windows open," she said.

Angela looked stricken. "I did," she admitted. "Oh, Jessie, honey, I'm so sorry. It was hot. I just wanted to get a breeze, I didn't mean..."

"The windows are too high to reach from the sidewalk," Donald pointed out. "He'd have needed a ladder or something to stand on. He'd have needed to do it in broad daylight, from a busy street, with people coming and going all the time. He'd have had to have left the same way. There's the problem of the screens. He doesn't look like a very athletic sort, either."

"He did it," Jessie insisted. "He was here, wasn't he?"

"I know you think so, and I'm not trying to deny your feelings, just explore them. Has this Pear-shaped Man ever been invited into the apartment?"

"Of course not!" Jessie said. "What are you suggesting?"

"Nothing, Jess. Just consider. He climbs in through the windows with these cheese curls he intends to secrete in your drawers. Fine. How does he know which room is yours?"

Jessie frowned. "He…I don't know…he searched around, I guess."

"And found what clue? You've got three bedrooms here, one a studio, two full of women's clothes. How'd he pick the right one?"

"Maybe he did it in both."

"Angela, would you go check your bedroom, please?" Donald asked.

Angela rose hesitantly. "Well," she said, "okay." Jessie and Donald stared at each other until she returned a minute or so later. "All clean," she said.

"I don't know how he figured out which damned room was mine," Jessie said. "All I know is that he did. He had to. How else can you explain what happened, huh? Do you think I did it *myself*?"

Donald shrugged. "I don't know," he said calmly. He glanced over his shoulder into the studio. "Funny, though. That painting in there, him and you, he must have done that some other time, after you finished it but before you sent it to Pirouette. It's good work, too. Almost as good as yours."

Jessie had been trying very hard not to think about the painting. She opened her mouth to throw something back at him, but nothing flew out. She closed her mouth. Tears began to gather in the corners of her eyes. She suddenly felt weary, confused, and very alone. Angela had walked over to stand beside Donald. They were both looking at her. Jessie looked down at her hands helplessly and said, "What am I going to do? God. What am I going to *do*?"

God did not answer; Donald did. "Only one thing *to* do," he said briskly. "Face up to your fears. Exorcise them. Go down there and talk to the man, get to know him. By the time you come back up, you may pity him or have contempt for him or dislike him, but you won't fear him any longer; you'll see that he's only a human being and a rather sad one."

"Are you sure, Don?" Angela asked him.

"Completely. Confront this obsession of yours, Jessie. That's the only way you'll ever be free of it. Go down to the basement and visit with the Pear-shaped Man."

"There's nothing to be afraid of," Angela told her again.

"That's easy for you to say."

"Look, Jess, the minute you're inside, Don and I will come out and sit on the stoop. We'll be just an earshot away. All you'll have to do is let out the teeniest little yell and we'll come rushing right down. So you won't be alone, not really. And you've still got that knife in your purse, right?"

Jessie nodded.

"Come on, then, remember the time that purse snatcher tried to grab your shoulder bag? You decked him good. If this Pear-shaped Man tries anything, you're quick enough. Stab him. Run away. Yell for us. You'll be perfectly safe."

"I suppose you're right," Jessie said with a small sigh. They *were* right. She knew it. It didn't make any sense. He was a dirty, foul-smelling, unattractive man, maybe a little retarded, but nothing she couldn't handle, nothing she had to be afraid of, she didn't want to be crazy, she was letting this ridiculous obsession eat her alive and it had to end now, Donald was perfectly correct, she'd been doing it to herself all along and now she was going to take hold of it and stop it, certainly, it all made perfect sense and there was nothing to worry about, nothing to be afraid of, what could the Pear-shaped Man do to her, after all, what could he possibly *do* to her that was so terrifying? Nothing. Nothing.

Angela patted her on the back. Jessie took a deep breath, took the doorknob firmly in hand, and stepped out of the building into the hot, damp evening air. Everything was under control.

So why was she so scared?

Night was falling, but down under the stairs it had fallen already. Down under the stairs it was always night. The stoop cut off the morning sun, and the building itself blocked the afternoon light. It was dark, so dark. She stumbled over a crack in the cement, and her foot rang off the side of a metal garbage can. Jessie shuddered, imagining flies and maggots and other, worse things moving and breeding back there where the sun never shone. *No, mustn't think about that, it was only garbage, rotting and festering in the warm, humid dark, mustn't dwell on it.* She was at the door.

She raised her hand to knock, and then the fear took hold of her again. She could not move. *Nothing to be frightened of,* she told herself, *nothing at all.* What could he possibly *do* to her? Yet still she could not bring herself to knock. She stood before his door with her hand raised, her breath raw in her throat. It was so hot, so suffocatingly hot. She had to breathe. She had to get out from under the stoop, get back to where she could breathe.

A thin vertical crack of yellow light split the darkness. *No,* Jessie thought, *oh, please no.*

The door was opening.

Why did it have to open so slowly? Slowly, like in her dreams. Why did it have to open at all?

The light was so bright in there. As the door opened, Jessie found herself squinting.

The Pear-shaped Man stood smiling at her.

"I," Jessie began, "I, uh, I…"

"*There* she is," the Pear-shaped Man said in his tinny little squeak.

"What do you want from me?" Jessie blurted.

"I knew she'd come," he said, as though she wasn't there. "I knew she'd come for my things."

"No," Jessie said. She wanted to run away, but her feet would not move.

"You can come in," he said. He raised his hand, moved it toward her face. He touched her. Five fat white maggots crawled across her cheek and wriggled through her hair. His fingers smelled like cheese curls. His pinkie touched her ear and tried to burrow inside. She hadn't seen his other hand move until she felt it grip her upper arm, pulling, pulling. His flesh felt damp and cold. Jessie whimpered.

"Come in and see my things," he said. "You have to. You know you have to." And somehow she was inside then, and the door was closing behind her, and she was there, inside, alone with the Pear-shaped Man.

Jessie tried to get a grip on herself. *Nothing to be afraid of,* she repeated to herself, a litany, a charm, a chant, *nothing to be afraid of, what could he do to you, what could he do?* The room was L-shaped, low ceilinged, filthy. The sickly sweet smell was overwhelming. Four naked lightbulbs burned in the fixture above, and along one wall was a row of old lamps without shades, bare bulbs blazing away. A three-legged card table stood against the opposite wall, its fourth corner propped up by a broken tv set with wires dangling through the shattered glass of its picture tube. On top of the card table was a big bowl of Cheez Doodles. Jessie looked away, feeling sick. She tried to step backward, and her foot hit an empty plastic Coke bottle. She almost fell. But the Pear-shaped Man caught her in his soft, damp grip and held her upright.

Jessie yanked herself free of him and backed away. Her hand went into her purse and closed around the knife. It made her feel better, stronger. She moved close to the boarded-up window. Outside she could make out Donald and Angela talking. The sound of their voices, so close at hand— that helped, too. She tried to summon up all of her strength. "How do you live like this?" she asked him. "Do you need help cleaning up the place? Are you sick?" It was so hard to force out the words.

"Sick," the Pear-shaped Man repeated. "Did they tell you I was sick? They lie about me. They lie about me all the time. Somebody should make them stop." If only he would stop smiling. His lips were so wet. But he never stopped smiling. "I knew you would come. Here. This is for you." He pulled it from a pocket, held it out.

"No," said Jessie. "I'm not hungry. Really." But she was hungry, she realized. She was famished. She found herself staring at the thick orange twist between his fingers, and suddenly she wanted it desperately. "No," she said again, but her voice was weaker now, barely more than a whisper, and the cheese curl was very close.

Her mouth sagged open. She felt it on her tongue, the roughness of the powdery cheese, the sweetness of it. It crunched softly between her teeth. She swallowed and licked the last orange flakes from her lower lip. She wanted more.

"I knew it was you," said the Pear-shaped Man. "Now your things are mine." Jessie stared at him. It was like in her nightmare. The Pear-shaped Man reached up and began to undo the little white plastic buttons on his shirt. She struggled to find her voice. He shrugged out of the shirt. His undershirt was yellow, with huge damp circles under his arms. He peeled it off, dropped it. He moved closer, and heavy white breasts flopped against his chest. The right one was covered by a wide blue smear. A dark little tongue slid between his lips. Fat white fingers worked at his belt like a team of dancing slugs. "These are for you," he said.

Jessie's knuckles were white around the hilt of the knife. "Stop," she said in a hoarse whisper.

His pants settled to the floor.

She couldn't take it. No more, no more. She pulled the knife free of her bag, raised it over her head. "*Stop!*"

"Ahh," said the Pear-shaped Man, "there it is."

She stabbed him.

The blade went in right to the hilt, plunged deep into his soft, white skin. She wrenched it down and out. The skin parted, a huge, meaty gash. The Pear-shaped Man was smiling his little smile. There was no blood, no blood at all. His flesh was soft and thick, all pale dead meat.

He moved closer, and Jessie stabbed him again. This time he reached up and knocked her hand away. The knife was embedded in his neck. The hilt wobbled back and forth as he padded toward her. His dead, white arms reached out and she pushed against him and her hand sank into his body like he was made of wet, rotten bread. "Oh," he said, "oh, oh, oh." Jessie opened her mouth to scream, and the Pear-shaped Man pressed those heavy wet lips to her own and swallowed at her sound. His pale eyes sucked at her. She felt his tongue darting forward, and it was round and black and oily, and then it was snaking down inside her, touching, tasting, feeling all her things. She was drowning in a sea of soft, damp flesh.

She woke to the sound of the door closing. It was only a small click, a latch sliding into place, but it was enough. Her eyes opened, and she pulled herself up. It was so hard to move. She felt heavy, tired. Outside they were laughing. They were laughing at her. It was dim and far-off, that laughter, but she knew it was meant for her.

Her hand was resting on her thigh. She stared at it and blinked. She wiggled her fingers, and they moved like five fat maggots. She had something soft and yellow under her nails and deep dirty yellow stains up near her fingertips.

She closed her eyes, ran her hand over her body, the soft heavy curves, the thicknesses, the strange hills and valleys. She pushed, and the flesh gave and gave and gave. She stood up weakly. There were her clothes, scattered on the floor. Piece by piece she pulled them on, and then she moved across the room. Her briefcase was down beside the door; she gathered it up, tucked it under her arm, she might need something, yes, it was good to have the briefcase. She pushed open the door and emerged into the warm night. She heard the voices above her: "…were right all along," a woman was saying, "I couldn't believe I'd been so silly. There's nothing sinister about him, really, he's just pathetic. Donald, I don't know how to thank you."

She came out from under the stoop and stood there. Her feet hurt so. She shifted her weight from one to the other and back again. They had stopped talking, and they were staring at her, Angela and Donald and a slender, pretty woman in blue jeans and work shirt. "Come back," she said, and her voice was thin and high. "Give them back. You took them, you took my things. You have to give them back."

The woman's laugh was like ice cubes tinkling in a glass of Coke.

"I think you've bothered Jessie quite enough," Donald said.

"She has my things," she said. "Please."

"I saw her come out, and she didn't have anything of yours," Donald said.

"She took all my things," she said.

Donald frowned. The woman with the sandy hair and the green eyes laughed again and put a hand on his arm. "Don't look so serious, Don. He's not all there."

They were all against her, she knew, looking at their faces. She clutched her briefcase to his chest. They'd taken her things, he couldn't remember exactly what, but they wouldn't get her case, he had stuff in there and they wouldn't get it. She turned away from them. He was hungry, she realized. She wanted something to eat. He had half a bag of Cheez Doodles left, she remembered. Downstairs. Down under the stoop.

As she descended, the Pear-shaped Man heard them talking about her. He opened the door and went inside to stay. The room smelled like home. He sat down, laid his case across his knees, and began to eat. He stuffed the cheese curls into his mouth in big handfuls and washed them down with sips from a glass of warm Coke straight from the bottle he'd opened that morning, or maybe yesterday. It was good. Nobody knew how good it was. They laughed at him, but they didn't know, they didn't know about all the nice things he had. No one knew. No one. Only someday he'll see somebody different, somebody to give his things to, somebody who would give him all their things. Yes. He'd like that. He'd know her when he saw her.

He'd know just what to say.

THE NIGHT THEY MISSED THE HORROR SHOW

JOE R. LANSDALE

(*For Lew Shiner. A story that doesn't flinch.*)

IF THEY'D GONE TO the drive-in like they'd planned, none of this would have happened. But Leonard didn't like drive-ins when he didn't have a date, and he'd heard about *Night Of The Living Dead*, and he knew a nigger starred in it. He didn't want to see no movie with a nigger star. Niggers chopped cotton, fixed flats and pimped nigger girls, but he'd never heard of one that killed zombies. And he'd heard too that there was a white girl in the movie that let the nigger touch her, and that peeved him. Any white gal that would let a nigger touch her must be the lowest trash in the world. Probably from Hollywood, New York or Waco, some godforsaken place like that.

Now Steve McQueen would have been all right for zombie killing and girl handling. He would have been the ticket. But a nigger? No sir.

Boy, that Steve McQueen was one cool head. Way he said stuff in them pictures was so good you couldn't help but think someone had written it down for him. He could sure think fast on his feet to come up with the things he said, and he had that real cool, mean look.

Leonard wished he could be Steve McQueen, or Paul Newman even. Someone like that always knew what to say, and he figured they got plenty

105

of bush too. Certainly they didn't get as bored as he did. He was so bored he felt as if he were going to die from it before the night was out. Bored, bored, bored. Just wasn't nothing exciting about being in the Dairy Queen parking lot leaning on the front of his '64 Impala looking out at the highway. He figured maybe old crazy Harry who janitored at the high school might be right about them flying saucers. Harry was always seeing something. Bigfoot, six-legged weasels, all manner of things. But maybe he was right about the saucers. He'd said he'd seen one a couple nights back hovering over Mud Creek and it was shooting down these rays that looked like wet peppermint sticks. Leonard figured if Harry really had seen the saucers and the rays, then those rays were boredom rays. It would be a way for space critters to get at earth folks, boring them to death. Getting melted down by heat rays would have been better. That was at least quick, but being bored to death was sort of like being nibbled to death by ducks.

Leonard continued looking at the highway, trying to imagine flying saucers and boredom rays, but he couldn't keep his mind on it. He finally focused on something in the highway. A dead dog.

Not just a dead dog. But a DEAD DOG. The mutt had been hit by a semi at least, maybe several. It looked as if it had rained dog. There were pieces of that pooch all over the concrete and one leg was lying on the curbing on the opposite side, stuck up in such a way that it seemed to be waving hello. Doctor Frankenstein with a grant from Johns Hopkins and assistance from NASA couldn't have put that sucker together again.

Leonard leaned over to his faithful, drunk companion, Billy—known among the gang as Farto, because he was fart lighting champion of Mud Creek—and said, "See that dog there?"

Farto looked where Leonard was pointing. He hadn't noticed the dog before, and he wasn't nearly as casual about it as Leonard. The puzzle piece hound brought back memories. It reminded him of a dog he'd had when he was thirteen. A big, fine German Shepherd that loved him better than his Mama.

Sonofabitch dog tangled its chain through and over a barbed wire fence somehow and hung itself. When Farto found the dog its tongue looked like a stuffed, black sock and he could see where its claws had just been able to scrape the ground, but not quite enough to get a toehold. It looked as if the dog had been scratching out some sort of coded message in the dirt. When Farto told his old man about it later, crying as he did, his old man laughed and said, "Probably a goddamn suicide note."

Now, as he looked out at the highway, and his whisky-laced Coke collected warmly in his gut, he felt a tear form in his eyes. Last time he'd felt that sappy was when he'd won the fart lighting championship with a four-inch burner that singed the hairs of his ass and the gang awarded him with a pair of colored boxing shorts. Brown and yellow ones so he could wear them without having to change them too often.

So there they were, Leonard and Farto, parked outside the DQ, leaning on the hood of Leonard's Impala, sipping Coke and whisky, feeling bored and blue and horny, looking at a dead dog and having nothing to do but go to a show with a nigger starring in it. Which to be up front, wouldn't have been so bad if they'd had dates. Dates could make up for a lot of sins, or help make a few good ones, depending on one's outlook.

But the night was criminal. Dates they didn't have. Worse yet, wasn't a girl in the entire high school would date them. Not even Marylou Flowers, and she had some kind of disease.

All this nagged Leonard something awful. He could see what the problem was with Farto. He was ugly. Had the kind of face that attracted flies. And though being fart lighting champion of Mud Creek had a certain prestige among the gang, it lacked a certain something when it came to charming the gals.

But for the life of him, Leonard couldn't figure his own problem. He was handsome, had some good clothes, and his car ran good when he didn't buy that old cheap gas. He even had a few bucks in his jeans from breaking into washaterias. Yet his right arm had damn near grown to the size of his thigh from all the whacking off he did. Last time he'd been out with a girl had been a month ago, and as he'd been out with her along with nine other guys, he wasn't rightly sure he could call that a date. He wondered about it so much, he'd asked Farto if he thought it qualified as a date. Farto, who had been fifth in line, said he didn't think so, but if Leonard wanted to call it one, wasn't no skin off his dick.

But Leonard didn't want to call it a date. It just didn't have the feel of one, lacked something special. There was no romance to it.

True, Big Red had called him Honey when he put the mule in the barn, but she called everyone Honey—except Stoney. Stoney was Possum sweets, and he was the one who talked her into wearing the grocery bag with the mouth and eye holes. Stoney was like that. He could sweet talk the camel out from under a sand nigger. When he got through chatting Big Red down, she was plumb proud to wear that bag.

When finally it came his turn to do Big Red, Leonard had let her take the bag off as a gesture of good will. That was a mistake. He just hadn't known a good thing when he had it. Stoney had had the right idea. The bag coming off spoiled everything. With it on, it was sort of like balling the Lone Hippo or some such thing, but with the bag off, you were absolutely certain what you were getting, and it wasn't pretty.

Even closing his eyes hadn't helped. He found that the ugliness of that face had branded itself on the back of his eyeballs. He couldn't even imagine the sack back over her head. All he could think about was that puffy, too-painted face with the sort of bad complexion that began at the bone.

He'd gotten so disappointed, he'd had to fake an orgasm and get off before his hooter shrivelled up and his Trojan fell off and was lost in the vacuum.

Thinking back on it, Leonard sighed. It would certainly be nice for a change to go with a girl that didn't pull the train or had a hole between her legs that looked like a manhole cover ought to be on it. Sometimes he wished he could be like Farto who was as happy as if he had good sense. Anything thrilled him. Give him a can of Wolf Brand Chili, a big moon pie, Coke and whisky and he could spend the rest of his life fucking Big Red and lighting the gas out of his asshole.

God, but this was no way to live. No women and no fun. Bored, bored, bored. Leonard found himself looking overhead for space ships and peppermint-colored boredom rays, but he saw only a few moths fluttering drunkenly through the beams of the DQ's lights.

Lowering his eyes back to the highway and the dog, Leonard had a sudden flash. "Why don't we get the chain out of the back and hook it up to Rex there? Take him for a ride."

"You mean drag his dead ass around?" Farto asked.

Leonard nodded.

"Beats stepping on a tack," Farto said.

They drove the Impala into the middle of the highway at a safe moment and got out for a look. Up close the mutt was a lot worse. Its innards had been mashed out of its mouth and asshole and it stunk something awful. The dog was wearing a thick, metal-studded collar and they fastened one end of their fifteen foot chain to that and the other to the rear bumper.

Bob, the Dairy Queen manager, noticed them through the window, came outside and yelled, "What are you fucking morons doing?"

"Taking this doggie to the vet," Leonard said. "We think this sumbitch looks a might peaked. He may have been hit by a car."

"That's so fucking funny I'm about to piss myself," Bob said.

"Old folks have that problem," Leonard said.

Leonard got behind the wheel and Farto climbed in on the passenger side. They maneuvered the car and the dog around and out of the path of a tractor-trailer truck just in time. As they drove off, Bob screamed after them, "I hope you two no-dicks wrap that Chevy piece of shit around a goddamn pole."

As they roared along, part of the dog, like crumbs from a flakey loaf of bread, came off. A tooth here. Some hair there. A string of guts. A dew claw. And some unidentifiable pink stuff. The metal-studded collar and chain threw up sparks now and then like fiery crickets. Finally they hit seventy-five and the dog was swinging wider and wider on the chain, like it was looking for an opportunity to pass.

Farto poured him and Leonard up Cokes and whisky as they drove along. He handed Leonard his paper cup and Leonard knocked it back, a lot happier now than he had been a moment ago. Maybe this night wasn't going to turn out so bad after all.

They drove by a crowd at the side of the road, a tan station wagon and a wreck of a Ford up on a jack. At a glance they could see that there was a nigger in the middle of the crowd and he wasn't witnessing to the white boys about Jesus. He was hopping around like a pig with a hotshot up his ass, trying to find a break in the white boys so he could make a run for it. But there wasn't any break to be found and there were too many to fight. Nine white boys were knocking him around like he was a pinball and they were a malicious machine.

"Ain't that one of our niggers?" Farto asked. "And ain't that some of them White Tree football players that's trying to kill him?"

"Scott," Leonard said, and the name was dogshit in his mouth. It had been Scott who had outdone him for the position of quarterback on the team. That damn jig could put together a play more tangled than a can of fishing worms, but it damn near always worked. And he could run like a spotted ass ape.

As they passed, Farto said, "We'll read about him tomorrow in the papers."

But Leonard drove only a short way before slamming on the brakes and whipping the Impala around. Rex swung way out and clipped off some tall, dried sunflowers at the edge of the road like a scythe.

"We gonna go back and watch?" Farto said. "I don't think them White Tree boys would bother us none if that's all we was gonna do, watch."

"He may be a nigger," Leonard said, not liking himself, "but he's our nigger and we can't let them do that. They kill him they'll beat us in football."

Farto saw the truth of this immediately. "Damn right. They can't do that to our nigger."

Leonard crossed the road again and went straight for the White Tree boys hit down hard on the horn. The White Tree boys abandoned beating their prey and jumped in all directions. Bullfrogs couldn't have done any better.

Scott stood startled and weak where he was, his knees bent in and touching one another, his eyes big as pizza pans. He had never noticed how big grillwork was. It looked like teeth there in the night and the headlights looked like eyes. He felt like a stupid fish about to be eaten by a shark.

Leonard braked hard, but off the highway in the dirt it wasn't quite enough to keep from bumping Scott, sending him flying over the hood and against the glass where his face mashed to it then rolled away, his shirt snagging one of the windshield wipers and pulling it off.

Leonard opened the car door and called to Scott who lay on the ground. "It's now or never."

A White Tree boy made for the car, and Leonard pulled the taped hammer handle out from beneath the seat and stepped out of the car and hit him with it. The White Tree boy went down on his knees and said something that sounded like French but wasn't. Leonard grabbed Scott by the back of the shirt and pulled him up and guided him around and threw him into the open door. Scott scrambled over the front seat and into the back. Leonard threw the hammer handle at one of the White Tree boys and stepped back, whirled into the car behind the wheel. He put the car in gear again and stepped on the gas. The Impala lurched forward, and with one hand on the door Leonard flipped it wider as if he were flexing a wing and popped a White Tree boy. The car bumped back on the highway and the chain swung out and Rex clipped the feet out from under two boys as neatly as he had taken down the dried sunflowers.

Leonard looked in his rearview mirror and saw two White Tree boys carrying the one he had clubbed with the hammer handle to the station wagon. The others he and the dog had knocked down were getting up. One had kicked the jack out from under Scott's car and was using it to smash the headlights and windshield.

"Hope you got insurance on that thing," Leonard said.

111

"I borrowed it," Scott said peeling the windshield wiper out of his tee-shirt. "Here, you might want this." He dropped the wiper over the seat between Leonard and Farto.

"That's a borrowed car?" Farto said. "That's worse."

"Nah," Scott said. "Owner don't know I borrowed it. I'd have had that flat changed if that sucker had had him a spare tire, but I got back there and wasn't nothing but the rim, man. Say, thanks for not letting me get killed, else we couldn't have run that ole pig together no more. Course, you almost run over me. My chest hurts."

Leonard checked the rearview again. The White Tree boys were coming fast. "You complaining?" Leonard said.

"Nah," Scott said, and turned to look through the back glass. He could see the dog swinging in short arcs and pieces of it going wide and far. "Hope you didn't go off and forget your dog tied to the bumper."

"Goddamn," said Farto, "and him registered too."

"This ain't so funny," Leonard said, "them White Tree boys are gaining."

"Well speed it up," Scott said.

Leonard gnashed his teeth. "I could always get rid of some excess baggage, you know."

"Throwing that windshield wiper out ain't gonna help," Scott said.

Leonard looked in his mirror and saw the grinning nigger in the backseat. Nothing worse than a comic coon. He didn't even look grateful. Leonard had a sudden horrid vision of being overtaken by the White tree boys. What if he were killed with the nigger? Getting killed was bad enough, but what if tomorrow they found him in a ditch with Farto and the nigger. Or maybe them White Tree boys would make him do something awful with the nigger before they killed them. Like making him suck the nigger's dick or some such thing. Leonard held his foot all the way to the floor; as they passed the Dairy Queen he took a hard left and the car just made it and Rex swung out and slammed a light pole then popped back in line behind them.

The White Tree boys couldn't make the corner in the station wagon and they didn't even try. They screeched into a car lot down a piece, turned around and came back. By that time the taillights of the Impala were moving away from them rapidly, looking like two inflamed hemorrhoids in a dark asshole.

"Take the next right coming up," Scott said, "then you'll see a little road off to the left. Kill your lights and take that."

Leonard hated taking orders from Scott on the field, but this was worse. Insulting. Still, Scott called good plays on the field, and the habit of following instructions from the quarterback died hard. Leonard made the right and Rex made it with them after taking a dip in a water-filled bar ditch.

Leonard saw the little road and killed his lights and took it. It carried them down between several rows of large tin storage buildings and Leonard pulled between two of them and drove down a little alley lined with more. He stopped the car and they waited and listened. After about five minutes, Farto said, "I think we skunked those father rapers."

"Ain't we a team?" Scott said.

In spite of himself, Leonard felt good. It was like when the nigger called a play that worked and they were all patting each other on the ass and not minding what color the other was because they were just creatures in football suits.

"Let's have a drink," Leonard said.

Farto got a paper cup off the floorboard for Scott and poured him up some warm Coke and whisky. Last time they had gone to Longview, he had peed in that paper cup so they wouldn't have to stop, but that had long since been poured out, and besides it was for a nigger. He poured Leonard and himself drinks in their same cups.

Scott took a sip and said, "Shit, man, that tastes kind of rank."

"Like piss," Farto said.

Leonard held up his cup. "To the Mud Creek Wildcats and fuck them White Tree boys."

"You fuck 'em," Scott said. They touched their cups, and at that moment the car filled with light.

Cups upraised, the Three Musketeers turned blinking toward it. The light was coming from an open storage building door and there was a fat man standing in the center of the glow like a bloated fly on a lemon wedge. Behind him was a big screen made of a sheet and there was some kind of movie playing on it. And though the light was bright and fading out the movie, Leonard, who was in the best position to see, got a look at it. What he could make out looked like a gal down on her knees sucking this fat guy's dick (the man was visible only from the belly down) and the guy had a short, black revolver pressed to her forehead. She pulled her mouth off of him for an instant and the man came in her face then fired the revolver. The woman's head snapped out of frame and the sheet seemed to drip blood, like dark condensation on a window pane. Then Leonard couldn't see anymore because another man had appeared in the doorway, and like the first he was fat. Both looked like huge bowling balls that had been set on top of shoes. More men appeared behind these two, but one of the fat men turned and held up his hand and the others moved out of sight. The two fat guys stepped outside and one pulled the door almost shut, except for a thin band of light that fell across the front seat of the Impala.

Fat Man Number One went over to the car and opened Farto's door and said, "You fucks and the nigger get out." It was the voice of doom. They had only thought the White Tree boys were dangerous. They realized now they had been kidding themselves. This was the real article. This guy would have eaten the hammer handle and shit a two-by-four.

They got out of the car and the fat man waved them around and lined them up on Farto's side and looked at them. The boys still had their drinks in their hands, and sparing that, they looked like cons in a line up. Fat Man Number Two came over and looked at the trio and smiled. It was obvious the fatties were twins. They had the same bad features in the same fat faces. They wore Hawaiian shirts that varied only in profiles and color of parrots and had on white socks and too-short, black slacks and black, shiny, Italian shoes with toes sharp enough to thread needles.

Fat Man Number One took the cup away from Scott and sniffed it. "A

114

nigger with liquor," he said. "That's like a cunt with brains. It don't go together. Guess you was getting tanked up so you could put the old black snake to some chocolate pudding after while. Or maybe you was wantin' some vanilla and these boys were gonna set it up."

"I'm not wanting anything but to go home," Scott said.

Fat Man Number Two looked at Fat Man Number One and said, "So he can fuck his mother."

The fatties looked at Scott to see what he'd say but he didn't say anything. They could say he screwed dogs and that was all right with him. Hell, bring one on and he'd fuck it now if they'd let him go afterwards.

Fat Man Number One said, "You boys running around with a jungle bunny makes me sick."

"He's just a nigger from school," Farto said. "We don't like him none. We just picked him up because some White Tree boys were beating on him and we didn't want him to get wrecked on account of he's our quarterback."

"Ah," Fat Man Number One said, "I see. Personally, me and Vinnie don't cotton to niggers in sports. They start taking showers with white boys the next thing they want is to take white girls to bed. It's just one step from one to the other."

"We don't have nothing to do with him playing," Leonard said. "We didn't integrate the schools."

"No," Fat Man Number One said, "that was old Big Ears Johnson, but you're running around with him and drinking with him."

"His cup's been peed in," Farto said. "That was kind of a joke on him, you see. He ain't our friend, I swear it. He's just a nigger that plays football."

"Peed in his cup, huh?" said the one called Vinnie. "I like that, Pork, don't you? Peed in his fucking cup."

Pork dropped Scott's cup on the ground and smiled at him. "Come here, nigger. I got something to tell you."

Scott looked at Farto and Leonard. No help there. They had suddenly become interested in the toes of their shoes; they examined them as if they were true marvels of the world.

Scott moved toward Pork, and Pork, still smiling, put his arm around Scott's shoulders and walked him toward the big storage building. Scott said, "What are we doing?"

Pork turned Scott around so they were facing Leonard and Farto who still stood holding their drinks and contemplating their shoes. "I didn't want to get it on the new gravel drive," Pork said and pulled Scott's head in close to his own and with his free hand reached back and under his Hawaiian shirt and brought out a short, black revolver and put it to Scott's temple and pulled the trigger. There was a snap like a bad knee going out and Scott's feet lifted in unison and went to the side and something dark squirted from his head and his feet swung back toward Pork and his shoes shuffled, snapped and twisted on the concrete in front of the building.

"Ain't that sometin," Pork said as Scott went limp and dangled from the thick crook of his arm. "The rhythm is the last thing to go."

Leonard couldn't make a sound. His guts were in his throat. He wanted to melt and run under the car. Scott was dead and the brains that had made plays twisted as fishing worms and commanded his feet on down the football field were scrambled like breakfast eggs.

Farto said, "Holy shit."

Pork let go of Scott and Scott's legs split and he sat down and his head went forward and clapped on the cement between his knees. A dark pool formed under his face.

"He's better off, boys," Vinnie said. "Nigger was begat by Cain and the ape and he ain't quite monkey and he ain't quite man. He's got no place in this world 'cept as a beast of burden. You start trying to train them to do things like drive cars and run footballs it ain't nothing but grief to them and the whites too. Get any on our shirt, Pork?"

"Nary a drop."

Vinnie went inside the building and said something to the men there that could be heard but not understood, then he came back with some crumpled newspapers. He went over to Scott and wrapped them around the bloody head and let it drop back on the cement. "You try hosing down that shit when it's dried, Pork, and you wouldn't worry none about that gravel. The gravel ain't nothing."

Then Vinnie said to Farto, "Open the back door of that car." Farto nearly twisted an ankle doing it. Vinnie picked Scott up by the back of the neck and seat of his pants and threw him into the floorboard of the Impala.

Pork used the short barrel of his revolver to scratch his nuts, then put the gun behind him, under his Hawaiian shirt. "You boys are gonna go to the river bottoms with us and help us get shed of this nigger."

"Yes sir," Farto said. "We'll toss his ass in the Sabine for you."

"How about you?" Pork asked Leonard. "You trying to go weak sister?"

"No," Leonard croaked. "I'm with you."

"That's good," Pork said. "Vinnie, you take the truck and lead the way."

Vinnie took a key from his pocket and unlocked the building door next to the one with the light, went inside, and backed out a sharp-looking, gold Dodge pickup. He backed it in front of the Impala and sat there with the motor running.

"You boys keep your place," Pork said. He went inside the lighted building for a moment. They heard him say to the men inside, "Go on and watch the movies. And save some of them beers for us. We'll be back." Then the light went out and Pork came out, shutting the door. He looked at Leonard and Farto and said, "Drink up, boys."

Leonard and Farto tossed off their warm Coke and whisky and dropped the cups on the ground.

"Now," Pork said, "you get in the back with the nigger, I'll ride with the driver."

Farto got in the back and put his feet on Scott's knees. He tried not to look at the head wrapped in newspaper, but he couldn't help it. When Pork opened the front door and the overhead light came on Farto saw there was a split in the paper and Scott's eye was visible behind it. Across the forehead the wrapping had turned dark. Down by the mouth and chin was an ad for a fish sale.

Leonard got behind the wheel and started the car. Pork reached over and honked the horn. Vinnie rolled the pickup forward and Leonard followed him to the river bottoms. No one spoke. Leonard found himself wishing with all his heart that he had gone to the outdoor picture show to see the movie with the nigger starring in it.

The river bottoms were steamy and hot from the closeness of the trees and the under and overgrowth. As Leonard wound the Impala down the narrow, red clay roads amidst the dense foliage, he felt as if his car were a crab crawling about in a pubic thatch.

He could feel from the way the steering wheel handled that the dog and the chain were catching brush and limbs here and there. He had forgotten all about the dog and now being reminded of it worried him. What if the dog got tangled and he had to stop? He didn't think Pork would take kindly to stopping, not with the dead burrhead on the floorboard and him wanting to get rid of the body.

Finally they came to where the woods cleared out a spell and they drove along the edge of the Sabine River. Leonard hated water and always had. In the moonlight the river looked like poisoned coffee flowing there. Leonard knew there were alligators and gars big as little alligators and water moccasins by the thousands swimming underneath the water, and just the thought of all those slick, darting bodies made him queasy.

They came to what was known as Broken Bridge. It was an old worn-out bridge that had fallen apart in the middle and it was connected to the land on this side only. People sometimes fished off of it. There was no one fishing tonight.

Vinnie stopped the pickup and Leonard pulled up beside him, the nose of the Chevy pointing at the mouth of the bridge. They all got out and Pork made Farto pull Scott out by the feet. Some of the newspaper came loose from Scott's head exposing an ear and part of the face. Farto patted the newspaper back into place.

"Fuck that," Vinnie said. "It don't hurt if he stains the fucking ground. You two idiots find some stuff to weight this coon down so we can sink him."

Farto and Leonard started scurrying about like squirrels, looking for rocks or big, heavy logs. Suddenly they heard Vinnie cry out, "Godamighty, fucking A. Pork. Come look at this."

Leonard looked over and saw that Vinnie had discovered Rex. He was standing looking down with his hands on his hips. Pork went over to stand by him, then Pork turned around and looked at them. "Hey, you fucks, come here."

Leonard and Farto joined them in looking at the dog. There was mostly just a head now, with a little bit of meat and fur hanging off a spine and some broken ribs.

"That's the sickest fucking thing I've ever fucking seen," Pork said.

"Godamighty," Vinnie said.

"Doing a dog like that. Shit, don't you got no heart? A dog. Man's best fucking goddamn friend and you two killed him like this."

"We didn't kill him," Farto said.

"You trying to fucking tell me he done this to himself? Had a bad fucking day and done this."

"Godamighty," Vinnie said.

"No sir," Leonard said. "We chained him on there after he was dead."

"I believe that," Vinnie said. "That's some rich shit. You guys murdered this dog. Godamighty."

"Just thinking about him trying to keep up and you fucks driving faster and faster makes me mad as a wasp," Pork said.

"No," Farto said. "It wasn't like that. He was dead and we were drunk and we didn't have anything to do, so we—"

"Shut the fuck up," Pork said sticking a finger hard against Farto's forehead. "You just shut the fuck up. We can see what the fuck you fucks did. You drug this here dog around until all his goddamn hide came off… What kind of mothers you boys got anyhow that they didn't tell you better about animals?"

"Godamighty," Vinnie said.

Everyone grew silent, stood looking at the dog. Finally Farto said.

"You want us to go back to getting some stuff to hold the nigger down?"

Pork looked at Farto as if he had just grown up whole from the ground. "You fucks are worse than niggers, doing a dog like that. Get on back over to the car."

Leonard and Farto went over to the Impala and stood looking down at Scott's body in much the same way they had stared at the dog. There in the dim moonlight shadowed by trees, the paper wrapped around Scott's head made him look like a giant papier-mâché doll. Pork came up and kicked Scott in the face with a swift motion that sent newspaper flying and sent a thonking sound across the water that made frogs jump.

"Forget the nigger," Pork said. "Give me your car keys, ball sweat." Leonard took out his keys and gave them to Pork and Pork went around to the trunk and opened it. "Drag the nigger over here."

Leonard took one of Scott's arms and Farto took the other and they pulled him over to the back of the car.

"Put him in the trunk," Pork said.

"What for?" Leonard asked.

"Cause I fucking said so," Pork said.

Leonard and Farto heaved Scott into the trunk. He looked pathetic lying there next to the spare tire, his face partially covered with newspaper. Leonard thought, if only the nigger had stolen a car with a spare he might not be here tonight. He could have gotten the flat changed and driven on before the White Tree boys even came along.

"All right, you get in there with him," Pork said, gesturing to Farto.

"Me?" Farto said.

"Nah, not fucking you, the fucking elephant on your fucking shoulder. Yeah, you, get in the trunk. I ain't got all night."

"Jesus, we didn't do anything to that dog, mister. We told you that. I swear. Me and Leonard hooked him up after he was dead…It was Leonard's idea."

Pork didn't say a word. He just stood there with one hand on the trunk lid looking at Farto, Farto looked at Pork, then the trunk, then back to

Pork. Lastly he looked at Leonard, then climbed into the trunk, his back to Scott.

"Like spoons," Pork said, and closed the lid. "Now you, whatsit, Leonard? You come over here." But Pork didn't wait for Leonard to move. He scooped the back of Leonard's neck with a chubby hand and pushed him over to where Rex lay at the end of the chain with Vinnie still looking down at him.

"What you think, Vinnie?" Pork asked. "You got what I got in mind?"

Vinnie nodded. He bent down and took the collar off the dog. He fastened it on Leonard. Leonard could smell the odor of the dead dog in his nostrils. He bent his head and puked.

"There goes my shoeshine," Vinnie said, and he hit Leonard a short one in the stomach. Leonard went to his knees and puked some more of the hot Coke and whisky.

"You fucks are the lowest pieces of shit on this earth, doing a dog like that," Vinnie said. "A nigger ain't no lower."

Vinnie got some strong fishing line out of the back of the truck and they tied Leonard's hands behind his back. Leonard began to cry.

"Oh shut up," Pork said. "It ain't that bad. Ain't nothing that bad."

But Leonard couldn't shut up. He was caterwauling now and it was echoing through the trees. He closed his eyes and tried to pretend he had gone to the show with the nigger starring in it and had fallen asleep in his car and was having a bad dream, but he couldn't imagine that. He thought about Harry the janitor's flying saucers with the peppermint rays, and he knew if there were any saucers shooting rays down, they weren't boredom rays after all. He wasn't a bit bored.

Pork pulled off Leonard's shoes and pushed him back flat on the ground and pulled off the socks and stuck them in Leonard's mouth so tight he couldn't spit them out. It wasn't that Pork thought anyone was going to hear Leonard, he just din't like the noise. It hurt his ears.

Leonard lay on the ground in the vomit next to the dog and cried silently. Pork and Vinnie went over to the Impala and opened the doors and stood so they could get a grip on the car to push. Vinnie reached in and moved the gear from Park to Neutral and he and Pork began to shove the car forward. It moved slowly at first, but as it made the slight incline that led down to the old bridge, it picked up speed. From inside the trunk, Farto hammered lightly at the lid as if he didn't really mean it. The chain took up slack and Leonard felt it jerk and pop his neck. He began to slide along the ground like a snake.

Vinnie and Pork jumped out of the way and watched the car make the bridge and go over the edge and disappear into the water with amazing quietness. Leonard, tugged by the weight of the car, rustled past them. When he hit the bridge, wooden splinters tugged at his clothes so hard they ripped his pants and underwear down almost to his knees.

The chain swung out once toward the edge of the bridge and the rotten railing, and Leonard tried to hook a leg around an upright board there, but that proved wasted. The weight of the car just pulled his knee out of joint and tugged the board out of place with a screech of nails and lumber.

Leonard picked up speed and the chain rattled over the edge of the bridge, into the water and out of sight, pulling its connection after it like a pull toy. The last sight of Leonard was the soles of his bare feet, white as the bellies of fish.

"It's deep there," Vinnie said. "I caught an old channel cat there once, remember? Big sucker. I bet it's over fifty feet deep down there."

They got in the truck and Vinnie cranked it.

"I think we did them boys a favour," Pork said. "Them running around with niggers and what they did to that dog and all. They weren't worth a thing."

"I know it," Vinnie said. "We should have filmed this, Pork, it would have been good. Where the car and that nigger lover went off in the water was choice."

"Nah, there wasn't any women."

"Point," Vinnie said, and he backed around and drove onto the trail that wound its way out of the bottoms.

LADY MADONNA

Nancy Holder

IT'S STARTING.

It's starting, and it doesn't even hurt that much. It hurts much less than I thought it would. Not that I mind. I don't care how much pain I endure for the sake of my baby.

I can't cry out. I can't make a noise. If they hear, they'll come. And they'll destroy us. I haven't forgotten what happened the first time. I will never forget.

Here it comes. The contraction. Oh, oh, shit, it *does* hurt. How could I have forgotten what it's like? What did Margaret say? It's like crapping a watermelon. Yes. An elephant, more like. God, I should call her. I'm not sure I can do this alone after all. But what if she tells them? I'm not sure I can trust her anymore. I don't think she believed me about Bryan.

I'm freezing. There's no heat in here and the mattress is soaked. I hope my water's broken. I hope it's not blood. It doesn't smell like blood —and believe me, I know what blood smells like. All I smell is dirt and rust and my own sweat. But I'm so wet! I wish I could check, but I can't even turn on my flashlight. I have to do this in the dark, like an animal. I'm furious. I'm terrified.

But it will be worth it. I have to remember, it'll definitely be worth it. But does it have to hurt so much?

I remember how it was, with Bryan. Clean and antiseptic, with starched sheets and broth afterwards and smiling faces. The nurses wore perfume and makeup and looked so happy for me. There was a picture of the Holy Mother on the wall, and a crucifix. The nuns were there, cloaked in black and white as they should be. Brides of Christ, but so old. Too old for a thirty-three-year-old man. Jesus, you know, is perpetually thirty-three.

Bryan. My lovely boy. I remember wanting him so badly. I tried everything. I remember walking in the snow to the cathedral to pray.

Hail Mary, full of grace. Heaven and earth are full of thy glory. A son, Holy Mother, give me a son. Give me a baby. Give me a child.

In the olden days, kings chopped off the head of their wives when they didn't give them sons. But you know, I didn't care if my baby was a boy or a girl. I just wanted someone to call my own. I had nothing in this world. I had no one. Surely the Holy Mother understood my plight. She had a family. She was loved. She was a queen who had everything. She stood on top of the world and she could give me what I wanted. I knew if I did my part, she would do hers.

Christ! This is tearing me apart inside. I can't do this. I have to get help.

But no one will help me. That's the terror. I can panic, I can call someone. But once they see, once they know —

Think about other things. Think about the Holy Mother.

Yes. I prayed to her. I screwed like crazy. I knew she'd understand. It wasn't lust; I wasn't enjoying it or anything. All I wanted was a baby. I wanted to feel the weight of a child in my belly, to feel it crawl from between my legs into the world. I wanted to carry it in my arms and suckle it at my breast. I wanted to smell that baby smell and see that baby smile. My child. My Sacred Infant.

So I prayed to the Holy Mother while I was having sex with some man—usually not very good-looking, not very intelligent, not even very clean—oomphing and umphing so he'd come and I'd get his good, sweet sperm. I thought about the Holy Mother's sweet, patient smile and I'd

126

move faster and harder. The guys loved it. Hundreds of them. I don't have any idea who Bryan's father was. I mean, his earthly father. Because I firmly believe Bryan was a gift from God.

Then the day came. Oh, god, oh, god, oh god. Hang on. Hang on. I can't do this.

The day. Came.

Yes. I knew I was pregnant before the doctor told me. I felt a spark of life deep inside me. It was like a spiritual orgasm. I lit a hundred candles to the Holy Mother and gave everything I had to the poor. I was the most radiant pregnant woman in the world. The doctor marvelled at my health, my happiness. He said it was nice to see a woman so unabashedly delighted to be pregnant. Unabashedly was the word he used. I wouldn't forget a thing like that.

Oh, God, *God*—

Why am I calling to God? That's over. Over.

I went into the cathedral and thanked the Holy Mother. The depths of the holy place swirled with incense and candlelight. I heard the choirboys practicing. And she stood there with her arms open wide, roses at her feet, and I got to thinking: she wasn't such a great mother after all. Look what she let them do to her son. Where was she when they flayed his back open? And drove nails through his palms? A real mother would have protected him. Would have done anything to keep him from harm.

Shit, shit, *shit*. I took Lamaze classes, but that was so long ago. I round my cheeks, I puff, puff, puff. It hurts too much. I can't.

Lady Mother. The Lady Mother was too much of a lady. A good Catholic, maybe—

Right before Bryan was born, Margaret was mugged. Mugged? Why do they call it mugged? The man beat her. He stole what little she had left. I think she was raped, but she never admitted it. She had a breakdown. She's never been the same.

I saw what an evil place the world was. The nuclear arms race, the pollution, the crime. I saw what could happen to a wonderful person like

Margaret. Was I supposed to stand by like the Holy Mother, smiling that sick, pathetic smile, and let my child grow up in a world like that?

Then he was born, and laid into my arms. I can't tell you how much I loved him. So sweet, so gentle, so helpless. I took him home and locked all the doors and windows. I didn't let anyone except the priest see him, not even Margaret. At night, I tied a rope around his little hand and hooked it into a belt I wore. I kept a knife and a gun under my pillow in case some one tried to attack him.

Blessed Mother, oh, help me. But I can't pray to the Holy Mother anymore. No matter; what use could she be?

We were watching TV one day; or rather, I was watching. Bryan was nursing. I think it was *Leave It to Beaver*. But it occurred to me that Bryan wouldn't stay a baby forever. And I wouldn't be able to protect him from the world because he would want to go out into it like the boy on TV.

No. No, no, no. He couldn't. He couldn't.

I think that's when I realized the Holy Mother's mistake. Now that I'm more sophisticated, I can't believe how dumb she was. Because if Jesus *couldn't* have gone out into the world…

I thought for a long time about if I was doing the right thing. I considered all kinds of methods. Cut off his pudgy, smooth legs? But there were wheelchairs. Sever his spine? I might kill him, and of course I didn't want to do that. I just couldn't decide what to do, so I prayed again to the Holy Mother.

And three words came to me: *the soft spot*. He was still a tiny baby, and very tender there, you see—

And it worked! He lived through it, and he would never care about going outside.

Things would have been perfect, but then I realized I'd made a terrible mistake: I had sinned. I was a sinner. Bryan had been baptized—foolish of me, I know, but I hadn't thought things out too well. He would never be held accountable—he would never be able to do anything construed as sin, anything intentional, you see. So I would go to hell and he would go to heaven.

The anguish! I've seen pictures of the Pieta. Where Jesus is lying across the Holy Mother's lap and she's still got that same, vacant smile on her face. She's supposed to be sorrowful, but you can see the smile. Because she expects to see him in heaven. She let him suffer—she thinks because she was born pure, she stayed pure, but God, in a way, well, God raped her. She is actually quite filthy.

She should be screaming, raging! What have you done to me? To my son? You bastard! She should be running after those Romans with an axe. She should have called down the wrath of God on them.

Passive. Unbelievably passive.

I, on the other hand, took action. I could congratulate myself on at least making an attempt. But the more I thought about what I'd done, the more obvious it became that I'd insured Bryan and I would be separated for all eternity.

I realized I would have to start over.

Oh, *no*! I'm going to scream. I am screaming! I am! I am!

Now I whimper. I listen. No one's coming, thank God. I've lived in this hovel for seven months—they were supposed to tear it down two months ago, but I know how bureaucracy works; I used to be a secretary for the planning commission—and I guess they're used to squatters and drug users making a stir now and then. Yes, there are drug dealers and other scum living in this building—hence the knife, and did I mention the gun? Did I mention the other day when one of them tried to get in here?

Perhaps I would've been safer back at Margaret's house. But I can't trust her, you see. And all those people she lives with—the man, the little children, her old granny. And I'm scared to death someone will find little Bryan underneath the dog house. The police are still looking for him, but if God is merciful, he will rest in peace.

Still, it would be wonderful to be somewhere clean and warm. I could be in the bed with the pink and green blankets, a pot of chocolate on the bed stand.

The Holy Mother delivered in a pig sty. I can do no less.

Giving birth is infuriating. It's one of the most passive activities there is—you lie there, screaming and panting while the doctors handle everything. That's how it was the first time, calling me "dear" and "honey" and telling me when to breathe, when to push. If I hadn't listened, if I'd just sat up and said, "No! I will not!"

Calm. I must stay calm.

I gave up on the Holy Mother, who wasn't smart enough or brave enough. She certainly didn't know how to love enough, with her foolish smiles and her roses and her hopes. So I prayed to the Devil instead. And he came to me.

He was beautiful, glowing red with a huge penis and round, firm testicles that I knew were loaded with sperm. No mortal man comes close to the devil. He's muscular and brawny and very tall. The color of his hair changes with his mood—blond when he's playful, black when he's angry or stern or amorous. The devil can be very amorous. I never enjoyed sex until I slept with the Devil.

The only time he hurt my feelings was when he called me Margaret. I can remember rolling away from him and saying, "Are you sleeping with her, too?"

"Of course not, love. Off course not, my darling. Come back to bed." Then he grabbed my wrist and practically dragged me onto the mattress. Actually, he did drag me. He takes what he wants. He's a real man. Not like Margaret's husband, who stood by and let those terrible things happen to her. I wouldn't be able to let a man like that touch me.

I got pregnant by the blessed Father of Hell, and he promised me he would take me and the baby down to dwell with him world without end, amen. "Just don't baptize the baby," he said.

I wasn't going to. I was blissfully happy. I did whatever he told me. I don't remember those weeks at all, but I do know we were happy.

But then I passed a church and the Holy Mother lured me in. I know now that she was jealous. I mean, having the child of God is like a life sentence in a harem. Into the purdah of the faceless nuns who tell you how to be good and sweet. To keep clean and tidy and think clean and tidy; and pick up after everyone, just pick up after them and if they make you bleed, just clean it up, stay clean—

My God! My God! It didn't hurt this much with Bryan.

Well, of course it didn't. Of course, of course.

The Holy Mother made me ask the priest if a baby wasn't baptized, would it go to hell. And the father asked me if I were a Catholic, because that was basic catechism. All the unbaptized babies used to go to limbo, and now they go to purgatory, and when the Lord returns, they will be gathered up into His arms and carried to heaven.

I got confused. No limbo? Since when is there no limbo? I tried to persist. I asked, what if the baby were…tainted? He looked at me strangely, asked me to explain.

I left. I was shaken. I thought about my past mistakes—about Bryan, especially—and I wondered if the Devil could be mistaken about things. What if I went to hell without our child? Can the son of the Devil go to limbo? I mean, purgatory?

Then it occurred to me that what I could have done with Bryan was repented. What I could still do. If I repented and was forgiven, then I could join little Bryan in heaven some day—

—ah, but only if I was forgiven. They say God forgives everything. But I have slept with his rival and I think his mother is a spineless idiot. And quite possibly, I bear the Antichrist.

Oh, no, I've been screaming again. Surely someone heard that time. It's echoing. My things are covered with blood, I think. It's pitch-black in here.

No, no, no, no.

Then *she* came to me. The beautiful woman who said she was a social worker. She said she wanted to talk to me about the baby. Had I considered adoption? It was obvious the priest had sent her. They were on to me, then. That's when I moved in here.

And I dreamed about her. I saw her with the Devil, my Devil, and she was kissing him and loving him, and I knew her for who she was: Lilith,

131

Adam's first wife, who was a witch. Eons ago, she became the Devil's consort and she reigns with him in hell—*and she steals children.* She is known the world over for snatching children's souls as they enter the world.

Deceiver! Lord of lies! The Devil had gotten me pregnant so he could give my baby to her. How he broke my heart, I who loved him so. I gave him myself, and all along he had another. He wanted to take my baby. He still wants it!

Well, I am not giving this baby to anyone. God took my first one. This one is mine. This one is for me to love. No one else has ever loved me, and I deserve someone, don't I?

I realized then I'd been passive with the devil, just as the Blessed Mother had been passive with God. I'd become his instrument. I remembered the blank days and nights when I did his bidding and felt nothing but sweet, unquestioning joy that he was pleased with me. Like some parent with a child, or frankly, like the Holy Mother and God. Who did he think he was?

"Try to get this baby from me!" I screamed at him. "Just try!"

"You misunderstand me," he said, but I had ceased to believe him. He can be very cunning, you know.

I was in despair. I didn't know what to do. And then, the miracle. The blessed miracle. For my Holy Child spoke to me, from my womb. She—for she is a girl—she said:

Hail, mother, full of grace. Blessed art thou among women, all blessed be the fruit of thy womb.

We communed. It was as if she lay in my arms already talking to me. There is a closeness between mother and child, between beings who are joined, as we are joined.

With Bryan, they told me to push. If they hadn't done that, if they'd helped me like this, I would have him now, my beautiful boy. I was too trusting, too hoping, too innocent. But his half-sister, my eternal baby, has told me what to do.

The pain is killing me, and I am glad of it. I'm going. Finally. The rope I tied around my thighs has cut into my skin. It's so tight my knees are mashes of bruises. My wrists bleed from the handcuffs. But it is blood gladly shed, for her, for the Lamb.

I am screaming. I am biting at my bonds. I am struggling to separate my legs. The contraction, oh, *God*!

But I can stand it. For love of my child, I can stand it. I can do it!

Through my tears I am smiling. I'm a real woman, not some faded rose of Sharon. Thanks to me, we're eternally joined, body and soul. We are one. We will always be one. We will never, ever be separated. What greater love is there?

I am smiling.

We're almost there, little darling.

We

I'm—

THE BOX

Jack Ketchum

"What's in the box?" my son said.

"Danny," I said. "Leave the man alone."

It was two Sundays before Christmas and the Stamford local was packed—shoppers lined the aisles and we were lucky to have found seats. The man sat facing my daughters Clarissa and Jenny and me, the three of us squeezed together across from him and Danny in the seat beside him.

I could understand my son's curiosity. The man was holding the red square gift box in his lap as though afraid that the Harrison stop, coming up next, might jolt it from his grasp. He'd been clutching it that way for three stops now—since he got on.

He was tall, perhaps six feet or more and maybe twenty pounds overweight and he was perspiring heavily despite the cold dry air rushing over us each time the train's double doors opened behind our backs. He had a black walrus mustache and sparse thinning hair and wore a tan Burbury raincoat that had not been new for many years now over a rumpled gray business suit. I judged the pant-legs to be an inch too short for him. The socks were gray nylon, a much lighter shade than the suit, and the elastic in the left was shot so that it bunched up over his ankle like the skin of one of those ugly pug-nosed pedigree dogs that are so trendy nowadays. The man smiled at Danny and looked down at the box, shiny red paper over cardboard about two feet square.

"Present," he said. Looking not at Danny but at me.

His voice had the wet phlegmy sound of a heavy smoker. Or maybe he had a cold.

"Can I see?" Danny said.

I knew exactly where all of this was coming from. It's not easy spending a day in New York with two nine-year-old girls and a seven-year-old boy around Christmas time when they know there is such a thing as F.A.O. Schwartz only a few blocks away. Even if you *have* taken them to the matinee at Radio City and then skating at Rockefeller Center. Even if all their presents had been bought weeks ago and were sitting under our bed waiting to be put beneath the tree. There was always something they hadn't thought of yet that Schwartz *had* thought of and they knew that perfectly well. I'd had to fight with them—with Danny in particular—to get them aboard the 3:55 back to Rye in time for dinner.

But presents were still on his mind.

"Danny..."

"It's okay," said the man. "No problem." He glanced out the window. We were just pulling in to the Harrison station.

He opened the lid of the box on Danny's side, not all the way open but only about three inches—enough for him to see but not the rest of us, excluding us three—and I watched my son's face brighten at that, smiling, as he looked first at Clarissa and Jenny as if to say *nyah nyah* and then looked down into the box.

"Gotta go," the man said. "My stop."

He walked past us and his seat was taken immediately by a middle-aged woman carrying a pair of heavy shopping bags which she placed on the floor between her feet—and then I felt the cold December wind at my back as the double-doors slid open and closed again. Presumably the man was gone. Danny looked at the woman's bags and said shyly, "Presents?"

The woman looked at him and nodded, smiling.

He elected to question her no further.

The train rumbled on.

Our own stop was next. We walked out into the wind on the Rye platform and headed clanging down the metal steps.

"What did he have?" asked Clarissa.

"Who?" said Danny.

"The man, dummy," said Jenny. "The man with the box! What was in the *box*?"

"Oh. Nothing."

"Nothing? What? It was *empty*?"

And then they were running along ahead of me toward our car off to the left in the second row of the parking lot.

I couldn't hear his answer. If he answered her at all.

And by the time I unlocked the car I'd forgotten all about the guy.

That night Danny wouldn't eat.

It happened sometimes. It happened with each of the kids. Other things to do or too much snacking during the day. Both my wife Susan and I had been raised in homes where a depression-era mentality still prevailed. If you didn't like or didn't want to finish your dinner that was just too bad. You sat there at the table, your food getting colder and colder, until you pretty much cleaned the plate. We'd agreed that we weren't going to lay that on *our* kids. And most of the experts these days seemed to agree with us that skipping the occasional meal didn't matter. And certainly wasn't worth fighting over.

So we excused him from the table.

The next night—Monday night—same thing.

"What'd you do," my wife asked him, "have six desserts for lunch?" She was probably half serious. Desserts and pizza were pretty much all our kids could stomach on the menu at the school cafeteria.

"Nope. Just not hungry, that's all."

We let it go at that.

I kept an eye on him during the night though—figuring he'd be up in the middle of a commercial break in one of our Monday-night sitcoms, headed for the kitchen and a bag of pretzels or a jar of honey-roasted peanuts or some dry fruit loops out of the box. But it never happened. He went to bed without so much as a glass of water. Not that he looked sick or anything. His color was good and he laughed at the jokes right along with the rest of us.

I figured he was coming down with something. So did Susan. He almost had to be. Our son normally had the appetite of a Sumo wrestler.

I fully expected him to beg off school in the morning, pleading headache or upset stomach.

He didn't.

And he didn't want his breakfast, either.

And the next night, same thing.

Now this was particularly strange because Susan had cooked spaghetti and meat sauce that night and there was nothing in her considerable repertoire that the kids liked better. Even though—or maybe because of the fact—that it was one of the simplest dishes she ever threw together. But Danny just sat there and said he wasn't hungry, contented to watch while everybody else heaped it on. I'd come home late after a particularly gruelling day—I work for a brokerage firm in the City—and personally I was famished. And not a little unnerved by my son's repeated refusals to eat.

"Listen," I said. "You've got to have something. We're talking *three days* now."

"Did you eat lunch?" Susan asked.

Danny doesn't lie. "I didn't feel like it," he said.

Even Clarissa and Jenny were looking at him like he had two heads by now.

"But you *love* spaghetti," Susan said.

"Try some garlic bread," said Clarissa.

"No thanks."

"Do you *feel* okay, guy?" I asked him.

"I feel fine. I'm just not hungry's all."

So he sat there.

Wednesday night Susan went all out, making him his personal favourite—roast leg of lemon-spiced lamb with mint sauce, baked potato and red wine gravy, and green snap-peas on the side.

He sat there. Though he seemed to enjoy watching *us* eat.

Thursday night we tried take-out—Chinese food from his favourite Szechuan restaurant. Ginger beef, shrimp fried rice, fried won ton and sweet-and-sour ribs.

He said it smelled good. And sat there.

By Friday night whatever remnants of depression-era mentality lingered in my own personal psyche kicked in with a vengeance and I found myself standing there yelling at him, telling him he wasn't getting up from his chair, *young man*, until he finished at least *one* slice of his favourite pepperoni, meatball and sausage pizza from his favourite Italian restaurant.

The fact is I was worried. I'd have handed him a twenty, gladly, just to see some of that stringy mozzarella hanging off his chin. But I didn't tell him that. Instead I stood there pointing a finger at him and yelling until he started to cry—and then, second-generation depression-brat that I am, I ordered him to bed. Which is exactly what my parents would have done.

Scratch a son, you always get his dad.

But by Sunday you could see his ribs through his teeshirt. We kept him out of school Monday and I stayed home from work so we could both be there for our appointment with Doctor Weller. Weller was one of the last of those wonderful old-fashioned GP's, the kind you just about never see anymore. Over seventy years old, he would still stop by your house after office hours if the need arose. In Rye that was as unheard-of as an honest mechanic. Weller believed in homecare, not hospitals. He'd fallen asleep on my sofa one night after checking in on Jenny's bronchitis and slept for two hours straight over an untouched cup of coffee while we tiptoed around him and listened to him snore.

We sat in his office Monday morning answering questions while he checked Danny's eyes, ears, nose and throat, tapped his knees, his back and chest, checked his breathing, took a vial of blood and sent him into the bathroom for a urine sample.

"He looks perfectly fine to me. He's lost five pounds since the last time he was in for a checkup but beyond that I can't see anything wrong with him. Of course we'll have to wait for the blood work. You say he's eaten *nothing*?"

"Absolutely nothing," Susan said.

He sighed. "Wait outside," he said. "Let me talk with him."

In the waiting room Susan picked up a magazine, looked at the cover and returned it to the pile. "*Why*?" she whispered.

An old man with a walker glanced over at us and then looked away. A mother across from us watched her daughter coloring in a Garfield book.

"I don't know," I said. "I wish I did."

I was aware sitting there of an odd detachment, as though this were happening to the rest of them—to them, not me—not *us*.

I have always felt a fundamental core of loneliness in me. Perhaps it comes from being an only child. Perhaps it's my grandfather's sullen thick German blood. I have been alone with my wife and alone with my children, untouchable, unreachable, and I suspect that most of the time they haven't known. It runs deep, this aloneness. I have accommodated it. It informs all my relationships and all my expectations. It makes me almost impossible to surprise by life's grimmer turns of fate.

I was very aware of it now.

Dr. Weller was smiling when he led Danny through the waiting room and asked him to have a seat for a moment while he motioned us inside. But the smile was for Danny. There was nothing real inside it.

We sat down.

"The most extraordinary thing." The doctor shook his head. "I told him he had to eat. He asked me why. I said, Danny, people die every day of starvation. All over the world. If you don't eat, you'll die—it's that simple. Your son looked me straight in the eye and said '*so?*' "

"Jesus," Susan said.

"He wasn't being flip, believe me—he was asking me a serious question. I said, well, you want to live, don't you? He said, '*should* I?' Believe me, you could have knocked me right off this chair. '*Should I!*' I said of course you should! *Everybody* wants to live.

" '*Why?*' he said.

"My God. I told him that life was beautiful, that life was sacred, that life was *fun!* Wasn't Christmas just around the corner? What about holidays and birthdays and summer vacations? I told him that it was everybody's duty to try to live life to the absolute fullest, to do everything you could in order to be as strong and healthy and happy as humanly possible. And he listened to me. He listened to me and I knew he understood me. He didn't seem the slightest bit worried about any of what I was saying or the slightest bit concerned or unhappy. And when I was done, all he said was, yes—yes, but *I'm not hungry.*"

The doctor looked amazed, confounded.

"I really don't know what to tell you." He picked up a pad. "I'm writing down the name and phone number of a psychotherapist. Not a psychiatrist, mind—this fellow isn't going to push any pills at Danny. A therapist. The only thing I can come up with pending some—to my way of thinking, practically unimaginable—problem with his blood work is that Danny has some very serious emotional problems that need exploring and need exploring immediately. This man Field is the best I know. And he's very good with children. Tell him I said to fit you in right away, today if at all possible. We go back a long time, he and I—he'll do as I ask. And I think he'll be able to help Danny."

"Help him do what, doctor?" Susan said. I could sense her losing it. "Help him do what?" she said. "*Find a reason for living?*"

Her voice broke on the last word and suddenly she was sobbing into her hands and I reached over and tried to contact that part of me which might be able to contact her and found it not entirely mute inside me, and held her.

In the night I heard them talking, Danny and the two girls.

It was late and we were getting ready for bed and Susan was in the bathroom brushing her teeth. I stepped out into the hall to go downstairs for one last cigarette from my pack in the kitchen and that was when I heard them whispering. The twins had their room and Danny had his. The whispering was coming from their room.

It was against the rules but the rules were rapidly going to hell these days anyway. Homework was being ignored. Breakfast was coffee and packaged donuts. For Danny, of course, not even that much. Bedtime arrived when we felt exhausted.

Dr. Field had told us that that was all right for a while. That we should avoid all areas of tension or confrontation within the family for at least the next week or so.

I was *not* to yell at Danny for not eating.

Field had spoken first to him for half an hour in his office and then, for another twenty minutes, to Susan and me. I found him personable and soft-spoken. As yet he had no idea what Danny's problem could be. The jist of what he was able to tell us was that he would need to see Danny every day until he started eating again and probably once or twice a week thereafter.

If he did start eating.

Anyhow, I'd decided to ignore the whispering. I figured if I'd stuck to my guns about quitting the goddamn cigarettes I'd never have heard it in the first place. But then something Jenny said sailed through the half-open door loud and clear and stopped me.

I opened it. They were huddled together on the bed.

"I still don't get it," she said. "What's it got to do with that *box*?"

I didn't catch his answer. I walked to the door. A floorboard squeaked. The whispering stopped.

"What's what got to do with *what* box?"

They looked at me. My children, I thought, had grown up amazingly free of guilty conscience. Rules or no rules. In that they were not like me. There were times I wondered if they were actually my children at all.

"Nothing," Danny said.

"Nothing," said Clarissa and Jenny.

"Come on," I said. "Give. What were you guys just talking about?"

"Just stuff," Danny said.

"*Secret* stuff?" I was kidding, making it sound like it was no big deal.

He shrugged. "Just, you know, stuff."

"Stuff that maybe had to do with why you're not eating? That kind of stuff?"

"D*aaaad*."

I knew my son. He was easily as stubborn as I was. It didn't take a genius to know when you were not going to get anything further out of him and this was one of those times. "Okay," I said, "back to bed."

He walked past me. I glanced into the bedroom and saw the two girls sitting motionless, staring at me.

"What," I said.

"Nothing," said Clarissa.

"G'night, daddy," said Jenny.

I said goodnight and went downstairs for my cigarettes. I smoked three of them. I wondered what this whole box business was.

The following morning my girls were not eating.

Things occurred rapidly then. By evening it became apparent that they were taking the same route Danny had taken. They were happy. They were content. And they could not be budged. To me, *we're not hungry* had suddenly become the three scariest words in the English language.

A variation became just as scary when, two nights later, sitting over a steaming baked lasagne she'd worked on all day long, Susan asked me how in the world I expected her to eat while all her children were starving.

And then ate nothing further.

I started getting takeout for one.

McDonald's. Slices of pizza. Buffalo wings from the deli.

By Christmas Day, Danny could not get out of bed unassisted.

The twins were looking gaunt—so was my wife.

There was no Christmas dinner. There wasn't any point to it.

I ate cold fried rice and threw a couple of ribs into the microwave and that was that.

Meantime Field was frankly baffled by the entire thing and told me he was thinking of writing a paper—did I mind? I didn't mind. I didn't care one way or another. Dr. Weller, who normally considered hospitals strictly a last resort, wanted to get Danny on an IV as soon as possible. He was ordering more blood tests. We asked if it could wait till after Christmas. He said it could but not a moment longer. We agreed.

Despite the cold fried rice and the insane circumstances Christmas was actually by far the very best day we'd had in a very long time. Seeing us all together, sitting by the fire, opening packages under the tree—it brought back memories. The cozy warmth of earlier days. It was almost, though certainly not quite, normal. For this day alone I could almost begin to forget my worries about them, forget that Danny would be going into the hospital the next morning—with the twins, no doubt, following pretty close behind. For her part Susan seemed to *have* no worries. It was as though in joining them in their fast she had also somehow partaken of their lack of concern for it. As though the fast were itself a drug.

I remember laughter that day, plenty of laughter. Nobody's new clothes fit but my own but we tried them on anyway—there were jokes about the Amazing Colossal Woman and the Incredible Shrinking Man. And the toys and games all fit, and the brand-new hand-carved American-primitive angel I'd bought for the tree.

Believe it or not, we were happy.

But that night I lay in bed and thought about Danny in the hospital the next day and then for some reason about the whispered conversation I'd overheard that seemed so long ago and then about the man with the box and the day it had all begun. I felt like a fool, like somebody who was awakened from a long confused and confusing dream.

I suddenly had to know what *Danny* knew.

I got up and went to his room and shook him gently from his sleep.

I asked him if he remembered that day on the train and the man with the box and then looking into the box and he said yes he did and then I asked him what was in it.

"Nothing," he said.

"Really *nothing*? You mean it was actually empty?"

He nodded.

"But didn't he...I remember him telling us it was a *present*."

He nodded again. I still didn't get it. It made no sense to me.

"So you mean it was some kind of joke or something? He was playing some kind of joke on somebody?"

"I don't know. It was just...the box was empty."

He looked at me as though it was impossible for him to understand why *I* didn't understand. Empty was empty. That was that.

I let him sleep. For his last night, in his own room.

I told you that things happened rapidly after that and they did, although it hardly seemed so at the time. Three weeks later my son smiled at me sweetly and slipped into a coma and died in just under thirty-two hours. It was unusual, I was told, for the IV not to have sustained a boy his age but sometimes it happened. By then the twins had beds two doors down the hall. Clarissa went on February 3rd and Jenny on February 5th.

My wife, Susan, lingered until the 27th.

And through all of this, through all these weeks now, going back and forth to the hospital each day, working when I was and *am* able and graciously being granted time off whenever I can't, riding into the City from Rye and from the City back to Rye again alone on the train, I look for him. I look through every car. I walk back and forth in case he should get on one stop sooner or one stop later. I don't want to miss him. I'm losing weight.

Oh, I'm eating. Not as well as I should be I suppose but I'm eating.

But I need to find him. To know what my son knew and then passed on to the others. I'm sure that the girls knew, that he passed it on to them that night in the bedroom—some terrible knowledge, some awful peace. And I think somehow, perhaps by being so very much closer to all of my children than I was ever capable of being, that Susan knew too. I'm convinced it's so.

I'm convinced that it was my essential loneliness that set me apart and saved me, and now of course which haunts me, makes me wander through dark corridors of commuter trains waiting for a glimpse of him—him and his damnable present, his gift, his box.

I want to know. It's the only way I can get close to them.

I want to see. I *have* to see.

I'm *hungry.*

For Neal McPheeters

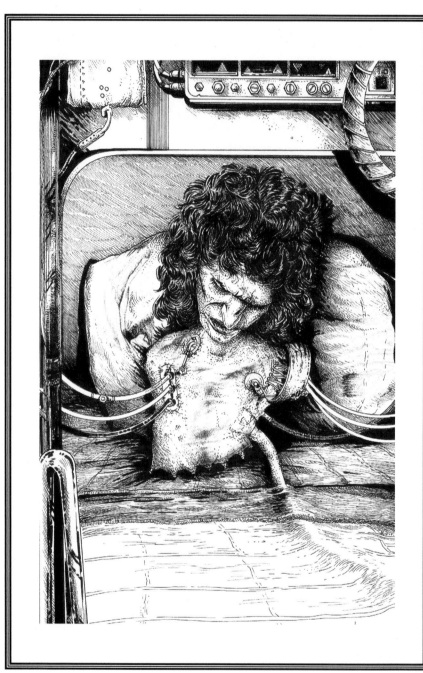

STEPHEN

ELIZABETH MASSIE

MICHAEL AND STEPHEN SHARED a room at the rehabilitation center. Michael was a young man with bright, frantically moving eyes and an outrageous sense of nonstop, bitter humor. He had been a student at the center for more than a year, and with his disability, would most likely be there much longer. This was true, also, for the others housed on the first floor of the west wing. Severe cases, all of them, living at the center, studying food services, auto mechanics, computer operating, art, and bookkeeping, none of them likely to secure a job when released because when hiring the disabled, businesses would usually go for the students who lived on east wing and on the second floor. The center had amazing gadgets that allowed people like Michael to work machines and press computer keys and dabble in acrylics, but the generic factory or office did not go in for space-age, human adaptive robotics. And Michael himself was a minor miracle of robotics.

Anne arrived at the center late, nearly ten thirty, although her meeting had been scheduled for ten o'clock. The cab dropped her off at the front walk and drove away, spraying fine gravel across her heels. Inside her shoes, her toes worked an awkward rhythm that neither kept them warm nor calmed her down. A cool November wind threw a piece of paper across the street before her. On its tail followed the crumbled remains of a dead oak leaf. Anne's full skirt flipped and caught her legs in a tight embrace. It tugged, as if trying to pull her backward and away. In her mouth she tasted hair and sour fear. When she raked her fingers across her face the hair was gone, but not the fear.

The center was large and sterile, a modern bit of gray stone architecture. The largest building was marked with a sign to the left of the walkway: ADMINISTRATION AND ADMISSIONS. Almost the entire front of this building was composed of plate glass with borders of stone. Anne could not see behind the glass for the harsh glare of morning sun, but in the wind the glass seemed to bulge and ripple.

Like a river.

Like water.

"Christ."

Anne scrunched her shoulders beneath the weight of her coat and glanced about for a place to sit and compose herself. Yes, she was late, but screw them if they wanted to complain about volunteer help. There were several benches just off the walkway on the lawn, but she didn't want to sit in full view. And so she took the walk leading to the right, following along until it circled behind the main building beside what she assumed was a long, gray storm dormitory. The walk ended at a paved parking lot, marked off for visitors and deliveries. She crossed the lot, skirting cars and food trucks and large vans equipped for hauling wheelchairs, heading for a grove of trees on the other side. A lone man pushing an empty wheeled cot crossed in front of Anne and gave her a nod. She smiled slightly and then looked away.

The trees across the lot encircled a park. Picnic tables were clustered beneath the largest of the oaks, and concrete benches made a neat border about the pond in the center. The pond itself was small, no more than two acres, but it was dark and clearly deep. Dead cattails rattled on the water's edge. A short pier jutted into the water from the shore, with a weathered rowboat tethered to the end. Leaves blew spastic patterns on the black surface.

Anne sat on the bench and wrapped her fingers about her knees. There was no one else in the park. She looked at the brown grass at her feet, then at her hands on her knees, and then at the pond. The sight of the bobbing boat and the dull shimmering of the ripples made her stomach clamp. What a raw and ugly thing the pond was.

A cold thing, enticing and deadly, ready to suck someone under and drag them down into its lightless depths. Licking and smothering with its stinking embrace.

Phillip would have loved this pond.

Phillip would have thought it just right.

The fucking bastard.

If she was to go to the water's edge, she thought she might see his reflection there, grinning at her.

But she did not go. She sat on the concrete bench, her fingers turning purple with the chill, her breath steaming the air. She did not look at the pond again, but at the grass and her knees and the picnic tables. She studied the gentle slopes the paths made about the park, all accessible to wheeled means of movement. Accessible to the people who lived here. To the people Anne's mother had protected her from as a child; who her mother had hurried Anne away from on the street, whispering in her ear, "Don't stare, now, Anne. Polite people don't react. Do you hear me?

"There but for the grace of God go you, Anne. Don't look now. It's not nice."

Anne closed her eyes, but the vision of the park and the tables and the sloped pathways stayed inside her eyes. She could hear the wind on the pond.

"Damn you, Mother," she said. "Damn you, Phillip."

She sat for another twenty minutes.

When she crossed the parking lot again, her eyes in the sun and her hands in her pockets, her muscles were steeled and her face carried a tight, professional smile.

Janet Warren welcomed Anne into the center at ten fifty-six, barely mentioning the tardiness. She took Anne into her office, and, as assistant administrator, explained the functions of the center. She gave Anne a brief summary of the students with whom Anne would work, then led her off to the west wing.

Anne entered Michael's room after Janet gave an obligatory tap on the door. Michael grunted and Anne walked in, still holding her coat, which Janet had offered to take, clutched tightly to her stomach.

"Michael," said Janet to the man on the bed. "This is Miss Zaccaria, the lady I said would be coming to help us out."

Michael propped up on his elbow, straightening himself, patting his blanket down about the urinary bag as if it were an egg in an Easter basket. He gave Anne a wide grin.

"Well, if it ain't my dream lady come to see me in the flesh!" he crowed. "Are you real or just a vision of delight?"

Anne licked her lips and looked back at Janet Warren. "Thank you, Mrs. Warren. I'll be fine now. I'll let you know if we need anything."

"Hell, I know what I need," said Michael. "And she's standing right in front of me."

Janet nodded, her motion seeming to be both acknowledgment of what Anne had said and a sisterly confirmation of what she had come to do. Janet turned and left the room.

"Come on," said Michael, and Anne looked back at him.

"Come on? What do you mean?" There was only a small comfort in her professional ability at conversation. It wasn't enough to overcome her discomfort at seeing the physical form of Michael before her. He was legless, with hipbones flattened into a shovel-shaped protrusion. The thin blanket emphasized rather than hid his lower deformity. He was missing his right arm to the elbow, and there was no left arm at all. A steel hook clipped the air in cadence with the blinking of Michael's eyes.

"Come on and tell me. You ain't really no shrink, are you? I was expecting some shrivelled-up old bitch. You really is my dream lady, ain't you?"

Anne focused on Michael's face and took a slow breath. "No, sorry,"

152

she said. "I'm from Associated Psychological. I'm a clinical social worker."

Michael grappled with a button and pressed it with the point of his hook. The bed rolled toward Anne. She held her position.

"No, you ain't. I dreamed about you last night. Dreamed I still had my parts and you was eating them nice as you please."

Anne's face went instantly hot. She could have kicked herself for not being ready for anything. "I was told you've had a rough time these past months," she said, "not getting along with the other students like you used to do. I'd like to help."

"Sure. Just sit on my face for a few hours."

Anne glanced at the withered body, then back at his face. Of all the students she would be working with through the volunteered-outreach program, Michael was the most disabled. "Is that all you think about, Michael? Sex?"

"When it comes to sex," he said, "all I can *do* is think." He laughed out loud and wheeled closer. "You like me?"

"I don't know you yet. I hope we'll like each other."

"Why you here? We got shrinks. Two of them. You on a field trip?"

"Field trip?"

"You know, like them school kids. Sometimes the local schools bring in their junior high kids. Show them around. Let them take little look-sees. Tell them if they are bad enough and dive into shallow lakes or don't wear seat belts, God'll make them just like us."

Anne cleared her throat and loosened her coat from her waist. "First of all, I'm here on a volunteer program. Until the new center is finished down state, there will continue to be more students than can be properly provided for. The center called on our association to help out temporarily. You are a student with whom I've been asked to work."

"Student." Michael spat out the word. "I'm thirty-one and I'm called a goddamn student."

"Second," Anne said, "I'm not on a field trip. I'm not here to stare. I'm here to help."

Michael shook his head, then eased off his elbow to a supine position. "So who else is on your list besides me?"

Anne opened the folded paper Janet had given her. "Randy Carter, Julia Powell, Cora Grant—"

"Cora'll drive you ape shit. She lost half her brain in some gun accident."

"And Ardie Whitesell. I might like Cora, Michael. Don't forget, I don't know her yet, either."

Michael sighed. "I don't need no shrink. What the fuck's your name?"

"Miss Zaccaria."

"Yeah, well, I'm okay. I don't need no shrink. Don't need one any more than old roomie over there." Michael tilted his head on his pillow, indicating a curtained corner of the room.

"Roomie?"

"Roommate. He don't need no shrink, neither. I don't 'cause I got things all figured out in this world. Nothing a little nookie can't cure." Michael looked at Anne and winked. "And roomie over there, he don't need one 'cause he's in some kind of damn coma. Not much fun to have around, you know."

Anne frowned, only then aware of the mechanical sounds softly emanating from the corner. The drawn curtain was stiff and white, hanging from the ceiling-high rod like a starched shroud. "What's wrong with your roommate?"

"Hell, what ain't wrong? Come over here." With a hissing of his arm, Michael rose again and clutched the bed switch, tapping buttons in a short series, and the bed spun around. The legless man rolled to the curtain. Anne followed.

Michael shifted onto his right side and took the curtain in his hook. "Stephen's been here longer'n me. He ain't on no shrink's list." Michael pulled the curtain back.

It was not registering what was before her that allowed her to focus on it as long as she did. There were machines there, a good number of them,

154

crowded around a tiny bed like rumbling and humming steel wolves about a lone prey. Aluminum racks stood on clawed feet, heavy bags of various colored liquids hanging from them, oozing their contents into thin, clear tubes. A portable heart monitor beeped. Behind it, a utility sink held to the wall, various antiseptics and lotions and balms cluttering the shelf above. The rails of the bed were pulled up to full height. At one end of the mattress was a thin blanket, folded back and tucked down. And at the other end, a thin pillow. And Stephen.

Anne's coat and paper dropped to the floor. "Oh, my dear God."

"Weird, huh? I call him Head Honcho. I think he must be some doctor's experiment, you know, keeping him alive and all. Don't it beat all?"

On the pillow was a head, with black curled hair. Attached to the head, a neck, and below that a small piece of naked, ragged chest, barely large enough to house a heart and single lung. The chest heaved and shuddered, wires pulsing like obscene fishermen's lines. That was all there was of Stephen.

Anne's heart constricted painfully. She stepped backward.

"Nurses don't like him. Can't stand to touch him, though they shave him every three days. Doctor checks him nearly every day. Head Honcho don't do nothing but breathe. He ain't much but at least he don't complain about my music." Michael looked at Anne.

Anne turned away. Her stomach clenched, throwing fouled bile into her throat.

"Hey, you leaving?"

"I need to see the others," she managed. And she went out of the west wing to the faculty restroom, where she lost her control and her lunch.

It was three days before Anne could bring herself to visit the center again. The AP partners were asking her for her volunteer hours chart, and as the newest member of the firm, she couldn't shrug it off. And so she returned. Her pulse was heavy in her neck and the muscles of her back were tight, but she decided she would not allow herself more than passing acknowledgment of them.

She talked to Cora in the art room. Cora had little to say, but seemed pleased with the attention Anne gave her painting. Randy was in the recreation hall with Ardie, playing a heated game of billiards, wheeling about the table with teeth gritted and chins hovering over cue sticks. Anne told them she'd visit later, after the match. Julia was shopping with her daughter, and Michael was in the pool on a red inner tube.

"Hey, Miss Zaccaria!" he called when he saw Anne peering through the water-steamed glass of the door. "Want to come in for a swim? I'm faster in the water. Bet I could catch you in a split second. What do you say?"

Anne pushed the door open and felt the onslaught of chlorine-heated mist. She did not go any closer to the pool. "I never learned to swim, Michael. Besides, I'm not exactly dressed for swimming."

"I don't want you *dressed* for swimming. What fun would that be?"

Anne wiped moisture from her forehead. "How long do you plan to swim? I thought we could visit outside. The day's turned out pretty fair. It's not as cold as it has been."

"I'm finished now, ain't I, Cindy?"

The pool-side attendant, who had been watching Michael spin around on his tube, shrugged. "If you say so." She pulled Michael's wheeled bed from the wall and moved it to the pool steps. "Get over to the side so I can get you out."

"Hey, Miss Zaccaria, do me a favor. My blue jacket is in my room. It's one of those Member's Only things. Anyway, I'm not really crazy about the wind, even when it's warm. Would you get my jacket for me? Door's unlocked."

Anne's head was nodding as she thought, Oh, Christ, yes, I mind. "No problem," she said. She left the pool, telling herself the curtain was drawn.

They would always keep the curtain drawn.

Michael's door was indeed unlocked. The students of the center kept valuables in a communal vault, and the staff moved about the floor frequently, so chances of theft were slim. Anne went into the room, expecting the jacket to be in plain sight, prepared to lift it coolly and leave with her self-esteem intact.

But she did not see the jacket.

She checked Michael's small dresser, behind the straight-backed visitor's chair, in the plastic laundry basket beside the vacant spot where Michael's bed rested at night. It was not there.

Anne looked at the curtained corner. Certainly the jacket would not be behind the curtain. There was no reason to go there, no reason to look.

She walked to the curtain and edged over to the hemmed corner of the heavy material. It's not over there, she thought. Her hands begun to sweat. She could not swallow.

She pulled the curtain back slowly. And let her gaze move to the bed.

Again, it was a flash image that recorded itself on her startled retinas before she looked away. The head was in the same place, eyes closed, dark hair in flat curls. The neck. The breathing, scarred half chest. Anne stared at the sink, counting, rubbing thumbs against index fingers, calming herself. She would look for Michael's jacket. There was a chair like that on Michael's side, and a laundry basket, although this one held no clothes, only white towels and washcloths. By the wall beside the sink was a pile of clothing, and Anne stepped closer to search through it. There were shirts, mostly, several pairs of shorts and underwear. And a blue jacket. Anne picked it up. She looked back at the small bed.

And the eyes in the head were open, and they were looking at her.

Anne's fingers clenched, driving nails into her palms. She blinked, and glanced back at the pile of clothes, pretending she hadn't seen the eyes. Chills raised tattoos up her shoulders, and adrenaline spoke loudly in her veins: leave now.

Her hands shook as they pawed through the clothes on the floor, acting as though she had more to find. Calm down. And leave.

But the voice made her stop.

"I didn't mean to stare," it said.

Anne flinched, and slowly stood straight. She looked at the bed.

The eyes were still open, still watching her.

Her own mouth opened before she had a chance to stop it, and she said, "I was looking for Michael's jacket." Leave now! cried the adrenaline. That thing did not say anything. It can't talk. It's comatose. It's brain-dead. Leave *now*!

The eyes blinked, and Anne saw the muscles on the neck contract in a swallowing reflex. "Yes," it said. And the eyes closed. The whole ragged body seemed to shudder and shrink. It had gone to sleep again.

The jacket worked in Anne's fingers. Michael was in the pool, waiting for her. It's brain-dead, Anne. Get ahold of yourself. "Stephen?" she whispered.

But it did not open its eyes, nor move, and Anne took the jacket down to the pool where Michael was fuming about on his bed, spinning circles around the yawning attendant.

"So I store my stuff on Stephen's side of the room, 'cause he don't complain none. And when I get visitors they don't think I'm a slob. Nurses don't care. I get the stuff from over there into my laundry basket when it's really dirty."

Anne was in Michael's visitor's chair. He was on his side, his gaze alternating between her, his hook, and the curtain.

"He's never complained to you?"

Michael chuckled shallowly. "You serious? He's in a coma, I told you already. Listen to this, if you don't believe me." Michael reached for the sleek black cassette player on the nightstand beside the bed. He pushed the switch, and an instant blast of heavy rock shattered the air. Above the shrieking guitars and pounding percussion, Anne could hear the sudden, angry calls from the neighboring students.

"Go, look, quick," Michael shouted over the music. "Go see before those damned nurses get here."

158

Anne shook her head, smiling tightly, brushing off the suggestion.

Michael would have none of it. "Shit, just go on and look at Dead-Head Honcho."

"I don't think it's my place to bother him."

"Get on now, the nurses are coming. I hear them damn squeaking shoes down the hall!"

Anne got up and looked behind the curtain. The head was silent and motionless. The eyes were closed.

"What'd I tell you? Dead, dumb, blind, and in a coma. Sounds like hell to me, and God knows I seen hell up close myself."

"You have?" Anne went back to her chair. "What do you mean, you've seen it up close?"

"Look at me, Miss Zaccaria. You think the love of the Lord do this to me?"

There were then three nurses' heads at the door, clustered on the frame like Japanese beetles on a rose stem. "Turn that down, Michael, or the player's ours for the next week."

"Shit," said Michael. He grappled the button; pushed it off. "I ain't no goddamn student!" he told the nurses who were already gone. "It's my business how loud I play my music!"

"Tell me about your accident," said Anne. But she was thinking: Hell, oh, yes, it must be hell, living in a coma.

But he's not in a coma. He is conscious. He is alive.

And when you are already in hell, what is hell to that?

Her next session with Michael was cancelled because he was in the infirmary with the flu. And so Anne sought out Julia and spent an hour with her, and then Cora, who did not want to talk but wanted Anne to paint a picture of a horse for her. Randy and Ardie were again at the billiard table and would have nothing to do with her. Then she visited the faculty lounge, and listened with feigned interest to the disgruntled banter and rehab shoptalk. A few questions were directed her way, and she answered them as cordially as possible, but she wanted to talk about Stephen. She wanted to know what they knew.

But she could not make herself bring up the subject. And so she went to the west wing, and let herself into Michael's unlocked room.

She went to the curtain and took the edge in her fingers. Her face itched but she shook it off. No, said the adrenaline. "Yes," she said. And she pulled the curtain back.

The tubes flowed, nutrients in, wastes out. The monitor beeped. Bags dripped and pumps growled softly. Anne moved to the end of the bed. She forced herself to see what was before her, what she needed to see, and not be distracted by the machinery about it.

The flesh of the chest twitched slightly and irregularly with the work of the wires. Every few seconds, the shuddering breath. It would be cold, Anne thought, yet the blanket was folded back at the foot of the bed, a regulatory piece of linen which served no purpose to the form on the pillow. With the wires and tubes, a blanket would be a hindrance. The neck did not move; swallowing was for the wakeful. The head as well did not move; except for the faint pulsing of the nostrils, working mindlessly to perform its assigned job.

Anne moved her hands to the railing of the bed. She slid around, moving along the side to the head of the bed. Her feet felt the floor cautiously as if the tiles might crack. She reached the pillow; her hands fell from the railing. Her face itched and again she refused to give in to it.

Through fear-chapped lips, she said, "Stephen?"

The monitor beeped. The chest quivered.

"Stephen?"

The sleeping face drew up as if in pain, and then the eyes opened. As the lids widened, the muscles of the cheeks seemed to ease. He blinked. His eyes were slate blue.

"I hope I'm not bothering you," she said.

"No," he said. And the eyes fluttered closed, and Anne thought he was

160

asleep again. Her hands went to her face and scratched anxiously. She pulled them down.

Stephen's eyes opened. "No, you aren't bothering me. Why would you think that?"

"You were sleeping."

"I always sleep."

"Oh," Anne said.

"You've been spending time with Michael. What do you think of him?"

"He's...fine. It's good to spend time with him."

The head nodded, barely, sliding up and down the pillow, obviously an effort. "You are Miss Zaccaria."

"Anne," she said.

"Anne," he repeated. His eyes closed.

"Do you want me to go now?"

His eyes remained closed. "If you wish."

"Do you want me to?"

"No."

And so she stood those very long minutes, watching Stephen slip into sleep, trying to absorb the reality of what was before her, counting the beepings of the heart monitor.

Again the eyes opened. "You are still here."

"Yes."

"How long has it been?"

"Only a few minutes."

"I'm sorry."

"No, that's all right. I don't mind."

Stephen sighed. "Why don't you sit? There is a chair over there somewhere."

"I'll stand."

"Michael is wrong. I do mind his music. I hate it."

"I could ask him to keep it down."

161

"It's not the volume. It is the music. Music was created for movement, for involvement. I feel a straightjacket around my soul when Michael plays his music."

Anne said nothing for a moment. Stephen looked away from her, and then back again.

"Why do you let them think you are comatose?" Anne asked.

"That way I can sleep. When I sleep, there are dreams."

"What kind of dreams?"

"Ever the clinical social worker," said Stephen. And for the first time, a small smile crossed his lips.

Anne smiled also. "That's me," she said.

"My dreams are my own," he said. "I would never share them."

"All right."

"And I would not ask you to share yours," he said.

"No," said Anne.

"I'm tired," he said.

And when she was certain he was asleep once again, Anne left.

"I liked college, my studies there. The psyche of the human is so infinite and fascinating. I thought I could do something with all I'd learned. But I wasn't smart enough to become a doctor."

"How do you know?"

Anne shrugged. "I know."

"And so you are a therapist," said Stephen.

"Yes. It's important. Helping people."

"How do you help?"

"I listen to them. I help them find new ways of seeing situations."

"Do you like your patients?"

"I don't call them patients. They are clients."

"Do you like them?"

"Michael asked me something like that when we first met. He wanted to know if I liked him."

"Do you?"

Anne crossed her feet and angled her face away from Stephen. There was a lint ball on the floor by the bed. The nurses and orderlies were obviously not quick about their business here.

"Of course I do," she answered.

"That's good. If you like people you can help them."

"That's not a prerequisite, though. Liking them."

Stephen closed his eyes momentarily. Then he looked at Anne again. "You have a husband?"

"No."

"A boyfriend, certainly."

"No, not really. I've not wanted one." Anne hesitated. "It's not what you think."

"What do I think?"

"That I'm a lesbian or something."

"I haven't thought that."

"I'm not."

"You have family, though."

Anne's crossed arms drew in closer. Family, yes, she did. God knows what wonders she could have accomplished had it not been for her beloved family.

"A mother," she said. "An older brother."

"What are their names?"

"My mother is Audrey. My brother..." Suddenly Anne was acutely aware of the utility sink behind her. She could see it brimming with water, cold water, stopped up and ready..."My brother's name is Phillip."

"Are you close?"

Anne's shoulders flinched at the nearness of the sink. Dark water; thick, stinking, and hungry water. Eager. She swallowed, then looked down at her hands. Pathetic things, she thought. She flexed them. Goddamn it all. She looked up at Stephen. His forehead was creased, with a barely discernible shadow over his eyes.

"Sure," she said. "We're close."

Then Stephen went to sleep. Anne stared at the dust ball and at the tubes running from beneath Stephen's ribs. And her fingers, wanting to move forward, were stopped, and were locked onto her lap like a colony of trapped souls.

Janet Warren was chuckling as she ushered Anne into the office. "It's no big deal," she said, obviously seeing through Anne's tight smile. "Honestly, I just want to talk with you for a minute."

Anne took one of the chairs that sat before the desk; Janet sat on the edge of the desk.

"It's Julia," Janet said.

Anne recrossed her arms and frowned slightly. "Julia? What's wrong with her?"

"Now, don't get me wrong. Sorry, I don't need to talk with you like that. You know what you're doing, you know how people react sometimes. I'm sure you've had clients freak out during sessions, things like that."

Anne said, "Certainly."

"Julia went a little crazy after your last visit. She started throwing things; she even threatened bodily harm to herself if you came back again."

"Mrs. Warren, certainly you don't think—"

"I don't think anything, Anne. We're in this together, remember? Julia has always been easily set off. It seems you remind her of someone she hated back when she was a child. In school, somewhere back then. You've done nothing wrong. As a matter of fact, you seem to be making real progress with Michael."

Anne tapped the rug lightly with the ball of her foot. "Michael likes to joke around. I seem to be a good receptacle for that."

"So be it," said Janet. "That could be just what he needs at this point."

"Yes, I believe so."

"So what I wanted to say was just forget about Julia for the time being. I'll get another volunteer assigned to her. With your own work at the association, I'm sure a smaller volunteer load won't disappoint you."

Anne nodded, stood, and started for the door. She turned back. "Mrs. Warren, what do you know about Stephen?"

"Stephen?"

"Michael's roommate."

"Ah, yes," Janet said. She slipped from the desktop and went around the desk to the swivel chair. She did not sit. "It may sound bad to say that we assigned Michael to that room because we didn't think any other student could tolerate Michael and his moods. Stephen's in a coma; you probably already know about that. We have brain waves, and they seem quite active, but who can figure what kinds of unconscious states the human mind can fall into? But whatever it is, Stephen is not to be disturbed. I would appreciate it if you would remind Michael to stay on his side of the curtain."

"Of course I will," said Anne.

"Thanks."

Anne looked out the office door, toward the activity in the main hall. Several wheelchaired students were talking with visitors; family, possibly. She looked again at Janet. "Before Stephen came here, who was he? I mean, what did he do?"

Janet sat and dug her fingers beneath a pile of manila folders, in search of a particular one. "What? Oh, music, he was a musician. A pianist. On the way up, I was told. Into classical concerts, things like that. A pity."

It felt as though cold water had been poured over Anne's lungs. She held her breath and slid her balled fists into her pockets. "And what," she began, "happened to him?"

The phone burred on the desk, and Janet raised an apologetic hand to Anne before picking up the receiver. She dropped to her seat with her "Hello," and Anne left the office.

Michael seemed glad to be out of the infirmary. He waggled his eyebrows at Anne as she came into the room and raised himself up on his elbow. "Miss Zaccaria! Did you miss me?"

Anne sat in the visitor's chair. "Sure, Michael. Are you feeling better?"

Michael snorted. "Not a whole *hell* of a lot better, but enough to get me out of there. God, you should see the nurses they have for us sick students. The old ones all look like marines, and the young ones look like willing virgins. Like going from hot to cold to hot again all the time. It's enough to pop your nads, if you got some."

"Are you well enough to start back into the electronics program? You haven't done anything for nearly a month; and you know you can't stay unless you are working toward a future."

"I've been sick. I had my emotional problems, right? I mean, you can vouch for that. That's why you're here."

Anne scratched her calf. "You have to look at your goals, Michael. Without goals you just stay put in time and don't make progress."

"I got a goal."

"What's that?"

"To get my butt scratched. You ever scratch your butt with a hook?"

Anne shook her head.

"You scratch my butt for me, Miss Zaccaria?"

"Michael, don't start—"

"I ain't trying to be gross, honest. I just got an itch."

"Michael, it's not my place to do that. There are nurses."

"Tell me about it. Okay, then my back. You scratch my back? Please?"

Anne felt her hands catch her elbows. She sat straight, shifting as far from Michael as she could without getting up from the chair. "I'm not supposed to."

"Why?"

"I just can't. It's not professional. Therapists aren't supposed to touch clients."

"I'm not talking like you being my shrink now. Just my friend. Please. My back itches."

"No, Michael."

Michael was silent for a moment. He looked away from Anne, and

166

studied a faint spot on his blanket. When he looked back, his face was pinched. "I ain't trying to be gross," he said softly. "How about my face? Can you scratch my nose for me?"

Anne, slowly, shook her head.

"Please," he said. "Nobody ever wants to touch me."

"I can't," said Anne.

Michael watched her, and then with a quick motion, he reached out and jabbed the play button on his tape player. Shrieking music cut the air. "Fine," he cried over it. "Sorry I asked. I didn't mean it, anyway. It was a joke. A butt scratch, shit, I just wanted a butt scratch for some jollies is all."

And then the nurses came and threatened Michael and he turned the music off.

"One of the last sets of visitors I had was quite a long time ago," said Stephen. "But it is one I'll never forget." He blinked, and his dark brows drew together, then apart. A strand of black, curled hair had been moved nearly into his eye, and Anne wondered what it would be like to reach out and push it back. "They were from a church. Pentecostal something. Holiness something. Young people, all of them. Neatly dressed, each in pure white outfit that made me think of angry young angels. Even their Bibles were white. They didn't want to be here; I could hear them whispering behind the curtain. They were frightened. But the leader, a young girl of about eighteen, quieted them saying, "Even as you do it unto the least of the flock you do it unto Jesus." And in they came, smiles flashing. The girl told me I needed to turn my life around, I needed to turn to the Lord. I told her I wasn't turning anywhere, couldn't she see that? She became flustered with my responses, then furious. I believe I was supposed to shake in the presence of their godly and bodily wholeness. Her face was as pale as her dress. When she finally ushered out her little group, she told me, 'You better accept the love of the Lord. There isn't anyone else in this world who would love something like you.' "

"Christ, Stephen."

"No, it's all right," he said. His eyes closed, held, then opened slightly. "It was a long time ago."

"You said one of the last sets of visitors were the church people. Who were the last?"

"Two insurance salesmen. I saw who they were, and went to sleep. I think they were more than relieved. I've been asleep most of the time since."

"Stephen."

"It's all right," he said. "Really."

Stephen shut his eyes. Anne watched his face. The nurses had done only a fair job of shaving. There was a small red cut on his chin. Then Stephen looked at her.

"Why wouldn't you touch Michael?"

Anne started. "You were listening."

"Yes."

"I can't. It's not part of the job, you know. People might take it the wrong way."

"Why are you a counsellor, Anne?"

"So I can help people."

"There are lots of ways to help. Doctors, physical therapists, teachers."

"Yes." But they have to touch people. I can't touch, not now, not ever. Phillip touched me. Sweet God, he touched me and touching is nothing but pain and...

"Your family hoped you'd be a counsellor?"

"No, I don't think it mattered to them."...anger and disgust. Touching is filth, degradation. It is losing control. Anne's feet were planted squarely on the floor. She was ready to run. Touching is cold and hateful, like putrid, black water.

"Tell me about your family."

"I already did."

"You have a mother. A brother."

"I already did!" Anne's hand flew to her mouth and pressed there. She had screamed. "Oh, God," she said then.

"I'm sorry."

"It's all right."

Anne's throat felt swollen. She swallowed and it hurt. "I didn't mean to shout. It was rude."

"It's all right."

"Stephen," Anne began, and then hesitated. She inched herself forward on her chair. Stephen's eyes watched her calmly, and they were not eyes of a blue and frightening ocean, but of a blue and clear sky. She saw an understanding there, and she wanted to reach out for it.

She wanted it, but knew the only way to have it was to touch it.

She sat back. "Good night, Stephen," she said.

"Good night," he answered. And he slept.

Randy was being released from the center. The staff threw him a good-bye party, complete with balloons and ridiculous hats and noisemakers which Randy pretended to hate but obviously loved. He made a point of hooting his paper horn into the ear of everyone present. Randy had landed a job in the camera room of the local newspaper. His going away gift was a framed, fake newspaper front page, complete with the headline "RANDY CARTER, AKA CLARK KENT, SECURES POSITION AT DAILY PRESS." Beneath the caption was a large black-and-white photo of Randy, cigar in teeth, leaning over the billiard table. A cue stick was in his hand.

"I taught him everything he knows," said Michael, as he looped about among the partiers. "He ought to take me with him, or he'll just make a mess of things."

Anne left in the midst of the hubbub and went down to the pond behind the administration building. The sky was overcast, and mist covered the algaed water.

Water, the dark trough of fears.

She stood beside the edge. The wind buffeted her.

Her mind, wearied, could not hold back the rush of memories.

Phillip, as a boy, touching Anne in secret. First as a game, then as an obsession. Anne growing up; Phillip growing up ahead of her, and his touching becoming even more cruel.

His body heavy and harsh; his immense organ tearing into her relentlessly. Anne crying each night, knowing he would come to her and would have no love for anything except the sensation of his own explosive release. Phillip swearing that if she told anyone, he would kill her.

Anne, promising herself over and over that if she was not killed, she would never let this happen again. She would not touch or be touched.

And then came the night Phillip decided blood would make it more rewarding. He was tired of the same old thing; he said he was going to change Anne just a little, like a sculptor changing a piece of clay to make it better. With the door locked and his underwear in Anne's mouth, he carved. He took off her little toes, stopping the blood with matches and suturing with his mother's sewing kit. He decorated her abdomen with a toothed devil face into which he rubbed ink from Anne's cartridge pen. Across her breasts he etched, "Don't fuck with me." The ink finished it off.

The next morning, Mother wanted to know why there were stains on the sheets. She accused Anne of having a boyfriend in at night. She shook Anne until the confession was made. Anne took off her nightgown and her slippers. Mother shrieked and wailed, clutching her hair and tearing hunks out. Then she said, "The grace of God has left you! You are one of those deformed creatures!"

Mother confronted Phillip.

Phillip killed Mother in the tub that evening with scalding water and an old shower curtain.

Then he had found Anne, hiding in the garage.

Anne doubled over and gagged on the bank of the pond. She could still taste the sludge and the slime from so many years ago. She drove her fists into the wall of her ribs, and with her head spinning, she retched violently. At her feet lay brown leaves, stirred into tiny, spiralling patterns by the wind and the spattering of her own vomit.

She wiped her mouth. She stood up. Her vision wavered, and it was difficult to stand straight.

She made her way to Michael's room.

Michael's tape player was on the bed table. Michael had left it on, though softly, and as Anne picked it up she could hear the faint hammering of the percussion. The player was slender and cool and Anne could wrap both hands about it easily. Much like Phillip's cock, when she was just a young girl. With a single jerk, she pulled the cord from the wall. The table teetered, then crashed to the floor. The music died in mid-beat.

Anne hauled the player, cord dragging, to Stephen's side of the room. There was sweat on her neck, and it dripped to her breasts and tickled like roach legs. She ignored it. Stephen was asleep. Anne threw the player into the sink and it shattered on the dulled enamel.

"This is for you, Stephen," she said. "No more music. You won't have to suffer it anymore."

She ran the water until the heat of it steamed her face and stung her eyes. She grabbed up the pieces of broken player and squeezed them. Sharp edges cut into her hands and she let the blood run.

"And this is for you, Phillip. Goddamn you to whatever hell there is in this world or the next."

She looked at Stephen's bed. He was awake, and watching her.

"Anne," he said.

Anne wiped her mouth with the back of her hand. Blood streaked her chin.

"Tell me, Anne."

"My brother killed my mother. Then he tried to kill me."

"Tell me."

Anne looked at the dead player in the sink. The hot water continued to run. Anne could barely catch her breath in the heat. She stepped back and licked the blood from her hands. "He tried to kill me. He was fucking me. Ever since I can remember, he was fucking me, hurting me, and enjoying it like any other boy would enjoy baseball." She turned to Stephen and held out her wounded hands. "Touching is wrong. And he knew it. When Mother found out, he killed her. He took me down the back road to the water treatment plant and threw me into the settling pool. It was not deep, but I could not swim, and the bottom was slick with sludge and it was rancid, Stephen, it was sewage and garbage, and I slipped under and under and every time I came up Phillip would lean over the rail and hit me with a broom handle. It was night, and I could no longer tell the difference between up and down, it was all black and putrid and I couldn't breathe. Phillip kept hitting me and hitting me. My blood ran into the sewage and when I screamed I swallowed the sludge."

Anne moved closer to Stephen's bed, her hand raised.

"Someone heard us. Phillip was stopped and arrested. I spent a good deal of time in the hospital, with concussions and infections."

Stephen watched between her bloodied hands and her face.

"I wanted to help people," Anne said. "I don't think I ever can. Phillip has seen to that."

"Yes, you can."

"Tell me, Stephen. What can I do for you?"

Stephen sighed silently, his chest lifting then falling. His head rolled slightly to the left, and he stared at the light above the bed.

"Love me," he said finally.

"I do, Stephen."

His eyes blinked, the light reflecting tiny sparks. He looked back at Anne. His mouth opened, then closed. His jaw flexed and he licked his lips with his dry tongue. "Love me," he said.

Anne hesitated. Then slowly, she lowered the side rail of the bed. She knelt beside the bed and put her head onto the pillow beside Stephen. For a moment she held still, and then she brought her hand up to touch Stephen's lips with her fingers. They did not move, yet she could feel the soft blowing of his breath on her skin.

She moved back then. Stephen watched her. Then he said, "You knew about my music."

Anne nodded.

"My dreams are different now."

Anne nodded.

After a long moment, he said, "Anne, love me." His voice was certain, kind, and sad.

Anne touched her face and it was hot and wet with the steam and her own sweat. She touched Stephen's face and it was fevered. She traced his cheekbone, his chin, his throat, and the damp, tendoned contour of his neck. She let her palm join her fingers, and felt slowly along his flesh among the myriad of tapes and tubes and wires. When she reached his heart, she pressed down. The beating quickened with the pressure, and Stephen moaned.

"That hurt," Anne said.

"No."

Anne stood straight. She unbuttoned her blouse and let it drop from her shoulders. She could not look at Stephen for fear of revulsion in his eyes. She removed her bra, and then slipped from her skirt and panties.

She looked at Stephen, and thought she saw him nod.

Anne climbed onto the foot of the bed. Beneath her knees the folded, unused blanket was cold. She moved forward, and bent over Stephen's body. Around her and beside her was the tangle of supports. Her body prickled; the veins in the backs of her hands flushed with icy fire. She tried to reach Stephen, but the web held her back.

"I can't," she said.

Stephen looked at her.

"These are in the way. I can't."

He said nothing.

And Anne, one by one, removed the web that kept her from him. She loosened the wires, she withdrew the needles, she pulled out the tubes. She touched the bruises and the marks on the pale skin. "I do love you," she said.

Anne lay with Stephen. Her hands were at first soft and tentative, then

173

grew urgent, caressing his body, caressing her own. As she touched and probed and clutched, her fingers became his fingers. Gentle, intelligent fingers studying her and loving her.

Healing her.

She rode the current, rising and falling, her eyes closed. Stephen kissed her lips as she brought them to him, and her breasts as well, and as she lifted upward, he kissed the trembling, hot wetness between her thighs. She stretched her arms outward, reaching for the world, and then brought them down and about herself and Stephen, pulling inward to where there was nothing but them both. His breathing was heavy; her heart thundered. It swelled and spread, moving downward. Anne opened her mouth to cry out silently to the ceiling. The charge stood her nerves on unbearable end, and it grew until it would hold no longer. The center of her being burst. She wailed with the pulses. And she fell, crumpled, when they were spent.

"Dear God," she whispered. She lay against Stephen, one hand entangled in the dark curls. Their warmth made her smile.

Her fear was gone.

Then she said, "Stephen, tell me. Only if you want. Why are you here? What put you in this place?"

Stephen said nothing. Anne hoped he had not slipped into sleep again.

"Stephen," she said, turning over, meaning to awaken him. "Tell me why you had to come over to the center. What happened to you?"

Stephen said nothing. His closed eyes did not open.

Anne pressed her palm to his heart.

It was still.

The party was over. Back in the recreation hall. Anne could hear Michael tooting his paper horn and calling out, "Hey, Miss Zaccaria, where are you? I'm ready to give you that swimming lesson. What about you?"

The water in the pond did not move. The breeze had died down, and the mist was being replaced by an impenetrable fog that sucked the form and substance from the trees and the benches around the surface of the blackness.

There were leaves at her feet, and she kicked them off the edge of the bank and into the pond. Small circles radiated from the disturbances, little waves moving out and touching other waves.

Anne took off her shoes and walked barefoot to the end of the pier. The boat was still moored there, full of leaves.

The deep water below was as dark as Stephen's hair.

Some have their dreams, others nightmares.

Stephen had his dreams now. Dreams without end.

Amen.

And Anne would now accept her nightmare.

The leaves on the water were kind, and parted at her entrance.

GLENN CHADBOORNE

THE RED TOWER

THOMAS LIGOTTI

THE RUINED FACTORY STOOD three stories high in an otherwise featureless landscape. Although somewhat imposing on its own terms, it occupied only the most unobtrusive place within the gray emptiness of its surroundings, its presence amounting to no more than a faint smudge of color upon a desolate horizon. No road led to the factory, nor were there any traces of one that might have led to it at some time in the distant past. If there had ever been such a road it would have been rendered useless as soon as it arrived at one of the four, red-bricked sides of the factory, no loading docks or entranceways allowed penetration of the outer walls of the structure, which was solid brick on all four sides without even a single window below the level of the second floor. The phenomenon of a large factory so closed off from the outside world was a point of extreme fascination to me. It was almost with regret that I ultimately learned about the factory's subterranean access. But of course that revelation in its turn also became a source for my truly degenerate sense of amazement, my decayed fascination.

The factory had long been in ruins, its innumerable bricks worn and crumbling, its many windows shattered. Each of the three enormous stories that stood above the ground level was vacant of all but dust and silence. The machinery, which densely occupied the three floors of the

177

factory as well as considerable space beneath it, is said to have evaporated, I repeat, *evaporated*, soon after the factory ceased operation, leaving behind it only a few spectral outlines of deep vats and tanks, twisting tubes and funnels, harshly grinding gears and levers, giant belts and wheels that could be most clearly seen at twilight — and later, not at all. According to these strictly hallucinatory accounts, the whole of the Red Tower, as the factory was known, had always been subject to *fadings* at certain times. This phenomenon, in the delirious or dying words of several witnesses, was due to a profound hostility between the noisy and malodorous operations of the factory and the desolate purity of the landscape surrounding it, the conflict occasionally resulting in temporary erasures, or fadings, of the former by the latter.

Despite their ostensibly mad or credulous origins, these testimonies, it seemed to me, deserved more than a cursory hearing. The legendary conflict between the factory and the grayish territory surrounding it may very well have been a fabrication of individuals who were lost in the advanced stages of either physical or psychic deterioration. Nonetheless, it was my theory, and remains so, that the Red Tower was not always that peculiar color for which it ultimately earned its fame. Thus the *encrimsoning* of the factory was a betrayal, a breaking-off, for it is my postulation that this ancient structure was in long-forgotten days the same pale hue as the world which encompassed it. Furthermore, with an insight born of dispassion to the point of total despair, I envisioned that the Red Tower was never solely devoted to the lower functions of an ordinary factory.

Beneath the three soaring stories of the Red Tower were two, possibly three, other levels. The one immediately below the ground floor of the factory was the nexus of a unique distribution system for the goods which were manufactured on all three of the floors above. This first subterranean level in many ways resembled, and functioned in the manner of, an old-fashioned underground mine. Elevator compartments enclosed by a heavy wire mesh, twisted and corroded, descended far below the surface into an expansive chamber which had been crudely dug out of the rocky earth and was haphazardly perpetuated by a dense structure of supports, a criss-crossing network of posts and pillars, beams and rafters, that included a variety of materials — wood, metal, concrete, bone, and a fine sinewy webbing that was fibrous and quite firm. From this central chamber radiated a system of tunnels that honeycombed the land beneath the gray and desolate country surrounding the Red Tower. Through these tunnels the goods manufactured by the factory could be carried, sometimes literally by hand, but more often by means of small wagons and carts, reaching near and far into the most obscure and unlikely delivery points.

The trade that was originally produced by the Red Tower was in some sense remarkable, but not, at first, of an extraordinary or especially ambitious nature. These were the gruesome array of goods that could perhaps best be described as novelty items. In the beginning there was a chaotic quality to the objects and constructions produced by the machinery at the Red Tower, a randomness that yielded formless things of no consistent shape or size or apparent design. Occasionally there might appear a particular ashen lump that betrayed some semblance of a face or clawing fingers, or perhaps an assemblage that looked like a casket with tiny irregular wheels, but for the most part the early productions seemed relatively innocuous. After a time, however, things began to fall into place, as they always do, rejecting a harmless and uninteresting disorder — never an enduring state of affairs — and taking on the more usual plans and purposes of a viciously intent creation.

So it was that the Red Tower put into production its terrible and perplexing line of unique novelty items. Among the objects and constructions now manufactured were several of an almost innocent nature. These included tiny, delicate cameos that were heavier than their size would suggest, far heavier, and lockets whose shiny outer surface flipped open to reveal a black reverberant abyss inside, a deep blackness roaring with echoes. Along the same lines was a series of lifelike replicas of internal organs and physiological structures, many of them evidencing an advanced stage of disease and all of them displeasingly warm and soft

179

to the touch. There was a fake disembodied hand on which fingernails would grow several inches overnight, every night like clockwork. Numerous natural objects, mostly bulbous gourds, were designed to produce a long deafening scream whenever they were picked up or otherwise disturbed in their vegetable stillness. Less scrutable were such things as hardened globs of lava into whose rough igneous forms were set a pair of rheumy eyes that perpetually shifted their gaze from side to side like a relentless pendulum. And there was also a humble piece of cement, a fragment broken away from any street or sidewalk, that left a most intractable stain, greasy and green, on whatever surface it was placed. But such fairly simple times were eventually followed, and ultimately replaced, by more articulated objects and constructions. One example of this complex type of novelty item was an ornate music box that, when opened, emitted a brief gurgling or sucking sound in emulation of a dying individual's death rattle. Another product manufactured in great quantity at the Red Tower was a pocket watch in a gold casing which opened to reveal a curious timepiece whose numerals were represented by tiny quivering insects while the circling "hands" were reptilian tongues, slender and pink. But these examples hardly begin to hint at the range of goods that came from the factory during its novelty phase of production. I should at least mention the exotic carpets woven with intricate abstract patterns that, when focused upon for a certain length of time, composed themselves into fleeting phantasmagoric scenes of the kind which might pass through a fever-stricken or even permanently damaged brain.

As it was revealed to me, and as I have already revealed to you, the means of distributing the novelty goods fabricated at the Red Tower was a system of tunnels located on the first level, not the second (or, possibly, third), that had been excavated below the three-story factory building itself. It seems that these subterranean levels were not necessarily part of the original foundation of the factory but were in fact a perverse and unlikely development that might have occurred only as the structure known as the Red Tower underwent, over time, its own mutation from some prior state until it finally became a lowly site for manufacturing. This mutation would then have demanded the excavating — whether from above or below I cannot say — of a system of tunnels as a means for distributing the novelty goods which, for a time, the factory produced.

As the unique inventions of the Red Tower achieved their final forms, they seemed to have some peculiar location to which they were destined to be delivered, either by hand or by small wagons or carts pulled over sometimes great distances through the system of underground tunnels. Where they might ultimately pop up was anybody's guess. It might be in the back of a dark closet, buried under a pile of undistinguished junk, where some item of the highest and most extreme novelty would lie for quite some time before it was encountered by sheer accident or misfortune. Conversely, the same invention, or an entirely different one, might be placed on the night-table beside someone's bed for near-immediate discovery. Any delivery point was possible, none was out of the reach of the Red Tower. There has even been testimony, either intensely hysterical or semi-conscious, of items from the factory being uncovered within the shelter of a living body, or one not long deceased. I know that such an achievement was within the factory's powers, given its later production history. But my own degenerate imagination is most fully captured by the thought of how many of those monstrous novelty goods produced at the Red Tower had been scrupulously and devoutly delivered — solely by way of those endless underground tunnels — to daringly remote places where they would never be found, nor ever could be.

Just as a system of distribution tunnels had been created by the factory when it developed into a manufacturer of novelty goods, an expansion of this system was required as an entirely new phase of production gradually evolved. Inside the wire-mesh elevator compartment that provided access between the upper region of the factory and the underground tunnels, there was now a special lever installed which, when pulled back, or possibly pushed forward (I do not know such details), enabled one to descend to a second subterranean level. This latterly excavated area was much smaller, far more intimate, than the one directly above it, as could be observed the instant the elevator compartment came to a stop and a full view of things was attained. The scene which now confronted the uncertain minds of witnesses was, in many ways, like that of a secluded graveyard, one surrounded by a rather crooked fence of widely spaced pickets held together by rusty wire. The headstones inside the fence all closely pressed against one another and were quite common, though somewhat antiquated, in their design. However, there were no names or dates inscribed on these monuments, nothing at all, in fact, with the exception of some rudimentary and abstract ornamentation. This could be verified only when the subterranean graveyard was closely approached, for the lighting at this level was dim and unorthodox, provided exclusively by the glowing stone walls enclosing the area. These walls seemed to have been covered with phosphorescent paint which bathed the graveyard in a cloudy, grayish haze. For the longest time — how long I cannot say — my morbid reveries were focused on this murky vision of a graveyard beneath the factory, a subterranean graveyard surrounded by a crooked picket fence and suffused by the highly defective illumination given off by phosphorescent paint applied to stone walls. For the moment I must emphasize the vision itself, without any consideration paid to the utilitarian purposes of this place, that is, the function it served in relation to the factory above it.

The truth is that at some point all of the factory functions were driven underground to this graveyard level. Long before the complete *evaporation* of machinery in the Red Tower, something happened to require the shut-down of all operations in the three floors of the factory which were above ground level. The reasons for this action are deeply obscure, a matter of contemplation only when a state of hopeless and devouring curiosity has reached its height, when the burning light of speculation becomes so intense that it threatens to incinerate everything on which it shines. To my own mind it seems entirely valid to reiterate at this juncture the longstanding tensions that existed between the Red Tower, which I believe was not always stigmatized by such a hue and such a title, and the grayish landscape of utter desolation that surrounded this structure on all sides, looming around and above it for quite incalculable distances. But below the ground level of the factory was another matter: it was here that its operations at some point retreated; it was here, specifically at this graveyard level, that they continued.

Clearly the Red Tower had committed some violation or offense, its clamouring activities and unorthodox products — perhaps its very existence — constituting an affront to the changeless quietude of the world around it. In my personal judgment there had been a betrayal involved, a treacherous breaking of a bond. I can certainly picture a time before the existence of the factory, before any of its features blemished the featureless country that extended so gray and desolate on every side. Dreaming upon the grayish desolation of that landscape, I also find it quite easy to imagine that there might have occurred a lapse in the monumental tedium, a spontaneous and inexplicable impulse to deviate from a dreary perfection, perhaps even an unconquerable desire to risk a move toward a tempting defectiveness. As a concession to this impulse or desire *out of nowhere*, as a minimal surrender, a creation took place and a structure took form where there had been nothing of its kind before. I pictured it, at its inception, as a barely discernible irruption in the landscape, a mere sketch of an edifice, possibly translucent when making its first appearance, a gray density rising in the grayness, embossed upon it in a most tasteful and harmonious design. But such structures or creations have their own desires, their own destinies to fulfil, their own mysteries and mechanisms which they must follow at whatever risk.

From a gray and desolate and utterly featureless landscape a dull edifice had been produced, a pale, possibly translucent tower, which, over time, began to develop into a factory and to produce, as if in the spirit of the most grotesque belligerence, a line of quite morbid and disgusting novelty goods. In an expression of defiance, at some point, it reddened with an enigmatic passion for betrayal and perversity. On the surface the Red Tower might have seemed a splendid complement to the grayish desolation of its surroundings, a unique, picturesque composition that served to define the glorious essence of each of them. But in fact there existed between them a profound and ineffable hostility. An attempt was made to reclaim the Red Tower, or at least to draw it back toward the formless origins of its being. I am referring, of course, to that show of force which resulted in the *evaporation* of the factory's dense arsenal of machinery. Each of the three stories of the Red Tower had been cleaned out, purged of its offending means of manufacturing novelty items, and the part of the factory that rose above the ground was left to fall into ruins.

Had the machinery in the Red Tower *not* been evaporated, I believe that the subterranean graveyard, or something very much like it, would nonetheless have come into existence at some point or another. This was the direction in which the factory had been moving, as was suggested by some of its later models of novelty items. Machines were becoming obsolete as the diseased mania of the Red Tower intensified and evolved into more experimental, even visionary projects. I have previously reported that the headstones in the factory's subterranean graveyard were absent of any names of the interred, or dates of birth and death. This fact is also confirmed by numerous accounts rendered in borderline-hysterical gibberish. The reason for these blank headstones is entirely evident as one gazes upon them standing crooked and closely packed together in the phosphorescent haze given off by the stone walls covered with luminous paint. None of these graves, in point of fact, could be said to have anyone buried in them whose names and dates of birth and death would require inscription on the headstones. These were not what might be called *burying graves*. This is to say that these were in no sense graves for burying the dead, quite the contrary: these were graves of a highly experimental design from which the newest productions of the Red Tower were to be born.

From its beginnings as a manufacturer of novelty items of an extravagant nature, the factory had now gone into business of creating what came to be known as "hyper-organisms." These new productions were also of a fundamentally extreme nature, representing an even greater divergence on the part of the Red Tower from the bland and gray desolation in the midst of which it stood. As implied by their designation as *hyper-organisms*, this line of goods displayed the most essential qualities of their organic nature, which meant, of course, that they were wildly conflicted in their two basic features. On the one hand, they manifested an ineluctable element of *decay* in these same areas. That is to say that each of these hyper-organisms, even as they scintillated with an obscene degree of vital impulses, also, and at the same time, had degeneracy and death written deeply upon them. In accord with a tradition of dumbstruck insanity, it seems the less said about these offspring of the *birthing graves*, or any similar creations, the better. I myself have been almost entirely restricted to a state of seething speculation concerning the luscious particularities of all hyper-organic phenomena produced in the subterranean graveyard of the Red Tower. Although we may reasonably assume that such creations were not to be called beautiful, we cannot know for ourselves the mysteries and mechanisms of, for instance, how these creations moved throughout the hazy luminescence of that underground world; what creaky or spasmic gestures they might have been capable of executing, if any; what sounds they might have made or specific organs used for making them; how they might have appeared when awkwardly emerging from deep shadows or squatting against those nameless headstones; what trembling stages of mutation they almost certainly would have undergone following the generation of their larvae upon the barren earth of the graveyard; what their bodies might have produced or emitted in the way of fluids and secretions; how they might have responded to the mutilation of their forms for reasons of an experimental or entirely savage nature. Often I picture to myself what frantically clawing efforts these creatures probably made to deliver themselves from that confining environment which their malformed or nonexistent brains could not begin to understand. They could not have comprehended, any more than can I, for what purpose they were bred from those graves, those incubators

185

of hyper-organisms, minute factories of flesh that existed wholly within and far below the greater factory of the Red Tower.

It was no surprise, of course, that the production of hyper-organisms was not allowed to continue for very long before a second wave of destruction was visited upon the factory. This time it was not merely the *fading*, and ultimate evaporation of machinery, that took place; this time it was something far more brutal. Once again, forces of ruination were directed at the factory, specifically the subterranean graveyard located at its second underground level, its three-story structure that stood above ground having already been rendered an echoing ruin. Information on what remained of the graveyard, and of its cleverly blasphemous works, is available to my own awareness only in the form of shuddering and badly garbled whispers of mayhem and devastation and wholesale sundering of the most unspeakable sort. These same sources also seem to regard this incident as the culmination, if not the conclusion, of the longstanding hostilities between the Red Tower and that grayish halo of desolation that hovered around it on all sides. Such a shattering episode would appear to have terminated the career of the Red Tower.

Nevertheless, there are indications that, appearances to the contrary, the factory continues to be active despite its status as a silent ruin. After all, the evaporation of the machinery which turned out countless novelty items in the three-story red-brick factory proper, and the ensuing obsolescence of its sophisticated system of tunnels at the first underground level, did not prevent the factory from pursuing its business by other and more devious means. The work at the second underground level (the graveyard level) went very well for a time. Following the vicious decimation of those ingenious and fertile graves, along with the merchandise they produced, it may have seemed that the manufacturing history of the Red Tower had been brought to a close. Yet there are indications that below the three-story above-ground factory, below the first and the second underground levels, there exists a *third* level of subterranean activity. Perhaps it is only a desire for symmetry, a hunger for compositional balance in things, that has led to a series of the most vaporous rumors of this third underground level, in order to provide a kind of complementary proportion to the three stories of the factory that rise into the gray and featureless landscape above ground. At this third level, these misty rumors maintain, the factory's schedule of production is being carried out in some new and strange manner, representing its most ambitious venture in the output of putrid creations, ultimately consummating its tradition of degeneracy, reaching toward a perfection of defect and disorder, according to every polluted and foggy rumor concerned with the issue.

Perhaps it seems that I have said too much about the Red Tower, and perhaps it has sounded far too strange. Do not think that I am unaware of such things. But as I have noted throughout this document, I am only repeating what I have heard. I myself have never seen the Red Tower — no one ever has, and possibly no one ever will. And yet wherever I go people are talking about it. In one way or another they are talking about the nightmarish novelty items or about the mysterious and revolting hyper-organisms, as well as babbling endlessly about the subterranean system of tunnels and the secluded graveyard whose headstones display no names and no dates designating either birth or death. Everything they are saying is about the Red Tower, in one way or another, and about nothing else but the Red Tower. We are all talking and thinking about the Red Tower in our own degenerate way. I have only recorded what everyone is saying (though they may not know they are saying it), and sometimes what they have seen (though they may not know they have seen it). But still they are always talking, in one deranged way or another, about the Red Tower. I hear them talk of it every day of my life. Unless of course they begin to speak about the gray and desolate landscape, that hazy void in which the Red Tower — the great and industrious Red Tower — is so precariously nestled. Then the voices grow quiet until I can barely hear them as they attempt to communicate with me in choking scraps of post-nightmare trauma. Now is just such a time when I must strain to hear the voices. I wait for them to reveal to me the new ventures of the Red Tower as it proceeds into ever

187

more corrupt phases of production, including the shadowy workshop of its third subterranean level. I must keep still and listen for them; I must keep quiet for a terrifying moment. Then I will hear the sounds of the factory starting up its operations once more. Then I will be able to speak again of the Red Tower.

THE BOY WHO CAME BACK FROM THE DEAD

Alan Rodgers

WALT FULTON CAME BACK from the grave Sunday evening, after supper but before his mom had cleared the table.

He was filthy, covered from head to toe with graveyard dirt, but all the things the car had crushed and broken when it hit him (things the mortician hadn't been quite able to make look right) were fixed.

"Mom," Walt called, throwing open the kitchen door, "I'm home!" His mother screamed, but she didn't drop and break the porcelain casserole dish she was holding.

⊣⊫

There's something in an eight-year-old boy that lets him understand his mother, though he could never know that he had it or put words to what it told him. Walt couldn't have told anyone how when his mother saw him first she wanted not to believe that it was him—the boy was dead and buried, by God, and let the dead rest—but because she was his mother and mothers *know*, she knew that it was him returned from the grave.

Then Walt saw the shock setting in, saw her begin to paralyze. But she was stronger than that; she set her teeth, shook off the numbness. She was a strong woman. His return brought her joy beyond words, for she loved him. But she wanted him to go away and never come back, because seeing him again meant remembering the moment at the highway rest stop when

191

she'd looked up to see him running off into traffic after his ball—and then suddenly splattered like a fly across the front bumper of a late model Buick. And she couldn't bear to have that dream again.

Walt didn't resent any of it, not even knowing that she felt that way about him. The same thing that let him know what she was thinking (despite the fact that it was impossible) made sure that he would always love her.

After a minute and a half she composed herself. "Walt," she said, "you're late for dinner and you're filthy. Wash your hands and face and sit down at the table." His father and sister smiled; dad had tears in his eyes, but he didn't say anything. Mom got up and set him a place at the table.

And Walt was home.

⸬

The morning after he came back Walt sat at the kitchen table for hours, coloring in coloring books, while his mother fussed about the house. There was a certain moodiness and elegance in his crayon-work; he wondered at the strangeness that grew on the pages as he colored.

"Walt," his mother said, peeking over his shoulder and humming in surprise, "you can't imagine how much trouble it's going to be to get back in school." She walked into the kitchen and bent down to look into the cabinet underneath the sink. "They're all certain that you're dead. People don't come back from the dead. No one's going to believe that it's you. They'll think we're both crazy."

Walt nodded. She was right, of course. It was going to be a lot of trouble. He looked down at the floor and scuffed his feet against the finish.

"I ought to tell someone," he said.

"What's that, Walt?" His mother's head was buried deep inside the cabinet under the sink, among the cleansers and the steel wool and the old rusty cans.

"About being dead," he told her. "I remember it."

192

Walt knew his mother wasn't listening. "That's nice. You all ready for school this afternoon? We have an appointment with the principal for one o'clock, right after lunch."

"Yeah," he said, "school's okay." He scratched his cheek. "I know people need to know what it's like, about being dead, I mean. It's one of those things that everybody has needed to know forever."

Walt's mother pulled her head out of the cabinet slowly. She turned to stare at him, her mouth agape.

"*Walt!* You'll do nothing of the sort. I won't have that." Her voice was frantic.

"But *why?* They need to know."

But she only clamped her lips and turned beet red. She wouldn't talk to him again until after lunch.

The principal, Mr. Hodges, was a man with dry red skin and greyblack hair who wore a navy blue suit and a red silk cloth in his breast pocket. Walt didn't like him and he never had. He never acted friendly, and Walt thought the man would do him harm if he only could.

"He's Walt all right," Mom told the man. "Never mind what I *know*; Sam and I went out to check the grave this morning as soon as the sun was up. All the dirt was broken, and you can see where he crawled up out of it."

"But it can't be done. We don't even have the files any more. They've been sent away to the fireproof vault downtown." He stopped for a moment to catch his breath. "Look, I know it's horrible to lose a child. Even worse to see him die while you're watching. Walt's not the first kid I've had die in an accident. But you can't let yourself delude yourself like this. Walt's dead and buried. I don't know who this young man is, much less why he's preying on this weakness of yours...."

Walt's mother looked outraged, so angry that she couldn't speak. He wanted to settle things, to quiet them: "What kind of proof do you want?" he asked the man. "What would make you certain that I'm me?"

Neither his mother nor the principal could respond to that at first. After a moment Mr. Hodges excused himself and left the room.

For twenty minutes Walt sat staring out the window of the principal's office, watching the other kids at recess. His mother never got out of the seat by the principal's desk. She stared at the wall with her eyes unfocused while her fingers twisted scraps of paper into tiny, hard-packed balls.

Finally, Mr. Hodges opened the door and came back into the room. He looked tired, now, and even shell-shocked, but he didn't look mean any more. He set two thick file folders onto his desk.

"Any proof I'd want could be manufactured, Walt. But it isn't right for me to try to stop you this way. If nothing else, you've got the right to call yourself anything you want." He opened one of the files. "I can't connect you to these files without moving heaven and earth. But I don't think you need them. There's nothing here that would make us treat you any differently than we'd treat a new student." He began to read. "You're in the third grade. The class you were in has gone on, now, but your teacher, Miss Allison, still works for us. You haven't been gone quite a year; you've already been through this part of the third grade, but I don't think the review will do you any harm."

Later, before Walt and his mother finished filling out the forms, the principal called Miss Allison in to see them. Walt looked up when she opened the door to Mr. Hodges' office, and he felt her recognize him when she saw him.

Miss Allison screamed, and her legs went limp underneath her. She didn't faint—she was never unconscious—but when she fell to the floor it looked as though she had.

She screamed again when he went over to help her up.

"*Wal—ter!*" Long and eerie, just like something out of an old horror movie.

"It's all right," Walt said. "I'm not a ghost."

"What are you?" Her voice was still shrill with terror.

"I'm just...just Walt. I'm Walt."

Miss Allison glared at him impatiently.

"Really. I'm Walt. Besides, Mom said I couldn't tell."

Walt heard his mother snap the pencil she was chewing on. "Tell her," she said. Her voice was furious. "Tell me."

Walt shrugged. "It was the aliens. They were walking all around the graveyard, looking into people's dirt."

"What aliens?"

"A whole bunch of them, all different kinds. They landed in a spaceship over in the woods. A couple of them looked kind of like fish—or snakes, maybe—one of them kind of like a bear, a couple looked like mole crickets when you see them in a magnifying glass. Others, too.

"But the one I paid attention to—he was the one telling all the rest what to do—that one was really gross. It had this big lumpy head—shaped like the head on that retarded kid Mrs. Anderson had—"

"Walt! Billy Anderson is a mongoloid idiot. You mustn't speak ill of those less fortunate than you."

Walt nodded. "Sorry. Anyways, the thing had this big, lumpy, spongy head, and this face that looked kind of like an ant's—with those big pincer things instead of a mouth—and kind of looked like something you dropped on the floor in the kitchen. It drooled all over the place—"

"*Walt!*"

"—and it kept making this gross sound like someone hawking up a great big clam. But it wasn't what it looked like that bothered me so much. What scared me was when it first got to my grave, and it looked down like it could see me right through the dirt. And its pincers clacked and rubbed against each other just exactly the way a cat licks its lips when it sees a mouse, and its elbows flexed backward like it wanted to pounce. It made this whining sound, like a dog when it begs, and I thought it was going to reach right through the dirt and eat my putrid body. And even though I knew I was dead and I couldn't get any deader, it scared me. It was bad enough being something trees couldn't tell from mulch, without being dinner for a ghoul. But then the thing turned away and went back to looking at other people's dirt. After they'd looked at everyone, they came back to me and broke up my dirt and shined their ray down on me. It didn't hurt, but nothing does when you're dead. After five minutes I was alive again, and I felt things but I couldn't just know them any more, and I pushed my way out of the dirt.

"But when I got up to the ground the aliens had already gone. So I went home."

It was Miss Allison who finally said it.

"Walt, that can't be. How could you know all that when you're dead, buried in the ground? Even if your eyes were open, how could you see through all the dirt?"

Walt shrugged. "That's what I need to tell them. About what it's like being dead. They've all been needing to know forever, because they're all afraid. It's like a feeling of your fingernails on a dusty chalkboard, like being awake so long you get dizzy and start hearing things. And you can't feel anything, and you know everything that's going on around you, and some things far away. It's bad, and it's scary, but not so terrible that you can't get used to it."

⚓

Neither Miss Allison nor his mother spoke to Walt again that afternoon.

No one saw any sense in disrupting things by bringing him into class in the middle of the day. Tomorrow morning was soon enough. (Maybe too soon, the look on Miss Allison's face said, but everyone did his best to ignore that.) When they got home Anne, his sister, had a hug for him, and they played cards until suppertime. After dinner Dad and Walt and Anne roughhoused and threw pillows at each other in the playroom.

It was fun.

Before bed Walt wanted Dad to tell him a story—he'd missed Dad's ghost stories—but Dad wouldn't. After a while, Walt stopped asking. He wasn't dumb; he knew why it scared his father.

But would could he do? He sure didn't want to go away, go back to being dead. He liked being alive. He liked having people see him, hear him, know he was there. The dead make poor companions. Almost all of them are quiet and tired, waiting for the resurrection, not so much world weary as exhausted by its absence.

Tuesday and Wednesday were quiet days in school. Almost no one in his new class had known Walt before the accident. Those few who did took a while to reason out that Walt was something they'd only seen on Saturdays on the afternoon horror movie.

But by Thursday word had got around, and the boldest of the boys from his class the year before—four of them—looked for him and found him in an empty corner of the school yard during recess.

"Hey Zombie," Frankie Munsen called at him from behind, throwing a dirt clod that caught Walt in the soft part of his shoulder, just below his neck.

"Count Dricula, I *prisume...*?" Donny James taunted him, stepping out from behind a tree on Walt's left. He draped his blue windbreaker over his forearm and shielded his chin with it, the way vampires do with their chins in the movies. "You got bats in your belfry, Walt? What's it like to be *un*dead?"

Walt flinched when a dirt clod hit him in the belly from the right. He looked over to see John Taylor and Rick Mitchell standing in a knot of pine trees throwing dirt clods. As he saw them a clod hit him on the forehead and the dust splattered in his eyes.

When he could finally open them again he saw four boys standing over him, surrounding him.

"What's the matter, Zom-boy? Smoke get in your eyes?" Donny jeered, shoving Walt by the shoulders so that he fell on his back. Donny straddled Walt's chest and pinned him by digging his knees into the muscles of his upper arms. "Aintcha gonna fight back, Zom-boy?" He snickered. "Too late now, sucker."

Walt's voice wasn't frightened, wasn't scared at all, just a little angry: "What's the matter with you? I haven't done anything to you."

"Don't like to see dead people walking around our school, Zom-boy." Donny drooled spit into Walt's eyes. "Want you to leave, sucker."

Walt rolled over, surprising Donny, throwing him off. As he stood up he wiped the spit from his eyes with one arm and grabbed Donny's collar with the other. Walt hauled the older boy to his feet.

"I'm not dead," he said. His voice was furious now, trembling. He threw Donny against a tree where his head made a liquid cracking sound.

None of the other boys said or did anything. They didn't run yet, either. Donny sat up, drooling bloody spit into the dirt.

"I bit my tongue," he said. He swayed back and forth unevenly.

Walt turned away. "Don't do anything like this again," he said. And he went home.

Someone should have done something about that: called his house, sent someone after him, marked him truant at least. But no one did. It was not as though no one noticed him gone. And certainly no one missed seeing what he'd done to Donny James. But Miss Allison couldn't bring herself to report him, and no one would contradict her.

When his mom got home, he was sitting by the TV with a coloring book spread out over the coffee table. He had the sound turned almost all the way down.

"You're home early, dear. Why's that?" she asked. Walt mumbled without using any real words, just low enough that she'd think his answer got lost in the sound of her walking.

"Sorry, dear, I didn't hear you. Why was it?"

Walt's hand pressed too hard, and his crayon left a dark, flaky wax mark on the paper. It looked like a scar to Walt.

"I got into a fight," he said. "I think I hurt Donny James pretty bad. He looked like he was going to have to see a doctor. I didn't want to have to talk to them any more. So I went home."

"You just left school? Just like that?"

"Mom, they think I'm a monster. They think I'm some sort of a vampire or something." Walt wanted to cry, mostly from frustration, but

198

he didn't. He set his head down onto his arms so that his nose rubbed against the coloring book.

Mom sat down beside him and lifted him up so that she could put her arms around him. In front of them, on the television with the sound turned down, the characters in a soap opera worried at each other silently, the way a dog worries a bone.

"You aren't a monster, Walt," she said as she held him, hugging him tighter to her. "Don't let them tell you that." But her voice was so uncertain that even though he wanted to more than anything else in the world, Walt couldn't make himself believe her.

⚌

Walt went out an hour before dinnertime, looking for something to do. He walked a long way, blocks and blocks into the neighbourhood, trying to find someone he knew, or a sandlot game to watch or even play in, or *something*, but all he found was some floating waterbugs (the ones his mom told him never to bring home because they were really *roaches*) in the creek down on Dumas Street. It wasn't much fun. Walking home, the stars were gloriously bright, even though it wasn't very dark out yet. Walt tried to find Betelgeuse—he loved the star's name, so he got his father to show him how to find it—but the star was nowhere Walt could see. Three stars turned to meteors as he watched. At first he just stared, marvelling at the pencil-marks of light that shooting stars left behind them—but then they all began to spiral down and each in turn to head toward him. Three blocks away there was a big woods, fifteen or twenty square blocks worth of land where no one had ever got around to putting in streets or building houses. Walt ran there, as hard and fast as he could. He ran deeper into the woods than he'd ever been before, until he couldn't see any houses or landmarks that he knew, and he wasn't sure where he was. When he heard the sound of people running toward him he climbed into the biggest, tallest, leafiest tree he could find. He hid there.

199

The aliens should have found him. Walt knew that.

There were seven of them, each one strange and different from every other. The only one he really saw was the one who held the gadget that looked like a Geiger counter, the one with the giant ant pincers for a mouth—it was a maw, really, not a mouth. (Walt knew that. He'd gone to the library on Tuesday and spent hours reading about bugs.)

That was the same one that'd stared at him right through the graveyard dirt when he was still dead. The thing came right up to the tree Walt had hidden in, where the widget in its hands beeped and whirred maniacally. He stared at the thing from above, chewing on his lower lip. So close, it was even uglier than when it'd looked into his grave. The things at the ends of its arms weren't hands at all, really. They didn't have palms or fingers, just muscle, wormy flaps of skin dangling and fluttering at the ends of its wrists. Its skin was just exactly the color a roach is when you squish it. It smelled kind of like rotten eggs and kind of like the mouse that nested in the TV one summer and chewed on the wrong wire and got itself electrocuted. Its arms looked ordinary at first (or something in Walt's eyes wanted to make them look ordinary) but then the thing reached out to lean on the tree trunk, and its arm bent *back* double-jointed, and then the thing leaned even harder and the arm wasn't just bent double, it was *bending* in an arc under the weight. The legs were like that, too, and they bent ass-backward in a half-crouch when it walked. It had a tunic on, so Walt mostly couldn't see its torso, but then it bent sideways and the cloth (or was it some stretchy, rubbery plastic?) stretched thin enough to see through, and Walt could see that it was twisted off like a sausage in the middle, two big, bulbous pieces connected only by a touch.

Its eyes were the worst thing, though. They were big, bigger than the saucers in Mom's good china, and they were sort of like what they say a spider's eyes look like when you see them up close. But not quite. More like a bowl full of eggs, broken and ready to scramble, but still intact. Around each eye's half-dozen yellow pupils, through the clear matter, Walt could see veins and nerve endings pulse against the eye socket. Phlegm dripped down steadily from the eyes, into the maw. That was why the thing kept making that sound like somebody hawking up a big wad of snot.

The thing spent a long time prowling around the base of Walt's tree, sifting through every log and bush and leaf pile, while the other aliens combed through the rest of the woods. But it never looked up. None of the aliens, not one of them, ever looked up.

They searched for him carefully, methodically, sticking electronic probes deep into the ground, turning every stone and rotted log, sifting every drift of mulch.

But not once did any of them check the branches of a tree.

Stupid aliens, Walt thought. Later, reflecting on it, he decided he was right.

After they'd prowled around him for three quarters of an hour they gave up and left. Walt stayed in the tree for twenty minutes longer, against the possibility that they were hiding, waiting for him. He'd meant to wait longer but he couldn't make himself be still.

That was just as well. No one came to get him when he climbed out of the tree.

The aliens are more impatient than me, Walt thought. The idea of jittery aliens made him want to laugh, but he didn't.

It was night, now, and Walt didn't know this part of the woods at all. The moon at least was already up and nearly full, so there was light enough to see by, to see the trail (not a very well used one at all; thick clumps of grass grew out of it in places) that led in both directions ways he didn't recognize.

He wasn't worried so much for himself—after all, he was lost not far from home, almost a silly thing to be—but he knew that his mother would be concerned. By the time he got home she'd be angry at him. He hurried as best he could.

After about fifteen paces the trail opened up into Walt's cemetery.

The one he'd spent eleven months and seven days buried in. The tree he stood by was the tree whose roots would almost tickle him on sunny mornings. In front of him was his headstone, desecrated with graffiti.

Even by the dim moonlight he could see it; bold strokes of spray paint crowding out the letters carved in the granite.

It had to be new. He'd looked back to see the stone the night he'd crawled out of the grave, and it was clean then.

And someone had packed the dirt back into his grave and tucked the sod grass back in above it.

Walt stood on the grave, kicking the toe of his shoe into the roots of the grass, staring at the gravestone, reading it over and over again. He tried to read the graffiti, too, but it wasn't made up of words or even letters, but of strange squiggles like the graffiti that covered the subways Walt had seen when Dad took him to New York. (Dad said the graffiti in the city was that way because the kids who painted it could never learn to read or write, that they were too dumb to ever even learn the alphabet. That seemed too incredible to believe, but Walt couldn't imagine any other reason why they didn't know how to use letters.) He thought maybe the aliens had left graffiti, but then he thought, *Why would the aliens use bright red spray paint?* And he knew it couldn't be them.

Looking at the grave made him feel sleepy and comfortable. It was getting late, and he knew he should go home. But he couldn't stop himself, not really. He lay down on his grave, rested his head on the headstone, (the paint was still fresh enough that Walt could smell it), and for an hour he stared into the sky, watching the stars. Not to search for alien starships, but because nothing in the world could be more comfortable.

His mom wasn't in when Walt got home. Just Dad and Anne, watching TV in the den.

"Hiya, Walt," Dad called when he walked in. "Late night with the Cub Scouts?"

Walt chuckled. "Yeah," he said. It wasn't *really* a lie; Dad was just being facetious. Walt sat down at the card table behind Dad's recliner. Anne, sitting in the love seat against the wall, didn't turn away from the TV until the commercial was on.

"Cards?" she asked him.

"No, I'm going to bed early, I think."

"There's dinner left over for you in the refrigerator, Walt," Dad said. "Stuffed pork chops and green beans."

Walt nodded. "Thanks." He got up and started toward the kitchen.

"Oh, and Walt," Dad said, "I forgot. The man from that newspaper called. *The Interlocutor*. He wants to come by and talk to you tomorrow morning. Before school."

"Huh." Walt wasn't certain what he thought.

"Yeah," Dad said. "It should be interesting. I wonder how they found out so soon."

Walt shrugged, then realized his father couldn't see that. "I don't know. Someone at school, I guess."

"Yes." His father nodded at the television set. "I guess that would have to be it."

In the kitchen he took the plate from the refrigerator and tried to eat what his mom had left him. Walt loved stuffed pork chops. Even cold. But he couldn't find the appetite to eat them or the green beans, and after twenty minutes he left the plate virtually untouched on the kitchen table, and went to bed.

His mom came in through the back door while he was on the stairs up to his room. He turned to say good night to her, and she was already on the stairway just below him, charging up to do God knew what, not seeing him at all in the dark.

"Mom," Walt said, trying to get her attention before she collided into him.

"*Oh my God!*" his mother screamed. In the darkness she swung her arm out and her fist hit Walt hard just below the right eye. That knocked him down; he would have rolled down the stairs if his left ankle hadn't jammed against her feet.

For five minutes, trembling and breathing deeply, she leaned into the banister that was screwed into the wall. Walt didn't move—it didn't seem safe to—he just lay on the stairs at her feet. In a moment his father and sister got to the foot of the stairs, and they could see. They stood there, watching. They didn't say anything.

"Walt," his mother said finally (her voice was colder and more inhuman than it would ever seem to any stranger). "A hundred times. I've told you to turn the lights on when you use the stairs and hallways."

"Sorry," he said, afraid she'd get angrier if he said anything else.

"*Don't* do it again."

He nodded. "I was going to bed. I meant to say good night."

"Good night," she said, her voice colder and lonelier than his grave had ever been.

In bed, drifting off to sleep, he realized that he'd hardly eaten all week, and that he hadn't been hungry since he came back from the dead.

⊁⊱⊰⊀

Dad woke him up real early in the morning, shaking him by the shoulder with his big soft hand. Walt took a shower and got dressed before he'd really woke up; later he discovered that he'd put on his shirt backward.

When he got to the kitchen his mom was already cooking breakfast—scrambled eggs and bacon—and the man from *The Interlocutor* was sitting at the kitchen table. He stared at Walt the way Walt remembered staring at the lizards in the House of Reptiles at the zoo when he was six. But the lizard couldn't see him, or it acted like it couldn't.

"Hi, Walt." The man held out his hand to shake, but he still stared. "I'm Harvey Adler from *The National Interlocutor*. I'm here to take your story." He smiled, but it reminded Walt of the lizard's smiles: more a fault in their anatomy than a true expression.

"Are you going to eat with us?" Walt asked. He wasn't sure why he did.

"Ahh," Adler began uncomfortably, but then Walt's mom set a plate in front of him and another in front of Walt. "Well. It looks like I am." Walt felt somehow betrayed.

"Coffee, Mr. Adler?" Walt's mom asked. That was even worse; Walt didn't know why.

"No thank you, Mrs. Fulton. I've already had two this morning." He turned back to Walt. "Did you really die, Walt? And come back from the dead? What was it like to die?"

Walt picked at his food with his fork. "I started to run across the highway, and I forgot to look. There was a screaming sound. I guess it was the car trying to stop. But I didn't see. I never turned my head. It happened too fast. Then everything was black for a while."

Adler had his tape recorder on, and he scribbled notes furiously. "Then what, Walt?"

Walt shrugged. "Then I was dead. I could see and hear everything around me. Just like the other dead people. But I couldn't move."

"You were like that for a year? It must have been pretty lonely."

"Well. You know. You don't care that much when you're dead. And the dead people can hear you. And can talk to you. But they don't much. They just don't ever want to."

They went on like that for an hour. He told the man everything about the aliens, about climbing out of his grave, about his friends and school and all. Finally, Walt was late for school. It probably wasn't a good day for that; when he finally got to class Miss Allison still wasn't talking to him from the day before.

At morning recess, Donny James (black and blue but not really hurt) found Walt and asked him to come to the Risk game they always had on Friday afternoons. He acted like nothing had happened, maybe even a little bit embarrassed. Walt could never understand that, and though later in life he knew that people could do such things, he could never expect or believe it.

It came to trouble with Miss Allison about an hour after recess. She asked the class a question (Where is Malagasy Republic?) that she meant no one to answer. But Walt raised his hand and answered it quite thoroughly (The Malagasy republic *is* the island of Madagascar off the southeast coast of Africa. The people are black, but they speak a language related to Polynesian), which made her look awfully silly, and the class giggled. Walt didn't mean to do it. But as soon as he opened his mouth he knew that he'd made her look silly. Answering questions was a compulsion for him, and he knew the answer because the old man in the grave next to his had been a sailor in the Indian Ocean for thirty years, and when he did talk (which was almost never) it was always about Africa or India or the Maldives or some such.

Miss Allison didn't take it well at all. She hadn't taken anything well since Walt got back. And it didn't help any when Walt (feeling bold since he'd explained everything to the man from *The Interlocutor* at breakfast) tried to explain how it was he knew such an odd fact and why, after all, it really wasn't so important. For the third time this week Miss Allison's expression was violent, and she pulled her hand back to strike him, and for the third time Walt glared at her as though if she did it might be the last thing she ever did. (Not that he meant it or even was able to carry out the threat. It was a bluff. But he knew her well enough to know that it would make her stop.) Miss Allison didn't go back to her desk, shaking, the way she did the times before, though. She ran out of the classroom and slammed the door behind her. She didn't come back for twenty minutes, and when she finally did Mr. Hodges, the principal, was with her.

He took Walt away from Miss Allison's class and moved him ahead a year—into the class he'd shared with Donny James, Rick Mitchell, and all the rest.

He liked it better there. Even if the fourth-grade teacher was a battleaxe, at least she wasn't hysterical.

In the afternoon he walked home with Donny and helped him set up the Risk game. Six boys showed up, all together Walt, Donny, Rick, Frankie, John, and Donny's little brother Jessie and the game went well enough. Walt didn't win, but he didn't lose, either. Nobody lost, really. It got to be dinnertime before anyone got around to conquering the world, so they left it at that.

When he got to the house, his father and sister weren't home yet. His mom was sitting at the kitchen table drinking coffee with the aliens.

─※─

He knew the things were there before he even banged into the kitchen; when he opened the front door he could smell electrocuted flesh and sulphury-rotten eggs, and he knew they were there for him. His first thought was that they'd taken his mother hostage, kidnapped her to make him go with them. He rushed into the kitchen (where the smell came from) on the tide of one of those brave reflexes a boy can have when there isn't time to think.

But there was no need for him to save her.

As soon as he opened the kitchen door he knew that he should turn around and run right then, but he didn't. Shock paralyzed him. He backed up against the wall by the door he'd just come through and stared at them with his eyes open wide and his mouth agape.

His mom sat at the kitchen table drinking coffee with the aliens. The ugly one, the one with skin the color of roach guts and eyes like a spider's corpse, he sat right there at the table with her. Behind them, in the hall that led from the garage, the rest of the aliens crowded together at the doorway to stare at him.

"Walt," his mom said, "this is Mr. Krant. He's going to take you with him."

Walt wanted to scream, but his throat cramped, jammed, and he couldn't make any sound. Something in his knees wanted to spring loose and let him fall to the ground, so he leaned his body into the wall enough for it to take his weight.

"That's why they woke you up, dear. They wanted you. They're here for you. They're here to help you."

Walt didn't believe a word of it, not for a minute. His mother's tone was saccharine and *too*-sincere; she lied to him just like that just after he had died.

207

"*No!*" he shouted. His voice was shrill. He still wanted to scream, but now he wanted to cry, too. *God,* why his mom? Why did *she* have to be with them?

"It's okay, Walt." She was still lying. "You don't have to go with them, if *you* don't want. But listen. Talk to them. Hear them out."

Right away he knew that was the last thing he should do. The alien reached into the purse he carried and took out a gadget that Walt got dizzy looking at.

A hypnotizer, Walt thought, and he turned his head away as fast as he could.

"Relax, Walter." The thing's voice sounded like the air that bubbles up in a toilet when the pipes are doing funny things. Walt could hear it tinkering with the gadget. "You can call me Captain Krant. We've come a long way to find you. From galaxies and galaxies away." Walt couldn't help himself; he turned to see it talking. The pincers didn't move much, but the maw jumped and squirmed crazily. That made booger-clotted mucous drool down the thing's chinless jaw. Walt watched it ooze down the cloth of the aliens tunic and feed into the stain-ring below the neck—

—and he had to puke, even though he hadn't eaten in days, and his legs propelled him through the aliens toward the bathroom—

—and he realized he could move again, could run—

—so where the hall split he went straight, through the garage and out the side door, to run and run and run without looking back at his mother's house.

Which, maybe, he should have done, because he never saw it again.

He didn't pay much attention where he ran to, so it didn't surprise him much when he found himself, moments later, panting and crying and leaning over his own headstone. The grave was his home, probably the best one he'd ever had—though there was an element of bias, of bitterness, in that thought. Walt didn't mind it. There was nothing wrong with bitterness when your mom turned against you like she was a rabid dog—maybe there was even something right about it. Mothers were supposed to be the ones who *protected* you, not the ones who sold you into slavery (worse: gave you away) when the aliens came for you.

"Walt?" and a hand on his shoulder. He jumped and nearly screamed, but stopped himself. He hadn't heard it coming. Not at all.

"Walt, are you okay?" His sister. No one else. No one with her. His heart stomped up and down like a lunatic inside his chest.

"Yeah." He took a deep breath, let it out real slow. "Okay. I ought to say good-bye, though. Got to run away."

"Huh? Why's that?"

"Mom—" He stopped. "You wouldn't believe me."

Anne shook her head.

"It's hard to believe you're alive. What could be worse?"

Walt tried to think about that for a moment, then decided he didn't want to. He shrugged. "The aliens, the ones who made me alive again. They came back for me. Mom wants me to go with them."

She shrugged. "Maybe she's right. Something is wrong. Hasn't been right since you came back."

"*God*! Not you, too. If you saw them, if *you* had to go with them…! They're *scary*!" Walt was trying not to cry, but it wasn't doing much good. "I don't want to go. I don't want Mom to try to get rid of me."

Anne stood there, empty-faced, not saying anything. Walt didn't really know why or how, but he knew there was no way she could respond to what he'd said.

And there was nothing left for him to say. "Yeah," he said, finally, because he needed to fill the space with something—he didn't really mean anything when he said it. "Well. I guess good-bye, then."

She nodded, and she hugged him and she wished him luck. She turned around and before she'd gone five paces he was in the woods, quietly skulking his way into the darkest place he could find. He didn't see her again for a long time.

‑‑‑

He sat in the woods for hours, trying to figure out what he was supposed to do next.

He still didn't know at midnight, when he heard his dad's footsteps. Dad didn't have to say anything for Walt to know who it was; he knew his walk by the sound of it.

"Son," Dad called, almost as though he could hear him breathing. "Walt…? Are you still out there, son?"

Walt tucked himself deeper into the niche between the two big rocks where he was resting.

"It's okay, son," Dad called. In the sound of his voice Walt heard everything he wanted to believe: that his dad loved him, wanted him, needed him. That his mom was just having a bad time, and that soon she'd be loving him just like she always had. Real soon next week, maybe the week after at the latest.

"It's all right, Walt," Dad called again. "Nobody's going to make you do anything you don't want to do. Really, son. Your mom's a little upset, sure, but it'll workout okay. Maybe you and me and Anne can take a week or two and rent a cabin up by the lake (Lake Hortonia, in Vermont, where they went every year for vacation since Walt was three), and let your mom have a little time to herself, time to get used to things."

Dad was real close, now, but Walt wasn't really trying to hide any more. He wasn't getting up and letting his dad know where he was, either, though. He'd gotten cautious. Reflex wouldn't let him just stand up. Then his leg twitched and made some dirt clods fall.

That gave him away.

"Walt?" His dad's voice was tense, now, sharper. The flashlight spun around, and there he was, trapped in it.

Walt wanted to scream in terror, in frustration at being caught. But what happened was a lot more like crying even though he tried hard as he could for it not to be, and then he was running to his dad with his arms stretched out, and calling Daddy, and hugging his dad with his arms around his waist and his face buried in Dad's big soft belly. And crying into his soft flannel shirt, and smelling clean laundry because his dad never sweated.

"Daddy," Walt said again, and he hugged him harder.

"Oh God, Walt, oh God, Walt, I love you son, you know that."

And Walt nodded into his dad's stomach even though it wasn't really a question.

"And I hope to God that some day you'll forgive me what I'm doing. God, your mother *made* me, she *made* me…!" And then his father's hands wrapped around his wrists, tight and hard as iron neck bands, and he shouted back in the direction of the cemetery, "I've got him, and…"

Something down inside Walt busted and without his even thinking, without his even knowing what he did, a scream bubbled up from some black, fireless pit at the base of him.

A scream so horrible and true that it shook the woods and, for weeks, the dreams of everyone who heard it.

His father's hands fell loose from Walt's hands.

And Walt *ran*.

⊣⊟⊢

Walt ran all night. He wasn't going anywhere. Not yet. He hadn't thought that far yet.

So he kept moving, because he knew they were looking for him. More than once he heard their walking just behind him—his mother, his father, the weird rhythms of the aliens. Others, later.

It was after moonset but before even the beginning of dawn when he heard the shrill, grating stage whisper of a hiss.

"*Hssit.* Walt."

He thought at first it came from Donny James's house, he was in the woods behind it but then he realized it came from Mr. Hodges's next door.

Walt couldn't imagine why the school's principal would call him. He went to the back window—it was open but it had a screen—to find out.

"What's happened, Walt? Your parents have been here, and then the police, looking for you. They must've gone to every house in the neighborhood, to watch them. What did you do?"

Walt shrugged. "I ran away, I guess. The aliens that made me alive again came back for me. Mom wants to give me to them."

Mr. Hodges didn't believe a word of it. "Even if that is what happened—I suppose it's no more preposterous than anything else about you these days—why would your mother call the police? They'd just complicate matters for her later."

Walt shrugged again. "Mom's tricky."

Mr. Hodges shook his head. "I don't know what you are, Walt, but you're strange." He looked out into the woods, back and forth. You want to come in for cocoa?"

Walt knew he shouldn't trust the man; he knew from experience that he shouldn't trust anyone tonight. But he was tired of being scared and bored of running, so he nodded and said, "Yes."

"Come around to the side door," Mr. Hodges told him, and he did.

Inside, it was still dark. They sat at the kitchen table while the principal made cocoa (he brewed coffee for himself) with only the light that came in through the windows from the street lamp out front.

"Best to leave the lights out," he said, "the way they're searching out there, they're sure to see you if we turn them on."

"Yeah." Walt nodded.

There was nothing, really, for them to talk about. Walt had already said more about himself and about the aliens than he ever meant to say to anyone. Besides, he didn't know much, really. There was school, but Walt felt uneasy telling the principal anything interesting; he might get someone in trouble.

"Miss Allison is in the hospital," Mr. Hodges said. "She had a breakdown yesterday afternoon. Right in her own classroom. The janitor came in at four o'clock to sweep and mop, and there she was, looking off into the distance just like she was waiting for something. And nothing anyone did would even make her blink—though if you watched long enough you might see her do that on her own."

Walt nodded and stirred his cocoa with his finger. "She was acting strange this morning."

Mr. Hodges lit his pipe, sucking in fire from a butane lighter three times with a hissing-sucking sound. Smoke billowed up to freeze in the street light. The smell was rich, but bitter and powdery.

Walt knew the sun would rise soon. He felt himself slipping away just like a fade out on a television set; felt his muscles let go bit by bit, felt his head sinking down to the cushion of his arm on the table beside the cocoa. He tried to make himself be taut, awake, but it didn't do any good.

"Walt? Are you going to be okay?"

Mr. Hodges' asking woke him up. He shook his head. "Sorry. I'm all right."

"Do you want to camp out on the couch here? Do you need to sleep?"

"Could I?" Walt was tired, but he was scared, too. He pictured his mother finding him while he slept, and giving him to the aliens without even waking him to let him know. He could see himself waking on a spaceship, already light-years from home, in the arms of some *thing* that looked and felt like tripe and smelled like rotten eggs. He tried not to shudder, but it didn't do any good.

"Walt? Should I get you a pillow and a blanket? Don't fall asleep there; you might fall off the chair and break your neck."

"Please." He stumbled into the living room, to the couch. He was almost asleep before Mr. Hodges got back.

The clean muslin of the pillowcase felt comfortable and wonderful but somehow alien to Walt. He'd got used to the satin of his coffin, even though he couldn't feel it when he was dead. Muslin seemed too coarse, too absorbent. He lay awake a lot longer than he wanted to, getting used to it.

◄⊟►

Walt woke in the early evening; Mr. Hodges wasn't home yet, and he hadn't left a note. Walt went to the bathroom to wash up as best he could without a change of clothes. He didn't know what he would do next; it seemed to him that there was no place to go, no life left for him to gather up the pieces of. He even thought for a moment that he would rather be dead, but he knew that wasn't so.

For the moment, at least, the doorbell decided him. Walt put down the towel he'd used to dry his face and looked around the corner where the hallway ended, into the living room.

Through the window in the alcove he could see three policemen, their hands clasped in front of them just like busboys at some fancy restaurant. His mother stood behind them.

Walt dropped the washcloth that he had in his hand. He had to go or they'd get him. He ran to the bedroom in the back, popped the screen out of the window frame, climbed out, and began to run.

"Walt!"

His heart lurched and tried to jump out of his throat. He thought they had him, but then he turned and recognized the voice at the same time: Donny James, sitting on a lawn chair in his backyard. The James's house was right next door to Mr. Hodges'.

"Quiet!" Walt stage-whispered. He tried to be quiet, but it didn't work. "They're looking for me. Don't shout."

"Huh…?" Donny was running to catch up to him. Over on the far side of the woods, where the storm drain passed under the interstate highway, there was a big concrete sewer pipe, big enough for a boy to walk through, but too small for an adult. He could hide there, and even if they found him they couldn't get in to catch him. Or even trap him. He could be long gone

214

before they could get around the nearest highway overpass and surround him at the far end of the pipe.

"Where're you going, Walt?" Donny asked. Walt didn't answer.

"Just come on," he said.

There still wasn't any sign of his mom or the policemen when they reached the pipe. Walt walked in first; duck-walked, half-squatting, really. In the middle of the pipe he sat down and leaned his back against the curved wall. It was cool and dry and dark. There weren't any bugs around, at least not that Walt could see.

"The police came to school today, looking for you," Donny said. "When they didn't find you they asked everybody questions."

Walt nodded. He'd kind of expected that.

"What happened to you? Why were you running? Why were they looking for you?"

Walt didn't know what to say; he kicked his pant leg against the far side of the pipe, trying to think.

"The aliens that made me alive again came back for me." He kept expecting people not to believe that, and they kept believing it. Strange. "I didn't want to go cause they're real gross. But mom wanted to make me. So I ran away."

Donny flicked a pebble at the entrance they'd come in through. "Where're you going to go now?"

Walt *still* hadn't thought about that. Not really. He shrugged. "I don't know, I guess."

Donny and Walt sat thinking about that, not talking, for a good five minutes.

"Well," Donny said, "you can't go back home, you know. She'll just pack you away with the aliens. But you got to have some place to stay."

"Yeah." Walt nodded. He hadn't thought that far before. He'd been avoiding it, he guessed.

"And wherever you go, it better be pretty far away. Or your mom'll find you."

"Yeah." It was true. It was why he'd been trying not to think about what he'd do. He didn't want to run away. He wanted to go home and stay there and grow up just like any other boy.

But there was just no way in hell. He felt like he needed to cry—more out of frustration than anything else—but he didn't want to do that where anybody could see it. Especially Donny.

"I guess I better go," Walt said.

Donny nodded. "Where're you going to go?"

"I don't know. I'll be back sooner or later, though. I'll see you again."

But he never did. By the time Walt got back to town Donny had been gone a long time.

In the window of the 7-Eleven by the on-ramp to the interstate, Walt saw himself on the cover of the *National Interlocutor*.

BOY CRAWLS OUT OF GRAVE

Walter Fulton, age 8, dug his way out of his grave last week, after being buried for more than a year. Walt died last year when a car hit him as he crossed a street. "Dying wasn't so bad," says Walt. "Two angels took my arms, lifted me from the car wreck, and brought me up to heaven." "Heaven's a great place, and everybody's happy there," Walt continues, "but it's no place for an 8-year-old boy. There isn't any mud, no baseball bats, and nobody ever gets hurt in the football games." Dr. Ralph Richards of the Institute for Psychical Research in Tuskegee, Alabama, speculated that Walt's experience may not have been mystical in nature at all. Its possible that young Fulton wasn't dead at all when he was buried, but suffering from a Thanatesque condition, from which he later recovered. *(continued on page 9)*

Walt marvelled at the newspaper, reading it again and again, staring at the photos. There were two of them: one a photo of the cemetery, focused on his tombstone. There was no graffiti on it yet, and the ground before it was still crumbled and spilling out from Walt's crawling out. Policemen—fifteen or twenty of them—milled about the cemetery. Walt had never seen the photo, but he knew it must have been taken not long after the caretaker found Walt's grave abandoned. That would be the Monday after his resurrection. The other photo was a head shot of Walt. He recognized it; it had to have been cut from his first-grade class picture, the group photo where the whole class had stood in three parallel lines and posed for the camera together.

Walt went into the 7-Eleven and bought a copy of the paper with some of the lunch money he'd hoarded this week. He hadn't been hungry at all at lunch.

The paper amazed him; it was as though they'd written the article before they'd sent the man to talk to him. He took the paper off the counter, paid the woman, walked out of the store, and wandered out to the street, still reading the article over and over again. He felt awed; the paper had the aura of The Mysteries—even things mystical—about it.

Out on the street, Walt set his teeth and pointed himself at the ramp to the interstate highway. He walked for thirty minutes, thumb out, hitchhiking along the grassy strip to the right of the southbound lane.

It was almost dark when the station wagon stopped for him.

"Where're you goin'?" the guy in the front passenger seat asked him. There were four people in the car already. The smell of burning marijuana drifted out from the window. Walt could see beer cans littering the floor, and at least one of the four men was drinking.

"South," Walt said. "A long way."

"You want to ride on the back shelf?"

It was mostly empty.

"Sure."

"Open the door and let him in, huh, Jack?"

Jack opened the door and leaned away from it enough for Walt to climb over him; Walt settled in among the duffel bags and piles of etcetera. He rode for hours lying on his back with his head on a pillow made of what felt like clothes. He stared up into the sky as he lay there, watching the stars.

Meteors whizzed back and forth over the highway in the sky above them. And three times police cars screamed by them, lights flashing, sirens wailing.

Once Jack asked him if he wanted a hit off a joint, but he didn't. Jack and everybody else in the car laughed uproariously.

At four in the morning they stopped at a rest area to use the men's room. When they stopped moving the odor in the car became unbearable.

"We're going to get off the highway at the next exit," Jack told him. He got back before the others did. "If you're still going south, this is probably a better place to get a ride than that is."

Walt nodded. "Yeah," he said. He started to climb out, relieved at the chance to get away from the stink. As he got up, he saw what it came from: the pile he'd been using for a pillow. Dirty socks and underwear. His stomach turned, he retched a little, but nothing came out. It'd been too long since he'd eaten, and thank God for that.

"Take it easy, kid," Jack said. He was awfully close when Walt's body was trying to puke. "You okay? You going to be all right?"

Walt got out of the car. He stood bent over with his hands on his knees. "I'll be all right," he said. The smell was horrible, and it was in his hair and clothes, and he was so *tired*. "Thanks for the ride."

He went to the water fountain by the picnic tables, and he drank water for ten minutes, hardly even pausing to breathe. When he looked up, the station wagon was gone.

Home was miles and miles away, and he was tired and he stank. He went into the men's room and tried to clean himself, but it didn't help. The smell had ground its way into his pores.

He needed someplace to sleep. He was sure his mom or someone would find him if he fell asleep on one of the benches in the little roadside park. If nothing else he'd be so conspicuous that some highway patrolman who had nothing to do with any of this would find him. But he couldn't stand the thought of trying to get another ride. He looked past the fence that wrapped itself around the rest stop and thought about the great thick woods that surrounded the highway. It was deep and dark and big; silent and endless. It extended as far as he could see.

The fence was three strands of barbed wire strung through rough wood posts. This far from any city there was no need for anything more elaborate. Walt pressed down the lowest wire and slipped between it and the wire above. His shirt snagged and tore on one of the barbs; another barb gave him a long bloody scratch on his upper arm. But he didn't care. He was too tired. He just wanted to find a dry, soft, comfortable bed of pine needles and sleep for a million years.

But he went much deeper into the forest than he meant to. He needed the hike, he guessed; at the same time he wanted to collapse, something like a nervous tick in his legs kept pushing him deeper and deeper into the woods. Maybe it was his body trying to bleed off excess adrenaline, or maybe it was a need to get as far away from the highway as he could, just to be safe.

Not long before dawn, his right foot caught on a gnarled, twisty root he hadn't seen, and he came down chest-first into an enormous heap of soft, wet, acid-smelling dung. It splattered all over the front of his shirt, onto his upper arms (even into the fresh cut), and under his chin. He started sobbing, then; it wasn't so bad to cry since no one was looking. He took his shirt off and used the back of it to wipe off his arms and neck. It didn't do any good. It took some of the clumps off him, but the shitty edges smeared him where he was clean. He threw the shirt onto a pile of rocks and crawled away from the bear shit, over to the base of a pine tree.

He sat there with his back to the tree until the sun came up, paralyzed with frustration and hopelessness. He thought about dying again, but he didn't think that would do any good, either.

219

Late in the morning he fell asleep, still filthy, his skin beginning to burn and itch where the shit was. He hadn't moved since he'd crawled over to the tree. He barely noticed the transition between wakefulness and sleep.

The touch of something cool and clean and wet woke him. Before he opened his eyes, while he was still waking up, he thought it was rain.

But it wasn't.

When his eyes finally focused he saw it was the alien, wiping Walt's body clean with a white cloth that smelled like lemons or something citrus. Its hands brushed him, and it felt just exactly like tripe in the refrigerator case in the grocery. Behind the citrus was the alien's smell of sulphur and... preserved meat. Walt's first impulse was to scream in stark raving bloody terror—was it cleaning him the way you clean an animal before you slaughter it?—but all the heart for screaming had worn out of him. If this was the end, then that was that: whether he'd meant it or not he'd already come to terms with it. He stared calm and cool into its drooling eyes.

"You are hurt?" the alien asked him, its voice bubbles in a fish tank, its breath rotten eggs. Walt turned his face away from it.

"No," Walt said. He sighed. "I'm okay."

The alien nodded its head back and forth slowly like a rocking chair. It finished wiping off Walt's right shoulder and reached over to clean the left. Walt could feel that under his chin was already clean. "Stop that," he said.

The alien looked startled, but it pulled its hand back. "It burns your skin," the thing said.

"Just don't."

The alien sat there staring at him for a long minute. "You can't go back home," it told him. "Your mother would be unhappy with you. She would hurt you."

"I know," Walt said. He'd known it for awhile now.

"Where will you go? Where will you have a life?"

Walt shrugged.

"You were unhappy being dead. That's strange for your people; almost

220

all of them rest content. We needed an assistant, so we woke you." The alien looked down into the dirt. "You don't have to come."

Walt could feel the bear shit, deep in his pores even where the creature had cleaned him. He could feel the filth matted into his hair in the station wagon. His clothes were filthy, kind of greasy; he'd been wearing them for three days now. And the alien—hands like tripe, smelling like something dead and something rotten—didn't seem gross or disgusting at all. Not in comparison.

He went with the aliens. Whether that was the right choice or not, he never regretted it.

And he had fun.

And when he grew up, he lived a great and full life out among the galaxies, a life full of stars and adventures and wonders. When he was forty he came home to the world to make his peace.

His father and he and his sister and her family spent a week of reunion and celebration. It was a good week, joyful as thirty Christmases at once.

But his mother was already dead when he came back. She hadn't lived a long life; she died not long after Walt left. He went to her grave to say good-bye to her.

She didn't answer. She did her best to ignore him.

THE NIGHT WE BURIED ROAD DOG

Jack Cady

I

BROTHER JESSE BURIED HIS '47 Hudson back in '61, and the roads got just that much more lonesome. Highway 2 across north Montana still wailed with engines as reservation cars blew past; and it lay like a tunnel of darkness before the headlights of big rigs. Tandems pounded, and the smart crack of downshifts rapped across grasslands as trucks swept past the bars at every crossroad. The state put up metal crosses to mark the sites of fatal accidents. Around the bars, those crosses sprouted like thickets.

That Hudson was named Miss Molly, and it logged 220,000 miles while never burning a clutch. Through the years, it wore into the respectable look that comes to old machinery. It was rough as a cob, cracked glass on one side, and primer over dents. It had the tough-and-ready look of a hunting hound about its business. I was a good deal younger then, but not so young that I was fearless. The burial had something to do with mystery, and Brother Jesse did his burying at midnight.

Through fluke or foresight, Brother Jesse had got hold of eighty acres of rangeland that wasn't worth a shake. There wasn't enough of it to run stock, and you couldn't raise anything on it except a little hell. Jesse stuck an old house trailer out there, stacked hay around it for insulation in

223

Montana winters, and hauled in just enough water to suit him. By the time his Hudson died, he was ready to go into trade.

"Jed," he told me the night of the burial, "I'm gonna make myself some history, despite this damn Democrat administration." Over beside the house trailer, the Hudson sat looking like it was about ready to get off the mark in a road race, but the poor thing was a goner. Moonlight sprang from between spring clouds, and to the westward the peaks of mountains glowed from snow and moonlight. Along Highway 2, some hot rod wound second gear on an old flathead Ford. You could hear the valves begin to float.

"Some little darlin' done stepped on that boy's balls," Jesse said about the driver. "I reckon that's why he's looking for a ditch." Jesse sighed and sounded sad. "At least we got a nice night. I couldn't stand a winter funeral."

"Road Dog?" I said about the driver of the Ford, which shows just how young I was at the time.

"It ain't The Dog," Jesse told me. "The Dog's a damn survivor."

You never knew where Brother Jesse got his stuff, and you never really knew if he was anybody's brother. The only time I asked, he said, "I come from a close-knit family such as your own," and that made no sense. My own father died when I was twelve, and my mother married again when I turned seventeen. She picked up and moved to Wisconsin.

No one even knew when, or how, Jesse got to Montana territory. We just looked up one day, and there he was, as natural as if he'd always been here, and maybe he always had.

His eighty acres began to fill up. Old printing presses stood gap-mouthed like spinsters holding conversation. A salvaged greenhouse served for storing dog food, engine parts, chromium hair dryers from 1930's beauty shops, dime-store pottery, blades for hay cutters, binder-twine, an old gas-powered crosscut saw, seats from a school bus, and a bunch of other stuff not near as useful.

A couple of tabbies lived in that greenhouse, but the Big Cat stood outside. It was an old D6 bulldozer with a shovel, and Jesse stoked it up from time to time. Mostly it just sat there. In summers, it provided shade for Jesse's dogs: Potato was brown and fat and not too bright, while Chip was little and fuzzy. Sometimes they rode with Jesse, and sometimes stayed home. Me or Mike Tarbush fed them. When anything big happened, you could count on those two dogs to get underfoot. Except for me, they were the only ones who attended the funeral.

"If we gotta do it," Jesse said mournfully, "we gotta." He wound up the Cat, turned on the headlights, and headed for the grave site, which was an embankment overlooking Highway 2. Back in those days, Jesse's hair still shone black, and it was even blacker in the darkness. It dangled around a face that carried an Indian forehead and a Scotsman's nose. Denim stretched across most of the six feet of him, and he wasn't rangy; he was thin. He had feet to match his height, and his hands seemed bigger than his feet; but the man could skin a Cat.

I stood in moonlight and watched him work. A little puff of flame dwelt in the stack of the bulldozer. It flashed against the darkness of those distant mountains. It burbled hot in the cold spring moonlight. Jesse made rough cuts pretty quick, moved a lot of soil, then started getting delicate. He shaped and reshaped that grave. He carved a little from one side, backed the dozer, found his cut not satisfactory. He took a spoonful of earth to straighten things, then fussed with the grade leading into the grave. You could tell he wanted a slight elevation, so the Hudson's nose would be sniffing toward the road. Old Potato dog had a hound's ears, but not a hound's good sense. He started baying at the moon.

It came to me that I was scared. Then it came to me that I was scared most of the time anyway. I was nineteen, and folks talked about having a war across the sea. I didn't want to hear about it. On top of the war talk, women were driving me crazy: the ones who said "no" and the ones who said "yes." It got downright mystifying just trying to figure out which was worse. At nineteen, it's hard to know how to act. There were whole weeks

225

when I could pass myself off as a hellion, then something would go sour. I'd get hit by a streak of conscience and start acting like a missionary.

"Jed," Jesse told me from the seat of the dozer, "go rig a tow on Miss Molly." In the headlights the grave now looked like a garage dug into the side of that little slope. Brother Jesse eased the Cat back in there to fuss with the grade. I stepped slow toward the Hudson, wiggled under, and fetched the towing cable around the frame. Potato howled. Chip danced like a fuzzy fury, and started chewing on my boot like he was trying to drag me from under the Hudson. I was on my back trying to kick Chip away and secure the cable. Then I like to died from fright.

Nothing else in the world sounds anywhere near like a Hudson starter. It's a combination of whine and clatter and growl. If I'd been dead a thousand years, you could stand me right up with a Hudson starter. There's threat in that sound. There's also the promise that things can get pretty rowdy, pretty quick.

The starter went off. The Hudson jiggled. In the one-half second it took to get from under that car, I thought of every bad thing I ever did in my life. I was headed for Hell, certain sure. By the time I was on my feet, there wasn't an ounce of blood showing anywhere on me. When the old folks say, "white as a sheet," they're talking about a guy under a Hudson.

Brother Jesse climbed from the Cat and gave me a couple shakes.

"She ain't dead," I stuttered. "The engine turned over. Miss Molly's still thinking speedy." From Highway 2 came the wail of Mike Tarbush's '48 Roadmaster. Mike loved and cussed that car. It always flattened out at around eighty.

"There's still some sap left in the batt'ry," Jesse said about the Hudson. "You probably caused a short." He dropped the cable around the hitch on the dozer. "Steer her," he said.

The steering wheel still felt alive, despite what Jesse said. I crouched behind the wheel as the Hudson got dragged toward the grave. Its brakes locked twice, but the towing cable held. The locked brakes caused the car to sideslip. Each time, Jesse cussed. Cold spring moonlight made the shadowed grave look like a cave of darkness.

The Hudson bided its time. We got it lined up, then pushed it backward into the grave. The hunched front fenders spread beside the snarly grille. The front bumper was the only thing about that car that still showed clean and uncluttered. I could swear Miss Molly moved in the darkness of the grave, about to come charging onto Highway 2. Then she seemed to make some kind of decision, and sort of settled down. Jesse gave the eulogy.

"This here car never did nothing bad," he said. "I must have seen a million crap-crates, but this car wasn't one of them. She had a second gear like Hydramatic, and you could wind to seventy before you dropped to third. There wasn't no top end to her—at least I never had the guts to find it. This here was a good hundred-mile-an-hour car on a bad night, and God knows what on a good'n." From Highway 2, you could hear the purr of Matt Simons' '56 Dodge, five speeds, what with the overdrive, and Matt was scorching.

Potato howled long and mournful. Chip whined. Jesse scratched his head, trying to figure a way to end the eulogy. It came to him like a blessing. "I can't prove it," he said, "'cause no one could. But I expect this car has passed The Road Dog maybe a couple hundred times." He made like he was going to cross himself, then remembered he was Methodist. "Rest in peace," he said, and he said it with eyes full of tears. "There ain't that many who can comprehend The Dog." He climbed back on the Cat and began to fill the grave.

Next day, Jesse mounded the grave with real care. He erected a marker, although the marker was more like a little signboard:

1947—1961
Hudson coupe—"Molly"
220,023 miles on straight eight cylinder
Died of busted crankshaft
Beloved in the memory of
Jesse Still

Montana roads are long and lonesome, and Highway 2 is lonesomest. You pick it up over on the Idaho border where the land is mountains. Bear and cougar still live pretty good, and beaver still build dams. The highway runs behind some pretty lakes. Canada is no more than a jump away; it hangs at your left shoulder when you're headed east.

And can you roll those mountains? Yes, oh yes. It's two-lane all the way across, and twisty in the hills. From Libby, you ride down to Kalispell, then pop back north. The hills last till the Blackfoot reservation. It's rangeland into Cut Bank, then to Havre. That's just about the center of the state.

Just let the engine howl from town to town. The road goes through a dozen, then swings south. And there you are at Glasgow and the river. By Wolf Point, you're in cropland, and it's flat from there until Chicago.

I almost hate to tell about this road, because easterners may want to come and visit. Then they'll do something dumb at a blind entry. The state will erect more metal crosses. Enough folks die up here already. And it's sure no place for rice grinders, or tacky Swedish station wagons, or high-priced German crap-crates. This was always a V-8 road, and V-12 if you had 'em. In the old, old days there were even a few V-16s up here. The top end on those things came when friction stripped the tires from too much speed.

Speed or not, brakes sure sounded as cars passed Miss Molly's grave. Pickup trucks fishtailed as men snapped them to the shoulder. The men would sit in their trucks for a minute, scratching their heads like they couldn't believe what they'd just seen. Then they'd climb from the truck, walk back to the grave, and read the marker. About half of them would start holding their sides. One guy even rolled around on the ground, he was laughing so much.

"These old boys are laughing now," Brother Jesse told me, "but I predict a change in attitude. I reckon they'll come around before first snowfall."

With his car dead, Jesse had to find a set of wheels. He swapped an old hay rake and a gang of discs for a '49 Chevrolet.

"It wouldn't pull the doorknob off a cathouse," he told me. "It's just to get around in while I shop."

The whole deal was going to take some time. Knowing Jesse, I figured he'd go through half a dozen trades before finding something comfortable. And I was right.

He first showed up in an old Packard hearse that once belonged to a funeral home in Billings. He'd swapped the Chev for the hearse, plus a gilt-covered coffin so gaudy it wouldn't fit anybody but a radio preacher. He swapped the hearse to Sam Winder, who aimed to use it for hunting trips. Sam's dogs wouldn't go anywhere near the thing. Sam opened all the windows and the back door, then took the hearse up to speed trying to blow out all the ghosts. The dogs still wouldn't go near it. Sam said, "To hell with it," and pushed it into a ravine. Every rabbit and fox and varmint in that ravine came bailing out, and nobody has gone in there ever since.

Jesse traded the coffin to Old Man Jefferson, who parked the thing in his woodshed. Jefferson was supposed to be on his last legs, but figured he wasn't ever, never, going to die if his poor body knew it would be buried in that monstrosity. It worked for several years, too, until a bad winter came along, and he split it up for firewood. But we still remember him.

Jesse came out of those trades with a '47 Pontiac and a Model T. He sold the Model T to a collector, then traded the Pontiac and forty bales of hay for a '53 Studebaker. He swapped the Studebaker for a ratty pickup and all the equipment in a restaurant that went bust. He peddled the equipment to some other poor fellow who was hell-bent to go bust in the restaurant business. Then he traded the pickup for a motorcycle, plus a '51 Plymouth that would just about get out of its own way. By the time he peddled both of them, he had his pockets full of cash and was riding shank's mare.

"Jed," he told me, "let's you and me go to the big city." He was pretty happy, but I remembered how scared I'd been at the funeral. I admit to being skittish.

From the center of north Montana, there weren't a championship lot of big cities. West was Seattle, which was sort of rainy and mythological. North was Winnipeg, a cow town. South was Salt Lake City. To the east....

"The hell with it," Brother Jesse said. "We'll go to Minneapolis."

It was about a thousand miles. Maybe fifteen hours, what with the roads. You could sail Montana and North Dakota, but those Minnesota cops were humourless.

I was shoving a sweet old '53 Desoto. It had a good bit under the bonnet, but the suspension would make a grown man cry. It was a beautiful beast, though. Once you got up to speed, that front end would track like a cat. The upholstery was like brand-new. The radio worked. There wasn't a scratch or ding on it. I had myself a banker's car, and there I was, only nineteen.

"We may want to loiter," Jesse told me. "Plan on a couple of overnights."

I had a job, but told myself that I was due for a vacation; and so screw it. Brother Jesse put down food for the tabbies and whistled up the dogs. Potato hopped into the backseat in his large, dumb way. He looked expectant. Chip sort of hesitated. He made a couple of jumps straight up, then backed down and started barking. Jesse scooped him up and shoved him in with old Potato dog.

"The upholstery," I hollered. It was the first time I ever stood up to Jesse.

Jesse got an old piece of tarp to put under the dogs. "Pee, and you're a goner," he told Potato.

We drove steady through the early-summer morning. The Desoto hung in around eighty, which was no more than you'd want, considering the suspension. Rangeland gave way to cropland. The radio plugged away with western music, beef prices, and an occasional preacher saying, "Grace" and "Gimmie." Highway 2 rolled straight ahead, sometimes rising gradual, so that cars appeared like rapid running spooks out of the blind entries. There'd be a little flash of sunlight from a windshield. Then a car would appear over the rise, and usually it was wailing.

230

We came across a hell of a wreck just beyond Havre. A new Mercury station wagon rolled about fifteen times across the landscape. There were two nice-dressed people and two children. Not one of them ever stood a chance. They rattled like dice in a drum. I didn't want to see what I was looking at.

Bad wrecks always made me sick, but not sick to puking. That would not have been manly. I prayed for those people under my breath and got all shaky. We pulled into a crossroads bar for a sandwich and a beer. The dogs hopped out. Plenty of hubcaps were nailed on the wall of the bar. We took a couple of them down and filled them with water from an outside tap. The dogs drank and peed.

"I've attended a couple myself," Brother Jesse said about the wreck. "Drove a Terraplane off a bridge back in '53. Damn near drownded." Jesse wasn't about to admit to feeling bad. He just turned thoughtful.

"This here is a big territory," he said to no one in particular. "But you can get across her if you hustle. I reckon that Merc was loaded wrong, or blew a tire." Beyond the windows of the bar, eight metal crosses lined the highway. Somebody had tied red plastic roses on one of them. Another one had plastic violets and forget-me-nots.

We lingered a little. Jesse talked to the guy at the bar, and I ran a rack at the pool table. Then Jesse bought a six-pack while I headed for the can. Since it was still early in the day, the can was clean; all the last night's pee and spit mopped from the floor. Somebody had just painted the walls. There wasn't a thing written on them, except that Road Dog had signed in.

Road Dog
How are things in Glocca Mora?

His script was spidery and perfect, like an artist who drew a signature. I touched the paint, and it was still tacky. We had missed The Dog by only a few minutes.

231

Road Dog was like Jesse in a way. Nobody could say exactly when he first showed up, but one day he was there. We started seeing the name "Road Dog" written in what Matt Simons called "a fine Spencerian hand." There was always a message attached, and Matt called them "cryptic." The signature and messages flashed from the walls of cans in bars, truck stops, and roadside cafés through four states.

We didn't know Road Dog's route at first. Most guys were tied to work or home or laziness. In a year or two, though, Road Dog's trail got mapped. His fine hand showed up all along Highway 2, trailed east into North Dakota, dropped south through South Dakota, then ran back west across Wyoming. He popped north through Missoula and climbed the state until he connected with Highway 2 again. Road Dog, whoever he was, ran a constant square of road that covered roughly two thousand miles.

Sam Winder claimed Road Dog was a Communist who taught social studies at U. of Montana. "Because," Sam claimed, "that kind of writing comes from Europe. That writing ain't U.S.A."

Mike Tarbush figured Road Dog was a retired cartoonist from a newspaper. He figured nobody could spot The Dog, because The Dog slipped past us in a Nash, or some other old-granny car.

Brother Jesse suggested that Road Dog was a truck driver, or maybe a gypsy, but sounded like he knew better.

Matt Simons supposed Road Dog was a traveling salesman with a flair for advertising. Matt based his notion on one of the cryptic messages:

Road Dog
Ringling Bros. Barnum and Toothpaste

I didn't figure anything. Road Dog stood in my imagination as the heart and soul of Highway 2. When night was deep and engines blazed, I could hang over the wheel and run down that tunnel of two-lane into the night.

The nighttime road is different than any other thing. Ghosts rise around the metal crosses, and ghosts hitchhike along the wide berm. All the mysteries of the world seem normal after dark. If imagination shows dead thumbs aching for a ride, those dead folk only prove the hot and spermy goodness of life. I'd overtake some taillights, grab the other lane, and blow doors off some partygoer who tried to stay out of the ditches. A man can sing and cuss and pray. The miles fill with dreams of power, and women, and happy, happy times.

Road Dog seemed part of that romance. He was the very soul of mystery, a guy who looked at the dark heart of the road and still flew free enough to make jokes and write that fine hand.

In daytime, it was different, though. When I saw Road Dog signed in on the wall of that can, it just seemed like a real bad sign.

The guy who owned the bar had seen no one. He claimed he'd been in the back room putting bottles in his cold case. The Dog had come and gone like a spirit.

Jesse and I stood in the parking lot outside the bar. Sunlight laid earthy and hot across the new crops. A little puff of dust rose from a side road. It advanced real slow, so you could tell it was a farm tractor. All around us, meadowlarks and tanagers were whooping it up.

"We'll likely pass him," Jesse said, "if we crowd a little." Jesse pretended he didn't care, but anyone would. We loaded the dogs, and even hung the hubcaps back up where we got them, because it was what a gentleman would do. The Desoto acted as eager as any Desoto could. We pushed the top end, which was eighty-nine, and maybe ninety-two downhill. At that speed, brakes don't give you much, so you'd better trust your steering and your tires.

If we passed The Dog, we didn't know it. He might have parked in one of the towns, and of course we dropped a lot of revs passing through towns, that being neighbourly. What with a little loafing, some pee stops, and general fooling around, we did not hit Minneapolis until a little after midnight. When we checked into a motel on the strip, Potato was sleepy and grumpy. Chip looked relieved.

233

"Don't fall in love with that bed," Jesse told me. "Some damn salesman is out there waitin' to do us in. It pays to start early."

Car shopping with Jesse turned out as fascinating as anybody could expect. At 7:00 A.M., we cruised the lots. Cars stood in silent rows like advertising men lined up for group pictures. It being Minneapolis, we saw a lot of high-priced iron. Cadillacs and Packards and Lincolns sat beside Buick convertibles, hemi Chryslers, and Corvettes ("Nice c'hars," Jesse said about the Corvettes, "but no room to 'em. You couldn't carry more than one sack of feed."). Hudsons and Studebakers hunched along the back rows. On one lot was something called "Classic Lane." A Model A stood beside a '37 International pickup. An L29 Cord sat like a tombstone, which it was, because it had no engine. But, glory be, beside the Cord nestled a '39 LaSalle coupe just sparkling with threat. That LaSalle might have snookered Jesse, except something highly talented sat buried deep in the lot.

It was the last of the fast and elegant Lincolns, a '54 coupe as snarly as any man could want. The '53 model had taken the Mexican Road Race. The '54 was a refinement. After that the marquee went downhill. It started building cars for businessmen and rich grannies.

Jesse walked round and round the Lincoln, which looked like it was used to being cherished. Matchless and scratchless. It was a little less than fire engine red, with a white roof and a grille that could shrug off a cow. That Linc was a solid set of fixings. Jesse got soft lights in his eyes. This was no Miss Molly, but this was Miss somebody. There was a lot of crap-crates running out there, but this Linc wasn't one of them.

"You prob'ly can't even get parts for the damn thing," Jesse murmured, and you could tell he was already scrapping with a salesman. He turned his back on the Lincoln. "We'll catch a bite to eat," he said. "This may take a couple days."

I felt sort of bubbly. "The Dog ain't gonna like this," I told Jesse.

"The Dog is gonna love it," he said. "Me and The Dog *know* that road."

By the time the car lots opened at 9:00 A.M., Jesse had a trader's light

234

in his eyes. About all that needs saying is that never before, or since, did I ever see a used-car salesman cry.

The poor fellow never had a chance. He stood in his car lot most of the day while me and Jesse went through every car lot on the strip. We waved to him from a sweet little '57 Cad, and we cruised past real smooth in a mama-san '56 Imperial. We kicked tires on anything sturdy while he was watching, and we never even got to his lot until fifteen minutes before closing. Jesse and I climbed from my Desoto. Potato and Chip tailed after us.

"I always know when I get to Minneapolis," Jesse said to me, but loud enough the salesman could just about hear. "My woman wants to lay a farmer, and my dogs start pukin.'" When we got within easy hearing range, Jesse's voice got humble. "I expect this fella can help a cowboy in a fix."

I followed, experiencing considerable admiration. In two sentences, Jesse had his man confused.

Potato was dumb enough that he trotted right up to the Lincoln. Chip sat and panted, pretending indifference. Then he ambled over to a ragged-out Pontiac and peed on the tire. "I must be missing something," Jesse said to the salesman, "because that dog has himself a dandy nose." He looked at the Pontiac. "This thing got an engine?"

We all conversed for the best part of an hour. Jesse refused to even look at the Lincoln. He sounded real serious about the LaSalle, to the point of running it around a couple of blocks. It was a darling. It had ceramic-covered manifolds to protect against heat and rust. It packed a long-stroke V-8 with enough torque to bite rubber in second gear. My Desoto was a pretty thing, but until that LaSalle, I never realized that my car was a total pussycat. When we left the lot, the salesman looked sad. He was late for supper.

"Stay with what you've got," Jesse told me as he climbed in my Desoto. "The clock has run out on that LaSalle. Let a collector have it. I hate it when something good dies for lack of parts."

I wondered if he was thinking of Miss Molly.

"Because," Jesse said, and kicking the tire on a silly little Volkswagen, "the great, good cars are dying. I blame it on the Germans."

Next day, we bought the Lincoln and made the salesman feel like one proud pup. He figured he foisted something off on Jesse that Jesse didn't want. He was so stuck on himself that he forgot that he had asked a thousand dollars, and come away with $550. He even forgot that his eyes were swollen, and that maybe he crapped his pants.

We went for a test drive, but only after Jesse and I crawled around under the Linc. A little body lead lumped in the left rear fender, but the front end stood sound. Nobody had pumped any sawdust into the differential. We found no water in the oil, or oil in the water. The salesman stood around, admiring his shoeshine. He was one of those easterners who can't help talking down to people, especially when he's trying to be nice. I swear he wore a white tie with little red ducks on it. That Minnesota sunlight made his red hair blond, and his face pop with freckles.

Jesse drove real quiet until he found an interesting stretch of road. The salesman sat beside him. Me and Potato and Chip hunkered in the backseat. Chip looked sort of nauseated, but Potato was pretty happy.

"I'm afraid," Jesse said regretful, "that this thing is gonna turn out to be a howler. A fella gets a few years on him, and he don't want a screamy car." Brother Jesse couldn't have been much more than thirty, but he tugged on his nose and ears like he was ancient. "I sure hope," he said real mournful, "that nobody stuck a boot in any of these here tires." Then he poured on some coal.

There was a most satisfying screech. That Linc took out like a roadrunner in heat. The salesman's head snapped backward, and his shoulders dug into the seat. Potato gave a happy, happy woof and stuck his nose out the open window. I felt like yelling, "Hosanna," but knew enough to keep my big mouth shut. The Linc shrugged off a couple of cars that were conservatively motoring. It wheeled past a hay truck as the tires started humming. The salesman's freckles began to stand up like warts while the airstream howled. Old Potato kept his nose sticking through the open window, and the wind kept drying it. Potato was so damn dumb he tried to lick it wet while his nose stayed in the airstream. His tongue blew sideways.

"It ain't nothing but speed," Jesse complained. "Look at this here steering." He joggled the wheel considerable, which at ninety got even more considerable. The salesman's tie blew straight backward. The little red ducks matched his freckles. "Jee-sus-Chee-sus," he said. "Eight hundred, and slow down." He braced himself against the dash.

When it hit the century mark, the Linc developed a little float in the front end. I expect all of us were thinking about the tires.

You could tell Jesse was jubilant. The Linc still had some pedal left.

"I'm gettin' old," Jesse hollered above the wind. "This ain't no car for an old man."

"Seven hundred," the salesman said. "And Mother of God, slow it down."

"Five-fifty," Jesse told him, and dug the pedal down one more notch.

"You got it," the salesman hollered. His face twisted up real teary. Then Potato got all grateful and started licking the guy on the back of the neck.

So Jesse cut the speed and bought the Linc. He did it diplomatic, pretending he was sorry he'd made the offer. That was kind of him. After all, the guy was nothing but a used-car salesman.

We did a second night in that motel. The Linc and Desoto sat in an all-night filling station. Lube, oil change, and wash, because we were riding high. Jesse had a heap of money left over. In the morning, we got new jeans and shirts, so as to ride along like gentlemen.

"We'll go to South Dakota," Jesse told me. "There's a place I've heard about."

"What are we looking for?"

"We're checking on The Dog," Jesse told me, and would say no more.

We eased west to Bowman, just under North Dakota line. Jesse sort of leaned into it, just taking joy from the whole occasion. I flowed along as best the Desoto could. Potato rode with Jesse, and Chip sat on the front seat beside me. Chip seemed rather easier in his mind.

A roadside café hunkered among tall trees. It didn't even have a neon sign. Real old-fashioned.

"I heard of this place all my life," Jesse said as he climbed from the Linc. "This here is the only outhouse in the world with a guest registry." He headed toward the rear of the café.

I tailed along, and Jesse, he was right. It was a palatial privy built like a little cottage. The men's side was a three-holer. There was enough room for a stand-up desk. On the desk was one of those old-fashioned business ledgers like you used to see in banks.

"They're supposed to have a slew of these inside," Jesse said about the register as he flipped pages. "All the way back to the early days."

Some spirit of politeness seemed to take over when you picked up that register. There was hardly any bad talk. I read a few entries:

On this site, May 16th, 1961, James John Johnson(John-John) cussed hell out of his truck.

I came, I saw, I kinda liked it.—Bill Samuels, Tulsa

This place does *know squat.—Pauley Smith, Odgen*

This South Dakota ain't so bad,
But I sure got the blues,
I'm working in Tacoma,
'cause my kids all need new shoes.—Sad George

Brother Jesse flipped through the pages. "I'm even told," he said, "that Teddy Roosevelt crapped here. This is a fine old place." He sort of hummed as he flipped. "Uh, huh," he said, "The Dog done made his pee spot." He pointed to a page:

238

Road Dog
Run and run as fast as you can
You can't catch me—I'm the Gingerbread Man.

Jesse just grinned. "He's sorta upping the ante, ain't he? You reckon this is getting serious?" Jesse acted like he knew what he was talking about, but I sure didn't.

II

We didn't know, as we headed home, that Jesse's graveyard business was about to take off. That wouldn't change him, though. He'd almost always had a hundred dollars in his jeans anyway, and was usually a happy man. What changed him was Road Dog and Miss Molly.

The trouble started awhile after we crossed the Montana line. Jesse ran ahead in the Lincoln, and I tagged behind in my Desoto. We drove Highway 2 into a western sunset. It was one of those magic summers where rain sweeps in from British Columbia just regular enough to keep things growing. Rabbits get fat and foolish, and foxes put on weight. Rattlesnakes come out of the ditches to cross the sun-hot road. It's not sporting to run over their middles. You have to take them in the head. Redwings perch on fence posts, and magpies flash black and white from the berm, where they scavenge road kills.

We saw a hell of a wreck just after Wolf Point. A guy in an old Kaiser came over the back of a rise and ran under a tanker truck that burned. Smoke rose black as a plume of crows, and we saw it five miles away. By the time we got there, the truck driver stood in the middle of the road, all white and shaking. The guy in the Kaiser sat behind the wheel. It was fearful to see how fast fire can work, and just terrifying to see bones hanging over a steering wheel. I remember thinking the guy no doubt died before any fire started, and we were feeling more than he was.

That didn't help. I said a prayer under my breath. The truck driver wasn't to blame, but he took it hard as a Presbyterian. Jesse tried to comfort him, without much luck. The road melted and stank and began to burn. Nobody was drinking, but it was certain-sure we were all more sober than we'd ever been in our lives. Two deputies showed up. Cars drifted in easy, because of the smoke. In a couple of hours, there were probably twenty cars lined up on either side of the wreck.

"He must of been asleep or drunk," Jesse said about the driver of the Kaiser. "How in hell can a man run under a tanker truck?"

When the cops reopened the road, night hovered over the plains. Nobody cared to run much over sixty, even beneath a bright moon. It seemed like a night to be superstitious, a night when there was a deer or pronghorn out there just ready to jump into your headlights. It wasn't a good night to drink, or shoot pool, or mess around in strange bars. It was a time for being home with your woman, if you had one.

On most nights, ghosts do not show up beside the metal crosses, and they sure don't show up in owl light. Ghosts stand out on the darkest, moonless nights, and only then when bars are closed and the only thing open is the road.

I never gave it a thought. I chased Jesse's taillights, which on that Lincoln were broad, up-and-down slashes in the dark. Chip sat beside me, sad and solemn. I rubbed his ears to perk him, but he just laid down and snuffed. Chip was sensitive. He knew I felt bad over that wreck.

The first ghost showed up on the left berm and fizzled before the headlights. It was a lady ghost, and a pretty one, judging from her long white hair and long white dress. She flicked on and off in just a flash, so maybe it was a road dream. Chip was so depressed he didn't even notice, and Jesse didn't either. His steering and his brakes didn't wave to me.

Everything stayed straight for another ten miles, then a whole peck of ghosts stood on the tight berm. A bundle of crosses shone all silvery white in the headlights. The ghosts melted into each other. You couldn't tell how many, but you could tell they were expectant. They looked like people lined up for a picture show. Jesse never gave a sign he saw them. I told

240

myself to get straight. We hadn't had much sleep in the past two nights, and did some drinking the night before. We'd rolled near two thousand miles.

Admonishing seemed to work. Another twenty minutes passed, maybe thirty, and nothing happened. Wind chased through the open windows of the Desoto, and the radio gave mostly static. I kicked off my boots because that helps you stay awake, the bottoms of the feet being sensitive. Then a single ghost showed up on the right-hand berm, and boy-howdy.

Why anybody would laugh while being dead has got to be a puzzle. This ghost was tall, with Indian hair like Jesse's, and I could swear he looked like Jesse, the spitting image. This ghost was jolly. He clapped his hands and danced. Then he gave me the old road sign for "roll 'em," his hand circling in the air as he danced. The headlights penetrated him, showed tall grass solid at the roadside, and instead of legs, he stood on a column of mist. Still, he was dancing.

It wasn't road dreams. It was hallucination. The nighttime road just fills with things seen or partly seen. When too much scary stuff happens, it's time to pull her over.

I couldn't do it, though. Suppose I pulled over, and suppose it wasn't hallucination? I recall thinking that a man don't ordinarily care for preachers until he needs one. It seemed like me and Jesse were riding through the Book of Revelation. I dropped my speed, then flicked my lights a couple times. Jesse paid it no attention, and then Chip got peculiar.

He didn't bark; he chirped. He stood up on the front seat, looking out the back window, and his paws trembled. He shivered, chirped, shivered, and went chirp, chirp, chirp. Headlights in back of us were closing fast.

I've been closed on plenty of times by guys looking for a ditch. Headlights have jumped out of night and fog and mist when nobody should be pushing forty. I've been overtaken by drunks and suiciders. No set of headlights ever came as fast as the ones that begun to wink in the mirrors. This Highway 2 is a quick, quick road, but it's not the salt flats of

241

Utah. The crazy man behind me was trying to set a new land speed record.

Never confuse an idiot. I stayed off the brakes and coasted, taking off speed and signalling my way onto the berm. The racer could have my share of the road. I didn't want any part of that boy's troubles. Jesse kept pulling away as I slowed. It seemed like he didn't even see the lights. Chip chirped, then sort of rolled down on the floorboards and cried.

For ninety seconds, I feared being dead. For one second, I figured it already happened. Wind banged the Desoto sideways. Wind whooped, the way it does in winter. The headlights blew past. What showed was the curve of a Hudson fender—the kind of curve you'd recognize if you'd been dead a million years—and what showed was the little, squinchy shapes of a Hudson's taillights; and what showed was the slanty doorpost like a nail running kitty-corner; and what showed was slivers of reflection from cracked glass on the rider's side; and what sounded was the drumbeat of a straight-eight engine whanging like a locomotive gone wild; the thrump, bumpa, thrum of a crankshaft whipping in its bed. The slaunch-forward form of Miss Molly wailed, and showers of sparks blew from the tailpipe as Miss Molly rocketed.

Chip was not the only one howling. My voice rose high as the howl of Miss Molly. We all sang it out together, while Jesse cruised three, maybe four miles ahead. It wasn't two minutes before Miss Molly swept past that Linc like it was foundation in cement. Sparks showered like the 4th of July, and Jesse's brake lights looked pale beside the fireworks. The Linc staggered against wind as Jesse headed for berm. Wind smashed against my Desoto.

Miss Molly's taillights danced as she did a jig up the road, and then they winked into darkness as Miss Molly topped a rise, or disappeared. The night went darker than dark. A cloud scudded out of nowhere and blocked the moon.

Alongside the road the dancing ghost showed up in my headlights, and I could swear it was Jesse. He laughed at like a good joke, but he gave the old road sign for "slow it down," his hand palm-down like he was patting an invisible pup. It seemed sound advice, and I blamed near liked him. After Miss Molly, a happy ghost seemed downright companionable.

"Shitfire," said Jesse, and that's all he said for the first five minutes after I pulled in behind him. I climbed from the Desoto and walked to the Linc. Old Potato dog sprawled on the seat in a dead faint, and Jesse rubbed his ears trying to warm him back to consciousness. Jesse sat over the wheel like a man who had just met Jesus. His hand touched gentle on Potato's ears, and his voice sounded reverent. Brother Jesse's conversion wasn't going to last, but at the time, it was just beautiful. He had the lights of salvation in his eyes, and his skinny shoulders weren't shaking too much. "I miss my c'har," he muttered finally, and blinked. He wasn't going to cry if he could help it. "She's trying to tell me something," he whispered. "Let's find a bar. Miss Molly's in car heaven, certain-sure."

We pulled away, found a bar, and parked. We drank some beer and slept across the car seats. Nobody wanted to go back on that road.

When we woke to a morning hot and clear, Potato's fur had turned white. It didn't seem to bother him much, but, for the rest of his life, he was a lot more thoughtful.

"Looks like mashed Potato," Jesse said, but he wasn't talking a whole lot. We drove home like a couple of old ladies. Guys came scorching past, cussing at our granny speed. We figured they could get mad and stay mad, or get mad and get over it. We made it back to Jesse's place about two in the afternoon.

A couple of things happened quick. Jesse parked beside his house trailer, and the front end fell out of the Lincoln. The right side went down, thump, and the right front tire sagged. Jesse turned even whiter than me, and I was bloodless. We had posted over a hundred miles an hour in that thing. Somehow, when we crawled around underneath inspecting it, we missed something. My shoulders and legs shook so hard I could barely get out of the Desoto. Chip was polite. He just yelped with happiness about being home, but he didn't trot across my lap as we climbed from the car.

Nobody could trust their legs. Jesse climbed out of the Linc and leaned against it. You could see him chewing over all the possibilities, then arriving at the only one that made sense. Some hammer mechanic bolted that front end together with no locknut, no cotter pin, no lock washer, no lock-nothin'. He just wrenched down a plain old nut, and the nut worked loose.

"Miss Molly knew," Jesse whispered. "That's what she was trying to tell." He felt a lot better the minute he said it. Color came back to his face. He peered around the corner of the house trailer, looking toward Miss Molly's grave.

Mike Tarbush was over there with his '48 Roadmaster. Matt Simons stood beside him, and Matt's '56 Dodge sat beside the Roadmaster, looking smug; which that model Dodge always did.

"I figger," Brother Jesse whispered, "that we should keep shut about last night. Word would just get around that we were alkies." He pulled himself together, arranged his face like a horse trying to grin, and walked toward the Roadmaster.

Mike Tarbush was a man in mourning. He sat on the fat trunk of that Buick and gazed off toward the mountains. Mike wore extra-large of everything, and still looked stout. He sported a thick red mustache to make up for his bald head. From time to time, he bragged about his criminal record, which amounted to three days in jail for assaulting a pool table. He threw it through a bar window.

Now his mustache drooped, and Mike seemed small inside his clothes. The hood of the Roadmaster gaped open. Under that hood, things couldn't be worse. The poor thing had thrown a rod into the next county.

Jesse looked under the hood and tsked. "I know what you're going through," he said to Mike. He kind of petted the Roadmaster. "I always figured Betty Lou would last a century. What happened?"

There's no call to tell about a grown man blubbering, and especially not one who can heave pool tables. Mike finally got straight enough to tell the story.

"We was chasing the Dog," he said. "At least I think so. Three nights ago over to Kalispell. This Golden Hawk blew past me sittin'." Mike watched the distant mountains like he'd seen a miracle, or else like he was expecting one to happen. "That sonovabitch shore can drive," he whispered in disbelief. "Blown out by a damn Studebaker."

"But a very swift Studebaker," Matt Simons said. Matt is as small as Mike is large, and Matt is educated. Even so, he's set his share of fence posts. He looks like an algebra teacher, but not as delicate.

"Betty Lou went on up past her flat spot," Mike whispered. "She was tryin'. We had ninety on the clock, and The Dog left us sitting." He patted the Roadmaster. "I reckon she died of a broken heart."

"We got three kinds of funerals," Jesse said, and he was sympathetic. "We got the no-frills type, the regular type and the extra-special. The extra-special comes with flowers." He said it with a straight face, and Mike took it that way. He bought the extra-special, and that was sixty-five dollars.

Mike put up a nice marker:

1948—1961
Roadmaster two-door—Betty Lou
Gone to Glory while chasing The Dog
She was the best friend of Mike Tarbush

Brother Jesse worked on the Lincoln until the front end tracked rock solid. He named it Sue Ellen, but not *Miss* Sue Ellen, there being no way to know if Miss Molly was jealous. When we examined Miss Molly's grave, the soil seemed rumpled. Wildflowers, which Jesse sowed on the grave, bloomed in midsummer. I couldn't get it out of my head that Miss Molly was still alive, and maybe Jesse couldn't, either.

Jesse explained about the Lincoln's name. "Sue Ellen is a lady I knew in Pocatello. I expect she misses me." He said it hopeful, like he didn't really believe it.

It looked to me like Jesse was brooding. Night usually found him in town, but sometimes he disappeared. When he was around, he drove real calm and always got home before midnight. The wildness hadn't come out of Jesse, but he had it on a tight rein. He claimed he dreamed of Miss Molly. Jesse was working something out.

And so was I, awake or dreaming. Thoughts of the Road Dog filled my nights, and so did thoughts of the dancing ghost. As summer deepened, restlessness took me wailing under moonlight. The road unreeled before my headlights like a magic line that pointed to places under a warm sun where ladies laughed and fell in love. Something went wrong, though. During that summer the ladies stopped being dreams and only imagination. When I told Jesse, he claimed I was just growing up. I wished for once Jesse was wrong. I wished for a lot of things, and one of the wishes came true. It was Mike Tarbush, not me, who got in the next tangle with Miss Molly.

Mike rode in from Billings, where he'd been car shopping. He showed up at Jesse's place on Sunday afternoon. Montana lay restful. Birds hunkered on wires, or called from high grass. Highway 2 ran watery with sunlight, deserted as a road ever could be. When Mike rolled a '56 Merc up beside the Linc, it looked like Old Home Week at a Ford dealership.

"I got to look at something," Mike said when he climbed from the Mercury. He sort of plodded over to Miss Molly's grave and hovered. Light breezes blew the wildflowers sideways. Mike looked like a bear trying to shake confusion from its head. He walked to the Roadmaster's grave. New grass sprouted reddish green. "I was sober," Mike said. "Most Saturday nights, maybe I ain't, but I was sober as a deputy."

For a while, nobody said anything. Potato sat glowing and white and thoughtful. Chip slept in the sun beside one of the tabbies. Then Chip woke up. He turned around three times and dashed to hide under the bulldozer.

"Now, tell me I ain't crazy," Mike said. He perched on the front fender of the Merc, which was blue and white and adventuresome. "Name of Judith," he said about the Merc. "A real lady." He swabbed sweat from his bald head. "I got blown out by Betty Lou and Miss Molly. That sound reasonable?" He swabbed some more sweat and looked at the graves, which looked like little speed bumps on the prairie. "Nope," he answered himself, "that don't sound reasonable a-tall."

"Something's wrong with your Mercury," Jesse said, real quiet. "You got a bad tire, or a hydraulic line about to blow, or something screwy in the steering."

He made Mike swear not to breathe a word. Then he told about Miss Molly and about the front end of the Lincoln. When the story got over, Mike looked like a halfback hit by a twelve-man line.

"Don't drive another inch," Jesse said. "Not until we find what's wrong."

"That can already cracked a hundred," Mike whispered. "I bought it special to chase one sumbitch in a Studebaker." He looked toward Betty Lou's grave. "The Dog did that."

The three of us went through that Merc like men panning gold. The trouble was so obvious we missed it for two hours while the engine cooled. Then Jesse caught it. The fuel filter rubbed its underside against the valve cover. When Jesse touched it, the filter collapsed. Gasoline spilled on the engine and the spark plugs. That Merc was getting set to catch on fire.

"I got to wonder if The Dog did it," Jesse said about Betty Lou after Mike drove away. "I wonder if the Road Dog is the Studebaker type."

Nights started to get serious, but any lonesomeness on that road was only in a man's head. As summer stretched past its longest days, and sunsets started earlier, ghosts rose beside crosses before daylight hardly left the land. We drove to work and back, drove to town and back. My job was steady at a filling station, but it asked day after day of the same old thing. We never did any serious wrenching; no engine rebuilds or transmissions, just tune-ups and flat tires. I dearly wanted to meet a nice lady, but no woman in her right mind would mess with a pump jockey.

247

Nights were different, though. I figured I was going crazy, and Jesse and Mike were worse. Jesse finally got his situation worked out. He claimed Miss Molly was protecting him. Jesse and Mike took the Linc and the Merc on long runs, just wringing the howl out of those cars. Some nights, they'd flash past me at speed no sane man would try in darkness. Jesse was never a real big drinker, and Mike stopped altogether. They were too busy playing road games. It got so the state cop never tried to chase them. He just dropped past Jesse's place next day and passed out tickets.

The dancing ghost danced in my dreams, both asleep and driving. When daylight left the land, I passed metal crosses and remembered some of the wrecks.

Three crosses stood on one side of the railroad track, and four crosses on the other side. The three happened when some Canadian cowboys lost a race with a train. It was too awful to remember, but on most nights, those guys stood looking down the tracks with startled eyes.

The four crosses happened when one-third of the senior class of '59 hit that grade too fast on prom night. They rolled a damned Chevrolet. More bodies by Fisher. Now the two girls stood in their long dresses, looking wistful. The two boys pretended that none of it meant nothin'.

Farther out the road, things had happened before my time. An Indian ghost most often stood beside the ghost of a deer. In another place a chubby old rancher looked real picky and angry.

The dancing ghost continued unpredictable. All the other ghosts stood beside their crosses, but the dancing ghost showed up anywhere he wanted, anytime he wanted. I'd slow the Desoto as he came into my lights, and he was the spitting image of Jesse.

"I don't want to hear about it," Jesse said when I tried to tell him. "I'm on a roll. I'm even gettin' famous."

He was right about that. People up and down the line joked about Jesse and his graveyard business.

"It's the very best kind of advertising," he told me. "We'll see more action before snow flies."

"You won't see snow fly," I told him, standing up to him a second time. "Unless you slow down and pay attention."

"I've looked at heaps more road than you," he told me, "and seeing things is just part of the night. That nighttime road is different."

"This is starting to happen at last light."

"I don't see no ghosts," he told me, and he was lying. "Except Miss Molly once or twice." He wouldn't say anything more.

And Jesse was right. As summer ran on, more graves showed up near Miss Molly. A man named McGuire turned up with a '41 Cad.

1941—1961
Fleetwood Coupe—Annie
304,018 miles on flathead V-8
She was the luck of the Irishman
Pat McGuire

And Sam Winder buried his '47 Packard.

1947—1961
Packard 2-door—Lois Lane
Super buddy of Sam Winder
Up Up and Away

And Pete Johansen buried his pickup.

1946—1961
Ford pickup—Gertrude
211,000 miles give or take
Never a screamer
But a good pulling truck.
Pete Johansen put up many a day's work with her.

Montana roads are long and lonesome, and along the highline is lonesomest of all. From Saskatchewan to Texas, nothing stands tall enough to break the wind that begins to blow cold and clear toward late October. Rains sob away toward the Middle West, and grass turns goldish amber. Rattlesnakes move to high ground, where they will winter. Every creature on God's plains begins to fat-up against the winter. Soon it's going to be thirty below and the wind blowing.

Four-wheel-drive weather. Internationals and Fords, with Dodge crummy-wagons in the hills; cars and trucks will line up beside houses, garages, sheds, with electric wires leading from plugs to radiators and blocks. They look like packs of nursing pups. Work will slow, then stop. New work turns to accounting for the weather. Fuel, emergency generators, hay-bale insulation. Horses and cattle and deer look fuzzy beneath thick coats. Check your battery. If your rig won't start, and you're two miles from home, she won't die—but you might.

School buses creep from stop to stop, and bundled kids look like colourful little bears trotting through late-afternoon light. Snowy owls come floating in from northward, while folks go to church on Sunday against the time when there's some better amusement. Men hang around town, because home is either empty or crowded, depending on if you're married. Folks sit before television, watching the funny, goofy, unreal world where everybody plays at being sexy and naked, even when they're not.

And nineteen years old is lonesome, too. And work is lonesome when nobody much cares for you.

Before winter set in, I got it in my head to run the Road Dog's route. It was September. Winter would close us down pretty quick. The trip would be a luxury. What with room rent, and gas, and eating out, it was payday to payday with me. Still, one payday would account for gas and sandwiches. I could sleep across the seat. I hocked a Marlin .30-30 to Jesse for twenty bucks. He seemed happy with my notion. He even went into the greenhouse and came out with an arctic sleeping bag.

"In case things get vigorous," he said, and grinned. "Now get on out there and bite The Dog."

It was a happy time. Dreams of ladies sort of set themselves to one side as I cruised across the eternal land. I came to love the land that autumn, in a way that maybe ranchers do. The land stopped being something that a road ran across. Canadian honkers came winging in vees from the north. The great Montana sky stood easy as eagles. When I'd pull over and cut the engine, sounds of grasshoppers mixed with birdcalls. Once, a wild turkey, as smart as any domestic turkey is dumb, talked to himself and paid me not the least mind.

The Dog showed up right away. In a café in Malta:

Road Dog
"It was all a hideous mistake."
Christopher Columbus

In a bar in Tampico:

Road Dog
Who's afraid of the big bad Woof?

In another bar in Culbertson:

Road Dog
Go East, young man, go East

I rolled Williston and dropped south through North Dakota. The Dog's trail disappeared until Watford City, where it showed up in the can of a filling station:

Road Dog
Atlantis and Sargasso

Full fathom five thy brother lies

And in a joint in Grassy Butte:

Road Dog
Ain't Misbehavin'

That morning in Grassy Butte, I woke to a sunrise where the land lay bathed in rose and blue. Silhouettes of grazing deer mixed with silhouettes of cattle. They herded together peaceful as a dream of having your own place, your own woman, and you working hard; and her glad to see you coming home.

In Bowman, The Dog showed up in a nice restaurant:

Road Dog
The Katzenjammer Kids minus one

Ghosts did not show up along the road, but the road stayed the same. I tangled with a bathtub Hudson, a '53, outside of Spearfish in South Dakota. I chased him into Wyoming like being dragged on a string. The guy played with me for twenty miles, then got bored. He shoved more coal in the stoker and purely flew out of sight.

Sheridan was a nice town back in those days, just nice and friendly; plus, I started to get sick of the way I smelled. In early afternoon, I found a five-dollar motel with a shower. That gave me the afternoon, the evening, and next morning if it seemed right. I spiffed up, put on a good shirt, slicked down my hair, and felt just fine.

The streets lay dusty and lazy. Ranchers' pickups stood all dented and work-worn before bars, and an old Indian sat on hay bales in the back of one of them. He wore a flop hat, and he seemed like the eyes and heart of the prairie. He looked at me like I was a splendid puppy that might someday amount to something. It seemed O.K. when he did it.

252

I hung around a soda fountain at the five-and-dime because a girl smiled. She was just beautiful. A little horsey-faced, but with the sun-blond hair, and with hands long-fingered and gentle. There wasn't a chance of talking, because she stood behind the counter for ladies' underwear. I pretended to myself that she looked sad when I left.

It got on to late afternoon. Sunlight drifted in between buildings, and shadows overreached the streets. Everything was normal, and then everything got scary.

I was just poking along, looking in store windows, checking the show at the movie house, when, ahead of me, Jesse walked toward the Golden Hawk. He was maybe a block and a half away, but it was Jesse, sure as God made sunshine. It was a Golden Hawk. There was no way of mistaking that car. Hawks were high-priced sets of wheels, and Studebaker never sold that many.

I yelled and ran. Jesse waited beside the car, looking sort of puzzled. When I pulled up beside him, he grinned.

"It's happening again," he said, and his voice sounded amused, but not mean. Sunlight made his face reddish, but shadow put his legs and feet in darkness. "You believe me to be a gentleman named Jesse Still." Behind him, shadows of buildings told that night was on its way. Sunset happens quick on the prairies.

And I said, "Jesse, what in the hell are you doing in Sheridan?"

And he said, "Young man, you are not looking at Jesse Still." He said it quiet and polite, and he thought he had a point. His voice was smooth and cultured, so he sure didn't sound like Jesse. His hair hung combed-out, and he wore clothes that never came from a dry-goods. His jeans were soft-looking and expensive. His boots were tooled. They kind of glowed in the dusk. The Golden Hawk didn't have a dust speck on it, and the interior had never carried a tool, or a car part, or a sack of feed. It just sparkled. I almost believed him, and then I didn't.

"You're fooling with me."

"On the contrary," he said real soft. "Jesse Still is fooling with *me*,

253

although he doesn't mean to. We've never met." He didn't exactly look nervous, but he looked impatient. He climbed in the Stude and started the engine. It purred like racing tune. "This is a large and awfully complex world," he said, "and Mr. Still will probably tell you the same. I've been told we look like brothers."

I wanted to say more, but he waved real friendly and pulled away. The flat and racey back end of the Hawk reflected one slash of sunlight, then rolled into shadow. If I'd had a hot car, I'd have gone out hunting him. It wouldn't have done a lick of good, but doing something would be better than doing nothing.

I stood sort of shaking and amazed. Life had just changed somehow, and it wasn't going to change back. There wasn't a thing in the world to do, so I went to get some supper.

The Dog had signed in at the café:

Road Dog
The Bobbsey Twins Attend The Motor Races

And—I sat chewing roast beef and mashed potatoes.

And—I saw how the guy in the Hawk might be lying, and that Jesse was a twin.

And—I finally saw what a chancy, dicey world this was, because without meaning to, exactly, and without even knowing it was happening, I had just run up against The Road Dog.

It was a night of dreams. Dreams wouldn't let me go. The dancing ghost tried to tell me Jesse was triplets. The ghosts among the crosses begged rides into nowhere, rides down the long tunnel of night that ran past lands of dreams, but never turned off to those lands. It all came back: the crazy summer, the running, running, running behind the howl of engines. The Road Dog drawled with Jesse's voice, and then The Dog spoke cultured. The girl at the five-and-dime held out a gentle hand, then pulled it back. I dreamed of a hundred roadside joints, bars, cafés, old-fashioned filling stations with grease pits. I dreamed of winter wind, and the dark, dark days of winter; and of nights when you hunch in your room because it's a chore too big to bundle up and go outside.

I woke to an early dawn and slurped coffee at the bakery, which kept open because they had to make morning doughnuts. The land lay all around me, but it had nothing to say. I counted my money and figured miles.

I climbed in the Desoto, thinking I had never got around to giving it a name. The road unreeled toward the west. It ended in Seattle, where I sold my car. Everybody said there was going to be a war, and I wasn't doing anything anyway. I joined the Navy.

III

What with him burying cars and raising hell, Jesse never wrote to me in summer. He was surely faithful in winter, though. He wrote long letters printed in a clumsy hand. He tried to cheer me up, and so did Matt Simons.

The Navy sent me to boot camp and diesel school, then to a motor pool in San Diego. I worked there three and a half years, sometimes even working on ships if the ships weren't going anywhere. A sunny land and smiling ladies lay all about, but the ladies mostly fell in love by ten at night and got over it by dawn. Women in bars were younger and prettier than back home. There was enough clap to go around.

"The business is growing like Jimsonweed," Jesse wrote toward Christmas of '62. "I buried fourteen cars this summer, and one of them was a Kraut." He wrote a whole page about his morals. It didn't seem right to stick a crap-crate in the ground beside real cars. At the same time, it was bad business not to. He opened a special corner of the cemetery, and pretended it was exclusive for foreign iron.

"And Mike Tarbush got to drinking," he wrote. "I'm sad to say we planted Judith."

255

Mike never had a minute's trouble with that Merc. Judith behaved like a perfect lady until Mike turned upside down. He backed across a parking lot at night, rather hasty, and drove backward up the guy wire of a power pole. It was the only rollover wreck in history that happened at twenty miles an hour.

"Mike can't stop discussing it," Jesse wrote. "He's never caught The Dog, neither, but he ain't stopped trying. He wheeled in here in a beefed-up '57 Olds called Sally. It goes like stink and looks like a Hereford."

Home seemed far away, though it couldn't have been more than thirty-six hours by road for a man willing to hang over the wheel. I wanted to take a leave and drive home, but knew it better not happen. Once I got there, I'd likely stay.

"George Pierson at the feedstore says he's going to file a paternity suit against Potato," Jesse wrote. "The pups are cute, and there's a family resemblance."

It came to me then why I was homesick. I surely missed the land, but even more, I missed the people. Back home, folks were important enough that you knew their names. When somebody got messed up or killed, you felt sorry. In California, nobody knew nobody. They just swept up broken glass and moved right along. I should have meshed right in. I had made my rating and was pushing a rich man's car, a '57 hemi Chrysler, but never felt it fit.

"Don't pay it any mind," Jesse wrote when I told about meeting Road Dog. "I've heard about a guy who looks the same as me. Sometimes stuff like that happens."

And that was all he ever did say.

Nineteen sixty-three ended happy and hopeful. Matt Simons wrote a letter. Sam Winder bought a big Christmas card, and everybody signed, "Merry Xmas, Jed—Keep It Between The Fence Posts." My boss didn't hold it against me that I left. In Montana a guy is supposed to be free to find what he's all about.

Christmas of '63 saw Jesse pleased as a bee in clover. A lady named

256

Sarah moved in with him. She waitressed at the café, and Jesse's letter ran pretty short. He'd put twenty-three cars under that year, and bought more acreage. He ordered a genuine marble gravestone for Miss Molly. "Sue Ellen is a real darling," Jesse wrote about the Linc. "That marker like to weighed a ton. We just about bent a back axle bringing it from the railroad."

From Christmas of '63 to January of '64 was just a few days, but they marked an awful downturn for Jesse. His letter was more real to me than all the diesels in San Diego.

He drew black borders all around the pages. The letters started out O.K., but went downhill. "Sarah moved out and into a rented room," he wrote. "I reckon I was just too much to handle." He didn't explain, but I did my own reckoning. I could imagine that it was Jesse, plus two cats and two dogs trying to get into a ten-wide-fifty trailer, that got to Sarah. "I think she misses me," he wrote, "but I expect she'll have to bear it."

Then the letter got just awful.

"A pack of wolves came through from Canada," Jesse wrote. "They picked off old Potato like a berry from a bush. Me and Mike found tracks, and a little blood in the snow."

I sat in the summery dayroom surrounded by sailors shooting pool and playing Ping-Pong. I imagined the snow and ice of home. I imagined old Potato mosing around in his dumb and happy way, looking for rabbits or lifting his leg. Maybe he even wagged his tail when that first wolf came into view. I sat blinking tears, ready to bawl over a dog, and then I did, and to hell with it.

The world was changing, and it wouldn't change back. I put in for sea duty one more time, and the chief warrant who ramrodded that motor pool turned it down again. He claimed we kept the world safe by wrenching engines.

"The '62 Dodge is emerging as the car of choice for people in a hurry." Matt Simons wrote that in February '64, knowing I'd understand that nobody could tell which cars would be treasured until they had a year or two on them. "It's an extreme winter," he wrote, "and it's taking its toll on many of us. Mike has now learned not to punch a policeman. He's doing ten days. Sam Winder managed to roll a Jeep, and neither he, nor I, can figure out how a man can roll a Jeep. Sam has a broken arm, and lost two toes to frost. He was trapped under the wreck. It took awhile to pull him out. Brother Jesse is in the darkest sort of mood. He comes and goes in an irregular manner, but the Linc sits outside the pool hall on most days.

"And for myself," Matt wrote, "I think, some summer, I'll drop by some revs. My flaming youth seems to be giving way to other interests. A young woman named Nancy started teaching at the school. Until now, I thought I was a confirmed bachelor."

A postcard came the end of February. The postmark said "Cheyenne, Wyoming," way down in the southeast corner of the state. It was written fancy. Nobody could mistake that fine, spidery hand. It read:

Road Dog
Run and run as fast as he can,
He can't find who is the Gingerbread Man

The picture on the card had been taken from an airplane. It showed an oval racetrack where cars chased each other round and round. I couldn't figure why Jesse sent it, but it had to be Jesse. Then it came to me that Jesse was The Road Dog. Then it came to me that he wasn't. The Road Dog was too slick. He wrote real delicate, and Jesse only printed real clumsy. On the other hand, The Road Dog didn't know me from Adam's off ox. Somehow it *had* to be Jesse.

"We got snow nut-deep to a tall palm tree," Jesse wrote at about the same time, "and Chip is failing. He's off his feed. He don't even tease the kitties. Chip just can't seem to stop mourning."

I had bad premonitions. Chip was sensitive. I feared he wouldn't be around by the time I got back home, and my fear proved right. Chip held off until the first warm sun of spring, and then he died while napping in the shade of the bulldozer. When Jesse sent a quick note telling me, I felt pretty bad, but had been expecting it. Chip had a good heart. I figured now he was with Potato, romping the hills somewhere. I knew that was a bunch of crap, but that's just the way I chose to figure it.

They say a man can get used to anything, but maybe some can't. Day after day, and week after week, California weather nagged. Sometimes a puny little dab of weather dribbled in from the Pacific, and people hollered it was storming. Sometimes temperatures dropped towards the fifties, and people trotted around in thick sweaters and coats. It was almost a relief when that happened, because everybody put on their shirts. In three years, I'd seen more woman skin than a normal man sees in a lifetime, and more tattoos on men. The chief warrant at the motor pool had the only tattoo in the world called "worm's-eye view of a pig's butt in the moonlight."

In autumn '64, with one more year to pull, I took a two-week leave and headed north chasing weather. It showed up first in Oregon with rain, and more in Washington. I got hassled on the Canadian border by a distressful little guy who thought, what with the war, that I wanted political asylum.

I chased on up to Calgary, where matters got chill and wholesome. Wind worked through the mountains like it wanted to drive me south toward home. Elk and moose and porcupines went about their business. Red-tailed hawks circled. I slid on over to Edmonton, chased on east to Saskatoon, then dropped south through the Dakotas. In Williston, I had a terrible want to cut and run for home, but didn't dare.

The Road Dog showed up all over the place, but the messages were getting strange. At a bar in Amidon:

Road Dog
Taking Kentucky Windage

At a hamburger joint in Belle Fourche:

Road Dog
Chasing his tail

At a restaurant in Redbird:

Road Dog
Flea and flee as much as we can
We'll soon find who is the Gingerbread Man

In a poolroom in Fort Collins:

Road Dog
Home home on derange

Road Dog, or Jesse, was too far south. The Dog had never showed up in Colorado before. At least, nobody ever heard of such.

My leave was running out. There was nothing to do except sit over the wheel. I dropped on south to Albuquerque, hung a right, and headed back to the big city. All along the road, I chewed a dreadful fear for Jesse. Something bad was happening, and that didn't seem fair, because something good went on between me and the Chrysler. We reached an understanding. The Chrysler came alive and began to hum. All that poor car had ever needed was to look at road. It had been raised among traffic and poodles, but needed long sight-distances and bears.

When I got back, there seemed no way out of writing a letter to Matt Simons, even if it was borrowing trouble. It took evening after evening of gnawing the end of a pencil. I hated to tell about Miss Molly, and about the dancing ghost, and about my fears for Jesse. A man is supposed to keep his problems to himself.

At the same time, Matt was educated. Maybe he could give Jesse a hand if he knew all of it. The letter came out pretty thick. I mailed it thinking Matt wasn't likely to answer real soon. Autumn deepened to winter back home, and everybody would be busy.

So I worked and waited. There was an old White Mustang with a fifth wheel left over from the last war. It was a lean and hungry-looking animal, and slightly marvellous. I overhauled the engine, then dropped the tranny and adapted a ten-speed Roadranger. When I got that truck running smooth as a Baptist's mouth, the Navy surveyed it and sold it for scrap.

"Ghost cars are a tradition," Matt wrote toward the back of October, "and I'd be hard pressed to say they are not real. I recall being passed by an Auburn boat-tail about 3:00 A.M. on a summer day. That happened ten years ago. I was about your age, which means there was not an Auburn boat-tail in all of Montana. That car died in the early thirties.

"And we all hear stories of huge old headlights overtaking in the mist, stories of Mercers and Deusenbergs and Bugattis. I try to believe the stories are true, because, in a way, it would be a shame if they were not.

"The same for road ghosts. I've never seen a ghost who looked like Jesse. The ghosts I've seen might not have been ghosts. To paraphrase an expert, they may have been a trapped beer belch, an undigested hamburger, or blowing mist. On the other hand, maybe not. They certainly seemed real at the time.

"As for Jesse—we have a problem here. In a way, we've had it for a long while, but only since last winter have matters become solemn. Then your letter arrives, and matters become mysterious. Jesse has—or had—a twin brother. One night when we were carousing, he told me that, but he also said his brother was dead. Then he swore me to a silence I must now break."

Matt went on to say that I must never, never say anything. He figured something was going on between brothers. He figured it must run deep.

"There is something uncanny about twins," Matt wrote. "What great matters are joined in the womb? When twins enter the world, they learn and grow the way all of us do; but some communication (or communion)

261

surely happens before birth. A clash between brothers is a terrible thing. A clash between twins may spell tragedy."

Matt went on to tell how Jesse was going over the edge with road games, only, the games stayed close to home. All during the summer, Jesse would head out, roll fifty or a hundred miles, and come home scorching like drawn by a string. Matt guessed the postcard I'd gotten from Jesse in February was part of the game, and it was the last time Jesse had been very far from home. Matt figured Jesse used tracing paper to imitate the Road Dog's writing. He also figured Road Dog had to be Jesse's brother.

"It's obvious," Matt wrote, "that Jesse's brother is still alive, and is only metaphorically dead to Jesse. There are look-alikes in this world, but you have reported identical twins."

Matt told how Jesse drove so crazy, even Mike would not run with him. That was bad enough, but it seemed the graveyard had sort of moved in on Jesse's mind. That graveyard was no longer just something to do. Jesse swapped around until he came up with a tractor and mower. Three times that summer, he trimmed the graveyard and straightened the markers. He dusted and polished Miss Molly's headstone.

"It's past being a joke," Matt wrote, "or a sentimental indulgence. Jesse no longer drinks, and no longer hells around in a general way. He either runs or tends the cemetery. I've seen other men search for a ditch, but never in such bizarre fashion."

Jesse had been seen on his knees, praying before Miss Molly's grave.

"Or perhaps he was praying for himself, or for Chip." Matt wrote. "Chip is buried beside Miss Molly. The graveyard has to be seen to be believed. Who would ever think so many machines would be so dear to so many men?"

Then Matt went on to say he was going to "inquire in various places" that winter. "There are ways to trace Jesse's brother," Matt wrote, "and I am very good at that sort of research." He said it was about the only thing he could still do for Jesse.

"Because," Matt wrote, "I seem to have fallen in love with a romantic.

Nancy wants a June wedding. I look forward to another winter alone, but it will be an easy wait. Nancy is rather old-fashioned, and I find that I'm old-fashioned as well. I will never regret my years spent helling around, but am glad they are now in the past."

Back home, winter deepened. At Christmas a long letter came from Jesse, and some of it made sense. "I put eighteen cars under this summer. Business fell off because I lost my hustle. You got to scooch around a good bit, or you don't make contacts. I may start advertising.

"And the tabbies took off. I forgot to slop them regular, so now they're mousing in a barn on Jimmy Come Lately Road. Mike says I ought to get another dog, but my heart isn't in it."

Then the letter went into plans for the cemetery. Jesse talked some grand ideas. He thought a nice wrought-iron gate might be showy, and bring in business. He thought of finding a truck that would haul "deceased" cars. "On the other hand," he wrote, "if a guy don't care enough to find a tow, maybe I don't want to plant his iron." He went on for a good while about morals, but a lawyer couldn't understand it. He seemed to be saying something about respect for Miss Molly, Betty Lou, and Judith. "Sue Ellen is a real hummer," he wrote about the Linc. "She's got two hundred thousand I know about, plus whatever went on before."

Which meant Jesse was piling up about seventy thousand miles a year, and that didn't seem too bad. Truck drivers put up a hundred thousand. Of course, they make a living at it.

Then the letter got so crazy it was hard to credit.

"I got The Road Dog figured out. There's two little kids. Their mama reads to them, and they play tag. The one that don't get caught gets to be the Gingerbread Man. This all come together because I ran across a bunch of kids down on the Colorado line. I was down that way to call on a lady I once knew, but she moved, and I said what the hell, and hung around a few days, and that's what clued me to The Dog. The kids were at a Sunday-school picnic, and I was napping across the car seat. Then a preacher's wife came over and saw I wasn't drunk, but the preacher was there, too, and they invited me. I eased over to the picnic, and everybody made me welcome. Anyway, those kids were playing, and I heard the gingerbread business, and I figured The Dog is from Colorado."

The last page of the letter was just as scary. Jesse took kids' crayons and drew the front ends of the Linc and Miss Molly. There was a tail that was probably Potato's, sticking out from behind the picture of Miss Molly, and everything was centered around the picture of a marker that said "R.I.P. Road Dog."

But—there weren't any little kids. Jesse had not been to Colorado. Jesse had been tending that graveyard, and staying close to home. Jesse played make-believe, or else Matt Simons lied; and there was no reason for Matt to lie. Something bad, bad wrong was going on with Jesse.

There was no help for it. I did my time and wrote a letter every month or six weeks pretending everything was normal. I wrote about what we'd do when I got home, and about the Chrysler. Maybe that didn't make much sense, but Jesse was important to me. He was a big part of what I remembered about home.

At the end of April, a postcard came, this time from Havre. "The Dog is after me. I feel it." It was just a plain old postcard. No picture.

Matt wrote in May, mostly his own plans. He busied himself building a couple of rooms onto his place. "Nancy and I do not want a family right away," he wrote, "but someday we will." He wrote a bubbly letter with a feel of springtime to it.

"I almost forgot my main reason for writing," the letter said. "Jesse comes from Boulder, Colorado. His parents are long dead, ironically in a car wreck. His mother was a schoolteacher, his father a librarian. Those people, who lived such quiet lives, somehow produced a hellion like Jesse, and Jesse's brother. That's the factual side of the matter.

"The human side is so complex it will not commit to paper. In fact, I do not trust what I know. When you get home next fall, we'll discuss it."

The letter made me sad and mad. Sad because I wasn't getting married, and mad because Matt didn't think I'd keep my mouth shut. Then I thought better of it. Matt didn't trust himself. I did what any gentleman would do, and sent him and Nancy a nice gravy boat for the wedding.

In late July, Jesse sent another postcard. "He's after me; I'm after him. If I ain't around when you get back, don't fret. Stuff happens. It's just a matter of chasing road."

Summer rolled on. The Navy released "nonessential personnel" in spite of the war. I put four years in the outfit and got called nonessential. Days choked past like a rig with fouled injectors. One good thing happened. My old boss moved his station to the outskirts of town and started an IH dealership. He straight-out wrote how he needed a diesel mechanic. I felt hopeful thoughts, and dark ones.

In September, I became a veteran who qualified for an overseas ribbon, because of work on ships that later on went somewhere. Now I could join the Legion post back home, which was maybe the payoff. They had the best pool table in the county.

"Gents," I said to the boys at the motor pool, "it's been a distinct by-God pleasure enjoying your company, and don't never come to Montana, 'cause she's a heartbreaker." The Chrysler and me lit out like a kyoodle of pups.

It would have been easier to run to Salt Lake, then climb the map of Havre, but notions pushed. I slid east to Las Cruces, then popped north to Boulder with the idea of tracing Jesse. The Chrysler hummed and chewed up road. When I got to Boulder, the notion turned hopeless. There were too many people. I didn't even know where to start asking.

It's no big job to fool yourself. Above Boulder, it came to me how I'd been pointing for Sheridan all along, and not even Sheridan. I pointed toward a girl who smiled at me four years ago.

I found her working at a hardware, and she wasn't wearing any rings. I blushed around a little bit, then got out of there to catch my breath. I thought of how Jesse took whatever time was needed when he bought the Linc. It looked like this would take awhile.

My pockets were crowded with mustering-out pay and money for unused leave. I camped in a ten-dollar motel. It took three days to get acquainted, then we went to a show and supper afterward. Her name was Linda. Her father was a Mormon. That meant a year of courting, but it's not all that far from north Montana to Sheridan.

I had to get home and get employed, which would make the Mormon happy. On Saturday afternoon, Linda and I went back to the same old movie, but this time we held hands. Before going home, she kissed me once, real gentle. That made up for those hard times in San Diego. It let me know I was back with my own people.

I drove downtown all fired-up with visions. It was way too early for bed, and I cared nothing for a beer. A run-down café sat on the outskirts. I figured pie and coffee.

The Dog had signed on. His writing showed faint, like the wall had been scrubbed. Newer stuff scrabbled over it.

Road Dog
Tweedledum and Tweedledee
Lonely pups as pups can be
For each other had to wait
Down beside the churchyard gate.

The café sort of slumbered. Several old men lined the counter. Four young gearheads sat at a table and talked fuel injection. The old men yawned and put up with it. Faded pictures of old racing cars hung along the walls. The young guys sat beneath a picture of the Bluebird. That car held the land speed record of 301.29 m.p.h. This was a racer's café, and had been for a long, long time.

The waitress was graying and motherly. She tsked and tished over the old men as much as she did the young ones. Her eyes held that long-distance prairie look, a look knowing wind and fire and hard times, stuff that either breaks people or leaves them wise. Matt Simons might get that

266

look in another twenty years. I tried to imagine Linda when she became a waitress's age, and it wasn't bad imagining.

Pictures of quarter-mile cars hung back of the counter, and pictures of street machines hung on each side of the door. Fifties hot rods scorched beside worked-up stockers. Some mighty rowdy iron crowded that wall. One picture showed a Golden Hawk. I walked over, and in one corner was the name "Still"—written in The Road Dog's hand. It shouldn't have been scary.

I went back to the counter shaking. A nice-looking old gent nursed coffee. His hands wore knuckles busted by a thousand slipped wrenches. Grease was worked in deep around his eyes, the way it gets after years and years when no soap made will touch it. You could tell he'd been a steady man. His eyes were clear as a kid.

"Mister," I said, "and beg pardon for bothering you. Do you know anything about that Studebaker?" I pointed to the wall.

"You ain't bothering me," he said, "but I'll tell you when you do." He tapped the side of his head like trying to ease a gear in place, then he started talking engine specs on the Stude.

"I mean the man who owns it."

The old man probably liked my haircut, which was short. He liked it that I was raised right. Young guys don't always pay old men much mind.

"You still ain't bothering me." He turned to the waitress. "Sue," he said, "has Johnny Still been in?"

She turned from cleaning the pie case, and she looked toward the young guys like she feared for them. You could tell she was no big fan of engines. "It's been the better part of a year, maybe more." She looked down the line of old men. "I was fretting about him just the other day...." She let it hang. Nobody said anything. "He comes and goes so quiet, you might miss him."

"I don't miss him a hell of a lot," one of the young guys said. "Johnny *always* blew you out."

"Because he's crazy," the first guy said. "There's noisy-crazy and quiet-crazy. The guy is a spook."

"He's going through something," the waitress said, and said it kind. "Johnny's taken a lot of loss. He's the type who grieves." She looked at me like she expected an explanation.

"I'm friends with his brother," I told her. "Maybe Johnny and his brother don't get along."

The old man looked at me rather strange. "You go back quite a ways," he told me. "Jesse's been dead a good long time."

I thought I'd pass out. My hands started shaking, and my legs felt too weak to stand. Beyond the window of the café, red light came from a neon sign, and inside the café, everybody sat quiet, waiting to see if I was crazy, too. I sort of picked at my pie. One of the young guys moved real uneasy. He loafed toward the door, maybe figuring he'd need a shotgun. The other three young ones looked confused.

"No offense," I said to the old man, "but Jesse Still is alive. Up on the highline. We run together."

"Jesse Still drove a damn old Hudson Terraplane into the South Platte River in spring of '52, maybe '53." The old man said it real quiet. "He popped a tire when not real sober."

"Which is why Johnny doesn't drink," the waitress said. "At least, I expect that's the reason."

"And now you are bothering me." The old man looked to the waitress, and she was as full of questions as he was.

Nobody ever felt more hopeless or scared. These folks had no reason to tell this kind of yarn. "Jesse is sort of roughhouse." My voice was only whispering. It wouldn't make enough sound. "Jesse made his reputation helling around."

"You've got that part right," the old man told me, "and youngest, I don't give a tinker's damn if you believe me or not, but Jesse Still is dead."

I saw what it had to be, but seeing isn't always believing. "Thank you, mister," I whispered to the old man, "and thank you, ma'am," to the waitress. Then I hauled out of there leaving them with something to discuss.

※

A terrible fear rolled with me, because of Jesse's last postcard. He said he might not be home, and now that could mean more than it said. The Chrysler bettered its reputation, and we just flew. From the Montana line to Shelby is eight hours on a clear day. You can wait it in seven, or maybe six and a half if a deer doesn't tangle with your front end. I was afraid, and confused, and getting mad. Me and Linda were just to the point of hoping for an understanding, and now I was going to get killed running over a porcupine or into a heifer. The Chrysler blazed like a hound on a hot scent. At eighty the pedal kept wanting to dig deep and really howl.

The nighttime road yells danger. Shadows crawl over everything. What jumps into your headlights may be real, and may be not. Metal crosses hold little clusters of dark flowers on their arms, and the land rolls out beneath the moon. Buttes stand like great ships anchored in the plains, and riverbeds run like dry ink. Come spring, they'll flow; but in September, all flow is in the road.

The dancing ghost picked me up on Highway 3 outside Comanche, but this time he wasn't dancing. He stood on the berm, and no mist tied him in place. He gave the old road sign for "roll 'em." Beyond Columbia, he showed up again. His mouth moved like he was yelling me along, and his face twisted with as much fear as my own.

That gave me reason to hope. I'd never known Jesse to be afraid like that, so maybe there was a mistake. Maybe the dancing ghost wasn't the ghost of Jesse. I hung over the wheel and forced myself to think of Linda. When I thought of her, I couldn't bring myself to get crazy. Highway 3 is not much of a road, but that's no bother. I can drive anything with wheels over any road ever made. The dancing ghost kept showing up and beckoning, telling me to scorch. I told myself the damn ghost had no judgment, or he wouldn't be a ghost in the first place.

That didn't keep me from pushing faster, but it wasn't fast enough to satisfy the roadside. They came out of the mist, or out of the ditches; crowds and clusters of ghosts standing pale beneath a weak moon. Some of them gossiped with each other. Some stood yelling me along. Maybe there was sense to it, but I had my hands full. If they were trying to help, they sure weren't doing it. They just made me get my back up, and think of dropping revs.

Maybe the ghosts held a meeting and studied out the problem. They could see a clear road, but I couldn't. The dancing ghost showed up on Highway 12 and gave me "thumbs up" for a clear road. I didn't believe a word of it, and then I really didn't believe what showed in my mirrors. Headlights closed like I was standing. My feelings said that all of this had happened before; except, last time, there was only one set of headlights.

It was Miss Molly and Betty Lou that brought me home. Miss Molly overtook, sweeping past with a lane change smooth and sober as an Adventist. The high, slaunch-forward form of Miss Molly thrummed with business. She wasn't playing Gingerbread Man or tag.

Betty Lou came alongside so I could see who she was, then Betty Lou laid back a half mile. If we ran into a claim-jumping deputy, he'd have to chase her first; and more luck to him. Her headlights hovered back there like angels.

Miss Molly settled down a mile ahead of the Chrysler and stayed at that distance, no matter how hard I pressed. Twice before Great Falls, she spotted trouble, and her squinchy little brake lights hauled me down. Once it was an animal, and once it was busted road surface. Miss Molly and Betty Lou dropped me off before Great Falls, and picked me back up the minute I cleared town.

We ran the night like rockets. The roadside lay deserted. The dancing ghost stayed out of it, and so did the others. That let me concentrate, which proved a blessing. At those speeds a man don't have time to do deep thinking. The road rolls past, the hours roll, but you've got a racer's mind. No matter how tired you should be, you don't get tired until it's over.

I chased a ghost car northward while a fingernail moon moved across the sky. In deepest night the land turned silver. At speed, you don't think, but you do have time to feel. The farther north we pushed, the more my feelings went to despair. Maybe Miss Molly thought the same, but everybody did all they could.

The Chrysler was a howler, and Lord knows where the top end lay. I buried the needle. Even accounting for speedometer error, we burned along in the low half of the second century. We made Highway 2 and Shelby around three in the morning, then hung a left. In just about no time, I rolled home. Betty Lou dropped back and faded. Miss Molly blew sparks and purely flew out of sight. The sparks meant something. Maybe Miss Molly was still hopeful. Or maybe she knew we were too late.

Beneath that thin moon, mounded graves looked like dark surf across the acreage. No lights burned in the trailer, and the Linc showed nowhere. Even under the scant light, you could see snowy tops of mountains, and the perfectly straight markers standing at the head of each grave. A tent, big enough to hold a small revival, stood not far from the trailer. In my headlights a sign on the tent read "chapel." I fetched a flashlight from the glove box.

A dozen folding chairs stood in the chapel, and a podium served as an altar. Jesse had rigged up two sets of candles, so I lit some. Matt Simons had written that the graveyard had to be seen to be believed. Hanging on one side of the tent was a sign reading "shrine," and all along that side hung road maps, and pictures of cars, and pictures of men standing beside their cars. There was a special display of odometers, with little cars beneath them: "330,938 miles"; "407,000 miles"; "half a million miles, more or less." These were the championship cars, the all-time best at piling up road, and those odometers would make even a married man feel lonesome. You couldn't look at them without thinking of empty roads and empty nights.

Even with darkness spreading across the cemetery, nothing felt worse than the inside of the tent. I could believe that Jesse took it serious, and had tried to make it nice, but couldn't believe anyone else would buy it.

The night was not too late for owls, and nearly silent wings swept past as I left the tent. I walked to Miss Molly's grave, half-expecting ghostly headlights. Two small markers stood beside a real fine marble headstone.

Potato
Happy-go-sloppy and good
Rest In Peace Wherever You Are

Chip
A dandy little sidekicker
Running with Potato

From a distance, I could see piled dirt where the dozer had dug new graves. I stepped cautious toward the dozer, not knowing why, but knowing it had to happen.

Two graves stood open like little garages, and the front ends of the Linc and the Hawk poked out. The Linc's front bumper shone spotless, but the rest of the Linc looked tough and experienced. Dents and dings crowded the sides, and cracked glass starred the windows.

The Hawk stood sparkly, ready to come roaring from the grave. Its glass shone washed and clean before my flashlight. I thought of what I heard in Sheridan, and thought of the first time I'd seen the Hawk. It hadn't changed. The Hawk looked like it had just been driven off a showroom floor.

Nobody in his right mind would want to look in those two cars, but it wasn't a matter of "want." Jesse, or Johnny—if that's who it was—had to be here someplace. It was certain-sure he needed help. When I looked, the Hawk sat empty. My flashlight poked against the glass of the Linc. Jesse lay there, taking his last nap across a car seat. His long black hair had turned gray. He had always been thin, but now he was skin and bones. Too many miles, and no time to eat. Creases under his eyes came from looking at road, but now the creases were deep like an old man's. His eyes showed that he was dead. They were open only a little bit, but open enough.

I couldn't stand to be alone with such a sight. In less than fifteen minutes, I stood banging on Matt Simons' door. Matt finally answered, and Nancy showed up behind him. She was in her robe. She stood taller than Matt, and sleepier. She looked blond and Swedish. Matt didn't know whether to be mad or glad. Then I got my story pieced together, and he really woke up.

"Dr. Jekyll has finally dealt with Mr. Hyde," he said in a low voice to Nancy. "Or maybe the other way around." To me, he said, "That may be a bad joke, but it's not ill meant." He went to get dressed. "Call Mike," he said to me. "Drunk or sober, I want him there."

Nancy showed me the phone. Then she went to the bedroom to talk with Matt. I could hear him soothing her fears. When Mike answered, he was sleepy and sober, but he woke up stampeding.

Deep night and a thin moon is a perfect time for ghosts, but none showed up as Matt rode with me back to the graveyard. The Chrysler loafed. There was no need for hurry.

I told Matt what I'd learned in Sheridan.

"That matches what I heard," he said, "and we have two mysteries. The first mystery is interesting, but it's no longer important. Was John Still pretending to be Jesse Still, or was Jesse pretending to be John?"

"If Jesse drove into the river in '53, then it has to be John." I didn't like what I said, because Jesse was real. The best actor in the world couldn't pretend that well. My sorrow choked me, but I wasn't ashamed.

Matt seemed to be thinking along the same lines. "We don't know how long the game went on," he said real quiet. "We never will know. John could have been playing at being Jesse way back in '53."

That got things tangled, and I felt resentful. Things were complicated enough. Me and Matt had just lost a friend, and now Matt was talking like that was the least interesting part.

"Makes no difference whether he was John or Jesse," I told Matt. "He was Jesse when he died. He's laying across the seat of Jesse's car. Figure it any way you want, but we're talking about Jesse."

273

"You're right," Matt said. "Also, you're wrong. We're talking about someone who was both." Matt sat quiet for a minute, figuring things out. I told myself it was just as well that he'd married a schoolteacher. "Assume, for the sake of argument," he said, "that John was playing Jesse in '53. John drove into the river, and people believed they were burying Jesse.

"Or, for the sake of argument, assume that it was Jesse in '53. In that case the game started with John's grief. Either way the game ran for many years." Matt was getting at something, but he always has to go roundabout.

"After years, John, or Jesse, disappeared. There was only a man who was both John and Jesse. That's the reason it makes no difference who died in '53."

Matt looked through the car window into the darkness like he expected to discover something important. "This is a long and lonesome country," he said. "The biggest mystery is: Why? The answer may lie in the mystery of twins, or it may be as simple as a man reaching into the past for happy memories. At any rate, one brother dies, and the survivor keeps his brother alive by living his brother's life, as well as his own. Think of the planning, the elaborate schemes, the near self-deception. Think of how often the roles shifted. A time must have arrived when that lonely man could not even remember who he was."

The answer was easy, and I saw it. Jesse, or John, chased the road to find something they'd lost on the road. They lost their parents and each other. I didn't say a damn word. Matt was making me mad, but I worked at forgiving him. He was handling his own grief, and maybe he didn't have a better way.

"And so he invented The Road Dog," Matt said. "That kept the personalities separate. The Road Dog was a metaphor to make him proud. Perhaps it might confuse some of the ladies, but there isn't a man ever born who wouldn't understand it."

I remembered long nights and long roads. I couldn't fault his reasoning.

"At the same time," Matt said, "the metaphor served the twins. They could play road games with the innocence of children, maybe even replay

274

memories of a time when their parents were alive and the world seemed warm. John played The Road Dog, and Jesse chased; and by God, so did the rest of us. It was a magnificent metaphor."

"If it was that blamed snappy," I said, "how come it fell to pieces? For the past year, it seems like Jesse's been running away from The Dog."

"The metaphor began to take over. The twins began to defend each other against each other," Matt said. "I've been watching it all along, but couldn't understand what was happening. John Still was trying to take over Jesse, and Jesse was trying to take over John."

"It worked for a long time," I said, "and then it didn't work. What's the kicker?"

"Our own belief," Matt said. "We all believed in The Road Dog. When all of us believed, John was forced to become stronger."

"And Jesse fought him off?"

"Successfully," Matt said. "All this year, when Jesse came firing out of town, rolling fifty miles, and firing back, I thought it was Jesse's problem. Now I see that John was trying to get free, get back on the road, and Jesse was dragging him back. This was a struggle between real men, maybe titans in the oldest sense, but certainly not imitations."

"It was a guy handling his problems."

"That's an easy answer. We can't know what went on with John," Matt said, "but we know some of what went on with Jesse. He tried to love a woman, Sarah, and failed. He lost his dogs—which doesn't sound like much, unless your dogs are all you have. Jesse fought defeat by building his other metaphor, which was that damned cemetery." Matt's voice got husky. He'd been holding in his sorrow, but his sorrow started coming through. It made me feel better about him.

"I think the cemetery was Jesse's way of answering John, or denying that he was vulnerable. He needed a symbol. He tried to protect his loves and couldn't. He couldn't even protect his love for his brother. That cemetery is the last bastion of Jesse's love." Matt looked like he was going to cry, and I felt the same.

"Cars can't hurt you," Matt said. "Only bad driving hurts you. The cemetery is a symbol for protecting one of the few loves you can protect. That's not saying anything bad about Jesse. That's saying something with sadness for all of us."

I slowed to pull onto Jesse's place. Mike's Olds sat by the trailer. Lights were on in the trailer, but no other lights showed anywhere.

"Men build all kinds of worlds in order to defeat fear and loneliness," Matt said. "We give all kinds of worlds in order to defeat fear and loneliness," Matt said. "We give and take as we build those worlds. One must wonder how much Jesse, and John, gave in order to take the little that they got."

We climbed from the Chrysler as autumn wind moved across the graveyard and felt its way toward my bones. The moon lighted faces of grave markers, but not enough that you could read them. Mike had the bulldozer warming up. It stood and puttered, and darkness felt best, and Mike knew it. The headlights were off. Far away on Highway 2, an engine wound tight and squalling, and it seemed like echoes of engines whispered among the graves. Mike stood huge as a grizzly.

"I've shot horses that looked healthier than you two guys," he said, but said it sort of husky.

Matt motioned toward the bulldozer. "This is illegal."

"Nobody ever claimed it wasn't." Mike was ready to fight if a fight was needed. "Anybody who don't like it can turn around and walk."

"I like it," Matt said. "It's fitting and proper. But if we're caught, there's hell to pay."

"I like most everything and everybody," Mike said, "except the government. They paw a man to death while he's alive, then keep pawing his corpse. I'm saving Jesse a little trouble."

"They like to know that he's dead and what killed him."

"Sorrow killed him," Mike said. "Let it go at that."

Jesse killed himself, timing his tiredness and starvation just right, but I was willing to let it go, and Matt was, too.

"We'll go along with you," Matt said. "But they'll sell this place for taxes. Somebody will start digging sometime."

"Not for years and years. It's deeded to me. Jesse fixed up papers. They're on the kitchen table." Mike turned toward the trailer. "We're going to do this right, and there's not much time."

We found a blanket and a quilt in the trailer. Mike opened a kitchen drawer and pulled out snapshots. Some looked pretty new, and some were faded: a man and woman in old-fashioned clothes, a picture of two young boys in Sunday suits, pictures of cars and road signs, and pictures of two women who were maybe Sue Ellen and Sarah. Mike piled them like a deck of cards, snapped a rubber band around them, and checked the trailer. He picked up a pair of pale yellow sunglasses that some racers use for night driving. "You guys see anything else?"

"His dogs," Matt said. "He had pictures of his dogs."

We found them under a pillow, and it didn't pay to think why they were there. Then we went to the Linc and wrapped Jesse real careful in the blanket. We spread the quilt over him, and laid his stuff on the floor beside the accelerator. Then Mike remembered something. He half-unwrapped Jesse, went through his pockets, then wrapped him back up. He took Jesse's keys and left them hanging in the ignition.

The three of us stood beside the Linc, and Matt cleared his throat.

"It's my place to say it," Mike told him. "This was my best friend." Mike took off his cap. Moonlight lay thin on his bald head.

"A lot of preachers will be glad this man is gone, and that's one good thing you can say for him. He drove nice people crazy. This man was a hellion, pure and simple; but what folks don't understand is, hellions have their place. They put everything on the line over nothing very much. Most guys worry so much about dying, they never do any living. Jesse was so alive with living, he never gave dying any thought. This man would roll ninety just to get to a bar before it closed." Mike kind of choked up and stopped to listen. From the graveyard came the echoes of engines, and from Highway 2 rose the thrum of a straight-eight crankshaft whipping in its bed. Dim light covered the graveyard, like a hundred sets of parking lights and not the moon.

"This man kept adventure alive, when, everyplace else, it's dying. There was nothing ever smug or safe about this man. If he had fears, he laughed. This man never hit a woman or crossed a friend. He did tie the can on Betty Lou one night, but can't be blamed. It was really The Dog who did that one. Jesse never had a problem until he climbed into that Studebaker."

So Mike had known all along. At least Mike knew something.

"I could always run even with Jesse," Mike said, "but I could never beat The Dog. The Dog could clear any track. And in a damn Studebaker."

"But a very swift Studebaker," Matt muttered, like a Holy Roller answering the preacher.

"Bored and stroked and rowdy," Mike said, "and you can say the same for Jesse. Let that be the final word. Amen."

IV

A little spark of flame dwelt at the stack of the dozer, and distant mountains lay white-capped and prophesied winter. Mike filled the graves quick. Matt got rakes and a shovel. I helped him mound the graves with only moonlight to go on, while Mike went to the trailer. He made coffee.

"Drink up and git," Mike told us when he poured the coffee. "Jesse's got some friends who need to visit, and it will be morning pretty quick."

"Let them," Matt said. "We're no hindrance."

"You're a smart man," Mike told Matt, "but your smartness makes you dumb. You started to hinder the night you stopped driving beyond your headlights." Mike didn't know how to say it kind, so he said it rough. His red mustache and bald head made him look like a pirate in a picture.

"You're saying that I'm getting old." Matt has known Mike long enough to not take offense.

"Me, too," Mike said, "but not that old. When you get old, you stop seeing them. Then you want to stop seeing them. You get afraid for your hide."

"You stop imagining?"

"Shitfire," Mike said. "You stop seeing. Imagination is something you use when you don't have eyes." He pulled a cigar out of his shirt pocket and was chewing it before he ever got it lit. "Ghosts have lost it all. Maybe they're the ones the Lord didn't love well enough. If you see them, but ain't one, maybe you're important."

Matt mulled that, and so did I. We've both wailed a lot of road for some sort of reason.

"They're kind of rough," Matt said about ghosts. "They hitch rides, but don't want 'em. I've stopped for them and got laughed at. They fool themselves, or maybe they don't."

"It's a young man's game," Mike said.

"It's a game guys got to play. Jesse played the whole deck. He was who he was, whenever he was it. That's the key. That's the reason you slug cops when you gotta. It looks like Jesse died old, but he lived young longer than most. That's the real mystery. How does a fella keep going?"

"Before we leave," I said, "how long did you know that Jesse was The Dog?"

"Maybe a year and a half. About the time he started running crazy."

"And never said a word?"

Mike looked at me like something you'd wipe off your boot. "Learn to ride your own fence," he told me. "It was Jesse's business." Then he felt sorry for being rough. "Besides," he said, "we were having fun. I expect that's all over now."

Matt followed me to the Chrysler. We left the cemetery, feeling tired and mournful. I shoved the car onto Highway 2, heading toward Matt's place.

"Wring it out once for old times?"

"Putter along," Matt said. "I just entered the putter stage of life, and may as well practice doing it."

In my mirrors a stream of headlights showed, then vanished one by one as cars turned into the graveyard. The moon had left the sky. Over toward South Dakota was a suggestion of first faint morning light. Mounded graves lay at my elbow, and so did Canada. On my left the road south ran fine and fast as a man can go. Mist rose from the roadside ditches, and maybe there was movement in the mist, maybe not.

There's little more to tell. Through fall and winter and spring and summer, I drove to Sheridan. The Mormon turned out to be a pretty good man, for a Mormon. I kept at it, and drove through another autumn and another winter. Linda got convinced. We got married in the spring, and I expected trouble. Married people are supposed to fight, but nothing like that ever happened. We just worked hard, got our own place in a few years, and Linda birthed two girls. That disappointed the Mormon, but was a relief to me.

And in those seasons of driving, when the roads were good for twenty miles an hour in the snow, or eighty under the sun, the road stood empty except for a couple times. Miss Molly showed up once early on to say a bridge was out. She might have showed up another time. Squinchy little taillights winked one night when it was late and I was highballing. Some guy jackknifed at Freightliner, and his trailer lay across the road.

But I saw no other ghosts. I'd like to say that I saw the twins, John and Jesse, standing by the road, giving the high sign or dancing, but it never happened.

I did think of Jesse, though, and thought of one more thing. If Matt was right, then I saw how Jesse had to die before I got home. He had to, because I believed in Road Dog. My belief would have been just enough to bring John forward, and that would have been fatal, too. If either one of them became too strong, they both of them lost. So Jesse had to do it.

The graveyard sank beneath the weather. Mike tended it for a while, but lost interest. Weather swept the mounds flat. Weed-covered markers tumbled to decay and dust, so that only one marble headstone stands solid beside Highway 2. The marker doesn't bend before the winter winds, nor does the little stone that me and Mike and Matt put there. It lays flat against the ground. You have to know where to look:

Road Dog
1931—1965
2 million miles, more or less
Run and run as fast as we can
We never can catch the Gingerbread Man

And now, even the great good cars are dead, or most of them. What with gas prices and wars and rumors of wars, the cars these days are all suspensions. They'll corner like a cat, but don't have the scratch of a cat; and maybe that's a good thing. The state posts fewer crosses.

Still, there are some howlers left out there, and some guys are still howling. I lie in bed of nights and listen to the scorch of engines along Highway 2. I heard them claw the darkness, stretching lonesome at the sky, scatting across the eternal land; younger guys running as young guys must; chasing each other, or chasing the land of dreams, or chasing into ghostland while hoping it ain't true—guys running into darkness chasing each other, or chasing something—chasing road.

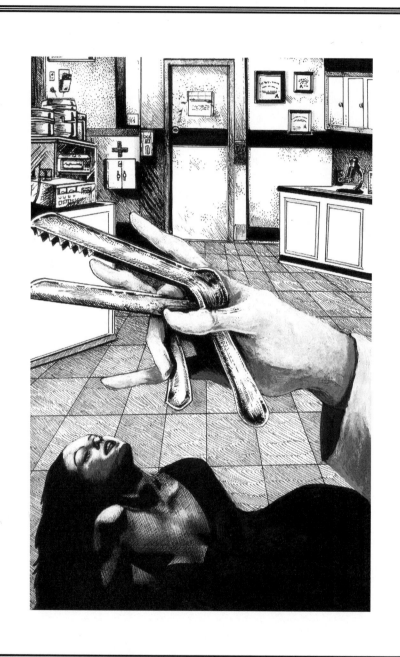

METALICA

P. D. Cacek

You wait in the cold white light, naked beneath the thin gown, knees pressed tightly together, hands clasped on your thighs. Waiting. Anticipating his touch and trembling as you remember the last time.

And the time before that.

And the time before that.

And the...

He enters, smiling, and the trembling stops. Everything stops except the working of your lungs and heart as you watch him close the door and walk toward you. The white light reflects off his gleaming flesh like diamonds.

His hands are cool as he places them over yours. Strong, capable of crushing you to a powder if he wants to. You begin to tremble again when he tells you to relax, that there's nothing to be afraid of.

He doesn't understand.

You tremble because he is with you again. And it's been so long since the last time. You can't relax for exactly the same reason.

You have been so long apart.

Lie back, he says, *and spread your legs*

And you do.

The trembling finally stops when he places a hand on your thigh and slides the gown out of the way.

"Ms. Dylan," the doctor said, nodding as he took her chart from its holder on the outside of the examination room door. "How do you do?"

He didn't know her from Adam...or, more correctly, from Eve. Not that he should, he'd never seen her before, didn't know anything about her except for those things she'd written down on the New Patient form. That was the way Kate liked it. Doctors weren't supposed to know you—not like the real people you had to deal with every day of your life. They existed only when you needed them and faded away when you didn't.

Kate smiled, and returned his nod.

"Just fine, Doctor."

"Good." He studied the form, his head doing little bobbing jerks. It reminded Kate of the way a pigeon's head moved when it walked. "So...you must be new to this area."

It was amazing how they always asked the same questions.

Accepted the same lies as answers.

"No. No, I've lived here almost all my life, but my regular doctor's office is becoming an HMO and..."

The doctor nodded, accepting the plausible lie. Shrugging, Kate made a great show of keeping the front of the disposable gown closed while at the same time smoothing down the thin paper sheet that covered her lower half. Her palms were already sweating.

And the doctor noticed.

"There's nothing to be nervous about," he said gently, fatherly, although Kate guessed he couldn't have been more than five years older than her own twenty-six years. "Finding a new doctor is probably one of the hardest things a person can do...and I should think it would be even more difficult for a woman. Sorry, I didn't mean to come off sounding like a politically incorrect poker just then."

Kate shrugged again and accidentally let the front of the gown gape open momentarily. It wasn't her job to tell him he was full of shit, even though he was. And not in it alone. Every new doctor she'd ever gone to voiced the same sentiment, as if lying naked with your legs spread while a strange man fiddled around was the worst thing a woman could suffer.

Jesus, it wasn't like they were *dating* or anything.

Kate noticed him chuckling and echoed it.

"But I can assure you I have never seriously injured anyone during a routine Pap smear," he went on. "Unless you consider that night watchman who happened to be bending over and...well, never mind. Besides that was before I got my astigmatism corrected."

This time Kate chuckled in earnest. He was funny! It was a shame she would never see him again.

"Thanks," she said. "I needed that."

Which was a lie. She didn't need that; she didn't need anything except the item he had just joked about...one of which was lying beneath the sterile drape on a tray directly across from her. A young nurse had brought it when she came to take Kate's temperature and blood pressure. Kate had convinced the woman the elevated readings were due to nerves.

"Okay, then," the doctor said, walking back to the door and opening it. "Let me just get a nurse in here and we can start. Now, why don't you lie back and relax?"

Kate swung her legs onto the table and lay back, but relaxing was out of the question. Her heart was pounding so hard she was surprised the doctor hadn't noticed. Keeping her eyes trained on the moronic poster of a smiling tabby kitten someone had taped to the ceiling at waist level so that it would be directly overhead during the pelvic exam, Kate heard the nurse's rubber-soled shoes squeak into the room at the same time a tap was turned on somewhere to her left.

The nurse who had taken her temperature appeared in Kate's periphery—as moral support and subpoenable witness should the matter of sexual misconduct be raised.

Kate took a deep breath and held it as the doctor threw back the gown's lapels to squeeze, poke, prod, and manipulate her breasts. His hands were warm and doughy.

"Fine," he muttered, first to one breast then the other. "Good. Any tenderness?"

"Only during my period," she answered automatically, realizing he would hear her only if she mentioned something negative.

"Fine. Good. Okay, this part's done."

He folded the gown back together, being very careful not to touch the same flesh he had, only a moment before, kneaded like clay, and accepted a white paper packet from the nurse. The words "Gloves, surgical—one pair" were printed along the side the doctor tore open.

"...ease."

"Excuse me?" Blinking, Kate glanced at the nurse and saw the reverse-color image of the kitten superimposed across her face. "I'm sorry, I didn't hear you."

"Scoot to the end of the table, please," she repeated—efficiently, effectively, and professionally detached as she extended the gynecological stirrups and positioned Kate's stocking feet in them. "There are hand grips on both sides of the table if you'd like something to hold on to."

Kate mumbled her thanks. At least she thought she did. She wasn't sure and didn't really care if she had or not. The doctor was smiling at her over the paper sheet covering her raised knees; one gloved hand already moving toward the hem.

"Okay, then. Spread your knees a little wider and try to relax. This won't hurt."

Kate caught her breath as the sheet fell back.

You gasp without thinking, raising your hips to meet him as he parts the tender folds of flesh and plunges into you. He is hard and cold as if he's been racing naked through freezing rain.

But that doesn't matter because at last you're together again.

The days and weeks of separation fade like a bad dream when you feel him grow...filling the emptiness inside you.

i'm here now...relax

You close your eyes and feel him begin to move—gentle, furtive strokes that you're not even sure you feel, not at first. Moaning, you wrap your legs around him and pull him closer until you're sure...until you can feel the hard knob of his cock against your cervix.

But now he knows what you're doing. He punishes you by stopping.

God, he can be so cruel.

It's the thing you love most about him.

are you alright? he asks, laughter in his voice.

You don't answer...wouldn't even if you had breath enough to form the words.

He teases you with his stillness until you open your eyes, until you succumb to the game he's playing. He smiles at the same time he thrusts forward...laughs when you whimper.

that's what happens to bad little girls, katie
and you're such a bad, bad girl
what am I going to do with you, katie
tell me

"Tell me if there's any discomfort," the doctor said, his voice muffled by the paper barrier between them. "But I have to say I don't think I've ever had a more relaxed patient. Just a couple more swabs and we should be all done. Nurse, may I have a slide, please?"

The woman left her position at the table long enough to get the sterile wafer of glass the doctor had asked for.

"Okay, Ms. Dylan, you may feel a little prick..."

your prick's not that *little,* you gasp, afraid for a moment until you hear him laugh...feel the vibrations of that laugh through his cock.

He's not little at all.

Unwrapping your legs from his waist, he grips them just below the knees and holds them apart. You reach out to him, caress his face, and he

287

takes your finger into his mouth, sucks greedily as he begins again to move.

Slowly.

Steadily.

The bones of his hips pummelling the backs of your thighs as he begins to move faster...faster...his hard flesh melting with yours...faster...harder...slamming himself against the closed door of your womb...

Closed and sealed forever, you told him. No babies to tear the door off the hinges and make the tight flesh he loves go loose.

No babies to take his place.

He bites down on your finger as if he can feel the orgasm building inside you. Head tipping back against the clean white sheet, you suck air into your already bursting lungs and taste salt on your lips.

i'm almost there don't stop don't

"Almost finished," the doctor said. Kate's eyes popped open. "But I think we can make you a little more comfortable in the meantime."

The doctor released the speculum's lock, and the pressure in Kate's vagina instantly vanished.

No!

"Better?" he asked and, without waiting for an answer, handed the closed speculum, its chrome dulled by Kate's cooling juices, to the nurse as he stood up between his patient's parted legs. "Now, compared to the last bit, this should be a snap. Just relax."

Kate closed her eyes before the nurse dropped the speculum into the sterilizing bath.

don't worry, he tells you as he pulls back...pulls out, gently lowers your legs to the bed. *I won't leave you like this*

His fingers slip easily into the place just vacated by his cock, but it isn't the same...never the same and never as good.

288

why do you always do this to me?

you know why, katie, he answers, fingers caressing her from the inside.
they won't let me stay long enough to finish you the right way.

and i want to, katie

i really want to

i hate them, you tell him, closing your eyes when you see your own
pain reflected in the polished metal of his face.

i know, katie

i know

but maybe someday

maybe

And you shush him, not wanting to hear the promises of a future that
can never come true and focus all your attention on the slippery, silken
touch of his fingers. He's good. A knuckle brushes against your clitoris and
you jump.

oops, he teases, *sorry*

just try to—

⚍⚌

"...relax, Ms. Dylan, are you okay? You jumped. Did I hurt you?"

"N-no, Doctor," Kate said from behind her closed eyelids. "Sorry, I-I
just had a toe cramp."

"Oh, okay, I just wanted to make sure *I* didn't hurt you. Hang in there
for a few more seconds... We're...almost...finished. O...kay, now if you'll
take a deep breath and..."

let it come, katie

let it come.

Your body jerks uncontrollably, plunging into the icy waves that sweep
up over your legs...your belly...your breasts...

Gasping for breath you arch your back, pivoting your back off the thin

289

mattress with only your shoulders, thrusting your hips against his questing fingers.

Hot and cold—fire and ice—you feel him growing warmer, incandescent as the orgasm builds.

Peaks.

Crashes down over you.

You shriek.

Exhaling slowly, Kate opened her eyes and smiled. She could hear the sound of her scream still vibrating off the room's disinfected walls and postpartum decor.

The giggle burst from her before she had a chance to stop it. The doctor was just standing there with his mouth hanging open and his fingers still crammed into her snatch, looking much less tanned than she remembered.

"You can let go now," she said, pointing between her legs. He looked down and faded another degree. Kate shivered when he finally pulled out.

"Sorry."

She didn't look at him until she'd scooted her rump fully back onto the table and pulled her feet out of the stirrups. No man liked to be laughed at after the fact. Sitting up slowly, Kate tucked one side of the gown over the other and made sure that nothing was showing from the waist down either.

The show of modesty seemed to help the doctor recover some, if not all, of his composure. By the time she looked up, he'd disposed of the gloves and washed his hands, and his tan was back to full color.

"That's all right. Nothing to be embarrassed about." He spoke so quickly it took a minute for Kate to separate the words from the supposed sentiment. "Um, okay. All finished, ah...we'll have the results of your Pap smear back from the lab in three days, so you can call the office then and get the results. Okay."

He didn't move, and Kate didn't answer.

"Okay. Get dressed and, um, if you won't mind stopping by my office before you leave? Ah, I always, um, like to, ah, talk with my new patients. Just getting acquainted.... You don't mind, do you?"

Kate looked long and hard at her wristwatch, making a point. In truth, the office didn't expect her back for another forty-five minutes, but she didn't want *him* to think she was easy.

"Uh, no. But I—"

"Great, no more than fifteen minutes. Tops," the doctor promised quickly. "Okay, then, uh, my office is straight down the corridor, last door on the right. I'll be waiting."

He didn't so much leave the examination room as flee. This time Kate was able to catch the giggle before it got away.

"Must be a busy man," she said to the nurse.

The woman didn't look amused.

You sigh and feel it quiver all the way down to your groin. Sighing again, you pull your clothes around you, suddenly cold, and stare at the closed door.

When you close your eyes you can hear the echoes of the promise he made...always makes even though you both know it can never be kept.

one day, he promised, *one day i won't have to go and we'll be together always*

One day.

i love you, the echoes say, even though neither of you has ever said that to the other.

The blank door mocks you, but you lift your chin and touch the moist flesh between your legs. The warm softness of your finger feels almost strange after his cool hardness, but you adapt.

Closing your eyes and spreading your legs, you pretend it's his hand stroking you...making you tremble.

Your clothes fall away as ice and fire sweep through your body, and in the fading echoes you hear him call out to you.

"Ah, Ms. Dylan, please come in. Take a seat." Back to normal and smiling, the doctor gestured to the pair of low-back chairs in front of his desk, then swept the air in a wide arch. "My inner sanctum, so to speak."

Kate looked around the cracker-box-sized office and nodded. The overall effect, with its white painted walls, acoustical-tile ceiling, framed kitten prints, and dark furnishings, was similar to that of the examination room. Only less comfortable.

"It's very nice," she said and took the chair closest to the door. If the nurse hadn't been standing in the hall when she finally came out of the examining room (panting shallowly), Kate would have paid her bill and been halfway to work already. "I like the cat pictures."

"Thank you. Yes, most of my patients like them." He nodded and followed the visual path Kate had just taken. When his gaze finally came back to her, his eyes were cold. "But then, you're not really my patient, are you, Ms. Dylan?"

Kate crossed one leg over the other. The post-orgasmic tingle was almost gone. She sighed before answering.

"Well, I filled out all that paperwork when I came in, and the physician's referral service I talked to gave you an excellent recommenda—"

"You should have checked the service's fine print, Ms. Dylan. Then you would have found out that they also produce a list *for* physicians. Its main purpose originally was to prevent one doctor from accidentally infringing on another doctor's patient. However, with the growing problem of substance abuse, especially in prescribed medicines, all a doctor has to do, if he or she suspects that a patient is obtaining multiple prescriptions..."

Leaning back, the doctor picked up a thick sheaf of fanfold computer printouts and flapped it at her. "I hadn't intended to pry into this particular...area of your private life, Ms. Dylan, you have to believe me."

"Then what *were* you trying to pry into, Doctor?"

His tan took on a rosy glow. "Your...reaction in the examination room startled me, and I swear I was only curious to see if you were under another doctor's care. There have been cases where some women who, after experiencing an orgasm during a pelvic exam, make appointments with new doctors to reassure themselves that what they...that their arousal was not caused by an unconscious desire for their primary gynecologist.

"But you, Ms. Dylan...Jesus, I don't know whether to applaud your energy or your stamina. If the printout is accurate, you're seeing twelve gynecologists on a monthly basis, and you've had non-repeat visits with fifty-three others."

He dropped the printout on the desk and laid one hand over it. The gesture gave Kate the impression of a cleric about to offer a blessing.

"Ms. Dylan, a pelvic exam once a year is all a healthy woman needs. Unless there's a problem or, for example, during pregnancy when more frequent exams are required, then..."

Kate derailed his train of thought by gasping out the litany that had served her many times before when one of her many gynecological studs began sticking his professionalism in places where it didn't belong. Terms like "cervical polyps," "precancerous conditions," "fibroid tumors," "hysterectomies," and "familial traits" fell from her lips like the names of the blessed saints.

Amen.

When she stopped, her mouth was drier than her panties.

Praise the Lord.

The doctor didn't look any more convinced than when she started.

"I can understand your concern, Ms. Dylan, and I have to warn you that I noticed scarring along the vaginal wall and a pronounced thickening of the cervix. Until I get the results back from the lab, I can't rule out the possibility that these may be indications of some specific pathology, but now that I'm aware of the number of exams you subject your body to, I can only assume..."

Yaddah, yaddah, yaddah. Kate glanced down at her watch and really checked the time. Unless he shut up within the next five minutes she wouldn't be able to get in a quick once-over rub in the ladies' room before having to turn back into a worker bee.

"...thought about seeking professional help for your problem?"

Kate stood up so slowly she could hear the bones realign themselves along her spine.

"Just what are you implying, Doctor?" she asked, letting the tone of her voice allude to the fact that if he answered she'd make sure the only beavers he'd see from that point on would be in the zoo.

He took the hint. "Nothing! I'm only suggesting that you might want to talk to...someone about...this."

"I don't think so," Kate said as she walked to the door. Hand on knob, she turned and gave him a look she generally saved for gropers on the bus. "Besides, I don't see anything wrong with a woman trying to stay healthy. Do you?"

Steepling his fingers, the doctor placed them over his lips and frowned.

"Of course not, Ms. Dylan, but tell me, have you ever had a *normal* sexual experience?"

Kate smiled, twisting the knob but keeping the door momentarily closed. He had more balls than her usual stable of metal-wielding studs.

"By that I take it you mean with a man?"

"Yes," he answered, "with a man."

You watch the patterns in the ceiling change shape, trying to make out shapes the way you used to see images in the clouds when you were a child—trying because it's easier than thinking about what he's doing.

If he'd just let you turn off the lights it might be all right, but he wants to *see* you and that means you can see him.

But you don't want to, so you look for shapes in the ceiling while he grunts and sweats and pushes back and forth, in and out of you.

God, you wish it was over.

Making love—it sounded so wonderful, and the touching was nice.

You liked that. The feel of his hands and lips on your naked flesh as you both undressed sent shivers into places you were never supposed to touch or even think about.

Yes, you tell yourself, *that* was nice.

And you really didn't even mind the pain when he parted your legs and crammed himself inside you. You still don't mind...not really...but you wish he would hurry up and finish.

So you watch the patterns in the ceiling and pretend you see a man riding a unicorn.

⌗

Kate opened the door and stepped into the hallway.

"Of course I have, Doctor," she said.

Kate cocked her head to one side and smiled at her own lopsided, elongated reflection in the curved metal. It was lying still and cool in her hands but part of her couldn't believe she'd taken it. An even bigger part didn't know *why* she'd taken it. Impulse? Maybe. Or maybe it was the doctor's final, insulting remark...as if she were some sort of sexual psycho or something.

Or maybe she'd finally decided to take matters into her own hands.

So to speak.

Kate laughed and hugged the cool metal to her breasts. It'd been so easy. A quick "Oops, I think I left something in the examination room"— and it was hers.

All hers.

She'd been lucky, just managing to get it into her purse before the next patient—a young woman with baby-swollen belly and milk-swollen breasts—waddled in.

Sorrys were exchanged, the payment for her visit made in cash, and Kate fled into the waning afternoon light.

"All mine," she whispered to it softly. Then a darker thought occurred. "At least I hope you're mine."

There'd been a total of three specula drowning in the purple sterilizing bath when she lifted the lid and they all looked alike—stainless-steel peas in a sanitized pod. Kate had played "eenie-meenie-mynie" then picked the topmost one, figuring it was most probably hers.

"Not that it really matters," she cooed to it. "I think we both could do with a nice hot bath. Then when we're all dry we can..."

Kate watched the blush spread across her flattened reflection and blew it a kiss. She'd phoned the office from the lobby of the Medical Arts Building, complaining about cramps and minor bleeding caused by a misguided vaginal swab and noting the lateness of the hour. "I thought I'd be done by now, but he poked me a little too hard, and..."

Sympathy poured through the phone line, that and a promise from the office gossip to tell "everyone" about "the bastard."

The perfect end to a perfect day. Well...not quite the end. Not yet.

Kate ran a thumb along the speculum's side until she came to the dilation wheel at the end. The size of a quarter, its edge had been scored for better traction, and just touching it made Kate's blood run hot and cold.

Fire and ice.

A drop of fluid that had somehow avoided capture by the discarded tissues and gum wrappers in her purse fell onto Kate's thumb like an amethyst tear.

Shivering, Kate wiped the drop into her skin.

"Definitely a bath first," she whispered.

Once at home, Kate laid the speculum back across her palms and carried it to the kitchen. She'd filled and set the spaghetti cooker on to boil a moment after she closed and locked her apartment door. The water was boiling—white, steam-filled bubbles churning the surface.

She'd decided against adding salt or vinegar. She preferred her lovers natural.

Taking a pair of rubber-handled tongs from the utensil drawer, Kate gently gripped the speculum just below its calibrated hinge, being careful not to scratch the mirror-smooth surface, and lowered it slowly into the steaming bath.

Thirty minutes, she decided, would be enough to kill anything that might have contaminated it. Besides, it had been soaking in a sterile solution when she liberated it. Boiling it now was just an added precaution, mostly to remove the lint and germs it might have picked up in her purse... and whatever trace remained of the other women who might have used it.

Kate watched the boiling water for another minute before heading for the bathroom. A quick shower and shampoo—maybe a little hand job to get the ball rolling—and she'd feel like a new woman.

A very horny new woman.

Fifteen minutes later she was beyond even that. Not even her usual method of tension release—for those times when she wasn't able to get to a doctor—brought any relief. Back pressed against the shower wall and standing on tiptoe, Kate had pulled the outer lips of her vagina apart until they throbbed and taken the full force of the shower's "massage" pulse right on the clit without getting so much as a warm glow.

The only chill she got was when the water went cold.

"Dammit to hell!"

It was as if her body had suddenly turned against her. Either that or it knew what it wanted and wouldn't settle for anything else.

Turning off the water, Kate patted the damp ringlets between her legs and stepped from the shower. She didn't bother drying off or throwing on a robe before hurrying to the kitchen. There was no need, her lover had already seen her naked...and wet...hundreds of times before.

He was waiting for her, a smile on his dolphinlike lips, as she reached over him to turn off the stove.

Using a dish towel as a makeshift pot holder, Kate carried the steaming pot to the sink and turned on the cold water tap. The exposed metal sizzled for only a few seconds.

While she waited for her lover to finish soaking, Kate rinsed off a wooden chopstick she'd gotten with a take-out order of kung-pao chicken and began wrapping one end in Saran Wrap. The chopstick was longer than the cotton swabs the doctors used. Sturdier, too. He would like that.

Her fingers shook as she worked the plastic into a knob the size of a golf ball.

He'd like *that* most of all.

You close your eyes and spread your legs, clutching him as he enters you.

He's warm, almost hot, and that startles you because your body remembers all the other times when he was so cold...so very cold.

Fire and ice.

because i'm yours now, he whispers, lying still, warm and hard between your legs.

only yours

And you answer, *yes*

only mine

You curl forward slightly and feel him grow, swell until he squeezes all the emptiness from you. Your internal flesh bruises and you whimper, but you don't ask him to stop because this is what you've longed for.

i love you, one of you whispers.

Smiling, knees spread so wide they tremble from strain instead of passion, toes curling into the bed's silken throw, you take a deep breath and nod.

please

you're ready? he asks.

And you answer without words, push his massive shaft further in and bite your lips to keep from crying out as your lovemaking begins in earnest.

i love you

This time there are to be no timid strokes. No teasing. No stopping. Red-tinted ecstasy dribbles from between your legs as he finally breaks down the door you've held closed for so long.

there'll be no babies, he promises you.

nothing to come between you and me
i love you
Pain-and-joy. Fire-and-ice.

You cry out, urging him on...driving him deeper and deeper until you miscalculate and he slips from your fingers...disappears into the cave of your flesh...his flesh becoming your flesh...your flesh swallowing him whole.

painandjoy fireandice

Ice-hot he comes before you, the sticky wash gushing from between your legs and spraying red hearts across the bed.

fireandice pain and joy

Groaning, your body heaves in agony, in ecstasy, as you come and come again, each orgasm building on the last until...until...

He comes again, you know he does, and your mixed juices flow from you in a crimson tide.

You curve your mouth into a dolphinlike smile and thumb the wheel on your jaw, opening your mouth so the sound of your love can fly free.

You're not surprised that it sounds like ice striking metal.

Shuddering, suddenly cold, you watch the bright white light darken and wait for the echoes to fade.

i

lov

...

ORANGE IS FOR ANGUISH, BLUE IS FOR INSANITY

DAVID MORRELL

VAN DORN'S WORK WAS controversial, of course. The scandal his paintings caused among Parisian artists in the late 1800s provided the stuff of legend. Disdaining conventions, thrusting beyond accepted theories, Van Dorn seized upon the essentials of the craft to which he'd devoted his soul. Color, design, and texture. With those principles in mind, he created portraits and landscapes so different, so innovative, that their subjects seemed merely an excuse for Van Dorn to put paint onto canvas. His brilliant colors, applied in passionate splotches and swirls, often so thick that they projected an eighth of an inch from the canvas in the manner of a bas-relief, so dominated the viewer's perception that the person or scene depicted seemed secondary to technique.

Impressionism, the prevailing avant-garde theory of the late 1800s, imitated as blurs. Van Dorn went one step further and so emphasized the lack of distinction among objects that they seemed to melt together, to merge into an interconnected, pantheistic universe of color. The branches of a Van Dorn tree became ectoplasmic tentacles, thrusting toward the sky and the grass, just as tentacles from the sky and grass thrust toward the tree, all melding into a radiant swirl. He seemed to address himself not to the illusions of light but to reality itself, or at least to his theory of it. The tree *is* the sky, his technique asserted. The grass is the tree, and the sky the grass. All is one.

Van Dorn's approach proved so unpopular among theorists of his time that he frequently couldn't buy a meal in exchange for a canvas upon which he'd labored for months. His frustration produced a nervous breakdown. His self-mutilation shocked and alienated such onetime friends as Cézanne and Gauguin. He died in squalor and obscurity. Not until the 1920s, thirty years after his death, were his paintings recognized for the genius they displayed. In the 1940s, his soul-tortured character became the subject of a best-selling novel, and in the 1950s a Hollywood spectacular. These days, of course, even the least of his efforts can't be purchased for less than three million dollars.

Ah, art.

It started with Myers and his meeting with Professor Stuyvesant. "He agreed...reluctantly."

"I'm surprised he agreed at all," I said. "Stuyvesant hates Postimpressionism and Van Dorn in particular. Why didn't you ask someone easy, like Old Man Bradford?"

"Because Bradford's academic reputation sucks. I can't see writing a dissertation if it won't be published, and a respected dissertation director can make an editor pay attention. Besides, if I can convince Stuyvesant, I can convince anyone."

"Convince him of...?"

"That's what Stuyvesant wanted to know," Myers said.

I remember that moment vividly, the way Myers straightened his lanky body, pushed his glasses close to his eyes, and frowned so hard that his curly red hair scrunched forward on his brow.

"Stuyvesant asked, even disallowing his own disinclination toward Van Dorn—God, the way that pompous asshole talks—why would I want to spend a year of my life writing about an artist who'd been the subject of countless books and articles, whose ramifications had been exhausted? Why not choose an obscure but promising Neo-Expressionist and gamble that *my* reputation would rise with his? Naturally the artist he recommended was one of Stuyvesant's favourites."

"Naturally," I said. "If he named the artist I think he did..."

Myers mentioned the name.

I nodded. "Stuyvesant's been collecting him for the past five years. He hopes the resale value of the paintings will buy him a town house in London when he retires. So what did you tell him?"

Myers opened his mouth to answer, then hesitated. With a brooding look, he turned toward a print of Van Dorn's swirling *Cypresses in a Hollow,* which hung beside a ceiling-high bookshelf crammed with Van Dorn biographies, analyses, and bound collections of reproductions. He didn't speak for a moment, as if the sight of the familiar print—its facsimile colors incapable of matching the brilliant tones of the original, its manufacturing process unable to recreate the exquisite texture of raised, swirled layers of paint on canvas—still took his breath away.

"So what did you tell him?" I asked again.

Myers exhaled with a mixture of frustration and admiration. "I said, what the critics wrote about Van Dorn was mostly junk. He agreed, with the implication that the paintings invited no less. I said, even the gifted critics hadn't probed to Van Dorn's essence. They were missing something crucial."

"Which is?"

"Exactly Stuyvesant's next question. You know how he keeps relighting his pipe when he gets impatient. I had to talk fast. I told him I didn't know what I was looking for, but there's something"—Myers gestured toward the print—"something there. Something nobody's noticed. Van Dorn hinted as much in his diary. I don't know what it is, but I'm convinced his paintings hide a secret." Myers glanced at me.

I raised my eyebrows.

"Well, if nobody's noticed," Myers said, "it *must* be a secret, right?"

"But if *you* haven't noticed..."

Compelled, Myers turned toward the print again, his tone filled with wonder. "How do I know it's there? Because when I look at Van Dorn's paintings, I *sense* it. I *feel* it."

I shook my head. "I can imagine what Stuyvesant said to that. The man deals with art as if it's geometry, and there aren't any secrets in—"

"What he said was, if I'm becoming a mystic, I ought to be in the School of Religion, not Art. But if I wanted enough rope to hang myself and strangle my career, he'd give it to me. He liked to believe he had an open mind, he said."

"That's a laugh."

"Believe me, he wasn't joking. He had a fondness for Sherlock Holmes, he said. If I thought I'd found a mystery and could solve it, by all means do so. And at that, he gave me his most condescending smile and said he would mention it at today's faculty meeting."

"So what's the problem? You got what you wanted. He agreed to direct your dissertation. Why do you sound so—?"

"Today there *wasn't* any faculty meeting."

"Oh," I said. "You're fucked."

Myers and I had started graduate school at Iowa together. That had been three years earlier, and we'd formed a strong enough friendship to rent adjacent rooms in an old apartment building near campus. The spinster who owned it had a hobby of doing watercolors—she had no talent, I might add—and rented only to art students so they would give her lessons. In Myers' case, she'd made an exception. He wasn't a painter, as I was. He was an art historian. Most painters work instinctively. They're not skilled at verbalizing what they want to accomplish. But words and not pigment were Myers' specialty. His impromptu lectures had quickly made him the old lady's favourite tenant.

After that day, however, she didn't see much of him. Nor did I. He wasn't at the classes we took together. I assumed he spent most of his time at the library. Late at night, when I noticed a light beneath his door and knocked, I didn't get an answer. I phoned him. Through the wall I heard the persistent, muffled ringing.

One evening I let the phone ring eleven times and was just about to hang up when he answered. He sounded exhausted.

"You're getting to be a stranger," I said.

His voice was puzzled. "Stranger? But I just saw you a couple of days ago."

"You mean, two weeks ago."

"Oh, shit," he said.

"I've got a six-pack. You want to—?"

"Yeah, I'd like that." He sighed. "Come over."

When he opened his door, I don't know what startled me more, the way Myers looked or what he'd done to his apartment.

I'll start with Myers. He'd always been thin, but now he looked gaunt, emaciated. His shirt and jeans were rumpled. His red hair was matted. Behind his glasses, his eyes looked bloodshot. He hadn't shaved. When he closed the door and reached for a beer, his hand shook.

His apartment was filled with, covered with—I'm not sure how to convey the dismaying effect of so much brilliant clutter—Van Dorn prints. On every inch of the walls. The sofa, the chairs, the desk, the TV, the bookshelves. And the drapes, and the ceiling, and, except for a narrow path, the floor. Swirling sunflowers, olive trees, meadows, skies, and streams surrounded me, encompassed me, seemed to reach out for me. At the same time I felt swallowed. Just as the blurred edges of objects within each print seemed to melt into one another, so each print melted into the next. I was speechless amid the chaos of color.

Myers took several deep gulps of beer. Embarrassed by my stunned reaction to the room, he gestured toward the vortex prints. "I guess you could say I'm immersing myself in my work."

"When did you eat last?"

He looked confused.

"That's what I thought." I walked along the narrow path among the prints on the floor and picked up the phone. "The pizza's on me." I ordered the largest supreme the nearest Pepi's had to offer. They didn't deliver beer, but I had another six-pack in my fridge, and I had a feeling we'd be needing it.

I set down the phone. "Myers, what the hell are you doing?"

"I told you..."

"Immersing yourself? Give me a break. You're cutting classes. You haven't showered in God knows how long. You look like shit. Your deal with Stuyvesant isn't worth destroying your health. Tell him you've changed your mind. Get another, an *easier*, dissertation director."

"Stuyvesant's got nothing to do with this."

"Dammit, what *does* it have to do with? The end of comprehensive exams, the start of dissertation blues?"

Myers gulped the rest of his beer and reached for another can. "No, blue is for insanity."

"*What?*"

"That's the pattern." Myers turned toward the swirling prints. "I studied them chronologically. The more Van Dorn became insane, the more he used blue. And orange is his color of anguish. If you match the painting with the personal crises described in his biographies, you see a correspondent use of orange."

"Myers, you're the best friend I've got. So forgive me for saying I think you're off the deep end."

He swallowed more beer and shrugged as if to say he didn't expect me to understand.

"Listen," I said. "A personal color code, a connection between emotion and pigment, that's bullshit. I should know. You're the historian, but I'm the painter. I'm telling you, different people react to colors in different ways. Never mind the advertising agencies and their theories that some colors sell products more than others. It all depends on context. It depends on fashion. This year's 'in' color is next year's 'out.' But an honest-to-God great painter uses whatever color will give him the greatest effect. He's interested in creation, not selling."

"Van Dorn could have used a few sales."

"No question. The poor bastard didn't live long enough to come into fashion. But orange is for anguish and blue means insanity? Tell that to Stuyvesant and he'll throw you out of his office."

Myers took off his glasses and rubbed the bridge of his nose. "I feel so... maybe you're right."

306

"There's no maybe about it. I *am* right. You need food, a shower, and sleep. A painting's a combination of color and shape that people either like or they don't. The artist follows his instincts, uses whatever techniques he can master, and does his best. But if there's a secret in Van Dorn's work, it isn't a color code."

Myers finished his second beer and blinked in distress. "You know what I found out yesterday?"

I shook my head.

"The critics who devoted themselves to analyzing Van Dorn..."

"What about them?"

"They went insane, the same as he did."

"*What?* No way. I've studied Van Dorn's critics. They're as conventional and boring as Stuyvesant."

"You mean, the mainstream scholars. The safe ones. I'm talking about the truly brilliant ones. The ones who haven't been recognized for their genius, just as Van Dorn wasn't recognized."

"What happened to them?"

"They suffered. The same as Van Dorn."

"They were put in an asylum?"

"Worse than that."

"Myers, don't make me ask."

"The parallels are amazing. They each tried to paint. In Van Dorn's style. And just like Van Dorn, they stabbed out their eyes."

I guess it's obvious by now—Myers was what you might call "high-strung." No negative judgment intended. In fact, his excitability was one of the reasons I liked him. That and his imagination. Hanging around with him was never dull. He loved ideas. Learning was his passion. And he passed his excitement on to me.

The truth is, I needed all the inspiration I could get. I wasn't a bad artist. Not at all. On the other hand, I wasn't a great one, either. As I neared the end of grad school, I'd painfully come to realize that my work never would be more than "interesting." I didn't want to admit it, but I'd probably end up as a commercial artist in an advertising agency.

That night, however, Myers' imagination wasn't inspiring. It was scary. He was always going through phases of enthusiasm. El Greco, Picasso, Pollock. Each had preoccupied him to the point of obsession, only to be abandoned for another favourite and another. When he'd fixated on Van Dorn, I'd assumed it was merely one more infatuation.

But the chaos of Van Dorn prints in his room made clear he'd reached a greater excess of compulsion. I was sceptical about his insistence that there was a secret in Van Dorn's work. After all, great art can't be explained. You can analyze its technique, you can diagram its symmetry, but ultimately there's a mystery words can't communicate. Genius can't be summarized. As far as I could tell, Myers had been using the word *secret* as a synonym for indescribable brilliance.

When I realized he literally meant that Van Dorn had a secret, I was appalled. The distress in his eyes was equally appalling. His references to insanity, not only in Van Dorn but in his critics, made me worry that Myers himself was having a breakdown. Stabbed out their eyes, for Christ's sake?

I stayed up with Myers till five A.M., trying to calm him, to convince him he needed a few days to rest. We finished the six-pack I'd bought from an art student down the hall. At dawn, just before Myers dozed off and I staggered back to my room, he murmured that I was right. He needed a break, he said. Tomorrow he'd call his folks. He'd ask if they'd pay his plane fare back to Denver.

Hungover, I didn't wake up till late afternoon. Disgusted that I'd missed my classes, I showered and managed to ignore the taste of last night's pizza. He probably felt as shitty as I did. But after sunset, when I called again, then knocked on his door, I started to worry. His door was locked, so I went downstairs to get the landlady's key. That's when I saw the note in my mail slot.

Meant what I said. Need a break. Went home. Will be in touch. Stay cool. Paint well. I love you, pal. Your friend forever,
Myers

My throat ached. He never came back. I saw him only twice after that. Once in New York, and once in...

Let's talk about New York. I finished my graduate project, a series of landscapes that celebrated Iowa's big-sky rolling, dark-soiled, wooded hills. A local patron paid fifty dollars for one of them. I gave three to the university's hospital. The rest are who knows where.

Too much has happened.

As I predicted, the world wasn't waiting for my good-but-not-great efforts. I ended where I belonged, as a commercial artist for a Madison Avenue advertising agency. My beer cans are the best in the business.

I met a smart, attractive woman who worked in the marketing department of a cosmetics firm. One of my agency's clients. Professional conferences led to personal dinners and intimate evenings that lasted all night. I proposed. She agreed.

We'd live in Connecticut, she said. Of course.

When the time was right, we might have children, she said.

Of course.

Myers phoned me at the office. I don't know how he knew where I was. I remembered his breathless voice.

"I found it," he said.

"Myers?" I grinned. "Is it really—? *How are you? Where have—?*"

"I'm telling you. I found it!"

"I don't know what you're—"

"Remember? Van Dorn's secret!"

In a rush, I did remember—the excitement Myers could generate, the wonderful, expectant conversations of my youth—the days and especially the nights when ideas and the future beckoned. "Van Dorn? You're still—"

"Yes! I was right! There *was* a secret!"

"You crazy bastard, I don't care about Van Dorn. But I care about you! Why did you—? I never forgave you for disappearing."

"I had to. Couldn't let you hold me back. Couldn't let you—"

"For your own good!"

"So *you* thought. But I was right!"

"Where *are* you?"

"The Metropolitan Museum of Art."

"Will you stay there, Myers? While I catch a cab? I can't wait to see you."

"I can't wait for you to see what *I* see!"

I postponed a deadline, cancelled two appointments, and told my fiancée I couldn't meet her for dinner. She sounded miffed. But Myers was all that mattered.

He stood beyond the pillars at the entrance. His face was haggard, but his eyes were stars. I hugged him. "Myers, it's so good to—"

"I want you to see something. Hurry."

He tugged at my coat, rushing.

"But where have you been?"

"I'll tell you later."

We entered the Postimpressionist gallery. Bewildered, I followed Myers and let him anxiously sit me on a bench before Van Dorn's *Fir Trees at Sunrise.*

I'd never seen the original. Prints couldn't compare. After a year of drawing ads for feminine beauty aids, I was devastated. Van Dorn's power brought me close to...

Tears?

For my visionless skills.

For the youth I'd abandoned a year before.

"Look!" Myers said. He raised his arm and gestured toward the painting.

I frowned. I looked.

It took time—an hour, two hours—and the coaxing vision of Myers. I concentrated. And then, at last, I saw.

Profound admiration changed to...

My heart raced. As Myers traced his hand across the painting one final time, as a guard who had been watching us with increasing wariness stalked forward to stop him from touching the canvas, I felt as if a cloud had dispersed and a lens had focused.

"Jesus," I said.

"You see? The bushes, the trees, the branches?"

"Yes! Oh, God, yes! Why didn't I—?"

"Notice before? Because it doesn't show up in the prints," Myers said. "Only in the originals. And the effect's so deep, you have to study them—"

"Forever."

"It seems that long. But I knew. I was right."

"A secret."

When I was a boy, my father—how I loved him—took me mushroom hunting. We drove from town, climbed a barbed-wire fence, walked through a forest, and reached a slope of dead elms. My father told me to search the top of the slope while he checked the bottom.

An hour later he came back with two large paper sacks filled with mushrooms. I hadn't found even one.

"I guess your spot was lucky," I said.

"But they're all around you," my father said.

"All around me? Where?"

"You didn't look hard enough."

"I crossed this slope five times."

"You searched, but you didn't really see," my father said. He picked up a long stick and pointed it toward the ground. "Focus your eyes toward the end of the stick."

I did...

And I've never forgotten the hot excitement that surged through my stomach. The mushrooms appeared as if by magic. They'd been there all along, of course, so perfectly adapted to their surroundings, their color much like dead leaves, their shape so much like bits of wood and chunks of rock that they'd been invisible to my ignorant eyes. But once my vision adjusted, once my mind reevaluated the visual impressions it received, I

311

saw mushrooms everywhere, seemingly thousands of them. I'd been standing on them, walking over them, staring at them, and hadn't realized.

I felt an infinitely greater shock when I saw the tiny faces Myers made me recognize in Van Dorn's *Fir Trees at Sunrise*. Most were smaller than a quarter of an inch, hints and suggestions, dots and curves, blended perfectly with the landscape. They weren't exactly human, though they did have mouths, noses, and eyes. Each mouth was a black, gaping maw, each nose a jagged gash, the eyes dark sinkholes of despair. The twisted faces seemed to be screaming in total agony. I could almost hear their anguished shrieks, their tortured wails. I thought of damnation. Of hell.

As soon as I noticed the faces, they emerged from the swirling texture of the painting in such abundance that the landscape became an illusion, the grotesque faces reality. The fir trees turned into an obscene cluster of writhing arms and pain-racked torsos.

I stepped back in shock an instant before the guard would have pulled me away.

"Don't touch the—" the guard said.

Myers had already rushed to point at another Van Dorn, the original *Cypresses in a Hollow*. I followed, and now that my eyes knew what to look for, I saw small, tortured faces in every branch and rock. The canvas swarmed with them.

"Jesus."

"And this!"

Myers hurried to *Sunflowers at Harvest Time*, and again, as if a lens had changed focus, I no longer saw flowers but anguished faces and twisted limbs. I lurched back, felt a bench against my legs, and sat.

"You were right," I said.

The guard stood nearby, scowling.

"Van Dorn did have a secret," I said. "These agonized faces give his work depth. They're hidden, but we *sense* them. We *feel* the anguish beneath the beauty."

"But why would he—?"

"I don't think he had a choice. His genius drove him insane. It's my guess that this is how he literally saw the world. These faces are the demons he wrestled with. The festering products of his insanity. And they're not just an illustrator's gimmick. Only a genius could have painted them for all the world to see and yet have so perfectly imposed them on the landscape that *no one* would see. Because he took them for granted in a terrible way."

"No one? *You* saw, Myers."

He smiled. "Maybe that means I'm crazy."

"I doubt it, friend." I returned his smile. "It does mean you're persistent. This'll make your reputation."

"But I'm not through yet," Myers said.

I frowned.

"So far all I've got is a fascinating case of optical illusion. Tortured souls writhing beneath, perhaps producing, incomparable beauty. I call them 'secondary images.' In your ad work I guess they'd be called 'subliminal.' But this isn't commercialism. This is a genuine artist who had the brilliance to use his madness as an ingredient in his vision. I need to go deeper."

"What are you talking about?"

"The paintings here don't provide enough examples. I've seen his work in Paris and Rome, in Zurich and London. I've borrowed from my parents to the limits of their patience and my conscience. But I've seen, and I know what I have to do. The anguished faces began in 1889, when Van Dorn left Paris in disgrace. His early paintings were abysmal. He settled in La Verge in the south of France. Six months later his genius suddenly exploded. In a frenzy, he painted. He returned to Paris. He showed his work, but no one appreciated it. He kept painting, kept showing. Still no one appreciated it. He returned to La Verge, reached the peak of his genius, and went totally insane. He had to be committed to an asylum, but not before he stabbed out his eyes. That's my dissertation. I intend to parallel his course. To match his paintings with his biography, to show how the faces increased and became more severe as his madness worsened. I want to dramatize the turmoil in his soul as he imposed his twisted vision on each landscape."

It was typical of Myers to take an excessive attitude and make it even more excessive. Don't misunderstand. His discovery was important. But he didn't know when to stop. I'm not an art historian, but I've read enough to know that what's called "psychological criticism," the attempt to analyze great art as a manifestation of neuroses, is considered off-the-wall, to put it mildly. If Myers handed Stuyvesant a psychological dissertation, the pompous bastard would throw Myers out of his office.

That was one misgiving I had about what Myers planned to do with his discovery. Another troubled me more. *I intend to parallel Van Dorn's course*, he'd said, and after we left the museum and walked through Central Park, I realized how literally Myers meant it.

"I'm going to southern France," he said.

I started in surprise. "You don't mean—"

"La Verge? That's right. I want to write my dissertation there."

"But—"

"What place could be more appropriate? It's the village where Van Dorn suffered his nervous breakdown and eventually went insane. If it's possible, I'll even rent the same room *he* did."

"Myers, this sounds too far out, even for you."

"But it makes perfect sense. I need to immerse myself. I need atmosphere, a sense of history. So I can put myself in the mood to write."

"The last time you immersed yourself, you crammed your room with Van Dorn prints, didn't sleep, didn't eat, didn't bathe. I hope—"

"I admit I got too involved. But last time I didn't know what I was looking for. Now that I've found it, I'm in good shape."

"You look strung out to *me*."

"An optical illusion." Myers grinned.

"Come on, I'll treat you to drinks and dinner."

"Sorry. Can't. I've got a plane to catch."

"You're leaving *tonight*? But I haven't seen you since—"

"You can buy me that dinner when I finish the dissertation."

I never did. I saw him only one more time. Because of the letter he sent two months later. Or asked his nurse to send. She wrote down what he'd said and added an explanation of her own. He'd blinded himself, of course.

You were right. Shouldn't have gone. But when did I ever take advice? I always knew better, didn't I? Now it's too late. What I showed you that day at the Met—God help me, there's so much more. I found the truth, and now I can't bear it. Don't make my mistake. Don't look ever again, I beg you, at Van Dorn's paintings. The headaches. Can't stand the pain. Need a break. Am going home. Stay cool. Paint well. I love you, pal. Your friend forever,

    Myers

In her postscript, the nurse apologized for her English. She sometimes took care of aged Americans on the Riviera, she said, and had to learn the language. But she understood what she heard better than she could speak it or write it, and hoped that what she'd written made sense. It didn't, but that wasn't her fault. Myers had been in great pain, sedated with morphine, not thinking clearly, she said. The miracle was that he'd managed to be coherent at all.

Your friend was staying at our only hotel. The manager says that he slept little and ate even less. His research was obsessive. He filled his room with reproductions of Van Dorn's work. He tried to duplicate Van Dorn's daily schedule. He demanded paints and canvas, refused all meals, and wouldn't answer his door. Three days ago, a scream woke the manager. The door was blocked. It took three men to break it down. Your friend used the sharp end of a paintbrush to stab out his eyes. The clinic here is excellent. Physically your friend will recover, although he will never see again. But I worry about his mind.

Myers had said he was going home. It had taken a week for the letter to reach me. I assumed his parents would have been informed immediately by phone or telegram. He was probably back in the States by now. I knew his parents lived in Denver, but I didn't know their first names or addresses, so I took a cab to the New York Public Library, checked the Denver phone book, and went down the list for Myers, using my credit card to call every one of them till I made contact. Not with his parents but with a family friend watching their house. Myers hadn't been flown to the States. His parents had gone to the south of France. I caught the next available plane. Not that it matters, but I was supposed to be married that weekend.

La Verge is thirty kilometres inland from Nice. I hired a driver. The road curved through olive trees and farmland, crested cypress-covered hills, and often skirted cliffs.

Passing an orchard, I had an eerie conviction that I'd seen it before. Entering La Verge, my déjà vu strengthened. The village seemed trapped in the nineteenth century. Except for phone poles and power lines, it looked exactly as Van Dorn had painted it. I recognized the narrow, cobbled streets and rustic shops that Van Dorn had made famous.

I asked directions. It wasn't hard to find Myers and his parents.

The last time I saw my friend, the undertaker was putting the lid on his coffin. I had trouble sorting out the details, but despite my burning tears, I gradually came to understand that the local clinic was as good as the nurse had assured me in her note. All things being equal, he'd have lived.

But the damage to his mind had been another matter. He'd complained of headaches. He'd also been increasingly distressed. Even morphine hadn't helped. He'd been left alone only for a minute, appearing to be asleep. In that brief interval he'd managed to stagger from his bed, grope across the room, and find a pair of scissors.

Yanking off his bandages, he'd jabbed the scissors into an empty eye socket and tried to ream out his brain. He'd collapsed before accomplishing his purpose, but the damage had been sufficient. Death had taken two days.

His parents were pale, incoherent with shock. I somehow controlled my own shock enough to try to comfort them. Despite the blur of those terrible hours, I remember noticing the kind of irrelevance that signals the mind's attempt to reassert normality. Myers' father wore Gucci loafers and an eighteen-karat Rolex watch. In grad school Myers had lived on as strict a budget as I had. I had no idea he came from wealthy parents.

I helped them make arrangements to fly his body back to the States. I went to Nice with them and stayed by their side as they watched the crate that contained his coffin being loaded onto the baggage compartment of the plane. I shook their hands and hugged them. I waited as they sobbed and trudged down the boarding tunnel. An hour later I was back in La Verge.

I returned because of a promise. I wanted to ease his parents' suffering—and my own. Because I'd been his friend. "You've got too much to take care of," I'd said to his parents. "The long trip home. The arrangements for the funeral." My voice had choked.

"Let me help. I'll settle things here, pay whatever bills he owes, pack up his clothes and..." I took a deep breath. "And his books and whatever else he had and send them home to you. Let me do that. I'd consider it a kindness. Please. I need to do *something.*"

True to his ambition, Myers had managed to rent the same room taken by Van Dorn at the village's only hotel. Don't be surprised that it was available. The management used it to promote the hotel. A plaque announced the historic value of the room. The furnishings were the same style as when Van Dorn had stayed there. Tourists, to be sure, had paid to peer in and sniff the residue of genius. But business had been slow this season, and Myers had wealthy parents. For a generous sum, coupled with his typical enthusiasm, he'd convinced the hotel's owner to let him have that room.

I rented a different room—more like a closet—two doors down the hall and, my eyes still burning from tears, went into Van Dorn's musty sanctuary to pack my dear dead friend's possessions. Prints of Van Dorn paintings were everywhere, several splattered with dried blood. Heartsick, I made a stack of them.

That's when I found the diary.

During grad school I'd taken a course in Postimpressionism that emphasized Van Dorn, and I'd read a facsimile edition of his diary. The publisher had photocopied the handwritten pages and bound them, adding an introduction and footnotes. The diary had been cryptic from the start, but as Van Dorn became more feverish about his work, as his nervous breakdown became more severe, his statements deteriorated into riddles. His handwriting—hardly neat, even when he was sane—went quickly out of control and finally turned into almost indecipherable slashes and curves as he rushed to unloose his frantic thoughts.

I sat at a small wooden desk and paged through the diary, recognizing phrases I'd read years before. With each passage my stomach turned colder. Because this diary *wasn't* the published photocopy. Instead, it was a notebook, and though I wanted to believe that Myers had somehow, impossibly, gotten his hands on the original diary, I knew I was fooling myself. The pages in this ledger weren't yellow and brittle with age. The ink hadn't faded till it was brown more than blue. The notebook had been purchased and written in recently. It wasn't Van Dorn's diary. It belonged to *Myers*. The ice in my stomach turned to lava.

Glancing sharply away from the ledger, I saw a shelf beyond the desk and a stack of other notebooks. Apprehensive, I grabbed them and in a fearful rush flipped through them. My stomach threatened to erupt. Each notebook was the same, the words identical.

My hands shook as I looked again to the shelf, found the facsimile edition of the original, and compared it with the notebooks. I moaned, imagining Myers at this desk, his expression intense and insane as he reproduced the diary word for word, slash for slash, curve for curve. Eight times.

Myers had indeed immersed himself, straining to put himself into Van Dorn's disintegrating frame of mind. And in the end he'd succeeded. The weapon Van Dorn had used to stab out his eyes had been the sharp end of a paintbrush. In the mental hospital, Van Dorn had finished the job by skewering his brain with a pair of scissors. Like Myers. Or vice versa.

When Myers had finally broken, had he and Van Dorn been horribly indistinguishable?

I pressed my hands to my face. Whimpers squeezed from my convulsing throat. It seemed forever before I stopped sobbing. My consciousness strained to control my anguish. ("Orange is for anguish," Myers had said.) Rationality fought to subdue my distress. ("The critics who devoted themselves to analyzing Van Dorn," Myers had said. "The ones who haven't been recognized for their genius, just as Van Dorn wasn't recognized. They suffered...And just like Van Dorn, they stabbed out their eyes.") Had they done it with a paintbrush? I wondered. Were the parallels that exact? And in the end, had they, too, used scissors to skewer their brains?

I scowled at the prints I'd been stacking. Many still surrounded me— on the walls, the floor, the bed, the windows, even the ceiling. A swirl of colors. A vortex of brilliance.

Or at least I once had thought of them as brilliant. But now, with the insight Myers had given me, with the vision I'd gained in the Metropolitan Museum, I saw behind the sun-drenched cypresses and hayfields, the orchards and meadows, toward their secret darkness, toward the minuscule, twisted arms and gaping mouths, the black dots of tortured eyes, the blue knots of writhing bodies. ("Blue is for insanity," Myers had said.)

All it took was a slight shift of perception, and there *weren't* any orchards and hayfields, only a terrifying gestalt of souls in hell. Van Dorn had indeed invented a new stage of Impressionism. He'd impressed upon the splendour of God's creation the teeming images of his own disgust. His paintings didn't glorify. They abhorred. Everywhere Van Dorn had looked, he'd seen his own private nightmare. Blue was for insanity, indeed, and if you fixated on Van Dorn's insanity long enough, you, too, became insane. ("Don't look ever again, I beg you, at Van Dorn's paintings," Myers had said in his letter.) In the last stages of his breakdown had Myers somehow become lucid enough to try to warn me? ("Can't stand the headaches. Need a break. Am going home.") In a way I'd never suspected, he'd indeed gone home.

Another startling thought occurred to me. ("The critics who devoted themselves to analyzing Van Dorn. They each tried to paint in Van Dorn's

319

style," Myers had said a year ago.) As if attracted by a magnet, my gaze swung across from me, where two canvas originals leaned against the wall. I shivered, stood, and haltingly approached them.

They'd been painted by an amateur. Myers was an art *historian*, after all. The colors were clumsily applied, especially the splotches of orange and blue. The cypresses were crude. At their bases, the rocks looked like cartoons. The sky needed texture. But I knew what the black dots among them were meant to suggest. I understood the purpose of the tiny blue gashes. The miniature, anguished faces and twisted limbs were implied, even if Myers had lacked the talent to depict them. He'd contracted Van Dorn's madness. All that had remained were the terminal stages.

I sighed from the pit of my soul. As the village's church bell rang, I prayed that my friend had found peace.

It was dark when I left the hotel. I needed to walk, to escape the greater darkness of that room, to feel at liberty, to think. But my footsteps and inquiries led me down a narrow cobbled street toward the village's clinic, where Myers had finished what he'd started in Van Dorn's room. I asked at the desk and five minutes later introduced myself to an attractive, dark-haired, thirtyish woman.

The nurse's English was more than adequate. She said her name was Clarisse.

"You took care of my friend," I said. "You sent me the letter he dictated and added a note of your own."

She nodded. "He worried me. He was so distressed."

The fluorescent lights in the vestibule hummed. We sat on a bench.

"I'm trying to understand why he killed himself," I said. "I think I know, but I'd like your opinion."

Her eyes, a bright, intelligent hazel, suddenly were guarded. "He stayed too long in his room. He studied too much." She shook her head and stared toward the floor. "The mind can be a trap. It can be a torture."

"But he was excited when he came here?"

"Yes."

"Despite his studies, he behaved as if he'd come on vacation?"

"Very much."

"Then what made him change? My friend was unusual, I agree. What we call high-strung. But he enjoyed doing research. He might have looked sick from too much work, but he thrived on learning. His body was nothing, but his mind was brilliant. What tipped the balance, Clarisse?"

"Tipped the—?"

"Made him depressed instead of excited. What did he learn that made him—?"

She stood and looked at her watch. "Forgive me. I stopped work twenty minutes ago. I'm expected at a friend's."

My voice hardened. "Of course. I wouldn't want to keep you."

Outside the clinic, beneath the light at its entrance, I stared at my own watch, surprised to see that it was almost eleven-thirty. Fatigue made my knees ache. The trauma of the day had taken away my appetite, but I knew I should try to eat, and after walking back to the hotel's dining room, I ordered a chicken sandwich and a glass of Chablis. I meant to eat in my room but never got that far. Van Dorn's room and the diary beckoned.

The sandwich and wine went untasted. Sitting at the desk, surrounded by the swirling colors and hidden horrors of Van Dorn prints, I opened a notebook and tried to understand.

A knock at the door made me turn.

Again I glanced at my watch, astonished to find that hours had passed like minutes. It was almost two A.M.

The knock was repeated, gentle but insistent. The manager?

"Come in," I said in French. "The door isn't locked."

The knob turned. The door swung open.

Clarisse stepped in. Instead of her nurse's uniform, she now wore sneakers, jeans, and a sweater whose tight-fitting yellow accentuated the hazel in her eyes.

"I apologize," she said in English. "I must have seemed rude at the clinic."

321

"Not at all. You had an appointment. I was keeping you."

She shrugged self-consciously. "I sometimes leave the clinic so late, I don't have a chance to see my friend."

"I understand perfectly."

She drew a hand through her lush, long hair. "My friend got tired. As I walked home, passing the hotel, I saw a light up here. On the chance it might be you..."

I nodded, waiting.

I had the sense she'd been avoiding it, but now she turned toward the room. Toward where I'd found the dried blood on the prints. "The doctor and I came as fast as we could when the manager phoned us that afternoon." She stared at the prints. "How could so much beauty cause so much pain?"

"Beauty?" I glanced toward the tiny, gaping mouths.

"You mustn't stay here. Don't make the mistake your friend did."

"Mistake?"

"You've had a long journey. You've suffered a shock. You need to rest. You'll wear yourself out as your friend did."

"I was just looking through some things of his. I'll be packing them to send them back to America."

"Do it quickly. You mustn't torture yourself by thinking about what happened here. It isn't good to surround yourself with the things that disturbed your friend. Don't intensify your grief."

"Surround myself? My friend would have said 'immerse.'"

"You look exhausted. Come." She held out her hand. "I'll take you to your room. Sleep will ease your pain. If you need some pills to help you..."

"Thanks. But a sedative won't be necessary."

She continued to offer her hand. I took it and went to the hallway.

For a moment I stared back toward the prints and the horror within the beauty. I said a silent prayer for Myers, shut off the lights, and locked the door.

We went down the hall. In my room, I sat on the bed.

"Sleep long and well," she said.

322

"I hope."

"You have my sympathy." She kissed my cheek.

I touched her shoulder. Her lips shifted toward my own. She leaned against me.

We sank toward the bed. In silence, we made love.

Sleep came like her kisses, softly smothering.

But in my nightmares there were tiny, gaping mouths.

Sunlight glowed through my window. With aching eyes I looked at my watch. Half past ten. My head hurt.

Clarisse had left a note on my bureau.

Last night was sympathy. To share and ease your grief. Do what you intended. Pack your friend's belongings. Send them to America. Go with them. Don't make your friend's mistake. Don't, as you said *he* said, "immerse" yourself. Don't let beauty give you pain.

I meant to leave. I truly believe that. I phoned the front desk and asked the concierge to send up some boxes. After I showered and shaved, I went to Myers' room, where I finished stacking the prints. I made another stack of books and another of clothes. I packed everything into the boxes and looked around to make sure I hadn't forgotten anything.

The two canvases that Myers had painted still leaned against a corner. I decided not to take them. No one needed to be reminded of the delusions that had overcome him.

All that remained was to seal the boxes, to address and mail them. But as I started to close the flap on a box, I saw the notebooks inside.

So much suffering, I thought. So much waste.

Once more I leafed through a notebook. Various passages caught my eye. Van Dorn's discouragement about his failed career. His reasons for leaving Paris to come to La Verge—the stifling, backbiting artists' community, the snobbish critics and their sneering responses to his early efforts. *Need to free myself of convention. Need to void myself of aesthete*

323

politics, to shit it out of me. To find what's never been painted. To feel instead of being told what to feel. To see instead of imitating what others have seen.

I knew from the biographies how impoverished Van Dorn's ambition had made him. In Paris he'd literally eaten slops thrown into alleys behind restaurants. He'd been able to afford his quest to La Verge only because a successful but very conventional (and now ridiculed) painter friend had loaned him a small sum of money. Eager to conserve his endowment, Van Dorn had walked all the way from Paris to the south of France.

In those days, you have to remember, the Riviera was an unfashionable area of hills, rocks, farms, and villages. Limping into La Verge, Van Dorn must have been a pathetic sight. He'd chosen this provincial town precisely because it *was* unconventional, because it offered mundane scenes so in contrast with the salons of Paris that no other artist would dare to paint them.

Need to create what's never been imagined, he'd written. For six despairing months he tried and failed. He finally self-doubted, then suddenly reversed himself and, in a year of unbelievably brilliant productivity, gave the world thirty-eight masterpieces. At the time, of course, he couldn't trade any canvas for a meal. But the world knows better now.

He must have painted in a frenzy. His sudden-found energy must have been enormous. To me, a would-be artist with technical facility but only conventional eyes, he achieved the ultimate. Despite his suffering, I envied him, when I compared my maudlin, Wyeth-like depictions of Iowa landscapes to Van Dorn's despair and epiphany. His victory had a price, to be sure. Insanity. Self-blinding. Suicide. But I had to wonder if perhaps, as he died, he'd have chosen to reverse his life if he'd been able. He must have known how remarkable, how truly astonishing, his work had become.

Or perhaps he didn't. The last canvas he'd painted before stabbing his eyes had been of himself. A lean-faced, brooding man with short, thinning hair, sunken features, pallid skin, and a scraggly beard. The famous portrait reminded me of how I always thought Christ would have looked just before he was crucified. All that was missing was the crown of thorns. But Van Dorn had a different crown of thorns. Not around but *within* him. Disguised among his scraggly beard and sunken features, the tiny, gaping mouths and writing bodies told it all. His suddenly acquired vision had stung him too much.

As I read the notebook, again distressed by Myers' effort to reproduce Van Dorn's agonized words and handwriting exactly, I reached the section where Van Dorn described his epiphany: *La Verge! I walked! I saw! I feel! Canvas! Paint! Creation and damnation!*

After that cryptic passage, the notebook—and Van Dorn's diary—became totally incoherent. Except for the persistent refrain of severe and increasing headaches.

I was waiting outside the clinic when Clarisse arrived to start her shift at three o'clock. The sun was brilliant, glinting off her eyes. She wore a burgundy skirt and a turquoise blouse. Mentally I stroked their cottony texture.

When she saw me, her footsteps faltered. Forcing a smile, she approached.

"You came to say good-bye?" She sounded hopeful.

"No. To ask you some questions."

Her smile disintegrated. "I mustn't be late for work."

"This'll just take a minute. My French vocabulary needs improvement. I didn't bring a dictionary. The name of this village. La Verge. What does it mean?"

She hunched her shoulders as if to say the question was unimportant. "It's not very colorful. The literal translation is 'the stick.'"

"That's all?"

She reacted to my frown. "There are rough equivalents. 'The branch.' 'The switch.' A willow, for example, that a father might use to discipline a child."

"And it doesn't mean anything else?"

"Indirectly. The synonyms keep getting farther from the literal sense.

A wand, perhaps. Or a rod. The kind of forked stick that people who claim they can find water hold ahead of them when they walk across a field. The stick is supposed to bend down if there's water."

"We call it a divining rod. My father once told me he'd seen a man who could actually make one work. I always suspected the man just tilted the stick with his hands. Do you suppose this village got its name because long ago someone found water here with a divining rod?"

"Why would anyone have bothered when these hills have so many streams and springs? What makes you interested in the name?"

"Something I read in Van Dorn's diary. The village's name excited him for some reason."

"But *anything* could have excited him. He was insane."

"Eccentric. But he didn't become insane until after that passage in his diary."

"You mean, his *symptoms* didn't show themselves until after that. You're not a psychiatrist."

I had to agree.

"Again, I'm afraid I'll seem rude. I really must go to work." She hesitated. "Last night..."

"Was exactly what you described in the note. A gesture of sympathy. An attempt to ease my grief. You didn't mean it to be the start of anything."

"Please do what I asked. Please leave. Don't destroy yourself like the others."

"*Others?*"

"Like your friend."

"No, you said, 'others.'" My words were rushed. "Clarisse, tell me."

She glanced up, squinting as if she'd been cornered. "After your friend stabbed out his eyes, I heard talk around the village. Older people. It could be merely gossip that became exaggerated with the passage of time."

"What did they say?"

She squinted harder. "Twenty years ago a man came here to do research on Van Dorn. He stayed three months and had a breakdown."

"He stabbed out his eyes?"

326

"Rumors drifted back that he blinded himself in a mental hospital in England. Ten years before, another man came. He jabbed scissors through an eye, all the way into his brain."

I stared, unable to control the spasm that racked my shoulder blades. "What the hell is going on?"

I asked around the village. No one would talk to me. At the hotel the manager told me he'd decided to stop renting Van Dorn's room. I had to remove Myers' belongs at once.

"But I can still stay in *my* room?"

"If that's what you wish. I don't recommend it, but even France is still a free country."

I paid the bill, went upstairs, moved the packed boxes from Van Dorn's room to mine, and turned in surprise as the phone rang.

The call was from my fiancée.

When was I coming home?

I didn't know.

What about the wedding this weekend?

The wedding would have to be postponed.

I winced as she slammed down the phone.

I sat on the bed and couldn't help recalling the last time I'd sat there, with Clarisse standing over me, just before we'd made love. I was throwing away the life I'd tried to build.

For a moment I came close to calling back my fiancée, but a different sort of compulsion made me scowl toward the boxes, toward Van Dorn's diary. In the note Clarisse had added to Myers' letter, she'd said that his research had become so obsessive that he'd tried to recreate Van Dorn's daily habits. Again it occurred to me—at the end, had Myers and Van Dorn become indistinguishable? Was the secret to what had happened to Myers hidden in the diary, just as the suffering faces were hidden in Van Dorn's paintings? I grabbed one of the ledgers. Scanning the pages, I looked for references to Van Dorn's daily routine. And so it began.

I've said that except for telephone poles and electrical lines, La Verge seemed caught in the previous century. Not only was the hotel still in existence, but so were Van Dorn's favourite tavern, and the bakery where he'd bought his morning croissant. A small restaurant he favored remained in business. On the edge of the village, a trout stream where he sometimes sat with a mid-afternoon glass of wine still bubbled along, though pollution had long since killed the trout. I went to all of them, in the order and at the time he recorded in his diary.

After a week—breakfast at eight, lunch at two, a glass of wine at the trout stream, a stroll to the countryside, then back to the room—I knew the diary so well, I didn't need to refer to it. Mornings had been Van Dorn's time to paint. The light was best then, he'd written. And evenings were a time for remembering and sketching.

It finally came to me that I wouldn't be following the schedule exactly if I didn't paint and sketch when Van Dorn had done so. I bought a notepad, canvas, pigments, a palette, whatever I needed, and for the first time since leaving grad school, I tried to *create*. I used local scenes that Van Dorn had favored and produced what you'd expect: uninspired versions of Van Dorn's paintings. With no discoveries, no understanding of what had ultimately undermined Myers' sanity, tedium set in. My finances were almost gone. I prepared to give up.

Except...

I had the disturbing sense that I'd missed something. A part of Van Dorn's routine that wasn't explicit in the diary. Or something about the locales themselves that I hadn't noticed, though I'd been painting them in Van Dorn's spirit, if not with his talent.

Clarisse found me sipping wine on the sunlit bank of the no longer trout-filled stream. I felt her shadow and turned toward her silhouette against the sun.

I hadn't seen her for two weeks, since our uneasy conversation outside the clinic. Even with the sun in my eyes, she looked more beautiful than I remembered.

"When was the last time you changed your clothes?" she asked.

A year ago I'd said the same to Myers.

"You need a shave. You've been drinking too much. You look awful."

I sipped my wine and shrugged. "Well, you know what the drunk said about his bloodshot eyes. You think they look bad to you? You should see them from *my* side."

"At least you can joke."

"I'm beginning to think that *I'm* the joke."

"You're definitely not a joke." She sat beside me. "You're becoming your friend. Why don't you leave?"

"I'm tempted."

"Good." She touched my hand.

"Clarisse?"

"Yes?"

"Answer some questions one more time?"

She studied me. "Why?"

"Because if I get the right answers, I might leave."

She nodded slowly.

Back in town, in my room, I showed her the stack of prints. I almost told her about the faces they contained, but her brooding features stopped me. She thought I was disturbed enough as it was.

"When I walk in the afternoons, I go to the settings Van Dorn chose for his paintings." I sorted through the prints. "This orchard. This farm. This pond. This cliff. And so on."

"Yes, I recognize these places. I've seen them all."

"I hoped if I saw them, maybe I'd understand what happened to my friend. You told me he went to them as well. Each of them is within a five-mile radius of the village. Many are close together. It wasn't difficult to find each site. Except for one."

She didn't ask the obvious question. Instead, she tensely rubbed her arm.

When I'd taken the boxes from Van Dorn's room, I'd also removed the two paintings Myers had attempted. Now I pulled them from where I'd tucked them under the bed.

"My friend did these. It's obvious he wasn't an artist. But as crude as they are, you can see they both depict the same area."

I slid a Van Dorn print from the bottom of the stack.

"*This* area," I said. "A grove of cypresses in a hollow, surrounded by rocks. It's the only site I haven't been able to find. I've asked the villagers. They claim they don't know where it is. Do *you* know, Clarisse? Can you tell me? It must have some significance if my friend was fixated on it enough to try to paint it *twice*."

Clarisse scratched a fingernail across her wrist. "I'm sorry."

"What?"

"I can't help you."

"Can't or won't? Do you mean you don't know where to find it, or you know but you won't tell me?"

"I said I can't help."

"What's wrong with this village, Clarisse? What's everybody trying to hide?"

"I've done my best." She shook her head, stood, and walked to the door. She glanced back sadly. "Sometimes it's better to leave well enough alone. Sometimes there are reasons for secrets."

I watched her go down the hall. "Clarisse..."

She turned and spoke a single word: "North." She was crying. "God help you," she added. "I'll pray for your soul." Then she disappeared down the stairs.

For the first time I felt afraid.

Five minutes later I left the hotel. In my walks to the sites of Van Dorn's paintings, I'd always chosen the easiest routes—east, west, and south. Whenever I'd asked about the distant, tree-lined hills to the north, the villagers had told me there was nothing of interest there, nothing at all to do with Van Dorn. What about cypresses in a hollow? I'd asked. There weren't any cypresses in those hills, only olive trees, they'd answered. But now I knew.

La Verge was in the southern end of an oblong valley, squeezed by cliffs to the east and west. To reach the northern hills, I'd have to walk twenty miles at least.

I rented a car. Leaving a dust cloud, I pressed my foot on the accelerator and started toward the rapidly enlarging hills. The trees I'd seen from the village were indeed olive trees. But the lead-colored rocks among them were the same as in Van Dorn's painting. I skidded along the road, veering up through the hills. Near the top I found a narrow space to park and rushed from the car. But which direction to take? On impulse, I chose left and hurried among the rocks and trees.

My decision seems less arbitrary now. Something about the slopes to the left was more dramatic, more aesthetically compelling. A greater wildness in the landscape. A sense of depth, of substance.

My instincts urged me forward. I'd reached the hills at quarter after five. Time compressed eerily. At once, my watch showed ten past seven. The sun blazed, crimson, over the bluffs. I kept searching, letting the grotesque landscape guide me. The ridges and ravines were like a maze, every turn of which either blocked or gave access, controlling my direction. I rounded a crag, scurried down a slope of thorns, ignored the rips in my shirt and the blood streaming from my hands, and stopped on the precipice of a hollow. Cypresses, not olive trees, filled the basin. Boulders jutted among them and formed a grotto.

The basin was steep. I skirted its brambles, ignoring their scalding sting. Boulders led me down. I stifled my misgivings, frantic to reach the bottom.

This hollow, this basin of cypresses and boulders, this thorn-rimmed funnel, was the image not only of Van Dorn's painting but of the canvases Myers had attempted. But why had this place so affected them?

The answer came as quickly as the question. I heard before I saw, though hearing doesn't accurately describe my sensation. The sound was so faint and high-pitched, it was almost beyond the range of detection. At first I thought I was near a hornet's nest. I sensed a subtle vibration in the otherwise still air of the hollow. I felt an itch behind my eardrums, a tingle on my skin. The sound was actually many sounds, each identical, merging, like the collective buzz of a swarm of insects. But this was high-pitched. Not a buzz but more like a distant chorus of shrieks and wails.

Frowning, I took another step toward the cypresses. The tingle on my skin intensified. The itch behind my eardrums became so irritating, I raised my hands to the sides of my head. I came close enough to see within the trees, and what I noticed with terrible clarity made me panic. Gasping, I stumbled back. But not in time. What shot from the trees was too small and fast for me to identify.

It struck my right eye. The pain was excruciating, as if the white-hot tip of a needle had pierced my retina and lanced my brain. I clamped my right hand across that eye and screamed.

I continued stumbling back, agony spurring my panic. But the sharp, hot pain intensified, surging through my skull. My knees bent. My consciousness dimmed. I fell against the slope.

It was after midnight when I managed to drive back to the village. Though my eye no longer burned, my panic was more extreme. Still dizzy from having passed out, I tried to keep control when I entered the clinic and asked where Clarisse lived. She'd invited me to visit, I claimed. A sleepy attendant frowned but told me. I drove desperately toward her cottage, five blocks away.

Lights were on. I knocked. She didn't answer. I pounded harder, faster. At last I saw a shadow. When the door swung open, I lurched into the living room. I barely noticed the negligee Clarisse clutched around her, or the open door to her bedroom, where a startled woman sat up in bed, held a sheet to her breasts, and stood quickly to shut the bedroom door.

"What the hell do you think you're doing?" Clarisse yelled. "I didn't invite you in! I didn't—!"

I managed the strength to talk: "I don't have time to explain. I'm terrified. I need your help."

She clutched her negligee tighter.

"I've been stung. I think I've caught a disease. Help me stop whatever's inside me. Antibiotics. An antidote. Anything you can think of. Maybe it's a virus, maybe a fungus. Maybe it acts like bacteria."

332

"*What happened?*"

"I told you, no time. I'd have asked for help at the clinic, but they wouldn't have understood. They'd have thought I'd had a breakdown, the same as Myers. You've got to take me there. You've got to make sure I'm injected with as much of any and every drug that might possibly kill this thing."

"I'll dress as fast as I can."

As we rushed to the clinic, I described what had happened. She phoned the doctor the moment we arrived. While we waited, she disinfected my eye and gave me something for my rapidly developing headache. The doctor showed up, his sleepy features becoming alert when he saw how distressed I was. True to my prediction, he reacted as if I'd had a breakdown. I shouted at him to humor me and saturate me with antibiotics. Clarisse made sure it wasn't just a sedative he gave me. He used every compatible combination. If I thought it would have worked, I'd have swallowed Drano.

What I'd seen within the cypresses were tiny, gaping mouths and miniscule, writhing bodies, as small and camouflaged as those in Van Dorn's paintings. I know now that Van Dorn wasn't imposing his insane vision on reality. He wasn't an Impressionist. At least not in his *Cypresses in a Hollow*. I'm convinced that this painting was his first after his brain became infected. He was literally depicting what he'd seen on one of his walks. Later, as the infection progressed, he saw the gaping mouths and writhing bodies like an overlay on everything else he looked at. In that sense, too, he wasn't an Impressionist. To him, the gaping mouths and writhing bodies *were* in all those later scenes. To the limit of his infected brain, he painted what to him *was* reality. His art was representational.

I know, believe me. Because the drugs didn't work. My brain is as diseased as Van Dorn's...or Myers'. I've tried to understand why they didn't panic when they were stung, why they didn't rush to a hospital to make a doctor understand what had happened. My conclusion is that Van Dorn had been so desperate for a vision to enliven his paintings that he gladly endured the suffering. And Myers had been so desperate to understand

Van Dorn that when stung, he'd willingly taken the risk to identify even more with his subject until, too late, he'd realized his mistake.

Orange is for anguish, blue for insanity. How true. Whatever infects my brain has affected my color sense. More and more, orange and blue overpower the other colors I know are there. I have no choice. I see little else. My paintings are *rife* with orange and blue.

My paintings. Because I've solved another mystery. It always puzzled me how Van Dorn could have suddenly been seized by such energetic genius that he painted thirty-eight masterpieces in one year. I know the answer now. What's in my head, the gaping mouths and writhing bodies, the orange of anguish and the blue of insanity, cause such pressure, such headaches that I've tried everything to subdue them, to get them out. I went from codeine to Demerol to morphine. Each helped for a time but not enough. Then I learned what Van Dorn understood and Myers attempted. Painting the disease somehow gets it out of you. For a time. And then you paint harder, faster. Anything to relieve the pain. But Myers wasn't an artist. The disease had no release and reached its terminal stage in weeks instead of Van Dorn's year.

But *I'm* an artist—or used to hope I was. I had skill without a vision. Now, God help me, I've got a vision. At first I painted the cypresses and their secret. I accomplished what you'd expect. An imitation of Van Dorn's original. But I refuse to suffer pointlessly. I vividly recall the portraits of Midwestern landscapes I produced in grad school. The dark-earthed Iowa landscape. The attempt to make an observer feel the fecundity of the soil. At the time the results were ersatz Wyeth. But not anymore. The twenty paintings I've so far stored away aren't versions of Van Dorn either. They're my own creations. Unique. A combination of the disease and my experience. Aided by powerful memory, I paint the river that flows through Iowa City. Blue. I paint the cornfields that cram the big-sky rolling country outside of town. Orange. I paint my innocence. My youth. With my ultimate discovery hidden within them. Ugliness lurks within the beauty. Horror festers in my brain.

Clarisse at last told me about the local legend. When La Verge was founded, she said, a meteor streaked from the sky. It lit the night. It burst upon the hills north of here. Flames erupted. Trees were consumed. The hour was late. Few villagers saw it. The site of the impact was too far away for those few witnesses to rush that night to see the crater. In the morning the smoke had dispersed. The embers had died. Though the witnesses tried to find the meteor, the lack of the roads that now exist hampered their search through the tangled hills to the point of discouragement. A few among the few witnesses persisted. The few of the few of the few who had accomplished their quest staggered back to the village, babbling about headaches and tiny, gaping mouths. Using sticks, they scraped disturbing images in the dirt and eventually stabbed out their eyes. Over the centuries, legend has it, similar self-mutilations occurred whenever someone returned from seeking the crater in those hills. The unknown had power then. The hills acquired the negative force to taboo. No villager, then or now, intruded on what came to be called the place where God's wand touched the earth. A poetic description of a blazing meteor's impact. La Verge.

I don't conclude the obvious: that the meteor carried spores that multiplied in the crater, which became a hollow eventually filled with cypresses. No—to me, the meteor was a cause but not an effect. I saw a pit among the cypresses, and from the pit, tiny mouths and writhing bodies resembling insects—how they wailed!—spewed. They clung to the leaves of the cypresses, flailed in anguish as they fell back, and instantly were replaced by other spewing, anguished souls.

Yes. Souls. For the meteor, I insist, was just the cause. The effect was the opening of hell. The tiny, wailing mouths are the damned. As *I* am damned. Desperate to survive, to escape from the ultimate prison we call hell, a frantic sinner lunged. He caught my eye and stabbed my brain, the gateway to my soul. My soul. It festers. I paint to remove the pus.

I talk. That helps somehow. Clarisse writes it down while her female lover rubs my shoulders.

My paintings are brilliant. I'll be recognized, as I'd always dreamed. As a genius, of course.

At such a cost.

The headaches grow worse. The orange is more brilliant. The blue more disturbing.

I try my best. I urge myself to be stronger than Myers, whose endurance lasted only weeks. Van Dorn persisted for a year. Maybe genius is strength.

My brain swells. How it threatens to split my skull. The gaping mouths blossom.

The headaches! I tell myself to be strong. Another day. Another rush to complete another painting.

The sharp end of my paintbrush invites. Anything to lance my seething mental boil, to jab my eyes for the ecstasy of relief. But I have to endure.

On a table near my left hand, the scissors wait.

But not today. Or tomorrow.

I'll outlast Van Dorn.